PEMBERLEY SHADES

PRIDE AND PREJUDICE CONTINUES

D.A. BONAVIA-HUNT

SOURCEBOOKS LANDMARK™
AN IMPRINT OF SOURCEBOOKS, INC.®
NAPERVILLE, ILLINOIS

Published by Sourcebooks Landmark, an imprint of Sourcebooks, Inc.
P.O. Box 4410, Naperville, Illinois 60567-4410
(630) 961-3900
FAX: (630) 961-2168
www.sourcebooks.com

This is a reprint of the first edition, written in 1913 and originally published in 1914 by Holden & Hardingham, London.

Library of Congress Cataloging-in-Publication Data

Bonavia-Hunt, D. A. (Dorothy Alice)
   Pemberley shades / D.A. Bonavia-Hunt.
      p. cm.
   "Originally published in 1949 by E.P. Dutton & Company, Inc."—T.p. verso.
   ISBN-13: 978-1-4022-1438-7
   ISBN-10: 1-4022-1438-3
   1. Bennet, Elizabeth (Fictitious character)—Fiction. 2. Married people—Fiction.
3. Darcy, Fitzwilliam (Fictitious character)—Fiction. 4. England—Fiction. I.
Title.
   PR6015.U52P46 2008
   823'.912—dc22
                                        2008013677

Printed and bound in the United States of America
VP   10   9   8   7   6   5   4   3   2   1

"Are the shades of Pemberley to be thus polluted?"

—Lady Catherine de I

Chapter 56, *Pride and Pre*

Chapter 1

WHEN OLD DR. ROBINSON, who had been Rector of Pemberley in Derbyshire for over fifty years, died one night in his sleep at the age of eighty-seven, a long life of little eventfulness and placid prosperity came to a not untimely end.

He had been presented to the living by the grandfather of the present patron, Fitzwilliam Darcy Esquire, of Pemberley House, whom he had christened as an infant, receiving on the occasion a present of ten pounds. Without prejudice to more congenial occupations in his house and garden he had generally done what was expected of him in church and parish, and was on the whole well liked by his parishioners, who spoke of him as a good, kind old gentleman. But in sober truth this was the most that could be said of him, particularly in his latter years when he had become sluggish both in body and mind. His reading of the services was a mumble, his sermons were so extremely dull that as soon as he ascended the pulpit Mr. Darcy stifled a yawn behind his hand, while Mrs. Darcy, though fixing her bright eyes on the preacher, as often as not slipped into meditations wholly unconnected with her surroundings. Who could have foretold that Dr. Robinson, who had done nothing of note in all his lifetime should, by the common and natural act of dying, set in motion a train of events so strange, so startling, so far removed from probability, as to emulate the riotous fancies of a disordered mind?

The funeral over, Mr. Darcy began to cast about for a successor to the benefice. In the meanwhile his friend, Robert Mortimer of Clopwell Priory, having taken orders before inheriting the family estate on the death of an elder brother, undertook to ride over to Pemberley on Sundays and at other times when a clergyman's ministrations were required. The arrangement suited Darcy very well as a temporary measure, for Mortimer, though an indifferent parish priest, having been ever more addicted to field sports, especially fox-hunting, than to the more sedentary pursuits associated with his cloth, was a most amiable, obliging young man and made an excellent stop-gap; Darcy was thus able to set about filling the vacancy at his leisure, partly out of consideration for the two elderly daughters of the late rector whose departure from the Parsonage he did not wish to hasten unduly, but chiefly that he might have time to find a clergyman who would answer all his requirements in being everything in which Dr. Robinson had been deficient.

He had settled in his own mind that the new rector should be under forty, of superior birth, breeding and education, a scholar without pedantry, or irreproachable life, but not too exigent in matters affecting the usages of the polite world, and preferably married to a gentlewoman who would be acceptable to the ladies of Pemberley, his wife Elizabeth and his sister

Georgiana. These demands appeared to him to be so moderate that he was hopeful of their attainment without difficulty or much delay. But that he should have exactly the sort of man he wanted he was thoroughly determined.

"As nearly every family of standing in the country has a younger son in the church it should not be impossible," said Mrs. Darcy. "But would not it be easier, and perhaps more expeditious, to prevail upon an angel to fly down to Pemberley? Seriously, Fitz, there must be plenty of charming young men in orders."

"I distrust charming young men," said Darcy.

"I comprehend perfectly. He must be agreeable and gentleman-like but not at all charming, of pleasing appearance but by no means handsome, endowed with sufficient under-standing to converse with his patron on serious subjects, but not so clever as to outshine him. That he should be a model of virtue and industry needs no saying. And if *I* am to be consulted, he must in no way resemble Mr. Collins, except in being a clergyman."

"Have you done?" enquired Mr. Darcy.

"No, for there is his wife, unless you can think of any young woman in the family for whom he would do as a husband."

"There may be in your family, but not in mine."

"If I did not so hate the trouble of matchmaking I might marry him off to poor Kitty who is still single, though twenty. However, he had better come with a ready-made wife, good, plain and serviceable, attractive to no one but himself. If they have children who are girls, they must be so much older than Richard that there can never be any question of his marrying one of them. Lastly—but I think that is all."

"While you are about it, let there be no reservations of any kind."

"I assure you I have not the least idea of anything further."

"As I see by your expression that you have a fit of modesty, shall I say it for you? She must regard you as perfection in everything—mind, manners and person."

Elizabeth burst out laughing. "Then you must banish the Miss Robinsons from Derbyshire, otherwise they would most certainly infect others with their strong disapprobation of the present mistress of Pemberley."

"I have never met your like for exaggeration, Elizabeth," said her husband.

"Whoever heeds the truth when it goes unembellished? On second thoughts, my love, I would prefer the new rector to be a confirmed bachelor. Such is my experience of Parsonage ladies, that I would rather have no more of them."

This conversation, though it may have afforded the Darcys some amusement, did not materially hasten the course of events. Owing to the perversity so often observable in human affairs, there was not at the death of Dr. Robinson any clergyman among Darcy's acquaintance to whom he cared to offer the living. Applications and recommendations there were in plenty, but none that he would entertain. And as the weeks hastened from March into April and towards May, the two Miss Robinsons, however irrationally, began to feel once more secure of the continued enjoyment of the home of their youth, and resumed that spring-cleaning of its apartments which the death of a parent had interrupted.

Darcy was first made aware of what was passing in their minds when one day the elder Miss Robinson, speaking with customary abruptness, asked him whether he had not noticed that the dining-parlour needed fresh papering. The spring sunshine and the clean curtains made the walls look absolutely faded, she complained. She had asked Mr. Groves, the Pemberley steward, to call and take her instructions, but he had never come.

"I am sorry to be obliged to speak ill of Mr. Groves, but he is not at all so attentive as he should be. I hope he is not so neglectful of *your* business, Mr. Darcy."

Darcy was so amazed that he hardly knew what to reply. After a moment's thought he observed that Mr. Groves probably thought it advisable to wait until the new rector had arrived in order that he might ascertain his wishes in the matter.

"He has no right to think anything of the sort," declared Miss Robinson, growing red with anger. "It is, besides, no excuse for his incivility. He never so much as answered my note."

"That indeed was wrong," said Darcy calmly. "He should have sent an acknowledgment. But he has much business to attend to, and he may have been waiting for an opportunity of consulting me."

"And, pray, why should he consult you? Has not he always taken my instructions in the past?"

"I am sorry to cause you any distress," Darcy replied, concealing some pardonable heat, "but if you reflect, you will see that he might justly consider he could do so no longer."

But Miss Robinson showed not the least disposition to reflect, or to do anything but grow more irritated, and Darcy could only hope that a seed of reason had been sown in the lady's mind, and would survive and grow. He had assumed that after their father's death she and her sister would shortly begin house-hunting; but enquiries now made of Mr. Groves disclosed that on his bringing a very eligible vacant residence to her notice, Miss Robinson had declined resolutely to view it. A second and even a third instance of this behaviour put it beyond doubt that the Miss Robinsons had been able to persuade themselves that they could continue to reside at the Parsonage as long as either of them should live.

Unhappily for the success of their design, Mr. Darcy was a match for the Miss Robinsons in obstinacy. That he had right and law on his side was something, but not everything; for it was unthinkable that he should have them forcibly ejected. Short of that, he resolved never to rest until the vexatious females were safely deposited under another roof. As soon as the next house within the Pemberley estates suitable to their degree and means became vacant, he resolved to offer it to them rent-free, on condition that they removed to it at once.

"What do you mean by a suitable house?" asked Elizabeth to whom he communicated his intention. "I am sure they would never consider anything less grand than the Parsonage."

"That is absurd," he replied. "It is almost a mansion."

"But they are absurd."

"They must be made to see reason."

"I should congratulate you or anyone else on so conspicuous an achievement. Did you know," she asked after a short pause, "that Mrs. Chichester is shortly to leave Yew Tree Cottage? I met her today in the village. She has received intelligence of her husband's return from abroad, and as he is now stationed at Portsmouth, he is urgent that she should join him without delay. He had advised Mr. Groves by the same post, she said."

"I have not seen Groves these three days," he answered, "and it is news so far as I am concerned. Yew Tree Cottage is very well, but I should have preferred a situation farther removed," he added seriously. "There cannot be any necessity for them to remain in the village. At Stowell or Kympton, or even at Lambton, they would be within driving distance of their acquaintance."

"But not within bullying distance," said Elizabeth. "Have you no concern for the morals of the villagers? What would become of them if Miss Robinson ceased to supervise them?"

Within a week Mrs. Chichester had quitted Pemberley and Yew Tree Cottage stood empty. Riding home from Kympton a day or two later, Darcy checked his horse beside the gate and surveyed it for some minutes. It lay charmingly secluded among trees without being solitary, for it was not far from the village street, and the garden, neither very trim nor too much neglected, was at this time full of spring flowers. Anyone with a taste for the picturesque would admire it exceedingly; but that was not the question to be debated. What would Miss Robinson say to it? He resolved to obtain a direct answer without delay, and rode on through the village to the Parsonage.

The church and Parsonage stood apart from the village and almost opposite to the entrance to the Park. The Parsonage was a substantial house built of stone, and set well back in grounds planted with a variety of trees and shrubs; it had an air of importance and was plainly a gentleman's residence. An elderly manservant admitted Darcy, and on his enquiring for the mistresses, led him at once to the dining-parlour where the two Miss Robinsons, dressed in deepest black, sat on either side of a great fire.

Darcy sat down between them, declined offers of refreshment and enquired with his usual grave civility after their health. These formalities over, while he sought a suitable opening for his proposal, Miss Robinson asked abruptly, "And when are we to have the pleasure of seeing Mrs. Darcy again?"

"But, sister," interposed Miss Sophia, "do not you remember that Mrs. Darcy called here last Monday?"

"True, she did call here last Monday. But I am sure she did not stay above five minutes, for no sooner was she in than she was out again. I do not consider *that* a visit."

Miss Robinson's habit of censoriousness had so grown upon her as the result of long indulgence that it was frequently unintentional. One could never be certain whether she intended offence or was conscious of giving it. Darcy knew this, but was nevertheless so angered by her manner of speaking of Elizabeth that he would not disguise his displeasure. He replied stiffly that Mrs. Darcy had been occupied with a hundred and one concerns. The little boy had been ill, and for some days they had feared the onset of an infectious fever. Then before the ladies could make any observations he commenced at once upon the business he had come about.

"You have doubtless heard that Mrs. Chichester has gone from Yew Tree Cottage."

"Dear me, yes," replied Miss Robinson. "That is no news to us. There are some who quite bemoan Mrs. Chichester quitting the neighbourhood, but I do not at all agree. She ruined all her maids, giving them her castoff finery; and after all Alice Brewer would not go with her to Portsmouth."

"But that was because she did not like to go so far from her family," said Miss Sophia.

"Pray do not contradict me, Sophia. Indeed she would have gone if I had not warned her mother that it was no proper place for her. How can you think of it, I said. A Pemberley girl at Portsmouth. The very idea! Do you suppose you would ever see her again? You should have more care than to let her run into such danger."

Darcy waited until she had finished her speech and then continued: "I was speaking of Yew Tree Cottage which is now empty. As you are under the painful necessity of removing from the Parsonage very shortly, I beg that you will seriously consider its suitability for your future abode. The house is not so large as this, but it is in fact more spacious than would appear from the first view. As soon as you can conveniently see him, Mr. Groves will wait upon you to give you all particulars."

The sisters looked at each other as if unable to credit their ears. Miss Robinson went purple with indignation and Miss Sophia pink with discomfiture; but the latter, not having lost all the effects of good breeding, commanded herself sufficiently to thank him.

"You are always kindness and consideration itself, Mr. Darcy. I am sure Yew Tree Cottage is a very pretty little house, but it would not take the half of our furniture—would it, Sister? And we do not think we need to leave the Parsonage after all, for with a little proper management it could be arranged for us to continue here, which would be so much better for us. Of course we know that we can no longer count upon the income from the living, but our dear Papa has most thoughtfully provided for us, and with care and economy we can still maintain ourselves in the same way as before. I am sure you would not want us to quit our dear home, for Sister could not be happy anywhere else."

"I am afraid," said Darcy speaking more gently, "that you do not altogether comprehend the matter. You have lived here so long that it is but natural for you to regard the house as your own. But the fact is that the Parsonage forms part of the benefice, and the new rector, whoever he may be, will expect to take possession of it as soon as he enters the parish, and most certainly to find it ready for the reception of himself, his family—should he have any—and his furniture."

"That would not be the case if you asked Mr. Mortimer to accept the living," said Miss Robinson. "I hear you have not got a new rector yet, so you can still do so. I wonder you have not thought of it, for I do not think he would take much pressing. Nothing could be more advantageous for everybody. He would continue in his own house at Clopwell, and we should not be turned out of our home to make way for a stranger. I am certain *he* would never desire it."

"I have no intention of offering the living to Mr. Mortimer."

Miss Robinson looked at him, but seemed not to have heard.

"Mr. Mortimer says that all could be done very well by a curate, and that it is quite the thing nowadays for a rector to reside away from the parish."

"I do not remember Mr. Mortimer saying that, Sister," Miss Sophia said in some surprise.

"I beg you will not interrupt, Sophia. It was the day you stayed in bed with a cold caught by going through the rain to see Mrs. Finch. You would go in spite of all I could say, and she was not at home, so back you had to come through the rain, and got your feet wet."

"Whatever Mr. Mortimer may have said on the subject is hardly to the point," said Darcy slightly raising his voice. "I am exceedingly sorry to add to your distresses, but you must allow me to be the best judge of what is for the good of the parish. The personal convenience of individuals—though friends—cannot weigh with me in comparison with that. Mr. Mortimer is all that is amiable, but he has no serious interest in a clergyman's duties, as he would be the first to avow."

"But surely, Mr. Darcy, there would be no objection to engaging a curate. A young man of no particular family and used to poverty would not want to be paid very much. He could lodge with some respectable, clean village woman."

"A curate," said Darcy firmly, "whether under Mr. Mortimer or anyone else, will not do for Pemberley. I must ask you to accept that as final and unconditional. As regards to another residence for yourselves, I do not wish to make any stipulation except as to removal within the usual period—I believe three months—observed in such cases. Any facilities that I can give are entirely at your service." He rose as he spoke for he was afraid that unless he ate his words nothing further could be said that would not call for repentance in a calmer mood.

"Indeed, yes," faltered Miss Sophia, looking thoroughly frightened. "I do not think that poor Papa had any opinion of curates either. If they are so poor, as they always are, they cannot be gentlemen, and that is a pity. It is very unfortunate that Mr. Mortimer has so little liking for making sermons. But there are so many beautiful ones written already that there is no need for him to put himself to any trouble. I am sure there are more than twenty volumes alone in Papa's study, for he would often take a paragraph from one of them to fill up what he had written himself. But of course whatever Mr. Darcy thinks is right should be done. Only as to Yew Tree Cottage, it would not take the half of our furniture unless by building on—"

"Do not talk such nonsense, Sophia," cried her sister. "By the time Yew Tree Cottage was large enough we should be in our graves."

Darcy, studiously polite, but also inflexibly determined to retract nothing of what he had said, now took his leave. Miss Robinson curtseyed with indignant ceremony. As the butler was ushering him to the front door he could hear her voice uplifted in castigation of poor Miss Sophia who had not yet learnt the wisdom of being silent, and never would.

Chapter 2

I<small>N</small> <small>MOMENTS OF EXTREME</small> emotion, especially of wrath or mortification, a gentleman in possession of a wife will rightly claim all her attention while he unburdens himself to the uttermost with that perfect freedom of expression which is his prerogative as a husband. The duty of a wife on such occasions is to listen, and when all has been said, to make observations of a consolatory nature, confirming the gentleman in his good opinion of himself and his bad opinion of all who thwart or vex him, and finally restoring him to good humour.

On reaching home, Darcy went in search of Elizabeth, expressly to acquaint her with all that had been unfolded during his visit to the Parsonage. As she was not in any of her accustomed places in the house, and none of the servants could say where she had gone, he went upstairs to his sister's sitting-room, hoping for information. Georgiana was seated at the pianoforte, and deep in the study of some very intricate music which she was reading for the first time, neither heard nor saw him until he had spoken twice over.

"Elizabeth?" she then replied. "She was here not very long ago. She did not stay a minute—I believe she said she was going out into the grounds. Perhaps she is walking with Richard."

"Have you no recollection at all where she said she was going?"

Georgiana thought for a moment or two and at length answered: "She asked me my favourite colour for a rose, and now I remember that she was going to see some new sorts of roses McGregor has grown which are coming into bloom in one of the greenhouses. She said he had asked her to name them."

This gave a probable direction to Elizabeth's whereabouts, and after lingering another moment or two looking at Georgiana's music and advising her not to study too hard, he went off in good hope of soon finding his wife. Making his way through the flower garden, he came upon her walking there attended by the Scotch head gardener. Both of them were surveying the severely pruned stumps of rose-bushes in a long bed with the deepest interest. While he was still some distance away Elizabeth looked up and gave him a smile of welcome. As soon as they were face to face something of urgency and constraint in his demeanour warned her that he had news to tell, that it would not wait, and that he was impatient of McGregor's presence. The old servant doubtless saw it likewise, for gravely saluting his master and mistress, he walked away to another part of the garden.

"What is the matter?" Elizabeth asked when they were alone. "You look disturbed. Has anything happened?"

"You shall hear," he replied, and while they paced slowly towards the terrace in front of the house he told her of all that had taken place at the Parsonage. He could repeat almost word for word the speeches of Miss Robinson, but the incoherencies of Miss Sophia must be left to Elizabeth's imagination.

"It is impossible to conduct a conversation where none but oneself observes the rules of logic," he said. "I did my best to make myself plain, but I doubt whether they paid me the compliment of believing me. All I know is that Miss Robinson became very angry."

"That is a foregone conclusion," said Elizabeth. "What a delightful scheme they have hatched up, to be sure. But I cannot believe that Mr. Mortimer is privy to it. And yet—is the Clopwell estate at all encumbered, do you know?"

"Between ourselves, I think it may be. Mortimer's brother was spendthrift and negligent, and Mortimer himself is too easy and indolent to retrieve what has been lost. But I am certain he is no schemer. He has his faults, doubtless—as we all have—but guile is not one of them. If he really desired the living, he would ask me for it outright."

"Are you so sure?" Elizabeth asked with a smile. "You are not so approachable as that implies."

"You are implying that I am a very disagreeable sort of person."

"Not at all, dearest, but you can be more intimidating than you probably know."

"Then I could wish I had been able to intimidate Miss Robinson into a more reasonable frame of mind. Argument is not enough; nothing will persuade her but action. Seriously, Elizabeth, the matter has gone on too long, and something must be done."

Elizabeth laughed. "Yes, up to now you have done nothing but reject one applicant after another."

"Not one was in any way suitable. They all desired to be comfortable and rich, and to have as little to do as possible. I begin to think that the kind of man I have set my mind upon must be sought before he can be found. I must prosecute enquiries farther afield than I have done hitherto. No stone must be left unturned . . . There is Richard. He does not look as if there were much amiss with him."

Walking slowly, they had traversed the length of the terrace and reached the western end as Richard's pony carriage guided by a young groom and attended by two nurses came into view round the corner of the house. The heir to Pemberley was about two years old, large, fair and handsome—in short, a thorough Darcy. He set up a clamour on seeing his parents and raised himself up in his seat in his impatience to be lifted out of it. No sooner had he got his way than he ran to his mother and walked a few steps holding her hand. But that could not satisfy him long, and he demanded next to be hoisted to his father's shoulder. He was already remarkable for the activity of his mind, his clear comprehension of what he wanted, and his directness of action in trying to get it. His parents affected to regard him as not extraordinary, but were secretly persuaded that he was probably more beautiful and intelligent than any other child that had ever been born. Like all much noticed and admired children he was tyrannous in exacting attention from those around him, and his amusing antics, his engaging attempts at intelligible speech, his adventurous impulses—as when he started to crawl between the fore and hind legs of his pony—caused such a diversion of ideas as to transport them to the remotest distance from the cares and vexations of church patronage.

At length the little boy was taken indoors and Darcy and Elizabeth left the terrace and strolled across the lawn towards the river which wound through the valley between the wooded heights enclosing the park.

It was that period of the day when the air is balmy after long hours of sunshine. The green of grass and trees was enriched with deepest gold, enhancing the beauty of a scene which held everything to charm the eye and tranquilise the mind. Elizabeth looked about her with delight at familiar objects of which she could never tire.

"I am not altogether easy in my mind about Georgiana," said Darcy, breaking the silence. "She is apt to spend too much time at her instrument. While she was under tuition it was no doubt right and proper—in fact, I encouraged it. But now it begins to verge on eccentricity, making her dreamy and unsocial."

"That is the result of permitting the free exercise of a real talent," answered Elizabeth. "You have done quite right and should not repent."

"Nevertheless there is a due proportion to be observed in all things."

"There is none in the dispensation of gifts, my dear Fitz. You must admit that Georgiana is gifted beyond the ordinary."

"I fear that I remain unconvinced. She is twenty and should be thinking of marriage."

"That she is twenty and not thinking of marriage or young men surely argues an exceptional young woman. You ought to be thankful, for with her simple, ardent nature she might so easily fall in love with quite the wrong sort of young man, in defiance of every rational consideration and normal prospect of happiness. If she is to marry, she would be happiest with a man much older than herself who would be ready to give everything and expect nothing in return—nothing, that is to say, that she did not yield of her own free will. But where such a man is to be found I do not know."

"Nor I," said Darcy with a smile. "Most men are selfish beings, and marriage often makes them more so, though it should have the contrary effect. Has it ever struck you that Mortimer is partial to her?"

"It is so apparent that Georgiana is beginning to be annoyed by it."

"He is a very good, honest fellow, yet I cannot imagine her settling down with him. Nor would it be the most desirable match in the prudential view. The family has declined in importance from what it was several generations ago."

"I like him very well," said Elizabeth, "but principally because there is nothing in him to dislike."

"And Georgiana?"

"She is not so tolerant of nonentity as I am become."

"Pray what does that mean?"

She laughed and slipped her hand inside his arm. "Something so extremely complicated that it can only be unravelled at leisure. In other words, I am not sure what I do mean."

"That is one of your fictions," said Darcy. "You do know perfectly well, but you like to tease me. Well, I am willing to oblige you. I am teased and you are amused. Are you now satisfied?"

"Not at all. You have left me with nothing to say."

"Another fiction."

They were now walking beside the stream, and Darcy fixed his eyes on the water. "There should be some very tolerable fishing for your uncle when he comes in June," he observed. "He and your aunt hope to arrive on the seventh or eighth of the month, so Mr. Gardiner wrote in his last letter."

"Yes, and the Bingleys and their children should be here by the fourth. My sister Kitty may come shortly, though I am not sure of the date. When I last heard she was still at Hunsford where she has been staying with the Collinses."

"The Collinses!"

"I fancy that Kitty is in training for a clergyman's wife under Charlotte Collins since Maria Lucas found a husband in a neighbouring parish. But of course Mr. Collins takes all the credit for that."

"Mr. Collins will always appropriate every good thing to himself."

"Then I wonder he has not applied for Pemberley. But no, nothing could exceed the advantages of Hunsford in his eyes, nor compensate for all the pains and labour he has bestowed on making the Parsonage a model of comfort and convenience. And how could he ever tear himself away from his beloved patroness, Lady Catherine de Bourgh?"

"She is perfectly welcome to keep him, but I am under the impression that she is not so well pleased with him as formerly."

The next day after breakfast Elizabeth was in the hall reading a letter when Darcy came out of the library to look for her.

"Here is an odd thing," he said. "We were talking only yesterday of Mr. Collins, and this morning a communication has come from him."

"Mr. Collins? What does he say? But I can guess. Do read it to me, however."

"You had better read it for yourself. I fear I cannot do justice to the rotundity of his phrases."

The letter was as follows:

Honoured and dear Sir,

Having received intelligence that the Rectory of Pemberley is presently vacant through the decease of the former incumbent, whereof I had unhappily remained ignorant until this forenoon, I take up my pen most respectfully to make application for the said benefice to be conferred upon me, upon favourable consideration of my special and peculiar claims to your notice, at the same time assuring you of my fervent gratitude and steadfast desire to serve you should you deem me worthy to hold and enjoy it.

As I have had the honour aforetime of officiating before you in Hunsford Church, it should be unnecessary for me to recommend myself on the score of either eloquence or delivery. Some years have passed, unfortunately, since you had the opportunity of judging my performance, but I can confidently assert that it has not in the interval suffered any deterioration in matter or expression, and I hereby state that it shall ever be my first aim and dearest object to inculcate in my humbler parishioners that respect for your illustrious person which is due to high lineage and great possessions, both by frequent and earnest exhortation, and by the constant example of a studied deference on my own part in all our personal intercourse.

I understand that the income from the living is eight hundred a year, a figure not much above that derived from Hunsford. My reasons for desiring to change my present abode are, however, briefly these. I have every confidence that your patronage will avail to procure my further advancement in the Church, the more so since my connection with your amiable lady, my cousin Elizabeth (née Bennet), will suggest to you the propriety of such steps as will attain that end. It will also be to the advantage of my children to be brought up in the vicinity of your own son, thus laying the foundations of a connection from which considerable benefits may be expected to accrue hereafter. Finally, through my cousinship with Mrs. Darcy, and owing to other circumstances which it does not become me to mention, I fear that I have lost that unqualified approbation with which your aunt, Lady Catherine de Bourgh, was wont to distinguish me. That I have endeavoured to support with all meekness and patience that withdrawal of her favour, now limiting our intercourse to the most distant civilities will not, I think, argue any want of desert on my part, but a truly Christian fortitude. There is, however, no merit in resignation where evils can be remedied, and in this persuasion I appeal to your sense of justice as well as to your compassion for such alleviation of my lot as lies in your power. Hoping therefore to receive a favourable reply to his communication, and ever praying for the continued health of yourself and your lady, I beg to subscribe myself

Your Humble and Obedient Servant,

—Wm. Collins

Elizabeth smiled more than once as she read this effusion, notwithstanding its tactless references to herself which testified to the writer's incurable stupidity. The scarcely veiled allusion to Lady Catherine's resentment at her marriage with Darcy was not likely to forward his cause, and how he could think it would passed comprehension.

If, however, he did sincerely believe that Lady Catherine's displeasure with him proceeded from a conviction that he had taken a hand in promoting the marriage of her nephew, whom she had designed for her own daughter, with a portionless young woman of no particular family related to himself, he might consider that nephew to be under an obligation to him with some show of reason on his side. Remembering that Miss Elizabeth Bennet had been in almost daily contact with Mr. Darcy that spring now four years ago when she was the guest of Mr. and Mrs. Collins at Hunsford Parsonage, and he was staying at Rosings Park, it was not an unwarrantable conclusion. And although a reconciliation had been patched up between aunt and nephew, Lady Catherine had never forgiven her niece-in-law for the frustration of her dearest hopes, nor by the same token, that young woman's cousin.

All these ideas hurried through her head even while the sentences of the letter passed under her eyes. Having read through to the end she looked up at her husband and asked, "How could he only just have heard of the vacancy? It was published in the newspapers at the time of its occurrence, I suppose."

"The how or the why does not much signify," Darcy replied. "He must have missed seeing the notice, and Lady Catherine of course would not deign to mention it."

"I am rather surprised that Lady Catherine has not proposed Mr. Collins to you of her own accord. If she is really so tired of him as appears, it is strange that she should neglect an opportunity of getting rid of him."

"She may write yet. But in that event I should reply that the recommendation comes too late."

"What?" cried Elizabeth, all amazement. "What on earth do you mean?"

Darcy smiled and, glancing at the servant who kept his station not far away, said, "If you will come into the library where we shall be more private, I will explain."

Elizabeth rose with alacrity and preceded him to the door of the library. When he had closed it behind them, he went to the writing-table, and took up a letter lying there.

"I had this at the same time as Mr. Collins. It is from an old schoolfellow—Lord Egbury of Mentmore in Yorkshire—and is written on behalf of a younger brother, Stephen Acworth."

"Is this brother known to you?"

"Only by repute. I was at Eton with Lord Egbury—George Acworth as he was then—and the second son Walter; but Stephen never came there. I did stay once at Mentmore Castle, but he was away with a private tutor, so I have not at any time set eyes on him."

"Then you are not really intimate with the family."

"No. George and Walter Acworth were not very particular friends of mine and I do not know why I was invited to Mentmore. I went there and did not much like it. The old Lord Egbury revolted me with his coarseness. He set his sons a shocking example of drunkenness and profanity, and besides treated his wife shamefully, making no secret of his infidelities. The two elder Acworths were good-natured and dull-witted, but from what Lady Egbury told me of her youngest son Stephen I formed the opinion that he was of a wholly different stamp from his brothers—gentle, retiring, serious, and studiously inclined."

"And in flight from coarseness and profanity he took orders?"

"It was understood that the family living was to be nursed for him until he was of an age to hold it. After I left Eton I saw no more of the Acworths and heard nothing more until it was reported that the eldest son had succeeded to the title and estates on the death of his father. And now after these many years he asks me to do him a favour. About a year ago Stephen married, he says, and his wife has lately died. Lord Egbury describes him as overwhelmed with grief, and expresses the fear that his reason may give way under it. Change of surroundings with some occupation is prescribed, and hearing by a side wind that the living of Pemberley is still vacant, Lord Egbury requests it for his unfortunate brother."

"But how can you accede to his request without some positive assurance as to his brother's suitability? You have never seen him and know nothing but what you have heard. Hearsay is no very reliable guide."

"True, madam, that has struck me as forcibly as it has yourself. Hearsay is certainly not enough. And so I propose making

Stephen Acworth's acquaintance before offering him the living. Lord Egbury mentions that he has left Mentmore and is staying at the family town house in Cavendish Square.

"You mean that you will go to London?"

"There is no alternative, I fear. I shall stay not an hour longer than is necessary for the prosecution of the business, for I abominate being at Berkeley Square without you—any place, for that matter. I would not go if I did not expect to find in Stephen Acworth the very person I have been looking for, and so have this long-drawn-out uncertainty put to an end."

"When shall you go? Do not forget that the Vernons are dining with us tomorrow."

"No, I had not forgotten. Unless anything unforeseen occurs to prevent me, I shall travel the following day."

"Let us hope that Mr. Collins in the meantime does not arrive in person to throw himself at your feet, or that Lord Egbury has not discovered another and healthier locality for his brother."

"As to Mr. Collins, I shall forestall him by replying at once. Lord Egbury's ideas and wishes I can by no means influence, but I do remember of him that once he took a notion into his head, it was not easily dislodged."

"Has it struck you," asked Elizabeth, "that a man whose reason is staggering is not in a fit state to take up the burden of a parish?"

"That is my principal reason for wishing to see him. Egbury may have exaggerated his condition, however. There is a passage in his letter which interests me very much, coming from him. He says—here it is—'I feel sure that my poor brother would have a great deal in common with yourself. He has suffered much at Mentmore from having no one to converse with on the sort of subjects he prefers. Unlike the rest of us he is a greater reader.'"

"That does quite unconsciously convey the character of Stephen Acworth," she said, "for it implies a comparison with yourself. It is both a compliment and a recommendation. I do not think Lord Egbury can be quite so stupid as you make him out."

Darcy smiled and made some light rejoinder from which Elizabeth inferred that he regarded that matter as virtually settled. It was unlike his usual cautiousness which often held him in long and anxious debate upon a question before coming to a final decision, and she who was impatient of all such deliberation was the more relieved and pleased. The uncertainty to which he had alluded had gone on far too long, and was already showing evil effects. Miss Robinson had begun to scheme and plot to continue at the Parsonage, and Mr. Mortimer was becoming tiresome to Georgiana. Elizabeth's enjoyment of her lot was therefore no longer unqualified, and she wished for it to be restored with the least possible delay. She desired, in fact, as we all do, to be forever perfectly happy.

Chapter 3

NOTHING OCCURRED TO PREVENT or put off Darcy's departure for London on the day appointed. Mr. Collins made no untoward appearance, nor was Lord Egbury visited by second thoughts on the desirability of Derbyshire as a place of residence for his brother. The last commissions given and the final adieus said, Elizabeth saw his carriage go off and disappear among the trees with a sense of being deserted for those particular pleasures which cannot be enjoyed in the country. For though he was gone on business, it could not fully engross his time. At this season all the theatres were open; Mrs. Siddons was playing at Drury Lane; there were concerts to be heard, and exhibitions of pictures to be seen.

The days passed and Sunday came. Elizabeth and Georgiana drove in customary state to church and occupied their seats in the family gallery. The service over, Mr. Mortimer hurriedly doffed his surplice and hastened to the church door to meet Mrs. and Miss Darcy. It had become established that he spent the interval between the morning and afternoon services at

Pemberley House, but Darcy's absence created a doubt in his mind as to Mrs. Darcy's wishes, and after the usual civilities had passed, he ventured upon a question which should resolve it. Elizabeth assured him that she looked for his returning with them, whereupon his countenance cleared and he thanked her with visible relief and gratification.

The young man was at this time in the full mood of his enjoyment of an unrequited passion. He kept his eyes most perseveringly fixed on Georgiana whenever he was not obliged to direct them upon someone else, and listened with bated breath to the least word that fell from her lips; while Georgiana as perseveringly ignored his glances and maintained a gravity and stiffness of manner towards him as far removed from complaisance as any young woman could contrive. In so gentle a creature, ever anxious to avoid giving pain, it was the more remarkable and spoke either a general determination against love, or a special aversion for the gentleman.

The Miss Robinsons, next to the Family in consequence, had now come out of church and must be spoken to. Elizabeth walked beside Miss Robinson down the path towards the lych-gate, where the Pemberley carriage was drawn up. Georgiana, Miss Sophia Robinson and Mr. Mortimer came behind, while the lesser residents, farmers, tradespeople and villagers streamed through the porch in their wake and spread out over the church-yard to wait until the equipage had driven off. Elizabeth acknowledged the salutations of the people who stood nearest her as she passed them, and having satisfied Miss Robinson's curiosity concerning Darcy's absence from church, and parried a question as to the nature of the business that had taken him to

London, she entered the carriage. Georgiana and Mortimer followed her.

The drive back to the house passed without very much being said beyond observations on the fineness of the weather and the forwardness of the season. Mortimer was too much engaged in watching for a sign of relenting on the part of Georgiana to ask any questions of his own about Darcy's journey; but while they sat in the dining-parlour eating their cold meat, Elizabeth thought it only fair to give him a hint of what was impending. He took it very quietly, without evincing surprise, and if his ingenuous countenance clouded a little, it was probably owing to the reflection that he would soon no longer come riding over to Pemberley so frequently as in the past month or two. His involuntary glance round the room showed what he was thinking.

Elizabeth went on to give the account of Mr. Stephen Acworth she had received from Darcy. Mortimer listened dejectedly, no doubt comparing her summary of super-excellent attainments with his own shortcomings.

"I knew Darcy would be uncommon hard to please," he said at length. "He is all for scholarship. He likes a man who can string together Latin tags by the dozen."

"I am sure that is not at all my brother's idea of scholarship," said Georgiana very decidedly. "He says that a man of real learning never displays it in that manner."

This was Georgiana's sole contribution to the conversation. After she had uttered it she cast down her eyes and appeared lost in thought. Mortimer looked dumbfounded. Elizabeth laughed and said immediately, "Mr. Darcy would never inflict too learned a theologian upon us, nor at least one who could not bring himself down to the level of our less instructed understandings; for we poor females, though without Latin or Greek, have also souls to be saved."

"Oh, certainly," said Mortimer very seriously. "What is wanted at Pemberley is a quiet gentleman-like man who is not too clever, but clever enough. I daresay that with all his learning this Mr. Acworth will not set himself up too much above the rest of us."

After the meal was over and there was no further necessity for remaining at the table, Georgiana escaped to her own apartment and Elizabeth, maintaining the custom when Darcy was at home, went out with Mortimer on a tour of the gardens and stables. Mortimer admired everything he saw, but especially the horses.

"I shouldn't wonder if Darcy has not some of the best horses in the country. Why don't he breed for racing? I should in his place."

"He has no interest in the sport."

"I daresay not. His mind is set on higher matters. You know, Mrs. Darcy, he used to be held up to us as a model of what a young man should be, and we didn't much like it. But he is vastly changed since he married; you wouldn't know him for the same. That is one of the effects of having a wife, I suppose."

"And what do you suppose are the effects of having a wife?" enquired Elizabeth, unable to refrain from drawing him out for her own amusement.

"If I am to speak for myself, I think it would do me a great deal of good. You can see without my telling you that I am an awkward, backward sort of man, and though you may not believe it, I often feel at a horrid disadvantage in the presence of ladies. True, I am not uncomfortable with you, for you know how to put a man at his ease. But with others! Sometimes I have not a word to say for myself, and then when I do think of something that comes naturally, I am afraid to say it for fear of displeasing female ears. For men, I am sorry to tell you, Mrs. Darcy, talk very differently among themselves. When the wine goes round, out come words and expressions you would not like to hear. Now if a man has a wife, he will get into the way of accommodating his speech to her taste. And then a wife orders the house in such a manner that her husband has to mind his behaviour, which is what he should do. When I go home after visiting at Pemberley where there is order and elegance in every part, I think what a difference a lady in the house would make." He paused at last, but after a moment said solemnly, "I don't think I should make a bad husband either."

"I am sure you would not," said Elizabeth warmly.

"It is very handsome of you to say so, Mrs. Darcy, for after Darcy I must seem monstrously stupid and countrified. I wish others could think so too." He heaved a great sigh, and looked at her with eloquent eyes.

"Perhaps someone will one day."

"But there is only one I would like to think so."

"You know, Mr. Mortimer, the first choice of our hearts is often a mistaken one."

"I was afraid you would say something like that. Then you think there is no hope for me."

Elizabeth made no disclaimer and they proceeded in silence until he burst out anew.

"I know I am not good enough for Miss Darcy."

"It is not that at all," she said gently. Truly sorry for his disappointment, she began to depict Georgiana as an extraordinary girl who cared for nothing but study and was indifferent to the society of any but the members of her own family. By some exaggeration of these traits she hoped to convince him that he had fixed his heart upon a very unpromising object, in the belief that he was not the man to nurse for long a one-sided attachment. But Mortimer, who was of a sanguine temperament and rebounded from each blow with like force, began to argue his own case with more ardour than cogency, until his hostess, though still commiserating him, lost patience and longed for the seclusion of her dressing-room. For in spite of all that the romantic novelists have written, nothing can be so dull to the onlooker as a respectable love. When the clock over the archway to the stables was heard striking the half-hour after two, a reminder that it was time to be preparing for the afternoon service, she felt an exquisite relief.

The following Tuesday her impatience for news from her husband was at last satisfied. He had written on his arrival at Berkeley Square promising a further letter when he had seen Mr. Acworth, and she came to breakfast from a survey of her flower garden to find it awaiting her. Eager to learn all that he had to tell she opened it forthwith, but saw that he had written at such length and so closely that a much more careful perusal would be required than was possible at the table. The first sentence informed her that he would reach home on the morrow, and this important question answered to her satisfaction, she cast a hurried glance over the rest of the page and then at the last one, and set the letter aside to be read in private and at leisure.

Georgiana had likewise heard from her brother, though briefly, and she looked up from her own letter and said, "Fitzwilliam has found nearly all the music we asked for, and now he is to hunt the bookshops. He says the spring fashions for women are ugly beyond words. Have you, too, a letter from him, Elizabeth?"

"Yes, and there is so much packed into it that I have not had time yet to read it properly. I collect, however, that he is returning tomorrow and bringing a visitor with him."

"A visitor! We have had none these six weeks, and how pleasant it has been."

"True. But this is no ordinary visitor. I believe that the new Rector of Pemberley is to be introduced into our midst."

"Is that all? There must be a new rector in any case, and we cannot escape his being introduced to us. How I wish we could make the acquaintance of some person unlike any we have known before. If only Fitzwilliam would bring us a musician, or a poet, or an actor of genius. But he would never do it because such people are not of our station and cannot be admitted to our society. And yet I am sure they must be on the whole more interesting than the people who do stay here, or come calling."

"That is very possible," said Elizabeth. "But you should remember that acquaintance does not only consist in interesting conversation, and the kind of people you mention, with some exceptions no doubt, lead irregular, and often disreputable lives."

"Do you know, Elizabeth, I have observed that when my brother is absent, you talk just as he would on any debatable subject. But when he is here, you fly to the opposite opinion. If *he* had said that musicians and poets and actors lead disreputable lives, *you* would have maintained the contrary."

"As to that, my dear Georgiana, you seem *not* to have observed that your brother frequently makes a statement with the sole object of provoking an argument, and if I did not immediately dissent from him, he would think I was either ill or out of humour. Besides, you are to remember that the simplest statement—as about the weather or somebody's taste in dress—is so highly controversial, and so many divergent opinions can be rationally advanced upon the same subject, that it is well nigh impossible to decide what is true."

"At that rate," said Georgiana, with more acuteness than most of her acquaintance would have given her credit for, "you cannot believe what anyone says, and your own statements least of all."

Elizabeth smilingly admitted the impeachment. "You see what comes of having to talk willy-nilly whenever you or your brother fall into one of your silences in dull company. One must say something, so long as it is not instantly detected as nonsense."

Breakfast over, the sisters separated, Georgiana to go to her sitting-room and her pianoforte, Elizabeth with her letter to the library. Here, sitting at the writing-table, with the letter pages spread out in front of her, she was soon immersed in what Darcy had to say. Her cursory survey, lighting upon a word or two here and there in his small and even handwriting, had by no means taught her what was to be unfolded, and she now learnt that she was not only to receive Mr. Acworth, but another visitor as well.

"I am happy to say," Darcy wrote, "that the business which brought me to town is now concluded so far as it can be, and I shall leave London early tomorrow—Wednesday—expecting to be with you in the afternoon of the next day. This is slow travelling for my natural impatience to be at home; but as I am bringing Mr. Acworth on his journey hither, it is not fair to one in his state of health to hasten the journey unduly. There will also be a third person in the carriage—Major Wakeford—whom I have induced to return with me to Pemberley for a long stay.

"You have heard me speak of Francis Wakeford, I know. He is a cousin of ours on my father's side, and on several occasions spent his school holidays here. We were of the same age, shared the same tastes and became firm friends. After he entered the army we saw one another only infrequently, but this happened without any fault on either side. He subsequently went abroad with his regiment, and I ceased to hear from him, except once after my father's death. I replied, but never knew whether my letter had reached him. Thus matters stood when two days ago I heard by mere chance that he was in town, in lodgings in Upper Seymour Street. My informant, a fellow officer of the same regiment, told me that he had been severely wounded in action, losing an arm, besides sustaining an injury to the left leg which rendered him very lame, and that in consequence he was invalided out of the army on half-pay. At the first opportunity I sought him out. His condition as described had in some measure prepared me for some change in him, apart from that wrought by the passage of time, but I must confess that on first seeing him he appeared so altered as almost to defy recognition. At thirty-two he is prematurely grey, his face seamed with lines and bearing the stamp of all he has suffered. But there is always that in persons with whom we have been truly intimate which survives all physical change, and after we had been talking together a short while, the Francis Wakeford I had known as a young man returned once more to view.

"I stayed for some time talking with him, and he seemed so cheered that although he spoke of his desire for solitude, I became convinced that his need is for companionship. I asked him what he was doing in London among strangers when he could be better cared for in his father's house. He replied that his surroundings had most cruelly reminded him of tastes and pursuits he could no longer indulge, and that the commiseration his state excited in his mother and sisters, so far from soothing him, served only to augment his wretchedness and weaken his self-command. When you have read thus far I know you will not blame me for pressing him to come to Pemberley and remain as our guest for as long as he chooses. He had not previously heard that I was married, and professed to be greatly surprised at the news, whereupon I told him that when he saw you he would no longer wonder. To conclude, I know that between us we shall find the means to rescue him from his present dejection of spirits and restore him to a happier frame of mind.

"And now to turn to Mr. Acworth. I find it difficult to express in few words what I think of this man, or perhaps it would be truer to say that I am at a loss to know what I do think. As you will recall, I was prepossessed in his favour by the good report I had of him formerly, the truth of which there was no reason to doubt since it came from those who had no motive for deception. Everyone at Mentmore spoke of him with praise and affection. Having now for the first time seen him in the flesh, I cannot say that he pleases me; but it may be that the discrepancy between the creature formed of my imagination and the actual man accounts for my disappointment. It will not do to give way to first unfavourable impressions, for he may prove to be one of those men who never do themselves justice before strangers. We must not judge him, therefore, until closer acquaintance has revealed more of his character.

"Having conceded this much, I can speak the more frankly. I have always flattered myself on being able to form a tolerably correct estimate of a person at a first meeting, particularly when it has for its purpose some business which demands candour on both sides. Mr. Acworth had a great deal to say, he spoke well and his sentiments were all that they should be, yet I found myself at every turn questioning his sincerity. Methought he did protest too much. Even if he had anything to gain in the pecuniary sense by exchanging the living of Mentmore for that of Pemberley, there could be no disgrace in avowing it; but he laboured the point that all he desired was a change of scene and a new direction to his thoughts. This is self-evident, and need only have been touched upon, instead of which he was copious in self-disclosure. That perhaps, Elizabeth, is at the bottom of my distrust. I cannot comprehend how he could speak of his inmost feelings to a man he had never seen before and can know next to nothing of, as he did to me.

"At a second interview which took place, this time at my house, although he had previously expressed the strongest desire to come to Pemberley, he begged that any decision affecting permanent residence might remain in suspense for at least six weeks. My original intention had been to allow a fortnight at most, on consideration of all the evils which a longer delay might produce, and had I consulted my own inclination it would have been strictly to adhere to it. But his request, though inconvenient, could not be judged unreasonable, and I agreed to a period of what might be called mutual probation, not to be extended beyond the six weeks desired, and terminable on his side beforehand on any new circumstance arising. In this I was moved as much by a sense of obligation to his brother who had approached me in the name of friendship, as by his own unhappy situation. Whether I have acted wisely in my own interest time will show. Expediency might point to another course, but on the whole my conscience approves what I have done.

"Well, now I have written out all my mind to you, and feel the clearer for it. Could I have acted otherwise? At the worst some time will have been gained, for I shall not in the meanwhile give over enquiries in other quarters. Acworth will, of course, stay with us for the present, and you will have ample opportunities of studying his character in all its intricacy. It is doubtless as complicated as you could wish; but that will be all in its favour, for, it will spur you on to solve the riddle, if such there be."

The remainder of the letter dealt with purely personal matters. At the end Darcy had added this postscript:

"Stephen Acworth bears a striking facial resemblance to his father, the late Lord Egbury. That may be the reason why I do not take to him."

Having read all that her husband had written, Elizabeth knew not what to think except that uncertainty must continue—no very happy reflection. Francis Wakeford she was thoroughly disposed to welcome warmly. His character and disposition as portrayed by Darcy left no room for doubt and she was eager to play her part in his restoration to health and better spirits. With regard to Stephen Acworth she was sensible of the misgivings imparted by Darcy, but also felt a lively curiosity. She knew her husband's mind too well to suppose for a moment that the several impressions made upon him by this man had not been long and carefully pondered before being committed to paper. He strove always to be generous, rather than exact and impartial in his estimate of any person, the more so as he knew himself prone to dislike a new acquaintance upon sight. Yet that he should have gone to the interview with Stephen Acworth, prepossessed in his favour, prepared to be cordial, and came away dissatisfied was extraordinary upon any supposition save that of good reason. Her second reading of certain phrases in no way varied this conclusion. Such sentences as—"I find myself questioning his sincerity at every turn—he was copious in self-disclosure"—could admit of only one interpretation.

The rest of the day was full of those occupations and engagements which hinder recollection. As on every Tuesday, soup and dumplings were dispensed to the sick and aged poor of Pemberley, and a cluster of men, women and children stood at a back door waiting for their empty basins to be replenished. Mrs. Reynolds, the housekeeper, and Baxter, the butler, were in attendance; Elizabeth moved among the people, talking to them, ascertaining their needs and their difficulties. Young as she was, and of a sphere beyond their knowledge, the villagers had discovered that however freely they spoke of their troubles, she never rebuked them, but understood immediately whatever they wished to say, even though words failed them. And when Mrs. Stone, a widow with a large family of children, said, "I ask your pardon, ma'am, but Miss Robinson have told my Rachel as she is to go into service with Mrs. Bridges at Kympton," she comprehended without questioning that the poor woman was begging that Rachel should not go to Mrs. Bridges, but should be taken into service at the Great House where she herself had been a serving-maid. This indeed was what Mrs. Stone and the fourteen-year-old Rachel did hope for. Mrs. Bridges had the reputation of being a very harsh, strict mistress, but how could they gainsay Miss Robinson? When Elizabeth promised to speak to Miss Robinson herself, informing her that she considered she had a prior claim to Rachel's services, the poor woman could hardly express all her gratitude and went away overjoyed.

This fresh instance of Miss Robinson's highhandedness made Elizabeth extremely indignant. That, as the late rector's eldest daughter, she should have assumed the airs and authority of a patroness during the many years Pemberley had been without a mistress was to be understood, though deplored; but that she should continue to give the law to the parishioners, when she no longer had any standing but that of sufferance, was intolerable. Mrs. Darcy determined to act in such a way that Miss Robinson should no longer remain under any misapprehension of her intention to put an end to this state of affairs.

When all the people had gone away she had some conversation with Mrs. Reynolds about Rachel Stone.

"You wish her to be taken into the house, ma'am?" said the housekeeper. "Her mother was an excellent needlewoman and could act maid when required. I hear Rachel is good with her needle, good for her age, that is, and she could be put to work in the linen-room."

There was something in Mrs. Reynold's aspect that spoke disapprobation, and Elizabeth said at once, "What else do you know of the girl?"

"Well, ma'am, no harm exactly. She is a fine well-grown girl of her age, and looks older and behaves older than she is. It is a pity, ma'am, that the children have no father. Sarah Stone is what I would call weak with them. Rachel must learn to mind her manners when she comes here."

"I dare say she will do tolerably well under proper guidance," said her mistress. It was thus settled that Rachel Stone was to enter service at Pemberley House as a serving-maid.

Elizabeth awoke next morning with a sense of the liveliest expectation. Never before during the whole three and a half years of their married life had she and Darcy been separated for so long, and on this day of his return, the hours which must elapse before he came seemed insupportably slow. It struck her that he might arrive sooner than he had given her to expect, so although she had at first intended to call at the Parsonage during the morning and beard Miss Robinson upon the subject of Rachel Stone, she gave up the project and resolved not to go beyond the grounds immediately surrounding the house. She kept, in fact, to the terrace where she spent some time with Richard and listened to some new words he had learnt to say. The child seemed well enough, but a rash on his neck and arms prompted her to consult Mrs. Reynolds. The housekeeper gave it as her opinion that the spots were an effect of the great heat they were having, and then, for it did not need much to set her off talking, she gave her mistress a history of all the complaints suffered by Darcy and Georgiana during their nursery years. Coughs and colds and biliousness had afflicted them both, and at one time Miss Darcy had been a prey to constant sickness. Unripe apricots were the cause, and after the most minute enquiry it was discovered that they had been taken from the greenhouse by her brother, then a boy of twelve or thirteen, and conveyed to her secretly. On being questioned he had confessed to it all.

"For I never knew Mr. Darcy to tell a lie," declared Mrs. Reynolds, "and what he did was in ignorance and the affection of his heart for his little sister. But, oh, how relieved we all were! A little senna put everything right, and I would not wonder, ma'am, but what a small dose would be good for Master Richard."

At three o'clock, Elizabeth being then indoors, the arrival of a carriage was heard. But, alas, it brought callers—a mother and two daughters. They stayed fortunately but twenty minutes and then departed. Towards four o'clock she went into the breakfast-parlour to look for a book missing from the library which she thought might have been left lying on one of the window seats. The book was not there, but she stood awhile at the window looking out, and her eyes roved over the prospect of lawn, and river, and wooded slopes beyond, and as far as the avenue of beech trees on the extreme left from which the carriage-road issued on its descent into the valley. In the same instant that her eyes reached this point, Darcy's carriage came into view and down the steep incline towards the river. Now it had crossed the bridge and, though she could see it no longer, as she darted into the hall she could hear its approach. By the time it had drawn up with a clatter of hooves upon the gravel she was standing at the top of the flight of steps outside the entrance.

Darcy got out first, but there was only time for a look and a smile before he turned to assist someone inside the carriage to alight. Elizabeth next saw a man, not much less tall than her husband, neither handsome nor plain, neither dark nor fair, but tanned by exposure to every sort of weather. An empty sleeve was pinned to the breast of his coat; he mounted the steps to the door with a decided limp. His face was grave and careworn, but on being presented to her by her husband as Major Wakeford, his smile transformed as it illumined his countenance.

She said a few words of cordial welcome to him and then turned to receive her second guest. Mr. Stephen Acworth stood before her, very dark, spare, of little more than middle height. His darkness was indeed to the degree of swarthiness; as he removed his hat his hair was seen to be black and curly. His nose was large and aquiline, his mouth wide but not unhandsome in its curves. His dark, sunken eyes had a bright intensity of gaze. As Elizabeth gave him her hand, because she had given it to Major Wakeford, he bowed over it with an excessive gesture of gallantry.

She recalled afterwards that there had been the light either of curiosity or recognition in his eyes—she could not determine which—as he approached her. In the agitation of the arrival, of having to command the variety of emotions it called forth and to appear most completely mistress of the occasion, she did not discern it until later when she had time to think over every minute circumstance of the introduction. For what chiefly struck her at the moment of first beholding him was her instant conviction of having seen him before, though the when and the where escaped recollection, and try as she would, could not be brought to mind.

Chapter 4

THE LATE ARRIVAL OF the travellers gave Elizabeth no opportunity for any private talk with her husband before they were all to meet at dinner. She was therefore unable to relate her astonishing conviction that Mr. Acworth's physiognomy was not that of a complete stranger. The few minutes they might have had alone together on descending to the hall, there to await their guests, were interrupted by Georgiana who followed them almost immediately. In her shyness of the strangers she was about to meet, she kept as close to her brother and sister as possible. Darcy could only ask Elizabeth whether she had received his letter, and she could only reply with an expressive look that indeed she had, before. Mr. Acworth also made his appearance from the staircase and came towards them. She was then in a position to judge whether the long journey with its enforced intimacy, the opportunities it gave of close observation, and its leisure to discuss almost every subject under the sun, had in any degree softened Darcy's opinion of the young man. It was instantly apparent by

the change in his demeanour from happy, domestic ease to digni-
fied gravity that no such alteration had taken place.

At dinner, with Major Wakeford and Mr. Acworth on either
side of her, so that she had continually to look from one to the
other, she could not but mark the contrast between the two
men, which was so complete that it could truly be said that
whatever the one was, the other was not. Major Wakeford was
serious and quiet; his expression varied little; he had the austere
aspect of a man of action who is also a thinker. When he spoke
it was in the fewest possible words and was directly intelligible,
admitting of only one significance. He was as spare of movement
as of speech; he made no fuss of his maimed condition, and
showed no self-consciousness in accepting the assistance which
the loss of an arm made necessary.

Mr. Acworth, on the other hand, was seen to be of a naturally
vivacious temperament. He had a quick-glancing eye, a mobile
mouth, and his whole countenance reflected every passing
thought and emotion. Elizabeth had the continuous impression
that every look, every movement, and that very many of his
speeches were the result of previous deliberation and were so
designed as to produce a certain effect upon those before him.
There was no doubt that he was trying to please. When, as not
infrequently happened, he could take no direct part in the conversation, he fell into a drooping, moping silence, and then looked
extremely melancholy. This would last until some chance remark,
usually from Elizabeth herself, roused him and his face would
instantly light up and his eyes sparkle with renewed animation.

The talk ran at first upon the journey from town and then
discussed travelling in general. There was comparison of routes,

roads and inns; everyone had some dire or amusing experience to relate. It was agreed that the route to Derbyshire through Oxford and Warwick was the pleasantest, though not the most direct.

"I am always happy to stay the night at Oxford," said Elizabeth, "but I remember one occasion, several years ago, when we were kept from sleeping by some horrid disturbance in the street outside the inn."

"Some town and gown affair, probably," said Darcy. "It may be a time-honoured custom that the two parties should periodically come to blows, but it is none the less annoying to the blameless, peaceable traveller." He then turned to Acworth and asked him whether he had not been a student of Balliol College.

"Yes," replied Acworth. But immediately afterwards he exclaimed, "No, no, what am I saying? I was at Magdalen."

To Elizabeth her husband appeared to be trying not to look surprised. The gentleman's consternation at being mistaken for a member of a college not his own struck her, however, as being merely laughable. She knew that certain colleges at the University ranked higher in consequence than others, either from being considered more fashionable, or from having a greater reputation for learning, but there was no horrifying difference that she had ever heard of between the two that had been mentioned. Nevertheless there are sentiments harboured by the male heart that are forever incomprehensible to female intelligence, and this rivalry of scholastic institutions was undoubtedly one of them.

Exerting herself to break the rather uncomfortable silence which followed, Elizabeth asked Major Wakeford whether in the course of his campaigning he had ever come so near Bonaparte as to be sensible of his proximity. She was afraid the question might sound downright silly to a soldier of experience, but she knew that as a rule one had but to mention Bonaparte for all the gentlemen present to become loquacious.

"Never," Major Wakeford replied. "Wherever I have fought, I have always known him to be hundreds of miles away. We soldiers have to think only of our immediate task, whatever it may be."

"I can understand that," said Darcy. "But to the Englishman at home whose view, though deficient in many particulars yet comprehends the whole, the idea that a man sprung from the people has in a comparatively short time assumed control over vast territories, and in consequence the lives and destinies of millions of human beings, does very powerfully affect his imagination, besides affronting his sense of justice."

"When I had time to reflect, which was seldom, I thought exactly as you do," Major Wakeford replied. "But as another artillery officer, I confess that I admired him. His use of the arm was masterly."

"While we stay-at-homes regard him as evil incarnate," said Elizabeth. "You must know that we are half-persuaded that he cannot be human, for in that case how could he perform such prodigies as he has done? Whence his invincibility, if not from the fact that his uniform conceals the cloven hoof, not to mention the other distinguishing marks of a fiend—horns, and tail?"

"Excellent, upon my word!" said Mr. Acworth, laughing rather affectedly.

"But," she continued, ignoring the compliment, "I dare say there is some good in him. I defy anyone to be wicked without one redeeming trait."

"Most certainly," agreed Acworth, "just as it would hardly be human to be undeviatingly virtuous. We look for a little leaven of wickedness, even in our dearest friends. The man or woman whose conduct appears impeccable must come under suspicion of hypocrisy."

It struck Elizabeth that this was a curious sentiment to come from a clergyman. She glanced at her husband and met his eye. Evidently the same thought had visited them both.

"The question surely is which is to predominate," said Darcy. "Even a murderer may have an amiable side to his character."

"And there are persons who pass for being everything that is good, and yet can and do commit the most atrocious acts," said Georgiana, speaking for the first time. "A governess I once had threw a half-grown kitten into the water to drown. She not only did that, but could stand and watch it struggle."

Darcy turned towards her interrogatively, while Major Wakeford regarded her flushed face with interest. "That was atrocious and inexcusable," he said. "No less barbarous than murder."

"Cruelty remains cruelty, whatever the object," said Mr. Acworth with a moralising air. "And suffering also," he added in a different tone. "Indeed there is a latent savagery in the human breast which too often seeks an outlet for just such actions as the one described by Miss Darcy, for the good reason that they go unpunished, the victims having neither voices nor rights. For the protection of the law is reserved for its framers and administrators—the rich and powerful." He spoke towards the end with such bitterness—almost venom—that Elizabeth's heart beat faster. Darcy said nothing, but he looked indignant and his colour rose. The conversation had taken such a decidedly wrong turn that something must be done, and Elizabeth made haste to smooth all over.

"Cruelty, suffering—are not these relative terms? We all differ as much in our susceptibilities as in our aptitudes. What is tolerable to one is torture to another. If I were to confess to that which afflicts me most you would think it so unreasonable that I shall say nothing about it. But, Major Wakeford, I am sure that above all things you detest being questioned about your campaigns."

"It depends upon the questions and who asks them," he replied with one of his rare smiles. "But since Mrs. Darcy has discovered and published my weakness, it is surely very ungenerous in her to conceal her own."

"Her discovery arises from a fellow feeling," said Darcy. "There is more than one sort of campaign, and she very much dislikes being questioned about hers."

Elizabeth laughed and exclaimed, "As for Mr. Darcy, he says nothing about his own abhorrences because they are too many. Possibly there is an arch-abhorrence, but it has a hundred competitors in the field—all striving for first place."

"You cannot expect me to be any more candid than you are yourself."

She let the provocation pass with a smile and a shake of the head.

"Speaking for myself," said Mr. Acworth, "I would say that a woman who sings out of tune enrages me more than anything else in the world."

"That is the most effectual silencer I ever heard," said Elizabeth with mock gravity. "But I have always understood that the offenders are never conscious of their guilt and continue the outrage. You must have suffered very much, and on many occasions."

Mr. Acworth appeared really delighted, but made a parade of his martyrdom. He cast up his eyes in a very foreign fashion, and in fact many of his gestures, such as his manner of shrugging his shoulders, recalled the antics of a Frenchman. At this point Darcy launched forth somewhat abruptly on a totally different subject, and the conversation became more general though less animated. Soon afterwards Elizabeth and Georgiana withdrew, leaving the gentlemen to their wine.

In the drawing-room they discussed their new acquaintances, with more unanimity than is usual with ladies when the other sex come up for judgment. They agreed in approving of Major Wakeford and being dubious about Mr. Acworth. As a state of doubt is more interesting than certainty, it is not surprising that the latter gentleman should receive the greater share of their attention.

"There is something very strange about him," said Georgiana, "but I cannot fix upon what it is. I can truly say that I have never seen anyone in the least like him before."

"Then you have your wish," said Elizabeth. "That was what you were desiring, you know. I think his strangeness comes in part from his variability. His character appears to shift from moment to moment, making him oddly inconsistent. One cannot in truth say what kind of a man he is, and for that reason should spare judgment until we know him better."

"He does not seem to be grieving for the death of his wife."

"Oh, Georgiana, how can you tell? He would not make a display of it before strangers." But as she spoke Elizabeth remembered that it was precisely what he had done in his first interview with Darcy. "One must not be too hasty in conjecture upon so slight an acquaintance," she continued, "but I will hazard the guess that at all times Mr. Acworth is very much the creature of his surroundings, on which his humour will depend. If so, that would explain his apparent insensibility on first coming among us."

"At any rate he is quite different from anyone who has ever stayed at Pemberley."

"So, for that matter, is Major Wakeford."

"Not *so* different," said Georgiana, walking away to the pianoforte. "The difference in Major Wakeford is owing to his—his condition, which is so dreadful. I could not bring myself to look at him, Elizabeth. Is that wrong in me?"

"No—not wrong, provided you try to overcome it. The loss of an arm is indeed a calamity. But if he can bear it bravely, so can you."

But the next moment Mr. Acworth and Major Wakeford were both forgotten. On reaching the pianoforte Georgiana had found a parcel containing some music she had commissioned her brother to bring from town. Partly unwrapped, it lay surmounted by the list she had made out. An exclamation from her brought Elizabeth to her side. Together they went through the pile, and below the pianoforte music came upon some songs inscribed with Elizabeth's name in Darcy's handwriting.

"Oh, Elizabeth, here is that Canzonetta we heard at Lady Fullerton's party—that Fitzwilliam was so much struck with."

"Yes, I remember—and by the Italian woman who sang it. Her voice was certainly very wonderful. But what does he propose by bringing it for me?"

"That you shall sing it, of course. Do try it, Elizabeth. There will be plenty of time before they come."

Seating herself at the instrument, Georgiana began to play the accompaniment with inviting glances at her sister. The spell worked as it was intended, and Elizabeth first came to look over her shoulder and then began to hum the air. When she had gone through it in this manner, she was easily persuaded to go through it again, enunciating the words with a firmer command of her voice. A further repetition enabled her to give a rendering guided by her recollection of the Italian singer's performance. The melody had a simple plaintiveness which Elizabeth, happy by nature and situation alike, enjoyed to the full, and she sang it with all the sadness it could be made to express. When she had come to the end, her voice held on the last soft note, she heard a man's 'Brava' behind her, and turned in astonishment to see that, all unnoticed, the three gentlemen had entered the room together. So quietly had they come that neither she nor Georgiana could know how long they had been there. Major Wakeford was seated in a chair, Darcy and Acworth were standing some distance apart.

Mr. Acworth now approached the ladies. "I must congratulate Mrs. Darcy on a very delightful performance," he said. "And may I say that never was intonation more true. You have indeed a charming voice, madam—not strong, perhaps, but perfectly musical; will you not give us the pleasure of hearing you again?"

Elizabeth was sensible of a tinge of patronage in his manner which surprised and displeased her. Happily she was saved from the necessity of deciding whether or not to comply by the diversionary entrance of tea. In the general conversation which ensued, Darcy asked Major Wakeford whether he was still as fond of card games as he used to be, probably with the intention of starting one later on. Major Wakeford, speaking exactly as he thought, said that while abroad he had got into the habit of playing chess with a fellow officer at odd times, and had become extremely interested in it.

"How fortunate for Mr. Darcy," said Elizabeth. "As an occupation demanding solitude, silence and the exercise of pure intellect, you could not hit upon anything more likely to answer his notions of perfect felicity."

Darcy always took his wife's pleasantries at his expense in good part, and usually returned a rejoinder designed to provoke a fresh sally from her. This was so well understood between them that when no reply came she glanced at him with a challenging smile to see him gravely considering his teacup as if she had not spoken. A moment later he said to Major Wakeford, "My wife thinks we mean to desert to the library and is determined to prevent it." As no such thought had occurred to her she was about to protest with energy when a belated understanding stayed the words upon her lips. In the presence of Mr. Acworth there was to be no levity; the domestic scene must be subdued to the hue of staidness and formality. This was a sobering reflection. She did not rebel, but she was silenced.

Had she seen what had already caught Darcy's eye more than once that evening—Mr. Acworth's deeply admiring gaze turned upon her, she would have been more embarrassed than ever. Mr. Acworth was seated beside her and she could not observe him unless by turning her head directly towards him, when he would either lower his eyes discreetly, or return her glance with a complaisance beaming in his countenance not so very much more than civil. That he did admire her she was aware, but most men did, and to this she was accustomed. None of them had ever transgressed the bounds of propriety, nor had Darcy before found fault with such admiration. But then all the gentlemen who resorted to their society were his friends and well-wishers, and their harmless gallantry to his wife was meant and taken as in part a compliment to himself, whereas Acworth's goodwill towards him was by no means certain, and appeared to diminish as acquaintance lengthened, instead of increasing.

When tea was over Darcy asked his sister to play to the company. She went directly to the pianoforte, but sat there for some moments silently considering what piece to choose, and while the others waited for her to begin Darcy said to Acworth, "You are an amateur of music, I collect, and have some knowledge of the art."

"I must confess that I have wasted rather more time with my violin than was to the advantage of other more serious studies," he replied. "But I can hardly remember the time when it was not my constant companion."

"It is strange that you should be the only musical member of your family," observed Darcy. "Your brother, Lord Egbury, used to declare that he hardly knew one note from another."

"That is so. Not one of my brothers has the least ear for anything."

"I remember hearing when I stayed at Mentmore many years ago, that you were extremely fond of music, but I did not know that you were a performer."

Acworth gave his host an odd, sharp look as Elizabeth, who had moved to a seat near Georgiana, could not but see. "No," he replied, "in England a fiddle-playing young man is regarded as very effeminate, almost a skeleton in the family cupboard. The Acworths have always prided themselves on their noble indifference to the arts."

Elizabeth said quietly, "I cannot conceive how the love or practice of art in any of its forms can be a matter for censure. You will find nothing of that sort at Pemberley."

To this Mr. Acworth returned a bow.

Georgiana now began to play, and continued at the instrument for over an hour. Her brother and sister had always regarded her performance as remarkable, both in taste and execution, but it remained for Mr. Acworth to reveal to them how truly remarkable it was. He commenced by looking all astonishment, then he spoke with enthusiasm of phrasing, rhythm, touch and tone with a kind of affectation that Darcy found obnoxious and Elizabeth amusing. Georgiana herself looked pleased, but not quite believing, and when her brother observed that she owed her proficiency to one of the best foreign masters in town, she instantly discounted Mr. Acworth's superlatives as decidedly overrating her accomplishment. She knew better than anyone else how much she had yet to learn, and how far she had to go before arriving within sight of that perfection which ever eluded her.

Major Wakeford was a silent, though attentive listener. On rising from the instrument, Georgiana came to a chair near him, and at this opportunity of paying his tribute he looked round and thanked her very simply. "I have never cared for such music before," he said, "but perhaps it is because I have never heard it really well played as you do."

After the party had separated for the night and Elizabeth and Darcy were at length alone and at liberty to say what they would, she attacked him upon the subject of Stephen Acworth.

"Upon extended knowledge I like him no better," said Darcy.

"You said in your letter that he resembled his father who was coarse and profane and habitually unfaithful to his wife. Are you not in danger of transferring your dislike of Lord Egbury to his son without due reason—for you do dislike him, that I can see? But though he may resemble his father in person, and in much else, Stephen Acworth is not coarse. He has good manners, though perhaps they are a little overdone. He is also a man of taste and education and evidently knows the world."

"To my mind a man of his profession should not have too much sophistication. Education and taste I grant, his birth is indubitable, therefore I find it strange that he should lack that something which marks the gentleman—which you have in Wakeford and even in Mortimer for all his rustic upbringing."

"Birth and breeding are not always the guarantee of a perfect product, it would seem. Do you know—" She was about to tell him of her persuasion of having seen Stephen Acworth before, but changed her mind. There was something of reserve in Darcy's manner which piqued her curiosity and determined her to gratify it if she could before anything else. "Do you know," she resumed, "that you appear to me to be holding something back. You say that you don't like his face, that he is too sophisticated for a clergyman and is not truly the gentleman. But that is not all. If you ask me to believe that it is, I do not."

"You think you are going to be very clever and worm some-thing out of me, Elizabeth."

"I? Certainly not. I am asking no questions but merely saying that you are not being perfectly frank. You are quite at liberty to keep your thoughts to yourself, however. Are they not your own? You did say that you would endow me with all your worldly goods—a rash promise, I have always thought—but that presumably did not include the furniture of your mind."

"You are welcome to anything worth having," said Darcy, vastly amused. "If I do not offer it to you without asking, it is because I am not certain of its value. However, as you desire to be particularly and precisely informed on all that at this moment is lodged in the secret recesses of my brain, I will confess everything." He went on more seriously. "As I have said, Stephen Acworth does resemble his father to a remarkable degree, but I will affirm that it is a circumstance which has not influenced me. In any case, he cannot help it. It is true, as you observed just now, that he is not coarse, and profanity seems far from his lips. But like his father, there is that in his manner to women which displeases me. He is of that class of man who cannot look at any woman without estimating her charms as they affect his senses. You may ask how I know that in such a short time as we have spent together, but I was an involuntary witness of more than one incident on the journey, trivial enough in itself, yet indicative of levity in such matters. Wakeford commented upon it unasked, though in a very guarded manner. When it is considered that he has not long since lost his wife, and is supposed to be broken with grief, it is all the more reprehensible."

"If that is so he is certainly very unsuitable for the living of Pemberley—or any living for that matter," said Elizabeth thoughtfully. "Are you really so committed to him that you cannot withdraw?"

"I am not committed except to the six weeks stay here, which arrangement, as a personal friend of his brother's, I can hardly depart from unless he gives me very good cause. That is, not likely, I fancy, for he made a great point of it and is not in the least foolish. If he does not stay out the full period, it will be because he chooses not to."

"Six weeks of discretion and circumspection and formality! That seems much too long. No more *jeux d'esprit*, and I may not even sing for fear of incurring a compliment. I must always think before I speak—especially to you."

"I do not ask impossibilities," said Darcy, smiling.

"No, but I do wonder whether someone has not been practising a deception of some sort, either Lord Egbury on you, or Mr. Acworth on his brother. *Is* the reason alleged for quitting Mentmore the true one? Is it not conceivable, in fact, that he may be running away from the effects of some indiscretion?"

"I should lay your imagination to rest, Elizabeth, or it will keep you awake half the night. When you begin wondering I know what to expect. A hectic fancy, besides, is no discoverer of the truth."

"I will make one more wild guess for the pleasure of contradicting you," said Elizabeth. "It is that, despite *your* superior faculties and *my* sole reliance upon a fevered imagination, I shall turn out to be right."

Chapter 5

AT AN EARLY HOUR next morning Darcy rode off with Acworth to view the parish. It was agreed between himself and Elizabeth that she should remain at home to entertain Major Wakeford until his return, when she and Georgiana were to drive over to Stowell to visit an elderly friend of the family, by name Lady Tyrrell, in fulfilment of a regular engagement. Elizabeth did debate with him whether, as this was Major Wakeford's first day at Pemberley, they had better not defer their visit until the following week, but Darcy saw not the least reason for their doing so, and assured her that he would be back long before they were to start.

After her daily conference with Mrs. Reynolds, and a short time spent in the nursery with Richard, Elizabeth went in search of Major Wakeford. She had seen him last in the hall with Darcy and Acworth, but he was there no longer, nor in the library, nor in the breakfast-parlour.

But on stepping outside a window which stood open, she saw him walking along a path leading away from the house, and making his way slowly with the help of a stick. It needed but a few moments to re-enter the house, despatch one of the servants for a parasol, and to overtake him going in the direction of a seat under a Spanish chestnut tree.

"We face the sun here; it may be too sunny for you," said Major Wakeford as they sat down together.

"Not at all," she replied. "I love the sun."

"I have always heard that ladies feared its effects upon their complexion."

Elizabeth smiled and said that of course women had to think of their appearance, but that she did not believe in sacrificing wholesome enjoyment for fear of a few freckles. "I snatch any excuse for staying out-of-doors in such weather as this," she added, "so I shall assume that you are in need of entertainment and that I am to supply it. But you will think that I am going about it very strangely when I begin asking you all manner of questions. You have known my husband a very long time, I believe."

"Since we were boys. The late Mr. Darcy used to invite me to Pemberley. We were about ten when we first met."

"So you came often?"

"I came nearly every summer holiday. When I was eighteen I entered the army and thenceforward we did not see much of one another."

"You had not met Georgiana before yesterday, I think."

"I had, but she was then so young that it is well-nigh impossible she should remember me. The last time I stayed at Pemberley she could not have been more than four or five years old."

"No doubt you find Pemberley much changed from what it was then."

"It is the same house, with the same prospect that I have often called to mind. Changes there are, but only such as the years must bring. Darcy is master here, and married, and Miss Darcy is grown up into a young lady. I, too, am changed, however."

Elizabeth fancied that he spoke with regret of the changes he had found. It occurred to her that he did not much relish coming upon Darcy again as a married man, or that he did not wholly approve of the wife he had chosen. Gallantry was not in his nature, perhaps, but almost any other man would have marked the occasion with a compliment.

"I cannot think that my husband is very much different from what he was formerly," she said. "His is a very consistent character."

"Yes, that is true."

"He has often spoken to me of you."

"Darcy does not forget his friends."

It struck Elizabeth that Major Wakeford had at least one trait in common with her husband. Neither was conversable with strangers. She was chagrined that he should treat her as one when she had intended him to be captivated by the simplicity of her manner, the warmth and sincerity of her address. Never before had she exerted herself to be agreeable with so little success. Fearing that he resented her enquiries as proceeding from a petty inquisitiveness, her cheeks grew hot and she could think of nothing to say that would not incur the criticism of so severe a man. But while she rejected this observation as inane, and that as too personal, he surprised her by saying as the fruit of his own pondering, "He is a very fortunate man. But so he always was."

"On that head we are agreed," she exclaimed. "He has had his own way in everything ever since he was born."

"But he deserves it. Or it may be truer to say that he has made the best possible use of his endowments."

"In that case he is justly fortunate, for as to natural endowments, they can be so abused as to bring their possessor to ruin. I have seen *that* more often than increase of good. Is not virtue more signally displayed in a struggle against adversity?"

"It is generally supposed that the practice of virtue is easier in prosperity. But we are getting into deep waters."

Elizabeth did her best to conceal her sense of affront to her intelligence; for how could he know that he was talking to one who was reputedly the cleverest and wittiest woman in Derbyshire? But bethinking herself that she would treasure up the circumstance to relate to Darcy the next time he wanted enlivening, she directed a sparkling gaze upon him and said archly, "Do you mean that we women get out of our depth directly we stray from the concrete and particular as my husband has sometimes informed me?"

"I am afraid I do not know how to talk to ladies," he replied humbly. "I am a soldier, and have lived for the most part among simple, ignorant men."

"I can assure you that women prefer sincerity to compliments," she said with a return to gravity.

After some further talk in the unforced strain of progressing acquaintance, Wakeford suggested they should walk down to the stream. "The sight of water is for me always a compulsion to go to it," he said.

They set off at a slow pace over the grass. Major Wakeford said that although many years had gone by since he had last visited Pemberley, he came back to it with a perfect recollection of its woods and hills, the course of the stream and even the bushes growing along its banks. "It is very little altered," he observed. "There was a pool where we used to bathe, but it lies beyond my walking powers. Yonder it is," and he pointed with his stick towards a part of the river where the woods on the farther side descended close to its verge. "And there was a tree higher than the rest that we climbed for a lookout over the surrounding country beyond the park—a tall ash. I see it no longer. Perhaps it has been cut down. There was a whole dead branch, I remember, and the foliage at the top was sparse and poor. But it served our purpose well."

He turned about with an awkward movement and Elizabeth fancied that he felt he had come far enough. She suggested that they should go back to the house. As they went, still walking beside the river that he might watch the movements of trout in the water, Richard was seen at some distance away in his pony carriage, attended as usual by his little groom and two nurses. Elizabeth made a sign for the child to be brought to her, and as soon as he was near enough she went to him, lifted him out of his carriage and held him up to see the stream. A trout leaped out of the water close beside them, and this so excited the child that he wriggled out of her arms and ran to a spot where rushes grew out from the brink into the river-bed itself. Instantly Major Wakeford dropped his stick, and snatching him away from the water's edge, held him struggling and kicking in his one hand until his mother could take him. On relinquishing the little boy, either his injured leg gave way or he lost his balance, and he fell heavily to the ground.

Bidding the nurses see to Richard, Elizabeth ran to Wakeford and endeavoured to help him to rise to his feet. He made a great effort to do so, but try as he might he could not; the injured leg was now powerless. As there was no means of moving him at hand, Richard's groom was sent to the house for assistance. Never did time seem to pass so slowly while he was gone. Major Wakeford lay on the ground, supporting himself on one elbow and Elizabeth knelt beside him, her horrified concern none the less acute for the wretched conviction that she alone was to blame for what had happened. She should have foreseen Richard's sudden movement and held him more firmly. A strong, vigorous child, he was already impetuous and active beyond his years. Thoughtlessness was answerable for all. Her imagination, flying on, beheld Major Wakeford continuing as helpless as he was now for the rest of his life. She controlled her agitation as well as she could for his sake, but even in his extreme pain he could not but be aware of it, and he begged her not to be distressed. "It was my fault entirely," said he. "I should not have thrown away my stick in attempting a movement to which my leg was unequal. The little boy could have been held back without that."

Again and again did she cast her eyes in the direction from which help should come. At last there appeared several of the outdoor servants, two of them carrying a hurdle between them. Behind them came Darcy and with his long stride soon outstripped the men. Elizabeth went to meet him and walking back beside him related how the injury to Major Wakeford had occurred. He asked a question or two, then spoke to his friend, and as soon as the servants came up, instructed them exactly what they should do. The hurdle was lowered to the ground and he himself helped to move Wakeford on to it with an experienced hand. More than once had he performed such an office on the hunting-field.

Carrying their burden slowly and with every precaution against jolting, the bearers walked back to the house and, upon Darcy's direction, straight upstairs to Wakeford's room where he was laid upon his bed. There was now much to be done. The housekeeper came hurrying to offer her services and the discreet advice of an old servant. Seeing that the poor gentleman looked quite spent, she went off to fetch some cordial of her own making. Elizabeth sat with the sufferer while Darcy went to the library to write a note to Mr. Roper, the family physician, and arrange for its delivery.

Major Wakeford lay silent with his eyes closed, maintaining a soldier's fortitude. Elizabeth watched him in anxiety not to fail of any service were it required, and every other thought was banished from her head. Presently a housemaid, sent by Mrs. Reynolds, entered the room to kindle a fire upon the hearth. Having performed her office, she left the room, but the next instant returned and approached her mistress, saying, "If you please, ma'am, I am bid to say that the carriage is at the door."

The engagement to Lady Tyrrell had been entirely forgotten. Elizabeth's first impulse was to send the carriage back to the stables, but before she could give the order, Darcy returned, and hearing what she proposed, expressed a contrary opinion.

She needed some persuasion, but he could see that she was agitated almost to tears, and was determined that she should not witness the suffering Mr. Roper must of necessity inflict upon his patient when attending to him. She consented at last to go. He appeared so calm, so hopeful even that no lasting injury had been sustained by their guest, that her conscience upbraided her less than it had done, and she could begin to give some thought to other matters. Before they parted she asked him how Mr. Acworth had behaved on the ride that morning.

"He was not very communicative," said Darcy, "at least not to me, and I do not think he trusted his horse. He has not a good seat and appears little accustomed to the saddle. It was for that reason probably that he did not display much interest in his surroundings. On our way back we called at the Parsonage and there I left him, for Miss Robinson insisted that he should see all over the house and garden, and I was in some haste to be at home again—rightly as it turned out. To my surprise he agreed with alacrity. There is no accounting for taste—he and Miss Robinson seemed absolutely charmed with one another."

"Old ladies can be very partial to young men," said Elizabeth.

"And insinuating young men will flatter old ladies to the top of their bent," rejoined Darcy.

"He could have nothing to gain by that," she said, looking surprised. "You should have warned him against such scheming women as they are."

"Any advice of the sort would have been thrown away," said he dryly. "I could see that he was laughing at them in his sleeve."

On the way to Stowell in the carriage Elizabeth and Georgiana talked chiefly of Major Wakeford. Georgiana had heard no more than that he had had a fall, and Elizabeth found some relief in giving her a detailed account of the accident and its effects, for she still could not acquit herself of blameworthiness in the matter. Georgiana did not express any great concern, since that was not her way, but her few words and thoughtful look betokened no lack of feeling. A most painful impression was made upon her by suffering in any form, and this fresh blow to one who had already endured so much horrified her.

They arrived nearly half an hour late at Stowell Lodge and to excuse their unpunctuality before all else, Elizabeth acquainted Lady Tyrrell with the reason for it, and the whole story was gone through again. The old lady's attention was caught by Major Wakeford's name, and being much addicted to genealogies and family histories, she began to connect him with all the Wakefords up and down the country. On hearing that he was of the Devonshire branch, she was able at once to confer upon him a very rich aunt, a widow and childless, who could be depended upon to leave him the greater part of her fortune, if not all. Happy in the glow of vicarious benefaction, she bequeathed him three thousand a year and a charming property near Bath. In the meantime she had no scruples in adding at least ten years to the age of her dear friend, Mrs. Chalmers, in order that the period of expectation might not be too protracted.

When they got home again they found that Mr. Roper had come and gone, having done all that was required for the present. He had found Major Wakeford's knee out of joint and had put it back into place, not without considerable pain to the patient. Wakeford had also sprained his ankle in falling, but not very severely, and it could be expected to mend in a week or ten days at most.

Concerning the knee there was astonishing and welcome news. It was thought that a slight displacement of the joint which had not before been discovered, and had therefore remained uncorrected, was the cause of all its former stiffness. In Mr. Roper's opinion, given with professional cautiousness, the dislocation having now been rectified, there was no reason why after a short period of rest Major Wakeford should not be able to walk as well as he had ever done.

Besides Mr. Roper there had been another caller. Mortimer had enquired for Mr. Acworth. Elizabeth heard from Mrs. Reynolds that the gentlemen had walked up and down the terrace for some time, and she could not help wondering what two such oddly contrasted persons could have found to say to one another. Enlightenment came later from Acworth himself. At dinner he spoke of his meeting with Mortimer, to whom he referred as remarkably agreeable.

"He entered so completely into my difficulties," he said to Darcy. "I told him that of late I had suffered from a nervous spasm of the throat which caught me unawares at critical moments, and prevented me from articulating distinctly. He said he would be only too happy to afford me any assistance in church short of preaching the sermon—an offer I gladly accepted."

Darcy looked astonished and not very well pleased, and his reply, though acquiescent, was coldly formal. Elizabeth thought it very strange that Mr. Acworth had not so far manifested any sign of the curious malady to which he laid claim, and that he should be less nervous of preaching the sermon than of reading the service. With Mr. Mortimer it was quite the other way about. He frankly confessed that getting up into the pulpit was for him like mounting the scaffold.

But the vagaries of Mr. Acworth could not long occupy her thoughts. For the time being Major Wakeford held foremost place in them, since she had much to do for him, and spent a great part of each day in his room. Her desire for his welfare embraced not only a speedy recovery from his present disablement, but the amendment of his fortunes, and she longed to see him happily settled in the fullest enjoyment of health, wealth and an amiable wife. They were now on such terms that she could say almost anything she chose to him without fear of misapprehension, and one day as she sat beside his couch she laid aside the book from which she had been reading aloud and told him he ought to marry. He smiled and shook his head.

"It would be great presumption on the part of a half-pay major—and maimed at that—to propose marriage to any young lady. To enter into an engagement! No, that would be inexcusable."

"Your circumstances may improve," she said.

"I see no likelihood of it at present," he replied.

Remembering Lady Tyrrell's prophecy of money coming to him, she resolved to find out the truth of it.

"Most of us have expectations, however modest," she continued, "though a small bequest may be merely a nuisance, involving more lawyer's business than profit. To be really worth while, a legacy should not be under ten thousand pounds—thirty thousand would be even better. There is also the question of the testator. A distant, unknown relative is to be preferred. A wealthy uncle, for instance, shut up for the last twenty years in a gloomy mansion, or an aunt—"

"I have a rich aunt," said Wakeford, "but her money is all to go to a nephew of her late husband."

"I would make it a law that rich aunts should divide their money among all their deserving nephews."

"And how would you assess a nephew's desert?" he enquired with a smile.

"That might be difficult, I admit," she replied. "But if it were to rest on a written testimonial, I would be happy to write one for you."

This conversation Elizabeth a little later repeated to Darcy. As she foresaw, he remonstrated with her for prying into Wakeford's private concerns. She defended herself by arguing that if Lady Tyrrell were to put into circulation a report of wealth coming to him, it behoved his friends to know and spread the truth. To this he replied that people commonly believed what pleased them best, and often in defiance of proof to the contrary.

"All I can say is that it is a most irrational world."

"Many of the men and women in it are."

"It would do him good to marry," she said. "Do not you agree?"

"The good of marriage depends on a man's choice."

"What I hope is that by and by he will meet with some good, sensible woman, someone as kind and unselfish as dear Jane, who will make him as truly happy as he deserves."

"Nothing could be better," said Darcy, "so long as you do not set about choosing the lady. I do assure you that men prefer choosing their wives for themselves."

"So I have heard, though by all accounts it is a method that does not always succeed. Fitz, tell me, what is a major's half-pay?"

When he told her she was horrified. "But that is indigence," she exclaimed.

"He will succeed to his father's estate in due course," said Darcy. "It is not a large one—under two thousand a year I believe—and there are several sisters to be provided for."

"But the father may live for many years to come."

"That no one can tell. He is already well over sixty. As soon as Wakeford is able to lead an active life again I have a notion that he will consider it his duty to return home and help with the management of the estate."

"He is the sort of man who would always do his duty, however difficult and disagreeable."

"That is his ruling characteristic."

"How strange it is that there should be two men in a state of affliction under our roof at one time. And yet how different they are in every other respect, not least in the way in which they bear their misfortune."

"They could not well be more different," said Darcy with some emphasis.

"Does your opinion of Mr. Acworth remain what it was?"

"I have not yet formed one," he replied gravely. "There is something I do not comprehend, but I am persuaded that it is from lack of proper knowledge. Never have I experienced so much discrepancy between this man as he was reputed to be and as he has shown himself on acquaintance. Either he has changed very much from what he was formerly, or—"

"What is the alternative?" she asked, as he checked himself.

He shrugged his shoulders. "None that I can think of," he answered.

It was so plainly evident that he did not wish to say anything further on the subject just then that Elizabeth forbore to press him, and began speaking of another matter. Her curiosity concerning Mr. Acworth which had slept of late was, however, revived. She had seen little of him for several days and how he spent his time she hardly knew. But from that time she began to observe him, to note his looks, his behaviour and any signs of unhappiness and ill-health. His unhappiness was soon not in doubt, but the motive was less certain, and she was disposed to agree with Georgiana that he appeared not so much afflicted by grief for the loss of his wife as out of humour with his surroundings or his company.

One evening after tea, Darcy having gone upstairs to Major Wakeford's room to play a game of chess with his friend, Elizabeth and Georgiana sat alone with Acworth in the little drawing-room. To make amends for any remissness towards him which he might have felt, she offered him an apology for her recent neglect of his entertainment, attributing it to her preoccupation with Major Wakeford's unfortunate condition. The effect upon him was immediate, almost startling. He smiled and begged her not to think that he had anything to complain of, and though in answer to her enquires he confessed to headaches and sleeplessness, all his vivacity of the first evening returned and he appeared most eager to converse. Elizabeth learnt for the first time that he paid an almost daily visit to the Parsonage where the Miss Robinsons had put at his disposal the late Rector's study and all his theological books. He disclosed that he had been begged to make himself completely at home, to treat the house, in fact, as if it were already his own. Such transparent tactics were extremely diverting, and Elizabeth allowed her amusement to become visible. Emboldened, perhaps, by something more of ease in her manner than he had before experienced, he proceeded to give an imitation of the ladies in one of their famous disputes—Miss Robinson angrily haranguing and bearing down her younger sister, the latter becoming sillier and sillier and finally completely losing her head—and with such success that Elizabeth was overcome with laughter. But seeing that Georgiana, though also laughing, was half scandalized by his mimicry, she exerted herself to recover her composure and with it her dignity. Turning to Georgiana, she asked for some music.

Georgiana was very willing to oblige, and sitting down at the pianoforte, gave a spirited rendering of a set of oldworld dances. Mr. Acworth professed himself enraptured. "How rare it is," he exclaimed, "to find a young lady able to enter into the mind of the composer and with an execution so perfectly at the command of the most exigent taste."

After Georgiana had played again he entreated Mrs. Darcy to sing, praising her voice in terms that Elizabeth found fulsome and absurd. She could not altogether refuse, but having sung one short song, she asked him whether he did not also perform, momentarily forgetting that he had once spoken of possessing a violin. Nothing could give him greater pleasure, so he assured her, and asking leave to fetch his instrument, he departed in quest of it.

While he was gone Elizabeth had time to reflect upon the change in his aspect from gloom and dissatisfaction to joyous animation. That a little music should work such a transformation seemed incredible. She began to think that what he really desired was to be taken notice of. Evidently, in spite all his protestations to the contrary, he had felt himself neglected.

He returned carrying his violin and a sheaf of music, and for an hour or more Georgiana tried over one piece after another. From frequent attendance at concerts while in London, Elizabeth had heard many famous musicians and had learnt to distinguish their particular merits and the varying degrees of their attainment. She perceived very soon that Acworth was no ordinary performer. Not only was he completely the master of his instrument, but also he possessed that power over the emotions of his hearers without which skill alone is of little value. She listened with the fullest enjoyment, but when her first astonishment had abated, her thoughts became busy with the man himself, trying to reconcile his unusual gifts with his birth and the sort of upbringing he must have had as a nobleman's son. His impersonation of the Miss Robinsons had been a perfect imitation of both, and had displayed an uncommon sense of character as well as a happy invention. In the course of conversation he displayed a wide, rather than a solid education, with much diversity of reading. And yet not infrequently he said and did what was not in good taste, and betrayed ignorance of the usages of polite society. Upon any consideration, viewed in any light, he was extraordinary.

Towards the end of a piece in which great demands were made upon the principal performer, Elizabeth saw Darcy come into the room. He advanced slowly and noiselessly until he reached the hearth, where he took up his station a little behind the players, and there composed himself to listen. The music reaching its conclusion, Acworth turned towards Elizabeth and made her a low bow.

"I salute my audience of one," he said with a smile of conscious pride.

"No, we are now two," she replied, indicating her husband. "Mr. Darcy came in a little while ago. We have been sharing a very great pleasure."

Darcy cordially assented. Nevertheless Acworth's countenance fell; he looked all at once as if he had eaten the sour grapes of which he had made mention in his sermon the previous Sunday.

Chapter 6

OVER A WEEK HAD passed since the arrival at Pemberley of Major Wakeford and Stephen Acworth, and the presence of these two very dissimilar guests was become established and familiar. The Darcys were now looking forward to welcoming other visitors who were to begin arriving early in June. The party when assembled was to include Elizabeth's sister, Jane Bingley and her husband; her uncle and aunt from London, Mr. and Mrs. Gardiner, her youngest unmarried sister, Kitty Bennet, and perhaps her father. Of the last's joining them there was yet no certainty; but she had sent him a pressing invitation, reminding him that it was many months since they had met, and she was in good hope that he would come.

The prospect of meeting once more all these dear friends of her girlhood was delightful, and promised much happiness, but her anticipations were thrown all awry when one morning Darcy received a letter from his aunt, Lady Catherine de Bourgh, proposing herself and her daughter for two weeks from the 9th of

June. No news could have been less welcome at such a time, but for her husband's sake she tried to make light of it. She could even smile on looking through Lady Catherine's letter, for her ladyship wrote with the same peremptory vigour as she spoke.

"The Gardiners will be here," she said. "They can take care of themselves, but won't Lady Catherine be affronted at being asked to consort with two such undistinguished citizens of London?"

"I trust she will behave with ordinary good breeding," replied Darcy.

"But that is what you can scarcely depend on. Perhaps you had better warn her whom she will find here."

"I cannot and will not apologise for anyone whom I invite to stay under my roof."

"She is to come then, and take the consequences. On the whole it is just as well that there will be other people here at the same time. The undiluted society of Lady Catherine might go to my head, and then who knows what would happen."

"You deserve great praise for being as patient as you usually are," said Darcy seriously.

"That is indeed encouragement to go on behaving well," said she, laughing and caressing his hand.

The course of events had been such as to drive all recollection of Rachel Stone out of Elizabeth's head, and with it her undertaking to speak to Miss Robinson about the change she had directed in the girl's employment. She was even unaware that Rachel was in the house until one day, coming from the nursery, she saw the new maid approaching her along the passage with a pile of linen in her arms. Instantly she dropped a curtsy and stood aside for her mistress to pass, but Elizabeth stopped to ask her some questions about her family, that she might form some opinion of her character, as well from her appearance as from her replies.

Rachel answered very respectfully, but her gaze was too unabashed and her manner too confident for her age and situation. She was a stout and well-grown girl of fourteen years, and with her black curly hair, bright rosy cheeks and dark eyes, was rather handsome. In spite of her simple maid's dress she was likely to be singled out for notice; her quick roguish glances, the carriage of her head, her perpetual smile—all invited attention.

Thus much Elizabeth saw and could not feel easy about. She resolved, however, to make further enquiries of Mrs. Reynolds, and on the next occasion of seeing the housekeeper, she asked her whether she was satisfied on the whole with Rachel's behaviour since coming into the house.

"I would not go so far as to call her a bad girl, ma'am. That she is not, but she might very well be better. I dare say she will behave as modest and pretty as the other maids do when she has been here a little longer, and learns to keep her place as she should."

"Have you had to reprimand her, then?"

"Well, ma'am, to speak the truth, I have had to tell her a few things—such as being seen and not heard. She is a great talker at all times and wanting to know everybody's business. 'A girl of your age to take such liberties,' I said to her only yesterday when I was having a little talk with Baxter, and turned round suddenly to find her listening. Oh, ma'am, I did give her a proper rating. And then, if you'll believe me, the very next thing Mason found her in the picture gallery, looking at your portrait. 'And who are you,' said I, 'to be looking at pictures? Even if you could under-stand them, which you cannot, they are no concern of yours. Do not you how that they are only for the gentry?' And then after speaking rather crossly, I told her how I had gone into service at the age of fourteen, and had always done what I was bid and minded my manners, and in that way had rose to what I am now."

"With such a good example before her she should improve," said Elizabeth, repressing a smile.

"She ought to, ma'am, but I have observed that young people do not always take kindly to good examples."

From what Mrs. Reynolds had said Elizabeth inferred that she did not think very well of Rachel Stone—in fact, thought badly of her. But having taken her stand against Miss Robinson on principle, she was determined to abide by her action, however awkward the consequences. In anticipation of what Rachel might do, of how she might turn out, she observed that a girl who needed so much supervision ought not to be sent away among strangers, but watched over by those who knew best her failings.

"Yes, indeed, ma'am," replied the housekeeper. "As I said to her, she ought to think herself very fortunate to be where she is. And I will say for her, ma'am, that she is quick and clever with her needle. When she is older and has learnt the ways here she might do for a waiting-maid, for she has the right sort of hands, and even now can tie a bow as well as ever I saw."

Later in the day Elizabeth spoke to her maid, Mason, about Rachel.

"I hear that you found her in the picture gallery," she said.

"Yes, ma'am, I did," Mason replied in shocked tones.

"What excuse did she give?"

"That she had lost her way, ma'am. But I hardly think it was true, for if it had been so, she would not have been standing and looking at the pictures, as I found her."

"Surely she ought to know her way about the house by this time."

"One would think so, ma'am."

"Mrs. Reynolds says that she is quick and clever for her age, in which case it seems most unlikely that she should have been so stupid in this particular instance."

"If I may make bold to say so, ma'am, I do not think she is at all stupid. I fancy she knows very well what she is about."

Mason's voice was so grave that Elizabeth, really disquieted, felt it necessary to find out everything she could relating to Rachel that she might have nothing to learn from Miss Robinson. She therefore pushed her enquiries to the limit of propriety as between mistress and maid. Although Mason was guarded in her replies, Elizabeth collected that Rachel was impatient of discipline, expressed her opinions with great freedom, was inclined to take liberties with the upper servants, and most improper of all, would engage in conversation with anyone of the other sex, though previously unknown to her. Such an awkward character was disclosed, in fact, that Mrs. Darcy had secretly to admit that if she had known more of Rachel Stone beforehand, she would not have had her in the house.

After some further thought, she took the unusual step of summoning Rachel to her presence. The girl was brought the next morning to her dressing-room by Mrs. Reynolds, who remained there at her mistress' request. She felt the expediency as well as the propriety of the housekeeper's being present, although she would have preferred to speak to Rachel in private. Rachel's rosy cheeks were scarlet and her eyes wide and gleaming with excitement, but she did not appear at all awed. She looked about her at the beautiful furniture, the flowers and ornaments and silk hangings. Such grandeur she could never have seen before, and her wonder swallowed up every other sensation.

Elizabeth spoke to her gravely but kindly. "You know, Rachel," she said, "I took you into my service because your mother begged it of me, not because I asked for you. You ought therefore to be all the more diligent and dutiful instead of which I hear that you are not always obedient and are apt to be above yourself. I am told, however, that you can do your work very well when you choose. It should be your aim so to improve, both in your work and your conduct, that you may in time be thought of well enough to be put to higher duties. From henceforth I shall hope to hear nothing but good of you."

Rachel curtseyed and answered very properly, "Thank you, ma'am," but before Mrs. Reynolds could finish exhorting her to be ever grateful to her kind mistress, she burst out, "Oh, please, ma'am, may I ask you a favour?"

"What is it?" asked Elizabeth, with a movement of her hand imposing silence on the housekeeper, who, excessively shocked at the interruption, was for taking the girl away at once.

"Please, ma'am, if I was to be a very good girl and do everything as I ought, would you consider of taking me to be your maid when Mason goes away? For I hear tell she is going to be wed come Michaelmas."

"For shame, Rachel," cried Mrs. Reynolds, aghast at the girl's temerity. "How can you dare to think of such a thing, let alone ask it? And after all the talking-to you have had. I declare I despair of you."

Elizabeth could not but be touched and amused, but she preserved to the full her gravity as she answered, "It will be many years before you are fit for such an office. And now go and see to it that no more complaints of your conduct are brought to me."

The next day Elizabeth drove into the village on her monthly inspection of the old people in the almshouses, and to dispense gifts of food and clothing. When that was done, she directed the coachman to take her as far as the Parsonage where she dismissed the carriage, saying that she would walk home through the woods.

At the door of the Parsonage she was informed that Miss Robinson was not at home, but that Miss Sophia was within, and before she could decide whether or not to step over the threshold, Miss Sophia herself came into the vestibule, and all smiles and delight, begged her to enter.

It so happened that this was the first occasion in which Elizabeth had held any conversation alone with Miss Sophia, and she very soon found that the younger Miss Robinson, encountered apart from her formidable sister, was a much different person from the silly, incoherent old lady she was usually accounted. It was certainly not in her to be clever or very entertaining, for her long subordination had kept her too timid and simple for that; but she could speak sensibly and connectedly on the subject of Rachel Stone, and show a proper understanding of the reasons for her retention at Pemberley House. It had, of course, been a little awkward for Sister having to disappoint Mrs.

Bridges when all had been settled for Rachel's going to her—here a shade overspread Miss Sophia's placid, plump features—but then everyone should know that Mrs. Darcy had first claim upon the Pemberley girls, and it was for her to say where they should go and what they should do.

Elizabeth did not dissent from this convenient article of faith, and having fulfilled the purpose of her visit, she turned from the subject of Rachel Stone and after a few minutes of harmless talk on recent events in the parish, began the business of leave-taking. But Miss Sophia was so urgent that Mrs. Darcy should try some cowslip-wine of her own brewing, that not to seem uncivil she sat down again for a short time longer. Miss Sophia rang the bell, and on its being answered by the manservant, she not only ordered him to bring the wine and some cake but pronounced these words:

"And, Thomas, if Mr. Acworth is still in the study tell him with my compliments that I shall be very pleased if he will favour us with his company."

A meeting with Mr. Acworth at the Parsonage! This had been furthest from Elizabeth's thoughts when she had decided to call there, but she wondered that the possibility had not occurred to her before. Without stopping to ask herself why, the idea displeased her. The truth was that his smiles and compliments and sometimes a too gallant approach made her uneasy. She had thought of it at first as the effect of a manner at all times exaggerated, but once or twice she had intercepted a look in his eyes that she did not like, and she was by no means pleased to come into close colloquy with him away from home, and with no greater protection than the simple, unsuspecting Miss Sophia.

No sooner was the door closed on Thomas than Miss Sophia began praising the gentleman.

"Mr. Acworth is such a very agreeable young man, is not he? He is so pleasant with us and so chatty. Sister told him he was welcome to use dear Papa's room whenever he chose, and he comes here very often—nearly every day. He does not always sleep very well at nights, he says, and the sight of dear Papa's books are so soothing to the mind that he often takes a little nap among them. And do you know what he said to me yesterday? I had gathered a few early strawberries, so I put them on a plate with some cream and sugar and carried them into the room, first knocking on the door as we always used to do when dear Papa was alive. And he said, 'you are so wonderfully kind and good, Miss Sophia. What do you say to our setting up housekeeping together?' He did indeed. Of course he did not really mean it, it was only intended as a compliment. But was not it agreeable of him?"

"A very charming compliment," said Elizabeth, "and thoroughly deserved, I am sure."

"It is not often that a young man will be so attentive to old ladies as he is to Sister and me. Sister and I were saying how much we should like to keep house for him if he stays. But he says he has not yet made up his mind, though if he does become rector here, he would like Sister and me to keep our home, for he wouldn't want such a large house all to himself."

These artless confidences were cut short by the entry of Thomas with the cake and wine. No sooner had the tray been placed on the table than Mr. Acworth made his appearance. That he was unprepared to see Elizabeth he showed by an involuntary start on beholding her. But his look of surprise was succeeded by one of pleasure, and he sat down between the ladies with an air of being prepared to enjoy himself.

The cowslip-wine was duly drunk and duly praised, and after a suitable interval Elizabeth rose for the second time. She had fancied that Mr. Acworth would return to the study to continue whatever labours he was carrying on there, but she found, on the contrary, that she was to have his company on the homeward way. Not the most positive assurances that she was perfectly accustomed to walking alone in the Park could dissuade him from escorting her. He protested that he would not think of letting her go by herself. And of course Miss Sophia threw her weight into the wrong scale.

"Walk home alone? I am sure Mr. Darcy would not dream of it. And besides there are such dangerous people about nowadays. Thomas saw a man going through the village yesterday that he had never seen in his life before."

"I should not be in the least alarmed though I did meet a stranger," said Elizabeth smiling.

"Mrs. Darcy's courage is unquestioned," said Acworth, "but beautiful ladies should beware how they tempt Providence."

The look which accompanied this speech made Elizabeth's cheeks grow hot with anger.

"As to that," she answered coldly, "if anyone should attempt to molest me, which is in the highest degree improbable, there would always be some woodman or other labourer within call. Surely I may count myself safe in my own Park."

"Mr. Darcy has been well advised to put angels with flaming swords round his Eden," he replied in the quietest of accents, the significance of which yet made her more indignant than ever.

"Mr. Acworth is quite the poet," said Miss Sophia, beaming with admiration. "It is wonderful what things he will think of to say. I am sure they are clever enough to go in a book."

Elizabeth now began for the third time to make her adieus, and summoning all her self-possession, expressed her gratitude to Mr. Acworth for his kind offer of walking with her, but also her desire that he would by no means interrupt his studies on her account. Acworth replied that he had finished his writing and was intending in any event to return to the House. As he was either not polite enough or too obtuse to take her hint, and good manners ruled out any overt refusal on her part, she could only acquiesce in his attending her, and a resolute movement was made towards the door. But at that very moment it was opened from without, and in sailed Miss Robinson dressed in her most towering bonnet and best pelisse.

Poor Miss Sophia at once lost her head and without waiting burst out, "Oh, Sister, how lucky you should come in and catch Mrs. Darcy before she went away. She has called to see you about Rachel Stone and was quite vexed to think that she had missed you. And I said how sorry you would be too."

"It is indeed most vexatious about Rachel Stone," said Miss Robinson, disdaining all civilities. "I had told her mother that she was to go into service with Mrs. Bridges, only to find that my instructions were to be overridden without a word of any sort said to me."

Although she had been ready to concede some degree of provocation on Miss Robinson's side, Elizabeth was so affronted by her rudeness that she did not scruple to show her resentment, which became instantly apparent in the heightened colour of her cheeks and the angry sparkle of her eyes.

"I do not consider that any such instructions should have been given," she said coldly. "I would by no means exercise so much authority myself as to order a girl into service contrary to the wishes of her mother. Such methods do not please me."

"Indeed, and how should such an ignorant foolish woman know what is for her daughter's good?" retorted Miss Robinson. But before she could obtain a reply Miss Sophia cried out, "Oh, but Sister, Mrs. Darcy has got Rachel Stone at the Great House now."

"Pray do not interfere in a matter which does not concern you," exclaimed her sister, turning upon her angrily. "As Mrs. Darcy should know, I am not accustomed to break my word, once given."

"I have endeavoured to show that no promise should have been given," answered Elizabeth with restraint. "If Mrs. Bridges has been incommoded I am sorry, and I will undertake to explain the matter to her. I beg that you will cease to feel that anything further is required of yourself."

Acworth, who had been a silent, though interested auditor throughout the colloquy, now suavely interposed.

"It is to be comprehended that Miss Robinson can with difficulty bring herself to relinquish the reins of authority in a place where for so long her position as the lady of the Parsonage conferred upon her certain rights and privileges. It takes time for all of us to accustom ourselves to a change in our situation. But the world at large is quick to apprehend it, and to base its expectations accordingly."

This intervention on her side was not perhaps in the best taste, but Elizabeth was sensible of gratitude, though she would rather have owed it to anyone else. Miss Robinson was so thunderstruck by her favourite's desertion of her that she could find nothing to say.

The pause which followed was terminated by the visitors' withdrawal. This was effected with all the usual ceremony on their side, imperfectly reciprocated by either of the sisters. Miss Robinson was too angry, and Miss Sophia too frightened.

As the door closed behind her Elizabeth drew a breath of relief, but she could not really rejoice. The routing of an adversary can sometimes be attended by regrets for the means used, however justifiable in the strict sense, and however important the cause to be served. She quitted the Parsonage looking extremely thoughtful and privately wishing her companion ten miles away.

Chapter 7

Mr. Acworth had the good sense not to offer any observations on the painful scene which had just been enacted at the Parsonage. He walked beside Mrs. Darcy in the most considerate silence, and not a word was spoken until they had issued from the Parsonage grounds and crossed the road to the Park gates. One of the lodge-keeper's children, a pretty little girl of about five, ran out as they passed and received from the gentleman a pat on the head. She looked up at him with a shy, dimpling smile.

"You have made the acquaintance of little Nancy Jones, I see," Elizabeth said as they turned aside from the carriage road and took the footpath through the wood.

"I have in general a fondness for children," he replied, "but particularly for little girls. Little girls and old ladies—they are the best of their sex, although," he added, with a sidelong glance, "old ladies can be monsters."

"Poor Miss Sophia," she said seriously, "I am indeed sorry for her, the victim of such a sister. I am afraid I—but let us not talk of it. She is so truly amiable, so exactly the reverse of the other."

"Ah," returned Acworth slyly, "but there is a road to Miss Robinson's heart if you look for it."

"It would seem that you have found it," she said, smiling. I fear I never should, even," she added truthfully, "if I wished it."

"No doubt you find that very extraordinary. You are not accustomed to being repulsed."

"It is impossible to go through life without meeting some people who do not find us all that is agreeable and charming."

"That is true enough of myself, madam. Wherever I go I seem to inspire either dislike or distrust."

"May not you impute to others sentiments which are not theirs?"

"It is impossible to be mistaken in such a case." His tone was charged with such bitterness that Elizabeth was made thoroughly uncomfortable. He seemed to be accusing her of coldness and unkindness—at any rate of some deficiency in her manner towards him. She could have said with perfect sincerity that she did not dislike him, that he interested her, but there was in his present demeanour an ill-concealed excitement which inspired distrust, and caution rather than honesty restrained the flattering protestations which might have flowed from her unalloyed charitableness. For an instant or two she knew not what to say; but silence she feared, and while they walked alone she must so converse as to carry their tête-à-tête to a safe and seemly conclusion.

"Perhaps we are apt to vex ourselves unduly about what others may think of us. Our actions cannot please everybody, and so we must learn to be satisfied with the approbation of conscience."

"Conscience," said Acworth, "is often another name for prejudice or self-esteem. We all like to be on good terms with the latter. When a man or woman begins to prate of conscience, I know what to think."

"But surely, Mr. Acworth, conscience supplies the corrective of errors of conduct to which we are all more or less prone."

"Has anyone ever told you, Mrs. Darcy, that you talk prodigiously like a book?"

The temerity, the presumption, the insolence of this speech took her breath away, and with it the power of effective retort. She wished to crush him, but as no words that occurred to her were forcible enough, she could only manifest her extreme displeasure by a haughty silence.

"I expressed myself badly," he said, with evident anxiety to make amends. "You have a remarkable command of language. If I mistake not, you read a great deal in your early youth and with an uncommonly good memory."

"Yes, that is so," she said, deciding to accept the olive branch. "I read a great deal, in fact everything that I could lay hands upon in my father's library. He encouraged me because he believed that a child should follow its bent."

"Perhaps I share that belief. In your case it has had the happiest results."

"But unfortunately for that theory some characters have bad tendencies. I am convinced that in childhood we ought to be guided not by our own inclinations, but by a good personal example."

"How absolutely true," Acworth exclaimed. "My own experience bears witness to that. If I were to tell you—"

"But we are guided not so much by the example of our elders," Elizabeth continued inflexibly, "as by persons of our own age—a brother or a sister."

"You have a brother?"

"No, only sisters. My eldest sister and her husband are coming here shortly. You will probably make their acquaintance. They live in Staffordshire, about thirty miles distant."

As Acworth did not reply, she went on talking in this unforced, desultory manner without seeming to notice his silence. But at length she paused, and he said in a light level tone which added to rather than detracted from the effect of his words.

"I do not think I can tolerate being at Pemberley much longer."

"Indeed! Our air does not suit you?"

"It is not that. Mrs. Darcy, I am a very unhappy man."

"I am very sorry," she said, with true feeling. "Perhaps only the lapse of time can bring you lasting relief, though your brother did hope, I know, that a complete change of scene might be beneficial."

"Wherever we are we cannot escape from ourselves—our memories, our past deeds, until we leave this life," he said, still quietly. "You can have no idea what the desire to escape is for me. At Pemberley a wretched lot is made still more so by contrast with a happier one. Yours is so desirable, so enviable in every single circumstance, that only a passing vexation can touch you. I could almost hate you for being so happy as you are."

It was difficult to reply except in the vein he had chosen. "I think I do understand," she answered gravely. "You have suffered so much that happiness must appear to you as heartlessness. But we are not heartless, we do feel for your affliction—a stroke of fate so unmerited."

"To what do you refer?"

"To your loss," she answered, wondering. "But do not speak of it if you had rather not."

"Why should I not speak of it? Speech is supposed to give relief. I know what you are thinking. You say to yourself, 'Here is a young man who has been bereft of his wife after one year of marriage.' But is death the worst of evils? Suppose, for example, that the woman he loved had been unfaithful, or that with the approval and assistance of everyone connected with her she had given herself to another man. Would that not be infinitely worse?"

"Perhaps—yes," Elizabeth said, amazed at him. "I can imagine it might be."

"Yes, you have imagination. Consider also that it by no means follows that a man will continue to love the woman he marries even if he succeeds in marrying the woman he loves. He who does is a dullard. Rather let him fall in love many times, believing each woman to be the one true love until he attains her. When that happens he must seek anew."

"Mr. Acworth!"

"You are shocked, Mrs. Darcy. You prefer not to believe me. You are all for romance in a circle of gold, not apprehending that a circle is a cage. But let me recall the experience of a not very reputable acquaintance of mine. He is a man of parts and some education, but without family, fortune or patronage. Circumstances have driven him into an irregular mode of life, driven him also to living by his wits. But never think that such a person does not admire the good, the beautiful, the true when he sees it. The contrasts that life have forced upon my friend have given him all the keener perception, the stronger admiration of the best and highest in every mode of existence, in art, in literature, in humanity. Particularly has he sought perfection enshrined in woman, in only one woman, believing that to find her would be to redeem him from the follies and despairs of a dissolute life.

"Some years ago he obtained employment at one of the theatres in town, and on a spring evening while he hung about the entrance after the play was over, he saw a young lady standing with her friends on the pavement waiting for their carriage to come up. There was a little delay before its arrival, long enough for him to observe her, to become entranced with her beauty and grace, ravished by her voice. Every word that she uttered fell upon his ears like a separate enchantment. Here at last was his dream, living, breathing, speaking. Once she turned her eyes upon him, but scarcely marked him. Why should she?

"The carriage appeared; she entered it with her friends, and was borne away out of his sight. Summoning a loiterer of the neighbourhood with whom he had some acquaintance, he commissioned the man to follow the carriage, ascertain where it deposited the lady and return to give him the particulars. Late that night the man came to his lodging with the information.

"From that time onwards my friend haunted the vicinity of the house which he believed the lady to inhabit, but he never so much as caught a glimpse of her. After some time, however, he got on speaking terms with a maidservant of the house, and this girl told him that the young lady did not live there, but occasionally came to stay with her relatives. In the hope of learning something further, he continued his acquaintance with the maid, beguiling her to talk of all that occurred in her master's family. One day he heard that his lady had indeed returned, but only for a few hours and had set off again for another part of the country. She might, however, come again, the girl said. She had listened to talk at the dinner-table which gave her the idea.

"The weeks passed; he lived but to see her just once more. In the meantime he lost his employment at the theatre through inattention, for in the fevered state of his being he plunged into courses which might procure him forgetfulness. He drank, he gambled, he did worse. Mad though he was, he was not so lost to all reason as not to know it, and he tried every way to erase her image from his mind. Vain was the attempt. Nothing could cure him.

"The autumn came. Having lost hope, he had ceased for some time to frequent the fatal spot. But one day he did return thither, drawn by intolerable longing. He wandered about the street filled with a melancholy of foreboding. The maid saw him from a window and ran out to tell him that she had news. The young lady was expected in a few days. She was to be married to a rich gentleman and was coming to town to buy her wedding-clothes.

"My poor friend was thunderstruck. Oddly enough he had never foreseen this conclusion to the business. He went back to his lodging and, I am sorry to say, drank himself into a stupor. Coming to himself again, he was filled with the desire to behold her with his eyes for the second, if for the last time of all, by some sophistry endeavouring to persuade himself that if he did, it would be to find her less than the perfection he had deemed her, and that thus his desire would be assuaged.

"He did see her. She passed along the street while he watched her from the opposite pavement. She was all joy, all animation, more beautiful than ever. He knew as he followed her with his eyes that to his dying day no other woman would ever command his heart.

"Mrs. Darcy, my friend was perhaps more fortunate than he knew. Closer acquaintance with the lady might have revealed flaws in character. She might even have come to look less beautiful than a discreet distance made her. What do you say? You were angry with me for representing the tender passion as fickle and fleeting—only constant while pursuit lasts. I too have lost the woman I loved, but that will not deter me from consoling myself as well as I can, because at the risk of incurring your contempt I have to confess that I am willing to accept any consolation that is offered me. I do not believe in wearing the willow for a memory I should be happy to forget. At the same time," his voice rose and became harsh and vehement, "never suppose that I shall know true happiness, or that I ever shall be able to forget."

Elizabeth had been deeply stirred by his narrative. At one time she had been briefly tempted to think that he spoke of himself under the veil of an imaginary third person, such was the passion and rapidity of his utterance. But his subsequent phrases undeceived her. Yet what did he wish to prove? Was it merely that a happy love cannot last? One thing was clear in all this mystification. He had suffered much and was still suffering.

"I sincerely hope that hereafter you may know at least relative happiness again," she said earnestly.

"I may know resignation. May I venture to think that you are sorry for me?"

"Indeed I am."

"You were moved by my friend's story, I think?"

"Yes, very much. But I cannot enter into his feelings. How could he hold in affection a being wholly unknown to him except by sight?"

"Affection and the passion of love are totally different sentiments. There are as many ways of loving as there are human beings."

"Yes," she returned, "that is perfectly true. The steadfast, rational way being one of them."

"I do not deny it. My friend, I suppose you think, followed a will-o'-the-wisp of his own brain. In my own case disillusionment followed—but I must not trouble you with that."

"I do feel every sympathy for you, Mr. Acworth," she said quietly, beginning to feel acutely the discomfort of the subject.

"It is proper to express sympathy for another's sorrow whether one feels it or not. But you are sincere. One would say that you had never experienced more than a trifling anxiety, yet you have a heart as well as an intelligence. You are sorry for my plight; nevertheless you distrust me, you withhold your friendship, you feel instinctively that I have no place among the denizens of Pemberley. The sincere cannot be blinded. You are not deceived, and though I would deceive anyone else, I would not you. If only I could lay bare my heart to you—this once—while we are alone."

Looking around her Elizabeth saw that they had some distance to go before issuing from the wood. The conversation had reached that point of danger when a single sentence that ought not to be uttered might fall upon her ears. She endeavoured to believe that Mr. Acworth was not responsible for what he said, having worked himself up into a state of mind bordering on frenzy. He had begun quietly, he had spoken with feeling, but also with restraint. But at last all restraint had been flung away, passion had inflamed his countenance, as a hurried glance had taught her, and had vibrated in his voice. It was necessary to curb him before he lost all self-control, and as soon as he paused sufficiently for any interruption, she said immediately, "It is always unwise to say what we may afterwards regret."

"You would regret it," he returned impetuously. "That is what you mean."

"Perhaps I should," she said coldly, "although of course I cannot know what you wish to say."

"You do, you do," he cried.

"Mr. Acworth," said Elizabeth, summoning all her courage and presence of mind, "let me speak plainly. You appear to wish to tell me, a comparative stranger, what should remain locked in your breast. You have already told me something. You have spoken equivocally, I admit, but in such a manner as to open up conjectures on a matter which concerns only yourself. Let me commiserate you for a misfortune which must evoke the sympathy of all people of right feeling. Do not go on to expose the past when it should remain buried in the grave. Your conscience—" she hesitated, remembering his derision of that faculty—"your conscience will tell you that you owe it to the dead."

"Do you really think—" he began. Further speech was suspended, an odd choking sound burst from his throat. For one dreadful moment Elizabeth thought he was weeping. Alone in the wood with a man of such unpredictable behaviour, such ungovernable emotion, what should she do? She listened eagerly for the sound of a woodman's axe, such as was often to be heard, or the least rustle of brushwood denoting human approach. But all around was silence. Mr. Acworth had stood still upon the path, and she, not at first perceiving it, had taken a few steps in advance of him. Now, on looking round, she saw him leaning against a tree, his face covered with his hands, shaken with uncontrollable laughter.

Her astonishment was so great that for a moment or two it took from her the power of connected thought, but at length she became sensible that it was the laughter of hysteria, not mirth, which convulsed him. A suspicion that he might be acting was instantly dispelled; he was plainly beyond self-mastery. She stood watching him in growing consternation, the while debating within herself what was best to be said or done until involuntarily she spoke his name. He seemed not to hear. The horrifying thought then struck her that he might be laughing at herself, and as his paroxysm showed no sign of abating, she said with some asperity, "I do not know what I have said to cause this outburst."

"Incomparable," he gasped. "Though you slay me, I must adore you. Oh, divinest creature, forgive me. You rob me of further speech."

"Mr. Acworth, this is not the way to talk to me," said Elizabeth calmly, though she trembled in every limb. "You are strangely forgetting yourself. Making all allowances as I am willing to do, there are bounds which should not be transgressed."

Suddenly he uncovered his face and looked at her with the utmost gravity. His cheeks were flushed and wet with tears, but his mouth still twitched oddly. "Well," he said, "what are you going to do, Mrs. Darcy? Are you going to denounce me?"

"I do not comprehend you," Elizabeth answered, with all the dignity of which she was capable. "You lost control of yourself for a few moments. That may be granted. Shall we continue our walk?"

"You do not blame me?" he cried. "And why should you? Is the heart to be blamed for beating? I speak equivocally, do I? You mean that thus you choose to hear me. Now you shall hear the truth, come what may of it."

He came towards her, and his aspect was so strange, his features so flushed, that Elizabeth shrank back and averted her eyes. For one instant she felt real fear, but with the necessity for it her spirit rose, and she looked up again with a firm gaze.

"I cannot think you wish me to denounce you," she said. Then turning upon the path, she added, "Let us in any case walk on."

They went some way farther in a silence that for her was filled with intolerable suspense. What her companion thought and felt, what he would say if he did speak again, agitated her in spite of herself, and it required a strong effort to sustain the appearance of composure that was so necessary. The silence continued, and became at length so embarrassing that she had resolved to break it with a commonplace observation, when he suddenly addressed her.

"Mrs. Darcy, I beg that you will forget anything I may have said in a moment of madness to distress or offend you. I ought not to speak of myself. When I do, it rouses in me such feelings of misery that they get the better of me, and I behave in a violent and unbridled manner. Let me assure you that I meant no disrespect."

"I trust not," she answered dryly.

"I hardly remember what I have said," he continued. "Sometimes I think that I must be going out of my mind. Can you imagine what it is to be haunted by the past without hope for the future? That is my condition. I implore you not to betray me."

Elizabeth hesitated before giving an assurance to a man so volatile and so little to be depended on.

"You are goodness and charity itself," he resumed, with increasing urgency of tone. "I know that I do not deserve that it should be extended to me, but I do entreat that what has lately passed between us should reach no other ears at all."

She had to consider before she could reply. He was in effect asking her to keep the matter from her husband to whom she owed the most perfect candour. The consequences of such candour in the present instance could not be in any doubt. Acworth would be asked to quit Pemberley at once. She had no fear of an open scandal, for Darcy was discretion and resourcefulness itself and could, and did, always act with consideration towards even the people who least deserved it. But she could not resist Acworth's plea. She was sensible of his hanging upon her decision in terror lest it should be adverse to him. Still distrusting him, and unwilling to show herself too compliant after the way he had behaved, she resorted to a question.

"Do I understand that you have no desire to remain at Pemberley?"

"To remain at Pemberley is to be on the rack. But although I ought for my own peace of mind to go away, there is nowhere I can go. I cannot explain, but I must ask you to believe that it is imperative for me to stay here, at least for some weeks longer."

"I can only accept your statement without comprehending it," she said. "This is an occasion when I would rather know too little than too much. I would wholly forget this conversation if I could, and for my part I am willing never to refer to it, if you do not."

"Thank you a thousand times," he cried. "You have lifted a load from my heart."

Elizabeth was saved any further reply by the sound of a voice in the distance. To her ears it was at once distinguishable as coming from Darcy, and as he approached, though still invisible behind the barrier of trees about the winding of the path, he could be heard speaking to a companion in his customary deliberate accents. He was speaking at such length, to judge by the absence of reply, that only a matter of public concern could be the theme. Had Elizabeth felt any curiosity to know who his companion was, which she had not from the rapturous relief of being rescued from a most uncomfortable situation, it would soon have been satisfied.

Darcy at length ceased and the tones of a beloved and well-known voice were heard, now close at hand.

"Well, Darcy, the state of the country being what it is, I feel myself fortunate in not being plagued with a sense of responsibility for setting it right."

"Papa!" cried Elizabeth. The next moment a turn in the path showed her husband and her father walking towards them.

Chapter 8

MR. BENNET HAD ARRIVED with his daughter Kitty not long after the return of Elizabeth's carriage from the Parsonage. He had come, as he nearly always did, without previous warning, for he never wrote a letter if he could help it, and delighting to arrive unexpectedly, seldom set out on a journey unless the whim seized him. He was therefore not in the least put out at finding nobody to receive him but Mrs. Reynolds. The good woman informed him, with many expressions of concern, that her master and mistress were both out, though in different directions, and Miss Darcy had gone riding. She did not think her mistress would be long in coming home, for she had but gone as far as the village to call on the Miss Robinsons. Joseph had driven her to the Parsonage, but she had told him not to wait as she would be walking home through the woods.

After some light refreshment Kitty, quite knocked up by the journey, went to her room to rest; but Mr. Bennet, having changed his travelling clothes and taken a peep at his grandson in the nursery, found his way to the library and gave himself up to his favourite occupation of reading. There he was discovered by Darcy on his return a little later and given a warm welcome. On Mr. Bennet's retailing the substance of Elizabeth's message, Darcy suggested that they should go and meet her. They set off directly and about a third of the way through the woods came upon her walking with Acworth.

Father and daughter exchanged an affectionate greeting, laconic on one side and lively on the other, and Mr. Acworth was made known to Mr. Bennet. Elizabeth then took her father's arm and walked the rest of the way with him while Darcy and Acworth followed close behind. At first Elizabeth, listening with half an ear to her father and straining the other half to catch what might be said by her husband, heard only her father's voice relating some circumstance of the journey. Presently Darcy made an observation about the trees in that part of the wood to which his companion mechanically replied. A somewhat one-sided conversation thus began, Darcy enumerating the many varieties of timber in the Park in a determination not to be silent, and Acworth making only the briefest rejoinders. Her father, on the other hand, was in an unusually talkative mood from the pleasure of being with her again, and she was soon obliged to give him all her attention.

"Well, Lizzie, my dear, I don't need to ask how you are. You look as blooming as one of your roses." Then lowering his voice, but not quite enough, he added, "That's a charming young man you were walking with. Where did you find him?"

"Oh, hush, Papa, did not you hear? He is a Mr. Stephen Acworth, a brother of Lord Egbury."

"Ah," replied Mr. Bennet, "I could see he was not just one of your plain gentlemen."

To lead away from the subject Elizabeth began enquiring for friends and acquaintances at her old home. "How are the Lucases?" she asked.

"In excellent health so far as I know," said her father. "The last time I saw Sir William he sent his dutiful respects to you and enquired whether you were not a great success in Derbyshire society. 'Tell her,' said he, 'that Derbyshire's gain is Hertfordshire's loss.' As to the rest, Kitty can detail all the particulars of their concerns. I pay no attention to anything that goes on around me nowadays, and am cultivating a very promising deafness, for otherwise I should hear nothing but talk about the neighbours. And as we have Solomon's word for it that there is nothing new under the sun, I prefer not to listen."

Elizabeth laughed. "You know, Papa, you will end like Diogenes by living in a tub."

"There are many worse places. The accommodation is so limited that it prohibits intrusion."

"Has not Kitty been staying until now with the Collinses at Hunsford?"

"She has. And to save her the trouble of unpacking her trunks on her return here, we set out for Pemberley the very next day."

"That was rather hard upon Kitty, for she hates travelling."

"But she loves change," said Mr. Bennet. "Between ourselves she has been crossed in love—at least so your mother informs me. Your mother is very enraged with Charlotte Collins about it. It appears that she gave her sister Maria Lucas all the opportunities for engaging the affections of a certain young gentleman that should have been Kitty's; for, as your mother pointed put in more words than I can remember, Charlotte Collins' prospective enjoyment of the Longbourn estate puts her very much in debt to the present owner and his family—especially the latter."

"You appear to have listened to Mamma, at all events."

"My dear," said her father, "as you yourself ought to know, there is no escaping the pertinacity of a spouse."

Elizabeth smiled but faintly. "But, Papa," she said, "it is stale news that Maria Lucas is engaged to a clergyman. I have known it these three weeks."

"That may be so, but in your mother's mind it is still fresh. If you could get Kitty settled in a matrimonial situation suitable to her looks and lack of fortune, I should be infinitely obliged, for I get sick of hearing of her rights and wrongs."

"Then you must prepare yourself to see a great deal of company, for it is not possible otherwise."

"Fiddlestick," replied her father. "You and Kitty can see as much company as you choose without dragging me by the heels."

On reaching the house Elizabeth went upstairs to see her sister. Kitty was lying down on her bed with her eyes closed and a handkerchief soaked in aromatic vinegar held to her forehead. She opened her eyes as Elizabeth came to her side, and sat up to kiss and be kissed, but sank back again immediately afterwards, looking haggard with headache and fatigue. In the three years or more since Elizabeth had been married, Kitty had, however, much improved in looks and manners, and from being thin and pale, with a peevish expression, she had grown into a slender, pretty girl with an air of delicacy and languor. She was neither clever nor well-educated, but she had learnt how to talk to different sorts of people and could make a little matter go a long way in keeping up a conversation. In general, her behaviour was of the most exemplary propriety.

Having enquired after her comfort Elizabeth would have left her again to continue her repose, but Kitty begged her to stay, so she sat down beside the bed prepared to chat for a little while. "You made a long stay at Hunsford," she observed.

"There was no getting away," Kitty replied. "I wanted to return home at the end of the six weeks for which Charlotte Collins had invited us, but Maria insisted on staying. She was determined not to go until she had secured Mr. Bullock, and so she hung on and on until she got him. And then Mr. Bullock, though invited to Lucas Lodge, could not immediately leave his parish, and Maria would not quit Hunsford until the date of his journey could be fixed."

"Was he really so wavering and uncertain as you make him appear?"

"He is so extremely dull that I do not think any notion of marriage entered his head until Charlotte put it there. In fact, he is the stupidest, backwardest young man I have ever known. However, he will be a husband for Maria, and of course the Lucases are pleased enough, and Charlotte is delighted that Maria will be living within three miles of her. For I can tell you that Charlotte is not at all happy since Lady Catherine has taken such a dislike to Mr. Collins. He is always in a bad temper, and Lady Catherine is insupportable."

"Did you see anything of Lady Catherine and Miss de Bourgh?"

"Not above once or twice. Charlotte and Mr. Collins are not often invited to Rosings now—only when Lady Catherine can get no one else for a game of quadrille—but she will call to see Charlotte now and again about something or other in the parish, and find fault with her and give her orders that I wonder Charlotte can bear it. Now I know what it is to be a clergyman's wife, I would not marry one for all the gold in Arabia."

"Poor Charlotte, her lot is indeed uncomfortable. When you did see Lady Catherine, how did she behave to yourself?"

"She seemed very angry with me for being your sister. Indeed, to hear her you would think it was a great impertinence on my part. The first time she called at the Parsonage after I was there, she asked me some questions about my age and place in the family, and then she said I could not hope to make so great a marriage as you had done. She said I was not so very ill-looking, but that I lacked your arts and allurements."

"They evidently made a great impression on her," said Elizabeth laughing. "She will always believe that they cheated her out of a son-in-law."

"Charlotte says Lady Catherine has never forgiven you for marrying Darcy. Is not it strange, Lizzie, that Miss de Bourgh has not been able to get a husband? I am sure Lady Catherine has tried all ways. And then she is so rich. One would have thought that with all the money she has, and what is coming to her, she could marry whom she pleased, even now when she must be nearly thirty. But she is so small and sickly looking and has such a cross expression, that who would look at her? And Lady Catherine has aimed so high for her that she has probably missed some chances. Charlotte says that at one time she would not consider anyone less than a viscount, but now she would be glad to marry her to any ordinary gentleman. There was talk at one time of Colonel Fitzwilliam. Of course he is only the younger son of an earl, and has not much money, but no doubt Lady Catherine would be glad to get him for her daughter. He used to come regularly to stay at Rosings, Charlotte says, and now he never does—at least he has not stayed there for the last two years—and Charlotte's opinion is that it is because he does not wish to be inveigled into marrying his cousin."

"That is only conjecture. Colonel Fitzwilliam is a man of the world and perfectly well able to take care of himself. It is besides by no means certain that Lady Catherine would make the attempt."

"But you cannot deny she is capable of it, for now she must be very nearly desperate. This last twelve months she and her daughter have been here and there—London, Bath, Brighton, Ramsgate and other places. They were to start on a round of visits when I quitted Hunsford."

"Yes," said Elizabeth, by this time thoroughly tired of Kitty's ill-natured gossip, "they are coming here on a visit in about ten days from now."

"Oh, Lizzy," cried Kitty, "why did you not tell me before?"

"I did not think to. I only knew it myself a few days ago. What difference would it have made had you known sooner?"

"Well, I don't know, but I must say I hate the very sight of Lady Catherine. My comfort is she will take no notice of me beyond 'good morning' and 'good night.' But what can they be coming here for? Does not Lady Catherine detest you?"

"I think it very likely that she does, but she still has an affection for Darcy and Georgiana."

Kitty closed her eyes and turned her face on her pillow in such a very suffering manner that Elizabeth offered to leave her alone. But Kitty hated to be alone at any time, and her headache, being of the nervous variety, engendered a strong desire to be talking. And beyond every motive in strength and urgency she had suddenly remembered that she had something to impart of such singular interest that further delay was not to be thought of.

"Pray, do not go just yet, Lizzy. It is such a comfort to have someone to speak to, and I have a prodigious deal to tell you. You cannot conceive what it is to travel with Papa. There he sits, as mum as a post, reading in one of his books, and pretending not to hear a word one says. We were talking of Lady Catherine and Miss de Bourgh, were not we? Well, there is something I must tell you, if you will promise not to repeat it to anybody else—not even Darcy. For I was vowed to silence, and you know it would be very wrong if anything came out through me."

This was the second time that day that Elizabeth had been urged to concealment from Darcy, and she replied with some indignation, "You may be quite certain that my husband can keep a secret as well as yourself. He is not interested in spreading tales."

"Well, come to think of it, I daresay he would not like to mention it, for it concerns his own cousin, Miss de Bourgh. I must tell you that Charlotte had it from a Mrs. Bevan who was wife to the rector before Mr. Collins. Mr. Bevan died and she went away to live in another part of the country, but there are some ladies, the Miss Fanshawes, who live in a pretty cottage outside the village, and she keeps friends with them and now and again comes to stay. Well, the last time she was here she told Charlotte in strict confidence that when Miss de Bourgh was about eighteen or nineteen she fell in love with a nephew of Mr. Bevan's that used to live with his uncle and aunt. He was an orphan and had been left so much money for his education and no more, and as he had no liking for the Church and was inclined to be rather wild, Mr. Bevan was going to put him into the Law. Mrs. Bevan said he was a fine, tall handsome young man and very lively, and in those days Miss de Bourgh was rather pretty. Of course they used to meet at church and at Rosings, and sometimes Mrs. Jenkinson, the companion, and Miss de Bourgh would come calling at the Parsonage, but Mrs. Bevan declared that there was never anything at all particular in their manner to one another that she could see, and to this day she cannot think how they contrived to meet in secret as they must have done. And so it might have gone on some time longer; but one day Mr. Bevan was going to Rosings on some business and walking by way of the grove instead of the carriage road because the sun was very hot, when suddenly he came upon them standing under a tree. He was holding her hands and talking and she was smiling up at him. I dare say that when Mr. Bevan walked up to them there was a fine scene. Mr. Bevan was very angry with his nephew and sent him away the very next day, and made him promise that he would never by any method whatever communicate with Miss de Bourgh, for if he did he would inform Lady Catherine. Mrs. Bevan says she was sure her nephew did not. He enlisted as a soldier and went to the war and was killed. And from that time Miss de Bourgh became what she is now."

As Elizabeth did not at once reply Kitty turned towards her impatiently and asked, "What do you say to that?"

"I think that if what you tell me is true it explains much that has hitherto suffered a wrong construction. I have not liked Anne de Bourgh because she has never been at pains to be even tolerably civil to me, but I have observed that she behaves with indifference to everyone alike, and as if she were wholly occupied with herself. I do not believe that any more spiritless being could be found, but if her feelings suffered such a blow in her early youth as would appear, it is hardly to be wondered at. In any circumstances to be the daughter of such a mother must have been a severe trial. I do hope that you will say nothing further on the subject to anyone else."

Having unburdened herself thus fully, Kitty had very possibly the less temptation to be indiscreet. She lay silent, her thoughts already wandering in another direction. Presently she said, "It seems quite an age since I saw Georgiana. I asked her to write to me, but she never has. Is there any likelihood of her becoming engaged yet?"

"Not the slightest."

"Does she intend never to marry then?" Kitty asked incredulously.

"I do not know. She may think of marriage in a few years time."

"A few years! Does no one pay court to her?"

"No one, unless it is Mr. Mortimer. But even he is becoming hopeless."

"Who is Mr. Mortimer?"

"Another clergyman," said Elizabeth mischievously.

"Then I am not surprised."

"But he is not in the least like Mr. Collins—or Mr. Bullock, either, from your description. He has an estate five miles from here about as large as Longbourn, and he lives on it like any other country gentleman. Georgiana cannot tolerate him, but you might find him very agreeable. He is indeed a most amiable young man, though not clever. I fancy he is only waiting for some young woman to be ordinarily pleasant to him to fall madly in love with her."

"He can wait as far as I am concerned," said Kitty with great indifference. "I am sure I do not vex my head about young men any more than Georgiana does. Seeing Maria Lucas ogling at Mr. Bullock gave me quite a disgust for that sort of thing."

Shortly afterwards Kitty began to show signs of having talked enough for that time, and Elizabeth could withdraw to her own room for rest and reflection. Her meditations were not of the most tranquil, for when she thought of Acworth she was filled with misgiving, and when she recalled her passage of arms with Miss Robinson her conscience upbraided her. In the one case she felt that she had disengaged herself from an unpleasant situation with dignity unimpaired, whereas in the other she had given way to provocation when she should have exercised patience.

Time passed and she began dressing for dinner. Rather earlier than usual Darcy entered to see if she were ready. As Mason was still attending to her mistress he took up a book that was lying on the dressing-table and turned its pages in discovery of what his wife had been reading. She had a taste for poetry and praised the new school of poets, while he still remained doubtful of their value and considered that certain poets of the past century had reached the summit of their art. But his action was mechanical, testifying only to a habit of mind, and when he had glanced at the first stanzas of a poem entitled "The Ancient Mariner" he let the book fall on his knee and rested his eyes on Elizabeth.

It had not escaped his observation that she was uncommonly flushed when he met her in the wood with Acworth. Not only was she flushed, but other traces of perturbation were visible to an eye instructed in all her moods and aspects. She had met his glance with one of candour, and he was perfectly satisfied that she would tell him anything he ought to hear as soon as she had the opportunity. Acworth had also been under scrutiny in the course of their walk together as far as the house. Distaste for the man made conversation with him a trial, but silence would have been a mistake, and so Darcy had exerted himself to talk. Although Acworth had responded as common civility directed, it was evident that he was in a state of extreme excitement and high resentfulness. His eyes glittered unpleasantly and his manner bordered on the discourteous. It looked, indeed, as if the rencontre with Elizabeth's husband had been the reverse of pleasing to him. All this Darcy perceived without appearing to notice anything extraordinary in his companion's behaviour. Only one interpretation presented itself, but until he heard what Elizabeth had to say he preferred not to accept it.

It was not long before Elizabeth dismissed Mason. As soon as the maid had quitted the room she looked round, her dark eyes wide with disquiet, and said, "Fitz, dearest, I fear I have irrevocably offended Miss Robinson."

This was so far from his expectation that he looked at her in silent astonishment. "What have you done?" he asked, recovering himself and beginning to smile, "or more pertinently, what did you say?"

She told him briefly of her action in regard to Rachel Stone. "I still maintain that it was justified," she said, "but of course I should have spoken to Miss Robinson much sooner. The truth is that all that has taken place of late—Major Wakeford's accident and other things—made me forget. I called at the Parsonage today to explain, but Miss Robinson was not in the least conciliatory. She was what she usually is—rude and brusque, and she so angered me that I was provoked into a stiff retort. But really I see nothing to laugh at! Surely you must be aware that all intercourse with the Parsonage is severed for the time being."

Darcy was seldom moved to laughter, but this revelation, so totally at variance with what he had conceived to be the cause of his wife's silence and abstraction struck him with the overpowering force of the incongruous and absurd. Subduing his hilarity, he asked her again what she had said. "Was it so very bad?" he enquired.

"I cannot remember the exact words I used, but I spoke with the perfect plainness which is all Miss Robinson can understand. I represented to her that it was no longer her business to interfere in parish matters, that she was arrogating to herself an authority that she did not possess. After I had spoken you could have heard a pin drop, and that poor, unfortunate Miss Sophia seemed on the verge of fainting. I can assure you it was a terrible moment, and I could have bitten out my tongue."

"To quote the Psalmist, 'the fire kindled and then you spoke.' Oh, Elizabeth, Elizabeth!"

"I have not your calm, your deliberation, your power of crushing with a look. But what is to be done?"

"Done? Nothing for the moment that I can see. You were perfectly right in acting as you did, though perhaps a little indiscreet in the way of doing it. In any case it is not for you to give way. You and Miss Robinson will no doubt meet at the Church door next Sunday, and curtsy coldly to one another. As the season advances the salutations will become slightly less distant, and by Christmas you will be able to command yourselves sufficiently to speak. But," recollecting himself, "by that time Miss Robinson will probably be honouring another church door."

Mention of the church door brought up the idea of Acworth. "Where did you meet Acworth?" he asked, with affected nonchalance.

"He was at the Parsonage when I arrived there. Miss Sophia says that he goes there every day."

"Was he present when you and Miss Robinson exchanged shots?"

"Yes, unfortunately. I do not know that his being there made it any worse, however. He was perfectly discreet and did his best to pour oil on troubled waters."

"So that was how he came to walk home with you?"

"I would much rather have walked home by myself, but Miss Sophia made such an outcry against it, and after that in spite of all I could say, he seemed to think it was his duty to escort me."

Darcy said nothing, and Elizabeth feeling the silence to be uncomfortable, continued, "He is evidently still very unhappy."

"Unquestionably," he replied, "but the source of his unhappiness is in some doubt."

"What do you mean?" she exclaimed, amazed that he should have for once formed the same conclusion as herself. It is a strange sort of unhappiness," she said almost without a pause, "a kind of restlessness. He told me this afternoon that he did not think he could support being here much longer."

Darcy kept moving about the room, constrained by some idea which he was uncertain whether to impart. Elizabeth, perceiving this, forbore to question him directly and waited for him to speak.

"Did he imply dislike of the place, or anything amiss on our side, or what?"

"He said—or seemed to say—that the spectacle of a happiness so enviable as ours was more than he could endure."

"That was hardly generous or delicate. Neither was it deserved. Real happiness is not for display and should offend no one."

"It made me rather uncomfortable, I must own," said Elizabeth. "Perhaps I have erred in being too high-spirited—too talkative."

"I have seen nothing of it," said Darcy smiling. "It is probably nearer the truth to say that our guest was making a bid for pity as a means of attracting attention to himself—the attention of a pretty woman."

Elizabeth laughed and looked aside. "You have reached one decision about him evidently," she said.

"One or two perhaps. I am convinced that there is more to know than he cares to divulge. It is apparent to me that he is the son of his father—more thoroughly than I like. But whatever I may suspect remains suspicion."

"What do you suspect?" she asked, taking his hand. "I believe you have something on your mind. You are hiding it— you cannot deceive me, for there is a look in your eyes that betrays you. If I wished to conceal anything from you, I could do it much better, you know."

"Indeed," he replied, endeavouring to preserve his gravity, "I am sorry to hear it. What do you suppose I am hiding from you?"

"Something relating to Mr. Acworth," she answered boldly. "You have discovered something to his discredit."

"Many things. There is very little about him that I do like."

"How tiresome you are, my love. You know I don't mean that. You have discovered something tangible to arouse suspicion."

"Any suspicions I may harbour are based on observation. And where, may I ask, are your eyes, Elizabeth?"

"I can see perfectly, but like yourself cannot always account for what I see. And after all I have seen very little of him, and then chiefly at breakfast and dinner when everyone is engaged in the business of eating."

"A most desirable state of affairs. Continue in the same by all means."

"How can I when you have provoked my curiosity? You are a most unreasonable creature, Fitz. You seem to forget that I am a woman."

"I do not think so," he replied, enfolding her. "That is the last thing I should ever do."

"Now you are throwing dust in my eyes."

"No, my dearest, it would be impossible. They are far too wide-awake for that. The only object they do not survey is yourself, except briefly, and perhaps not quite truly, in your mirror. You will never know how you look to me, to me especially—or to others. The best part of you is banished from your own vision, for it is in self-forgetfulness, in speaking, in listening, in looking upon a rose, upon your child that you are most beautiful."

"You speak as a poet would," she said softly, touched and also very much pleased. After a short but complacent silence, she asked archly, "Fitz, do I talk like a book?"

"Sometimes you do," he said startled.

"Alas, how dreadful!"

"Not at all. It was one of your most endearing charms."

"Was, indeed!"

"It is less extraordinary in a married woman who learns to converse with her husband and his friends on equal terms. But when you were still Elizabeth Bennet, very young, very pretty, inclined to be saucy, the polished fluency with which you at times expressed yourself was extremely diverting. But who, pray, has been telling you that you talk like a book?"

Elizabeth, enraged with herself for falling into her own trap, decided that it was best to reply without hesitation, "Mr. Acworth," adding immediately, "but it is only fair to say that he apologised when he saw I was displeased."

"Was this today, when he was walking with you in the wood?"

"Yes. One had to talk about something, you know, and I may have sounded formal and high-flown."

"Elizabeth, be frank with me. Is this the first time you have had to complain of his behaviour?"

"Indeed it is," she said, determined to finish with the subject once and for all lest what she had promised to be silent about should be dragged out of her. "I have never—there has never been any previous opportunity for him to be familiar. I will not deny," she continued in perfect sincerity, "that he interests me in a sense. His gifts alone render him interesting."

Darcy was silent, his brow contracted with anxious thought.

"Is it impossible to end the arrangement between you?" she asked, but said no more, remembering Acworth's statement that he had nowhere to go.

"I cannot very well depart from an agreement once entered into unless very good reason arises," he replied. "Before quitting London I wrote to Lord Egbury, acquainting him with the particulars of our interview, and I feel therefore as much bound to him in the matter as to Acworth. It is certain that Acworth will never become rector of Pemberley, but unless he behaves in such a way as to warrant extreme measures there can be no occasion for dismissing him before the time stipulated between us expires."

"It is not so much what he does, as what he is, that makes him undesirable."

"You are perfectly right. I have in fact had considerably more opportunity of observing him than yourself, and there has been much in what I have seen and heard that displeases me. When he is in the company of other men, especially when he has drunk a glass or two, his tongue is apt to run away with him and he will betray an acquaintance with a sort of life that he ought not to have. His knowledge of the world extends downwards rather than in his proper sphere, and I cannot find that he has any respectable friends. He speaks of seclusion from the great world, and yet knows too much of the lower ranks of society. He consorts with professional actors and musicians. He is a vain man, and his indiscretion matches his vanity, for to attract attention to himself he will tell a story that discloses inadvertently what he should be ashamed to relate. Now you know all that is weighing on my mind."

He smiled so frankly, with such full assurance of whole and undivided mutual understanding that Elizabeth had to force back the words of a confidence that at this moment came easily and naturally to her lips. It was almost an agony not to speak, and feeling that in reality she owed Acworth nothing, and that he deserved less, she bitterly repented having pledged herself to silence on his account. But she had pledged herself, and could not in honour break her promise.

"Do not tell me any more," she exclaimed impetuously. "It is better to know too little than too much." Remembering that she had used the same words to Acworth only an hour or two before, she coloured and looked down. "While he remains here," she said more quietly, "I must continue to behave to him as I have done hitherto. Any alteration in manner would not do. I cannot altogether avoid him."

"No," he agreed. "Fortunately he appears anxious to avoid our society. He doubtless finds the Miss Robinsons very much more congenial. From what I hear they make quite a pet of him."

The clock on the mantelpiece chimed the dinner hour. It was a premonitory announcement, for Elizabeth kept her timepiece expressly ten minutes fast. But it was high time to be downstairs. They quitted the room together.

Chapter 9

WHEN MORTIMER FIRST BEGAN to be a regular visitor at Pemberley House in the course of riding over for the Sunday duty, he was so shy of the ladies that he neither presented himself nor stayed more than was absolutely necessary for the prosecution of Darcy's purpose, being impelled only by the desire to oblige his friend and not by any form of self-gratification. But as he grew familiar with the ways of the great house and got on easier terms with Mrs. Darcy, it came to attract him so much that he would invent excuses for calling at odd times, and if Darcy were not at home would cheerfully spend an hour or more chatting with his wife and sister. It was not long before he imagined himself to be violently in love with Georgiana, and then he was drawn chiefly by the desire of securing her hand. Gradually his hope of that dwindled, but his constancy as a caller abated not at all, for he discovered that he could not stay away.

On Acworth's arrival he had assumed that his services in the parish would be no longer required. Darcy's request, made within a week, that he would continue them for the present surprised though gratified him, despite his hatred of preaching. He supposed that Acworth's health was not up to any exertion as yet, for after the first Sunday he was left to support the whole business alone, since it appeared that Acworth's first appearance in a surplice was not to be repeated. But although he affected to groan under the burden among his Clopwell acquaintance, he was really delighted to feel that he was still of use to the Darcys and was regarded by them as a tried and trusty friend from whom a favour was no longer a debt.

He was not the sort of young man to enquire what it was in particular that drew him to Pemberley so irresistibly. It was enough that with all its state there was no other house where he was so well entertained, where youth, beauty and gaiety reigned with such invincible charms. To be at Pemberley was to be happy. Riding home under the stars after an evening spent there, he would turn over in his mind all that had passed during his visit and contrast the animation of the scene he had lately quitted with the solitude and dullness of the house to which he was returning. Dark throughout, save for one solitary candle burning in the hall, and in melancholy silence, it received him, and thus he went to bed.

That there could be any charm of the picturesque in the ancient abode of the Mortimers did not occur to him. It was all neglect within, a wilderness without, not much worse than he ever remembered it, but none the less a reproach to its owners past and present. He wished to improve it, but did not know how to begin where so much was needed to be done and so much money must be spent. What he did know was that since he had been frequenting Pemberley his eyes had been opened, his ideas changed and his desires extended beyond anything he had ever before conceived for man's happiness and comfort.

One evening, as he wandered round the lake in front of the house, it struck him that for all the hospitality he had received from the Darcys he ought to make some return. Reflection upon the state of everything, the worn furniture and threadbare carpets, the clumsy and dilatory service of the few ancient servants bequeathed by his father made him seriously doubt the propriety of attempting to entertain them to dinner. He might succeed tolerably well with the gentleman of the Pemberley party, but how could he venture to ask the ladies! Yet that was precisely what he most desired to do, and the longer he dallied with the idea, the more it attracted him, great as were the obstacles in the way of execution, and not the least his own inexperience in the sort of hospitality he contemplated. In his perplexity the image of Mrs. Darcy floated before his eyes, all wisdom, kindness and beauty. He resolved to lay the matter before her to the last and most embarrassing detail, and be guided by her implicitly.

The next morning he took the road to Pemberley at an early hour when he might be tolerably sure of finding her at home. As he rode his horse up the steepest part of the carriage-road through the park he overtook Acworth strolling along in the same direction, and dismounted to walk beside him. Acworth looked so thoroughly out of sorts, so pale and depressed that Mortimer was really concerned to see it, and told him so.

"You don't look at all the thing, Acworth. Your health does not improve much, I fear. Do you still sleep badly?"

"I hardly closed my eyes last night," Acworth replied. "They have the habit here of retiring early—half after eleven at latest—and I have been used to very different hours, so that when I go to my room my brain is still too active for rest. The cocks are beginning to crow before sleep comes. I detest the country. For me London has charms superior to any place on earth."

"I went to Bath several times with my brother when he was alive, and I once stayed in London, but I never got much pleasure out of the town. I had rather be at home in Derbyshire where I can keep my money in my pocket."

"You are a wise man," said Acworth banteringly. "Speaking of money, can you lend me any?"

"How much do you require?" asked Mortimer, after some hesitation.

"I require a great deal, a much larger sum than you would be willing to part with."

"I dare say I can let you have fifty pound."

"Think no more about it, Mortimer. I was only joking. Fifty pounds would be the fiftieth part of the sum I need for my purpose."

"Why don't you apply to Darcy? He is not only rich, but very liberal, so I have always heard."

"Darcy! Never! He is the last man I should ask a favour of. It would be intolerable to be beholden to him."

"You do not like him?" exclaimed Mortimer, struck by the acrimony of his tone.

"I dislike him very much," answered Acworth more calmly. "And I have not the least doubt that he returns the sentiment."

Mortimer began warmly defending Darcy in the mistaken belief that Acworth could be reasoned into a better opinion of him. The latter bore with his praise of his friend for some moments in silence and with an unmoved countenance. Suddenly he raised a clenched fist and shook it in a paroxysm of fury.

"You do not, cannot, and never will comprehend what I hate in that man. He represents all that is directed against such as myself. Every adventitious superiority is found in him—wealth, rank, a handsome person—so that you all pay court to him. But the real superiority—of mind and talent—that you ignore and slight."

"I am sure I meant no offence," said Mortimer in surprise, for he could not believe that Acworth meant what he said. "After all a man cannot help being what he is. And I can tell you this much—Darcy does his duty by his tenants and servants as few men of his station do."

"Oh, for God's sake say no more," shouted Acworth, his face distorted by rage. "If he treats his servants well it is only that they may be the more willing slaves. What would he be without his money? It is that alone which enables him to cut a figure, to pick and choose among the best this earth has to offer. If he desires to take a wife, what woman will not be tempted by the jewels, the finery he can give her, and by the consequence which the being mistress of Pemberley confers? What but his wealth sets him upon his pinnacle from which he can look down upon everyone else? I tell you that I despise him for the inferior being he would appear were he denuded of his grandeur. I hold myself infinitely better than he is by natural endowment, in heart, in brain incomparably more gifted."

He ceased for want of breath. Mortimer had heard him, first with amazement, then with growing resentment. Despite his modest opinion of himself, he had a kind of hardihood, and he now said quietly but with decision, "I do not agree with you at all about Darcy, for I know him to be otherwise. If you dislike him so much as you say, why don't you quit Pemberley?"

"I cannot properly explain," Acworth returned in a lower voice and in halting accents. "It is too long, too difficult to relate why. I do not stay here by my own choice, but until I obtain money from a source at present closed to me I am extremely embarrassed and my movements are correspondingly restricted. I will not deny also that to be at Pemberley has its compensations. In short, I have exaggerated as usual. It is a malady of the nerves from which I suffer that I imagine any fancied contempt, slight, or ridicule into the grossest of its kind. Pray do not repeat anything I have said just now. I would not for the world have a misleading impression get about."

"I should not dream of it," said Mortimer with serious candour.

"Do not let me delay you any longer," Acworth said after a few moments. "You intend calling at the house, no doubt. I am not returning there at present."

Mortimer demurred politely, but on Acworth's again urging him to go forward, he mounted his horse and rode on. His relief at being rid of this strange companion was very great, and he straightway put him out of his mind which he now addressed to the purpose of his errand.

On reaching the house he was informed that Mrs. Darcy was in the garden and that the gentlemen had taken their rods down to the river. The circumstance, so favourable to a private interview with the lady, could not have better answered his wishes. Alas, he hastened to the garden only to find Mrs. Darcy accompanied by Miss Darcy and another young lady wholly unknown to him. Salutations in proper form followed, and having been introduced to the lately arrived Miss Catherine Bennet, Mortimer stationed himself beside Mrs. Darcy, and seizing the first opportunity which occurred, asked in a low voice whether he might have a private word with her.

Georgiana had wandered away of her own accord to another part of the garden, but Kitty kept close to her sister, and while affecting to be not in the least curious, was intent to observe the young man and hear as much as she could. At a sign from Elizabeth, however, she too strolled away, though not so far that under cover of cutting roses and transferring them to the basket hanging on her arm, she was unable to catch a good deal of what was said.

Elizabeth led the way to a stone bench in the shade cast by a yew hedge. Here they seated themselves, and she asked him what he wished to say to her. But the view of the great house in all its stateliness, the exquisite order of the gardens and the park beyond, the whole ravishing scene before his eyes scattered his thoughts and his command of appropriate language. At last, for he must speak, he said in his natural and unaffected style, "Mrs. Darcy, I believe you have never been to Clopwell, for there is really nothing to tempt you there, but it will give me the greatest pleasure in the world if you and Darcy and Miss Darcy—in short all at Pemberley—will do me the honour of spending an hour or so at my house one day soon."

Elizabeth replied immediately that she and her husband would be delighted to visit him. "But I ought to warn you that we shall be very numerous next week," she added, "for besides our present party of seven, my eldest sister and her husband will be with us then, and very possibly my uncle and aunt, making eleven all told. Oh, and I had forgot Lady Catherine de Bourgh and her daughter whom we are expecting on Friday week."

"But that will bring your party to thirteen," exclaimed Mortimer in genuine dismay. "Oh, Mrs. Darcy, had you thought of it?"

"Indeed I had not. It had quite escaped me that we should be a number of such ill-omen. Would you not rather that we visited you when we are nine and innocuous?"

"That would not trouble me in the least, for I should make a fourteenth. But, Mrs. Darcy, I do beseech you to add another guest or so to the number at Pemberley for your own sake."

"Come, Mr. Mortimer, you are not so superstitious as all that. I dare say you can muster a dozen shocking cases of catastrophe, but there must be dozens of others where nothing untoward has happened."

"Despise me if you will," said Mortimer, very red and distressed, "but it vexes me prodigiously to think of your sitting down thirteen to dinner. It will not do at all."

"In that case you must hold yourself in readiness to preserve us from calamity at any time should the need arise," said Elizabeth, simulating complete gravity. "We shall of course invite the Miss Robinsons occasionally, for the eldest Miss Robinson is a prime favourite with Lady Catherine de Bourgh, and perhaps Mr. Groves can sometimes be present to avert disaster."

Mortimer appeared greatly relieved. "There is no sense in taking risks," said he. "Even Darcy would see that, for all he is in general so much above that sort of thing, and professes to despise what he calls 'old wives' fables'."

"No doubt he would make some concession to our frailer understandings. The greatest minds are not always consistent, and even Mr. Darcy has been known to bow to superstition, for I do remember that once he went a great way round rather than walk under a ladder. I dare say he was not like that before he married; association with a wife has its dangers, you know, Mr. Mortimer, for if one of her uses is to keep her husband upon a common level, all her arts are employed to make him as silly and trivial as she is herself."

"Oh, Mrs. Darcy, how can you say such a thing," he protested vehemently. "It should be—must be quite the reverse. I have always thought Darcy so much to be envied— in a lady for his wife so accomplished—so very superior as well as—as beautiful."

Elizabeth laughed away her embarrassment. "Really, you are becoming famous with your compliments. But are not we straying from the point? We were talking of a visit to Clopwell. Did you mention a day? For if so, I have forgot what it was."

A further short discussion produced agreement on a date— Thursday in the following week. The next day was to see the arrival of Lady Catherine, and Elizabeth felt that not only was it inexpedient to engage for her participation in the visit before-hand, but also that beyond the strain it might put upon the condescension of so great a lady, everybody would be much more at their ease than if she were present. On the other hand, Mortimer had to bargain that due time be given for the vast amount of preparation the scheme would entail, and the cajoling of his spoilt servants into exerting themselves beyond their ordinary lazy habits.

As the business seemed to be concluded Elizabeth rose from the bench. Mortimer followed her example, but detaining her with his ingenuous gaze he began, "Mrs. Darcy, do you remember a conversation we had one Sunday some weeks ago when Darcy was in London?"

"What was the subject?"

"We spoke of Miss Darcy. You gave me some advice which at the time I did not like. And now I wish to tell you that I have come to think you were right. So I have given up thinking about her."

"I really do applaud your courage and good sense," said Elizabeth. "But"—a gleam of mischief sparkling in her eyes—"do not you feel a great deal happier in consequence?"

"Yes, I do," he replied in all seriousness. "So much so that I believe I was more wanting to be in love than in love itself."

"Mr. Mortimer," said she, matching his solemnity, "permit me to say that you are a very remarkable person. Never in my life have I met anyone who knew his own mind in such a case with such lucidity. How did the scales fall from your eyes, may I ask?"

"It is very curious," he said, after a little hesitation. "One day as I was looking at her, it struck me that she was not after all so beautiful as I had thought her. It couldn't be that *she* had changed, so after some thought, I concluded that *I* had done so."

"In other words, you had fallen *out* of love?"

"Yes," he agreed in a tone of depression. "And though it is a great relief not to be vexing myself with hopes and fears, I do feel at a loss. For I am still wanting to be married, that I may have a comfortable home as I see other men have. But I should not like to marry unless I was at least a little in love."

"That is very right and proper, since a woman prefers her husband to be partial to her, at least to begin with."

"Yes, it is only her due. But that is not all. A man ought to give his wife a home that she can take pleasure in, and when you come to Clopwell, you will see how very far it is from being what any lady of nice taste would wish for. There has been no new furniture brought into it these fifty years, I am sure, for my father never bought any to my knowledge unless it was a piece or two when he married my mother. I would very much like to lay out some money in improving it if I only knew how to set about it, but in truth I haven't the least notion, and so, Mrs. Darcy, I would be ever grateful if, when you have seen everything, you would tell me what ought to be done."

"I would gladly help you in any way I could," Elizabeth replied, "but would it not come better from the woman you propose to marry?"

"There is no such person at present," he answered seriously.

Elizabeth laughed as she returned, "I really cannot help you there, Mr. Mortimer; it would never do." At that moment Kitty in passing from one rosebush to another, flitted across their path. Elizabeth called to her, and she turned towards them smiling. Mortimer was so preoccupied with thoughts on marriage that at first he scarcely saw her. But in the sunlight, her cheeks faintly flushed in the shadow of her wide-brimmed straw bonnet, she looked her prettiest, and as occasionally happens between the members of a family, however little they in general resemble one another, a likeness to Elizabeth was suddenly, though transiently revealed. Mortimer, happening to look at her at that precise instant, was powerfully struck by it.

"Mr. Mortimer has invited us all to Clopwell on Thursday of next week," said Elizabeth. "It is a house such as you dote on, Kitty—very old, full of rambling passages according to what I have been told, and odd nooks and crannies. Is not that so, Mr. Mortimer?"

Mortimer confessed that his house was certainly old, but doubted whether Miss Bennet would dote upon it after being accustomed to the greater beauties of Pemberley. Kitty, nevertheless asked so many questions, and showed so much interest in his answers, that he was led on to give an account in some detail of its long history, in the development of which it transpired that Darcys and Mortimers had been neighbouring landowners for many generations. All that he recounted of past dignity and importance told greatly in favour of a very ordinary looking young man, and exalted his modesty and simplicity into extraordinary virtues in Kitty's eyes. She smiled upon him very graciously, and in her unwonted animation looked more than ever like Elizabeth. Thus encouraged, the gentleman began to spread his own plumage, and with increasing confidence in his power of pleasing, to converse with more point and spirit than was customary with him.

While they were thus engaged, Elizabeth drew their steps away from the garden and across the terrace to the lawn leading down to the river, where the spreading foliage of scattered trees cast a welcome shade from the rays of the sun. The anglers were not immediately visible, but shortly Mr. Bennet came in sight, rod in hand, walking along the bank in search of a likely place to cast his line. Having ascended to a mound where the stream could be surveyed over a farther distance than elsewhere, Elizabeth descried the figures of Georgiana and Major Wakeford not very far away, but beyond some bushes which had previously hidden them from view. Next she looked for her husband who, as she knew, was in attendance upon a visitor, and at last saw him a good way off. Darcy was not fishing himself and could therefore be spoken with, so she set off towards him, followed by Mortimer and Kitty who were finding so much to say to one another that their feet lagged behind hers.

She had not gone far when her eye fell upon Acworth as he lay stretched on the grass under a tree some way off up the slope. Resting on one side, and his head supported by his hand, he was reading from a book and appeared oblivious of everything around him. She averted her gaze directly as if merely to look at him were to attract his attention. Georgiana and Major Wakeford were now close at hand and she made haste to approach them.

Georgiana was fastening a fly on the end of Major Wakeford's line under his direction, and they were both so closely engaged by it that they remained unconscious of her presence.

"I do not use this kind of fly as a rule," Major Wakeford was saying. "In the past I have always made my own to my own pattern. We have excellent trout-fishing at my home in Devonshire. An old servant of my father's taught me the art when I was a lad."

"Is it difficult to make flies?" asked Georgiana. "Could I learn how to do it?"

"I am sure you could," he replied. "But few ladies, I imagine would give themselves the trouble. They have so many other accomplishments to practise."

"I should like to try," she said. "At any rate I could learn to make your sort of fly, if not any of the others. There now, will that do?"

"Perfectly. I thank you. It could not be better."

He turned and cast his line upon the stream, and from having often watched her husband, Elizabeth knew enough of the sport to admire the swift, effectual movement of his single wrist and arm. Georgiana remained where she had been—several feet back from the edge, as she had been schooled from childhood by her brother. Elizabeth had thoughts of staying with her, if only for a moment or two, but Darcy happened to catch sight of his wife, and Mortimer with her, and concluding that his presence might be desired, signalled that he was coming. She went to meet him.

Very soon they were together, the purpose of Mortimer's visit was explained, and on Mortimer and Kitty coming up, acceptance of the invitation most heartily ratified. Darcy then offered Mortimer a rod if he would care to stay and fish, but though he longed to do so, for never had Pemberley appeared so delightful to all his senses, the student of good manners fancied that having delivered his invitation, delicacy forbade him to linger, and he began to make excuses of urgent business at home. In his anxiety not to seem insensible of the charms of his present company, he almost conveyed the impression that what with the hay harvest and cherrypicking soon to be begun, and some young horses to be broken in, he would be fully occupied from morning till night for days to come.

"I hope this does not mean that we shall not see you again until next Sunday," said Elizabeth, for Kitty's sake rather than for her own.

He assured her earnestly that he hoped to be with them again very soon. While he was still speaking, Elizabeth caught sight of Acworth pacing along beside the stream. He passed onwards about twenty yards and then, circling round, came towards their group, and stood a little behind Darcy's elbow. There he stayed, fixing her with a mournful gaze. Indignant at such behaviour, she determined to take no notice of him, and assuming her gayest manner, she told Mortimer that she counted on seeing him on the morrow.

"And do not forget that from Friday week onwards we shall expect you to be with us very constantly," she added, smiling. "To be consistent, you ought to take up your abode at Pemberley until all danger is past."

"What is this?" enquired Darcy. "What danger are you speaking of?"

"Tell him, Mr. Mortimer, and you will see for yourself how he can scorn such superstitious folly as ours."

But Mortimer, not wishing to invite scorn in the presence of fair ladies, pretended not to understand what she was speaking about. It therefore fell to Elizabeth to ask her husband with mock concern whether he was aware that when all their guests were assembled under their roof, the inauspicious number of thirteen would be sitting down to table at every meal, unless Mortimer were there to avoid this happening. While enumerating the members comprising their party when complete, she saw him give her a quick, conscious glance at the mention of her uncle and aunt Gardiner. As soon as she had finished, he said rather more gravely than suited her own liveliness that he attached no importance to numbers—whether three or thirteen—provided the company were good.

"You see how we are reproved," said Elizabeth to Mortimer. "But for your consolation I will tell you that secretly he is as much alarmed as we are, and at this moment is very likely devising some deep scheme that will obviate any possible mischance."

"I must warn you, Mortimer, that ladies say what they please because they know that we may not contradict them," said Darcy, now falling in with her humour. "And whether they see a wedding in a row of cherry stones or seven years of misfortune in a cracked mirror they will not be cheated of it. It must happen as foretold even if they have to wait ten years."

As Elizabeth looked laughingly up at him, the voice of Acworth suddenly cried out, "Why do you jest at misfortune? Only those who have never known it could do such a thing."

The rebuke, for as such the speech was plainly intended, silenced everyone. Darcy, who until that moment had seemed not to know that Acworth was present, turned and looked at him. Seeing the glance, almost of hatred, which Acworth returned, Elizabeth was in terror of what might follow. But Darcy, with great presence of mind and without any alteration of manner, overcame the general awkwardness and constraint by saying, "What my wife actually means, Mortimer, is that we are all delighted to see you at any time that you care to visit us. We look for you now, and you must not disappoint us." Then turning again to Acworth, he said quietly, "We would never make a jest of real misfortune. Forgive us if we seemed to do so."

Acworth made a slight movement of the shoulders, but no

other reply. Mortimer, reddening with extreme pleasure, and stammering his thanks, most effectually drew attention away from Acworth to himself. The diversion would have been more grateful to Elizabeth's feelings had she not seen Acworth, all mortification, gazing at her in mute entreaty. She took care not to encounter his eyes again, but her sense of discomfort was acute.

A common movement was now made to return to the house, and Darcy, having first satisfied himself that his friend, Mr. Harrington, lacked for nothing, walked some part of the way thither, the while recounting the sport which each of the anglers had so far enjoyed. They had not gone more than a few yards when Acworth broke away and wandered down to the river. Not long afterwards Darcy excused himself and returned to his visitor.

On reaching the terrace Mortimer took leave of the ladies, mounted his horse and rode away. Before entering the house Elizabeth turned to survey the scene behind her. While Kitty, all excitement, chattered to an inattentive ear, she looked to see where everybody was and what each might be doing. Her father and Major Wakeford had both moved upstream; Georgiana, tired, perhaps, of watching a sport in which she had no real interest, was sitting on the river bank near the place where she had been before, and beside her, half recumbent upon the sward, was the figure of Acworth. He lay there, his face upturned towards his companion, and while Elizabeth looked, he raised his body and leaning forward and flinging out his arms in the manner of one declaiming, seemed to be speaking with eager vehemence. Elizabeth searched the river bend for Darcy, but he was now gone out of sight. She felt uneasy as she wondered whatever Acworth, so unaccountable in deed and word, so little to be trusted, could be saying to Georgiana. But nothing could well be done; no interference was really called for, and with a last backward glance she passed through the door into the house.

Chapter 10

ELIZABETH'S CURIOSITY AS TO the purport of the conversation between Acworth and Georgiana was not too severely strained, for enlightenment came voluntarily from Georgiana herself later in the day.

"Mr. Acworth has some very odd fancies," she said in her calm, reflective way. "When I was sitting by the river this morning, he suddenly appeared and sat down beside me. I did not particularly wish to talk, but he persisted, and presently he said, 'Oh, do look about you, Miss Darcy. Is it not exactly like a painted scene where everything conduces to pleasing the eye of the beholder? The figures that we see, the anglers at their posts along the stream, the two ladies in their light summer dresses with their attendant squire grouped on the terrace against the stately façade of a great mansion—what would happen to them if they attempted to step out of their frame? But they cannot; they are forever fixed in their paint. You and I are outside the picture. I know that I am alive, and I think that you are, too.'"

"What did you reply to all this?" asked Elizabeth, not very well pleased at being denominated a painted figure.

"I don't remember. Very likely nothing at all. He said next, 'All this is a fiction, a pretty piece of poetry!' Then he began reciting some verses about a cat that fell into a bowl of goldfish."

"I know them," said Elizabeth, "but do not perceive the connection."

"Perhaps none was intended. He has a prodigious memory for poetry and he went on repeating a great many sonnets of Shakespeare's that I had never heard before."

"I imagine them to be those that would hardly find their way into the course of a young lady's studies," said Elizabeth dryly.

"He said that Shakespeare knew what it was to love, whereas figures in a picture only went through the show of it."

"It is so easy to deceive oneself with a metaphor or so."

"He recites extremely well," Georgiana continued. "His voice and the play of his features lend beauty and life to the dullest, most ordinary words."

"What is your opinion of him viewed as a man, Georgiana—not as a reciter of poetry?"

"I think that he is extravagant and unpractical, a dreamer bemused with his own fancies."

Elizabeth could scarcely help laughing at such a judgment from one so fanciful and so little practical in herself. She observed, however, that Georgiana had spoken impartially, even in his praise, and while frankly admiring his gifts was not dazzled by them, and could moreover perceive some absurdity in his behaviour. Satisfied on a point which had been agitating her for the last several hours, she said no more beyond a word of cordial agreement by way of reinforcing a very salutary frame of mind. But she herself ceased not to think of the man for some time longer, for this latest illustration of his character served less to instruct than to perplex her.

The next morning she went to her husband's room to consult him about an invitation to dinner at a neighbouring great house which had just been brought by hand, and found him walking up and down with knitted brows and arms folded, deep in thought. A letter lay on the writing table; on seeing Elizabeth he turned and picked it up, and without waiting for her to speak said immediately:

"I am afraid you will be disappointed. I have had this morning a letter from Mr. Gardiner, and he writes that it is more than doubtful whether he and your aunt will be able to come to Pemberley on the day originally fixed for the journey."

"Why is this?" cried Elizabeth. "Surely it is not on account of Lady Catherine."

"Certainly not," he replied decidedly. "The fact is, that I had asked your uncle to undertake some business for me in London. It is keeping him longer than either of us had anticipated. I am as sorry as you are. But their visit will not be long postponed— only for a week or two."

"I trust so," she answered. Struck by another thought she exclaimed, "So that was in your mind when I was counting up the party to thirteen. You doubted whether they would be here with the others."

Darcy smiled. "I did foresee the possibility that they might not."

"But will their visit be shortened?"

"I sincerely hope not."

"And you say there is no certainty as to when they will be able to travel."

"The day cannot be fixed until the business I spoke of has been concluded."

It was on the tip of her tongue to ask idly what sort of business it could be which hung in so much uncertainty of despatch, but the invitation pressed for a decision and must be discussed, and she lost no further time in referring it to him. Directly she had obtained his agreement to acceptance, she went away to write her reply, for the servant who had brought the invitation was waiting. Darcy was thereby spared the awkwardness of refusing to show her Mr. Gardiner's letter which she might very naturally have expected to see. The occasion past, there was little chance of a renewal of questioning, for although he valued and often invited his wife's judgment on practical matters affecting the estate, she never intruded upon his business affairs unasked. While deception of any sort was abhorrent to him, circumstances might arise when to withhold information was expedient. Such circumstances were now present, and having weighed all the consequences of silence, he decided that the contents of Mr. Gardiner's letter were best kept secret, even from Elizabeth, until the time came when no evil could result from publishing them at large.

Mr. Gardiner wrote with all a business man's circumspection, omitting names of places and persons from a communication of confidential import lest it should fall into hands for which it was not intended. After the usual preliminaries he thus proceeded:

"Following your recommendation I went direct to the house and asked for the gentleman by name. Your suspicions received instant confirmation. The servant who answered the door informed me that his master was at home, but had only that day risen from a bed of sickness which had left him extremely weak. While he was speaking, the gentleman's physician, evidently on his way out of the house from seeing his patient, stopped in the doorway to say that although he was glad to be able to report a very material improvement in his patient's condition he could not sanction his seeing any visitors for some days more. Nothing therefore remained for me but to come away with the greater part of my errand still to perform.

"The matter to be dealt with thus stands in suspense for the period mentioned or perhaps longer. With your concurrence I propose to let several days elapse, then to write to the gentleman requesting the favour of an interview. How he will receive me depends on his part in the business which is still obscure, but as the major question to be resolved is no longer in any doubt, complete elucidation of all that pertains to the affair should follow in due course. When all that is to be known has been ascertained I will acquaint you with the whole without delay.

"I am afraid this halt in the action to be undertaken will entail some postponement of a visit to Pemberley to which Mrs. Gardiner and I have been looking forward this long while. Mrs. Gardiner had some thought of writing to Elizabeth to express her disappointment, but we have decided instead to leave it to yourself to break the news to her of our delayed arrival."

After Elizabeth had gone, Darcy continued in thought some while longer. His first impulse on reading her uncle's letter had been to act on it immediately, but as the result of further cogitation he decided that until the further information promised by Mr. Gardiner was in his possession nothing had better be done. A state of affairs highly distasteful to him must therefore continue for the present, and all he could permit himself was the exercise of a greater vigilance than ever upon the doings of a certain person under his roof.

The arrival next day of Mr. and Mrs. Bingley and their two little girls was an occasion that drove everything else temporarily out of Elizabeth's head. Although marriage had perforce divided them in space, Elizabeth and Jane were still firmly knit in each other's confidence, and for them to meet was to enter at once into the peculiar intimacy that had always bound them together. Bingley, with his natural and happy manners, was immediately on good terms with everyone in the house. As for little Harriet and Eleanor, they were charming, good-tempered children, not at all resentful of Richard's unfriendly manner of receiving them. To Elizabeth's chagrin he hid his face in her skirt, and for a whole hour would not so much as lift his eyes to look at either of them. By the next day, however, he had got over his aversion for Harriet and was induced to play with her, though nothing could persuade him to have anything to do with the infant Eleanor.

"My grandson is already so thoroughly spoilt that I have not the least compunction in continuing the process," said Mr. Bennet. "I shall therefore encourage him to think as meanly as possible of all little girls and of himself as more important than anyone else in the family."

"You exaggerate prodigiously, Papa," complained Richard's mother. "I can assure you that Richard is instantly corrected whenever he is naughty. But he knows perfectly well that he can take liberties with you."

"He is an extremely intelligent child," replied her father, "and we understand one another very well. I have some claim upon his affection, for apparently there is no one else who can tell him nursery fables as I do. His eyes grow larger and larger as the tale proceeds to the grand climax, and when it is reached— when the wolf leaps upon Red Ridinghood to devour her, or the ogre comes roaring out of his castle to chase Jack back to the beanstalk—the pupils snap in the most diverting manner."

Mr. Bennet took so much more notice of Richard than of the little Bingleys that Elizabeth thought it only due to Jane to put in a plea for Harriet and Eleanor.

"It is not quite fair to Jane's little girls to distinguish Richard so continually as you do, Papa. He has quite enough attention in the ordinary way. You admit that you spoil him, don't you?"

"Of course I do," said Mr. Bennet. "Have I not said so? If I do not, somebody else will. We are all either spoilt or spoiling. Look at the way Jane spoils Bingley. The fellow cannot even write a letter but she must advise him what to say and how to say it. As for you, Lizzy, you are become a thoroughly spoilt young woman."

"Indeed," exclaimed Elizabeth. "And pray, who spoils me?"

"Do you really need to be told? Who else but your husband? Every woman requires a dose of neglect now and then to keep her from being above herself."

"This would be very alarming if there were any truth in it."

"And not only your husband," continued Mr. Bennet inexorably, "but all these young men to whom you dispense smiles and advice as if you were to each his own particular goddess. Yes, yes, you may well blush."

"Really, Papa, you are preposterous," cried Elizabeth, scarlet between vexation, confusion and laughter. "I would like to know who all these admiring young men are, for I do not admit them."

Mr. Bennet only smiled, and resuming his spectacles went on reading his book.

His observations were sufficiently perturbing to his daughter to determine her upon seeking an opportunity for a good long talk alone with Jane that she might unburden herself upon the subject of Acworth, and get an honest opinion in return. But Jane's time never seemed to be her own. Either one of her children or her husband required her attention. It was but too true that Bingley, though an affectionate husband, was inclined to be selfish where Jane was concerned, perhaps because she had formed the habit of instantly acceding to any demands he might make on her. It was no use remonstrating with her, for she concluded that she was only doing her duty. Two days passed, therefore, before Elizabeth could get her sister to herself, and then some contrivance was needed. But the moment arrived when Bingley was out riding with Darcy for an hour or two, the children had been fed and had gone to sleep with exemplary punctuality, and Jane was free. Elizabeth proposed that they should go for a walk in the park. Once outside the house she drew her sister out of sight of everyone who might pursue them, by entering the woods at the nearest point.

"Now that we have got rid of our husbands we can talk at our ease," she said. "Do not look so shocked, Jane. If we do not desert them now and again for someone else's society, they will cease to value us, and come to regard us as mere appendages."

"I am not shocked," said Jane, "for I know you are not serious. Indeed, it is not true that we can ever have too much of the society of those we love."

"Seriously, I do not agree with you at all. Variety is the spice of life for every one of us. There are often days when my husband and I do not see each other from breakfast till dinner. And what is the result? Instead of having exhausted every topic of conversation, we have something left to talk about when we do meet."

Jane smiled, but did not look convinced.

"The truth is," continued Elizabeth, "that there are subjects we can only discuss with another woman. Surely that is self-evident. How many men, I ask you, will talk politics with their wives, or allow them to know anything about such matters? In general they do not, and not because women are any less acute than men on the whole, but as government is out of their reach, they wisely do not concern themselves with affairs which they have no power to influence. Generally speaking, though men have a wider grasp, women have a finer perception—they are seldom deceived in a character, for instance, while men often are. Perhaps that is why so many husbands are suspicious of their wive's friends, especially of the other sex."

"A married woman must be doubly careful," said Jane. "She has in many ways more freedom than when she was single, and greater scope for exercising it. The less apparent the danger, therefore, the more real it is. Our husbands have so much more knowledge of the world than we can ever attain to, that it is but natural they should seek to restrain us from exposing ourselves to temptation."

Elizabeth laughed. "What becomes of our vaunted freedom then? No, Jane, *your* discretion and delicacy are so utterly beyond question that I cannot believe for one instant that Charles ever troubles his head about what you may be doing in his absence. But with me it is different. It is unfortunately the fact that gentlemen of all ages do appear to enjoy my society, perhaps because I study to put them at their ease and so make them think well of themselves, for which any man will ever be grateful. My husband trusts me, and would scorn to lay injunctions upon me, nevertheless there have been occasions when a gentleman has so mistaken my liveliness of manner for an invitation to overstep the bounds of propriety."

"My dearest Lizzy," cried Jane. "What are you saying? You cannot really mean that you have been indiscreet?"

"Certainly not consciously or wantonly," replied Elizabeth. And having thus successfully led up to the subject of Acworth, she told her sister all that had occurred between them to the last particulars of their conversation in the wood. "And now that I have told you all, my dear Jane," she said in conclusion, "what do you think of it? Do not you agree that I have been placed in a very delicate situation?"

"I do think it most unfortunate that he should have spoken as he did. But his words—his expressions, must have been the effect of an excess of grief which we know can produce temporary derangement."

"Seriously and candidly, Jane, do you really think from what you have seen of him since you arrived that he is in a state of grief bordering on derangement?"

The suggestion conveyed was more appalling to Jane than to believe him mad, since it made him wicked. She knew not what to say, for it so happened that she had never detected anything eccentric in his demeanour. At length she replied that she was too inexperienced in such matters to give an opinion, adding cautiously, "But I have heard of instances where fits of the most violent lunacy alternate with periods of perfectly collected and rational behaviour."

"I have never seen him violent, except, perhaps, on the occasion I have described, but he does appear to be sometimes out of humour, more out of humour than sorrowing. But what do you advise me to do?"

"I can only counsel you to avoid him as much as possible," said Jane. "The time will soon come when he will quit Pemberley for ever, and every unpleasantness connected with him can then be buried in oblivion. Unhappy man, in spite of all, I must pity him."

"Do, by all means. He would be delighted if he only knew it. But Jane, you don't blame me, do you? Could I have acted otherwise in the circumstances?"

"I do not know that you could."

"You seem undecided. Perhaps you think I should not have pledged my word to repeat nothing of what he said to me."

"Then why have you told me?" asked Jane with a smile.

"It is the habit of a lifetime. You have always been the repository of confidences breathed to no other soul, for I knew that they would spread no further."

"But you can hardly be sure of it now. I make a point of telling Charles everything."

"I must beg you not to do so, Jane. It would be very wrong that your husband should know what mine is hitherto ignorant of."

"Is it fair to keep him in ignorance of what so nearly concerns himself?" asked Jane doubtfully.

"I shall not always keep him in ignorance. That indeed would be treacherous and deceitful. But to tell him now might well involve us all in the most painful consequences—it might even lead to a duel. How could I permit that? You must also remember, Jane, that Mr. Acworth was clearly alarmed at the prospect of what might ensue if I complained of his conduct, and seemed so full of contrition that I felt justified in deeming the incident to be closed."

"In that case, to be silent for the present is no doubt the right course."

"But," continued Elizabeth, "is it closed? Since that unfortunate incident I never see him but what I recall it, for whether it is my imagination or not, his words, his glances most frequently appear to offer a secondary construction meant for my ears alone. Blameless as I account myself, it makes me experience a sense of guilt."

Jane was silent for some moments from sheer dismay. "My beloved sister," she said at last, "this must make you very uncomfortable."

"It does, and I have to summon all my determination to endure it with sealed lips. Sometimes I feel impelled to broach the subject again with Mr. Acworth, to let him know at any rate that I see what he is about. But I might be mistaken, and then what an opening it would give him."

"At all costs that must be avoided. And, dear Lizzy, do not for anything let yourself be drawn into a clandestine interview. Should Mr. Acworth continue his persecution—for it is nothing less—I implore you to go to your husband and tell him everything."

"You know my reason for not doing that as yet. In the meantime I shall give the gentleman as wide a berth as possible, and I shall count on you to be always at hand to shield me from his ambiguous attentions."

"Of course I will gladly do what I can. But I cannot always dispose of my time as I would. With a husband and children I am always liable to be called upon."

"And now a sister calls upon you. Poor Jane, it is too bad."

At this point the path through the wood which had been descending some way brought them down to the stream. Here it flowed in the shadow of trees growing on either side of its course, but taking the direction of the house, they soon came into the open, and there saw Georgiana and Major Wakeford strolling ahead of them a good way off. They walked some distance apart, but for all that companionably, and now and again Georgiana could be observed turning her head to make a response to whatever Wakeford was saying. Wakeford had now arrived at walking without a trace of his former limp.

"I am glad that Georgiana is beginning to get over her shyness," said Elizabeth. "But Major Wakeford's manner is such as to put her at her ease. He has a plain, matter-of-fact way with him, wholly devoid of the gallantry she so much dislikes in general."

"I have thought," said Jane, "that he admires Georgiana very much. He always listens to anything she says with so much attention."

"But that is usual with him. He has an air of weighing very seriously what one says before deciding upon his reply. I find it disconcerting, for it checks my natural flow, but apparently it suits Georgiana."

"He is a very different kind of man from Mr. Acworth."

"Indeed he is. But what makes you say so?"

Jane hesitated before answering, "I had wondered whether Georgiana was becoming attracted to Mr. Acworth."

"They have a love of music in common," said Elizabeth, "but that is all." Then, as Jane did not reply, and conscious that her silence was of the negative sort, she exclaimed, "Have you any particular reason for what you have just said?"

"It was only that I came upon them yesterday in Georgiana's sitting-room. He must have gone there at her invitation I suppose, for he would hardly have ventured in without it. They had evidently just finished playing a piece, and were looking over it together. It struck me that their heads were closer than was really necessary and that Georgiana did not dislike his proximity. I will however say that they did not show the least surprise or awkwardness when I spoke to them."

"Is it your belief that the attraction is mutual?"

"I had assumed that it was more on Georgiana's side from the circumstance of his being so recently a widower."

"But now that you know what you do about him, what is your opinion?"

"Really," said Jane, quite distressed, "I am at a loss what to think."

"Shall I tell you what I think, then?—that he cannot approach a woman without pretending that he is captivated by her. It is very reprehensible in him, but in a way a source of comfort, for it shows that he intends nothing serious by anybody. Yet he will go as far as he dares, and when he found himself alone with me in the wood that day, the temptation to profit by the occasion was too strong."

"In that case do not you think that Georgiana ought to be warned against him?"

"If necessary she shall be. It would be unwise to embarrass her unless there is very good reason. But I have discussed Mr. Acworth with her and from her manner of speaking I am persuaded that she has no special feeling for him—none at all. It is easy to be deceived by Georgiana's air of inattention; on the contrary, she is capable of the most just discernment where persons of either sex come into question. She values the solid rather than the showy qualities. There are not many girls of her age, I fancy, who would voluntarily seek the society of Major Wakeford as she does now. Let us catch up with them and find out what they are talking about."

Accordingly the sisters quickened their pace and before very long came up with the gentleman and lady who, however, unreasonably, looked all astonishment at seeing them.

"How hot it is," exclaimed Elizabeth. "Jane and I have been walking in the woods, but the air is much cooler by the water. Major Wakeford, we accuse you and Georgiana of talking either botany or ornithology."

"We were talking about birds," replied Georgiana in mild surprise.

"I thought so!"

"But that is not necessarily ornithology," said Major Wakeford, with unaccustomed playfulness. "Is it, Miss Darcy?"

"No, there can be all the difference in the world."

"I bow to correction," said Elizabeth. "For Georgiana birds are objects of beauty and joy, and to introduce ornithological considerations into discourse about them is an irrelevance."

"I was telling Miss Darcy," said Major Wakeford, more seriously, "of some of the birds we have in my native Devonshire which I do not see here. But you have a very great variety also, and many which are not found in the south."

"No gun is ever raised against them within these precincts," said Elizabeth. Conversing about the many beauties surrounding them, they pursued their way back to the house. Georgiana did not contribute much to the conversation, but she looked tranquil and happy in the enjoyment of all that the scene afforded to delight the eye. She seemed also perfectly content with her present company, and if she did not say much, listened to all that was said and smiled often. Such behaviour spoke her heart-free, as Elizabeth subsequently forced Jane to admit.

But Jane still retained a slight doubt in her own mind, for she had seen with startled eyes how close Mr. Acworth's black locks had been to Georgiana's fair ones, whereas Elizabeth had not. Could any well-bred young woman suffer so very great a liberty if she did not believe herself to be decidedly encouraging unmistakable attentions? Anxious to oblige Elizabeth by agreeing with her entirely, poor Jane knew not what to think.

Chapter 11

AFTER HER HEART TO heart talk with Jane, Elizabeth's spirits rose higher than for some time, so great was the relief of sharing an uncomfortable secret with another person, and that her beloved and ever indulgent sister.

That evening after dinner, the ladies being still alone in the drawing-room, Georgiana and Jane entreated her to sing to them. Yielding to persuasion, she sat down at the pianoforte and having begun, found herself in better voice than usual. Thus encouraged, she needed little prompting to continue, and went from one song to another as fancy led her.

While she was in the middle of a song that suited her voice particularly well, Mortimer and Acworth entered the room together. Mortimer at once sat down by Kitty in response to the invitation of her eyes, but Acworth came and leant against the pianoforte, and without directly gazing at the singer, expressed in his countenance the utmost enjoyment. Elizabeth continued as if unaware of his presence, and when she had finished, Jane, with her unfailing tact, asked her to sing a certain duet with

Georgiana. The music was found after some searching; Georgiana took Elizabeth's place at the instrument and Elizabeth stood beside her, while Jane came to the other side to turn the pages.

"I had been hoping for some music this evening," said Acworth strolling round to them before they had begun. "My violin is here—" Thus saying, he took it from a chair close at hand, "And if these ladies will permit me, I will add another part to theirs."

There could be no objection to the proposal, and Georgiana appeared to welcome it. The duet was sung, and the violin blended so happily with the voices that at its conclusion it received great commendation from Mr. Bennet who, with Darcy, Bingley and Major Wakeford, had entered the room in time to hear the greater part of it.

"It is a novelty indeed to hear such first-rate singing and playing," said he, "and without the trouble and expense of going out to a public hall."

Major Wakeford asked for another duet, but Elizabeth said truthfully that her throat was tired and the field was left to Georgiana if she would hold it. This gave Acworth an opportunity he was not slow to take.

"Shall we play the piece we have lately been practising together?" he asked her. "I am sure we shall never play it better than we do now."

Georgiana gave a ready and eager assent, and after a murmured conference and a further tuning of the violin, they addressed themselves to the execution of a work which, though of extreme difficulty for both instruments, was most brilliantly played.

Major Wakeford had taken a chair near Mr. Bennet's. He listened and watched with more astonishment than pleasure, for the music was of a character that confused him, being full of rapid passages which he could by no means follow with his ear, and on that account was devoid for him of all significance or beauty. Probably no one enjoyed it quite so well as Georgiana and Acworth who threw themselves with evident zest into their performance. Darcy gave them his closest attention, but his thoughts were not wholly engaged with the sounds that he heard. Elizabeth, watching him for a moment or two, saw that he was in a reflective rather than an applauding frame of mind.

"If I am not mistaken," said Mr. Bennet to Wakeford as soon as the playing finished, "much practice has gone to such excellence. As the father of two daughters who have studied the pianoforte I may claim to know what such feats of dexterity mean to the performers, as well as to those who inhabit the same house."

"But I will swear that you never heard us practising, sir," said Acworth laughingly. "We took particular care not to make ourselves a nuisance, didn't we, Miss Darcy? We were always careful to choose those times when everyone was out of the way."

"You have given us a charming surprise," said Elizabeth, resolved not to show any concern for the degree of intimacy implied in a privately concerted arrangement only now for the first time mentioned. "Do, pray, play something else if you are not tired."

Her praise was intentionally formal in manner, but Acworth's eyes sparkled with delight. "What do you say, Miss Darcy?" he asked, smiling and bending towards her. "I am ready if you are. But what shall it be? Something sweet and sedative, able to soothe the savage breast?"

"I very much doubt whether the savage breast wishes to be soothed," said Mr. Bennet. "From all I have heard it prefers the martial strains of fife and drum. What is your opinion, Major Wakeford? As a soldier, you ought to know."

"I have no opinion on the subject," Wakeford answered shortly. "I have always been one of those unfortunates who scarcely know one note from another."

Georgiana looked round in surprise at a statement so much at variance with all that Major Wakeford had ever expressed before. Her lips parted; she seemed on the point of speaking when Acworth, who had turned aside to look through the scattered sheets of music lying on the lid of the pianoforte, found what he sought and placed it on the desk before her.

The piece was played and was followed by the polite thanks of the listeners. Acworth would most willingly have obliged with a further display of his talent, but Mr. Bennet, unconsciously betraying that he had listened long enough for one evening, turned to his neighbour and began a conversation, and Georgiana settled the matter by closing the pianoforte and coming to a chair near Elizabeth. Happily for Acworth's ruffled feelings the appearance of tea made an opportune diversion. When it was over Mr. Bennet went off to the library to be alone with a book, and Bingley called for a round game.

"Now let us be frivolous," said he, "for I am in a melancholy mood. Such singing and playing as we have been hearing constrains me to reflect upon a misspent youth."

"Have you, too, sown your wild oats?" asked Acworth, with a look of rather malicious amusement.

"Alas, no. I have sown no oats at all—not even wild ones. I am, I dare say, the most useless being in the world. I can neither sing nor play, nor paint in water colours."

"How you do enjoy running yourself down," said Elizabeth.

"You really should not speak so, for people might believe you," added his wife.

"I am sure there are many things you do very well," said Mortimer very seriously.

"A few things tolerably, a number of things very ill, and not one really well. A truce to such painful reflections. What shall we play at? If I know Kitty, she is all agog for a game of lottery tickets."

"Indeed, I am not, it is much too noisy," said Kitty pettishly, resenting what she considered an aspersion upon her genteelness.

"Nonsense, you love noise, and you are an inveterate gambler."

"So am I," said Acworth, "and not ashamed to own it."

A move was made to a table large enough to hold eight or nine persons, but although there was plenty of room for him, Wakeford stood aloof, and on being pressed by Elizabeth to sit down, quietly asked to be excused.

"Your party is already large enough," he said. "I will ask Darcy to give me a game of chess."

"The place for that is the library," said Darcy. "I do not think we shall disturb Mr. Bennet, but their game would most certainly disturb our play."

As soon as they had gone away, Bingley said in some

surprise, "What can be the matter with Wakeford? Has anything occurred to upset him?"

"Are not you indulging your fancy?" asked Elizabeth. But she, too, had observed that Wakeford seemed out of humour. It had been a fleeting impression, chiefly due to the contrast of his greater cheerfulness than usual during dinner. Unable to assign a cause for the change in his spirits, and not seriously apprehending any, she might have thought no more of the matter had not Acworth said to Georgiana, "I am afraid we were the offenders, Miss Darcy. Major Wakeford did not like our music, and for some people to dislike is to be displeased."

Georgiana made no reply, but she looked as distressed as though she had been accused of some fault in conduct or manners.

"I do not think for a moment that he would give way to any feeling so petty, and it is unjust to ascribe it to him," said Elizabeth. Fearing that she had spoken too roundly, she continued, "Speaking for myself, I know I am apt to read into a passing change of countenance a meaning it does not possess. It is fatally easy, indeed."

She did not look directly at Acworth, but in avoiding his gaze she turned her eyes on Georgiana and thus beheld the sudden change in her expression from anxious and apprehensive attention to one of relief.

"That is very true," said Acworth. "I once knew a man who would appear racked with grief on the most trifling occasion, such as the loss of a button from his coat, or the cook's inattention to the boiling of the potatoes."

The uncomfortable suspicion flashed through her mind that he was laughing at her. Such an idea was not to be dwelt upon; she repelled it instantly.

The game was begun and soon all else was forgotten in its varying fortunes. Mortimer, seated beside Kitty, gave all his attention to her play and scarcely any to his own, rejoicing when she won, and lamenting when she lost. Bingley was more venturesome than successful; Jane seemed chiefly concerned to give all her chances away; Elizabeth, from disinclination for what she privately considered a stupid waste of time, soon became interested in spite of herself. Acworth showed himself a spirited player who, while talking and laughing incessantly, nevertheless triumphed repeatedly to the amazement of the rest who were yet to learn that his success lay in their distraction. Now and then for a brief period he would fall silent and let, as it were, the game go past him in order that others might recover their losses. At such times he looked round about the table, directing a keen eye here and there, but casting it downwards as soon as he became observed. Elizabeth once caught him looking at herself with plainly expressed speculation. The next time she looked his way to bargain with Jane, he was regarding Georgiana in the spirit of curiosity, it seemed to her.

"It is fortunate that we are not playing for money," he said, rousing himself anew to be active. "I should force you all to sit up through the night until I had parted with my last penny."

"Ah," said Bingley, unthinkingly, "wait until you are a family man, Acworth. You will see soon enough who governs such recklessness." He looked at Jane and laughed; then warned of indiscretion by the steady gravity of her eyes, checked his laughter and turned red.

To Elizabeth's surprise Acworth showed not the least sign of discomposure or any painful feeling. He merely smiled in acknowledgment of Bingley's thrust.

It was getting late when Darcy returned to the room alone.

The players had some while since finished their game, but still sat at the table chatting. Mortimer had stated several times that he ought to go home, and on Darcy's appearance rose up with determination and began making his adieus. When he had departed the Bingleys, Acworth and Kitty sought their candles to go to their rooms. Darcy, however, said that Mr. Bennet was intending to sit up a half-hour or so longer and that he would rejoin him, and Elizabeth waited behind to have a word with her husband.

"Where is Major Wakeford?" she asked in surprise that he had not returned to say good-night, for as a rule he was punctilious in all such observances.

"He asked me to make his excuses and went upstairs to write a letter."

Georgiana was putting together her music and it struck Elizabeth that she was lingering to hear what was said. With the kind intention of gratifying her desire for information she immediately continued, "I thought that he looked out of spirits. Did he appear so when you were together in the library?"

"I do not recall that he did. But my eyes were on the board all the time. I remarked that he did not play so well as usual, that is all."

She did not think it worth while to pursue the subject, and shortly afterwards Georgiana quitted the room. Alone with her husband she would have detained him some minutes longer reviewing in unfettered talk the incidents of the evening, but although there was much to say, much that she would have liked to hear his opinion about, she could see that he was not in a listening temper, was evidently preoccupied with some matter weighing on his mind which he had no intention of imparting to her, and was even meaning to escape. Mortification, the injury to her vanity, held her silent.

"Are you going upstairs now?" he asked calmly, holding the door open for her.

Without a word and looking as unconcerned as possible, she approached him to pass out of the room. But suddenly he shut the door again and in a voice of some constraint said, "Elizabeth, I must give you a word of caution."

"Caution? What a very ill-sounding word!" she returned. "Pray, what have I said or done to deserve it?"

"I am serious," he said, smiling a little. "Where there is danger—as at the edge of a precipice or the skirts of a bog, it is usual to give warning by a notice to that effect. I wish merely to tell you that we have in our midst one who is very far from being a desirable acquaintance."

"You mean Mr. Acworth?" she said after a slight pause.

"I do."

"You have learnt something fresh concerning his character?"

"I have learnt just so much as confirms me in what I have long thought about him. I cannot say more at present. But I would ask you to see that Georgiana does not admit him to any degree of intimacy. I know that you do not."

"I certainly do not," she answered quietly. "As to Georgiana—it appeared this evening from what he himself said that they had been practising together in private. There did not seem to be anything to cavil at as it was so openly confessed. But it is to be prevented in the future. Is that what you mean?"

"More or less. But there should be no marked discrimination

made against the man, for that would be to raise questions in the minds of other people which, besides the awkwardness for ourselves, would embarrass them."

"Am not I to ask what you know?"

"I would rather that you did not press me for particulars just now. Later, most certainly you shall know all, and then you will see that I was right."

"You must have unbounded confidence in me if you think I am going to act blindly on your orders."

"I have."

"You are unanswerable as usual. You do not allow me the satisfaction of beating you down in argument."

"I did not know there was an argument," said Darcy lifting her hand and kissing it. "Come, Elizabeth, you are looking tired. It is late to be talking."

"Upon my word! But I tell you what, Fitz. Such concealment is a very bad precedent. What is sauce for the goose is sauce for the gander, don't forget."

"You are not going to bludgeon another word out of me," he said, embracing her. "Now, my love, there is just one more thing. In writing to your uncle lately I suggested that if he were much longer delayed by this business I mentioned to you some days ago, your aunt might be persuaded to come in advance of him. When she will come is at present uncertain, but to over-come at least one possible obstacle I have offered to send a carriage for her."

"Now that is to be charming, that is to be a good, kind, affectionate husband. I wish, though, that you had given me the chance of enclosing a letter to my aunt in yours to my uncle. I would have told her that her presence at Pemberley as a sober, discreet and experienced matron was sorely needed. I am sure that young married women are as much in need of a duenna as their unmarried sisters, don't you think so, Fitz? But perhaps that is what you have given her to understand. I have no doubt she will very quickly come. She cannot refuse you anything, you know."

"For once we are agreed," said Darcy.

Many are the proverbs instilling the unhappy truth that the first step upon any of the devious paths which lure us from the straight road of open conduct is but seldom retraced. Darcy was already becoming hardened in concealment from the wife of his bosom, for in speaking of a letter to be written to her uncle, he had purposely omitted to say that yet another letter had come from Mr. Gardiner. It had that day been delivered, not by the ordinary post, but by a business acquaintance of the latter's who happened to be passing through Lambton and was very happy to oblige a good customer by going a few miles out of his way.

"At last I have been able to gain admittance to the gentleman's presence," wrote Mr. Gardiner.

"I found that my fears of a painful interview were needless. He received me with great courtesy and heard all that I had to say with much patience, only interrupting me to request the elucidation of some point essential to comprehension of the whole. The awkwardness of explaining how enquiries came to be commenced was soon overcome; he was immediately sensible of the delicacy of your situation and expressed the utmost regret for the affront, as he termed it, which had been put upon you. Having thus paved the way to complete mutual understanding, he gave me certain information which may be held to explain what has occurred. *Here I may say that your conjecture as to the identity of the person in question has proved substantially correct.* To his certain knowledge his relative, among other consequences of foolish and irregular conduct, undoubtedly feared himself to be in danger of imprisonment for debt. The opportunity of escape which opened before him—as it would have seemed providentially—was such as would be grasped at by a man undeterred by scruple or stayed by reflection. I collect, indeed, that a rash impetuosity is one of the leading traits of a character which our friend would by no means allow to be altogether bad or unamiable.

"Before we parted, while expressing anew his horror at the deception which had been practised upon yourself, he entreated that no step should be taken which would expose his relation too painfully before the world. To quote his own words, he feels himself to be his brother's keeper. It was therefore left between us that until the enquiries necessary to the disentanglement and subsequent rehabilitation of his relation's affairs have been completed, nothing should openly be done. That this will involve a continuance of your hospitality to him for a further short period he is perfectly aware, but apart from his own shrinking from the publicity which his relative's open disgrace would bring upon the family in general, he is anxious that the young man should remain in a place where he is not only safe but accessible to be called upon when his presence in London is required. Saving only this proviso he earnestly begs that you will deal with him as you think proper. You may be sure I would not have agreed had I not been certain that you would have wished it.

"To press forward the business to as speedy a conclusion as may be, I have offered him any assistance that lies in my power. He is to employ his own lawyer, a man in whom he has every confidence, but in his still enfeebled state there may be tasks among the various transactions to be undertaken of which I can relieve him. The preliminary investigations must take some time, but in another week or so I shall be better able to judge of their scope and nature. As soon as I have more precise intelligence to send you I will write again.

"Mrs. Gardiner desires me to say with her compliments that she is indeed grateful for your kind offer of one of your carriages to bring her to Pemberley and is most happy to accept it. There is nothing to prevent her coming very shortly but her natural persuasion that I must not be left alone to the servants too long. I have done my best to reason her out of this strange notion, and now her chief uncertainty appears to turn upon when she can be ready. She has mentioned next Tuesday, but as Mr. Colquhoun stays for this letter, she purposes to write to Elizabeth by the ordinary post a little later to announce the precise date."

When Darcy returned to the library it was to find that Mr. Bennet had in the meantime vacated it, but he sat there for an hour or more re-reading Mr. Gardiner's letter and pondering its contents. Grossly as he had been abused, indignation was not his strongest emotion, nor was he sensible of disgust. His own lifetime had been long enough for him to have seen many men fall much below what was expected of them, or what they owed to others, and he had learnt to attribute such lack of principle to some hidden circumstance as, perhaps, a bad example in childhood or a defective education. This was not to condone error, but to understand it, and knowing now what he had learnt from Mr. Gardiner, as well as from other sources not available to the latter, he was less concerned to exact retribution for the offence than to mitigate its consequences to the innocent. In this frame of mind he gave some very concentrated thought to the question of what to do, and what to leave undone. Having come to a decision as to the immediate course to be taken, he sat down at his writing table and began a letter addressed to the Honourable Stephen Acworth at Lord Egbury's house in Cavendish Square. In the friendliest terms he assured that gentleman that he need be under no apprehension for his relative from any action proposed by his involuntary host.

"As I conceive the matter, it is of the first importance for both our families that what he has done here should lose nothing of its present secrecy. At this moment he is totally unaware that I am no longer deceived as to his identity, but now that every dubious point has been resolved I shall seek an early opportunity for an explanation with him, that he may know what has occurred between ourselves, what is being under-taken for him and how it behoves him to conduct himself in the meantime. Until your plans on his behalf are complete and while he remains under my roof, he must continue to bear a name to which he is not enti-tled, in the interests of that secrecy of which I have spoken. He is not particularly well affected towards me, which perhaps is not strange, but I hope he will be reasonable enough to do nothing which might embarrass our relations still further. You may, however, be certain that I should never exclude him from my house without making proper provision for his safety until he can once more stand forth before the world!"

Chapter 12

MRS. GARDINER DID ARRIVE not many days later to the general satisfaction of all her relations assembled at Pemberley. Sound principles are not always found in conjunction with a sweet temper, a superior understanding and elegant manners, but Mrs. Gardiner possessed all these attributes and more besides. She could enter alike into the cares and forebodings of age and the interests, amusements, and even frivolities of youth, and if her advice was not always taken it was seldom resented. Her sterling good sense was a proverb in the family, so much to be depended on that she was credited with never wanting the right answer to any and every doubtful question which could arise in a mixed society. Mr. Bennet found himself able to converse with her on serious subjects for a whole half-hour without weariness to himself. Darcy had the warmest regard for her and the fullest confidence in her discretion. As for Elizabeth and Jane, whatever Elizabeth might say to her husband about duennas for young married women, they both felt, Elizabeth particularly, that she supplied that maternal solicitude which had not always been bestowed on them by their own mother.

The day following her arrival had been fixed for the visit to Clopwell Priory. When the morning came, the younger of Jane's children was discovered to be rather ailing, and the fond and careful mother could not be prevailed upon to leave the little girl for so long a period as the expedition would last. Bingley offered to stay at home with his wife, but Jane would not hear of it. Her absence from the party was felt by all as a loss to be deplored, but neither argument nor entreaty could overcome Jane's strong sense of duty, nor her equally fervent desire that no one should forfeit one hour's pleasure for her sake.

The start for Clopwell was to be made an hour before noon, and it had been settled that the five gentlemen should ride ahead of the carriage conveying the ladies. While waiting for the carriage to be brought round, Elizabeth stood with Mrs. Gardiner at a window in the breakfast-room and watched the advance party mount and ride away. She was amazed at the ease with which Major Wakeford was able to control his horse, a spirited animal, single-handed.

"Is not he a superb horseman?" she said to her aunt. "But whatever he attempts he does well, without either fuss or display."

"I have always thought that character is most truly revealed in affliction," replied Mrs. Gardiner. "To some it affords an excuse, but to others it acts as a spur."

"There is little doubt that he will go through life undaunted," continued Elizabeth. "He is formed in the heroic mould, but that is scarcely calculated to recommend him in general, for most people prefer, though they may not admit it, the easy, amiable rather weak character. Every allowance is made for such people, but Major Wakeford's sort is seldom applauded, or if at all, with a grudging kind of praise. Perhaps it is not really very much to be wondered at in his case. Have you observed how he never speaks but to the purpose? It does not make conversation with him too easy, for one watches oneself to beware of tripping in logic. And yet, for all his sternness, one learns to value him sincerely. His simplicity and modesty are somehow disarming. If he were to leave us now, he would be genuinely missed by all—even Georgiana."

"Why do you say—even Georgiana?" asked her aunt with a smile.

"Because she is so little dependent on the society of other beings as a rule."

"She has a great affection for yourself, has she not?"

"Yes, I think she has. She attaches herself to very few, but to those most strongly. Affection with Georgiana takes time to grow and strike root."

"I do not think she is looking as well as when I was last here," said Mrs. Gardiner. "If I did not believe it to be impossible, I should say she had something on her mind."

Elizabeth considered before rebutting such an idea. It was not altogether new to her, but on that account no less unwelcome. As the sanguine will, she cast about for the most trivial reason to account for what would otherwise be an evil, and found it in the interference of Kitty with Georgiana's daily avocations. There was a thorough incompatibility of tastes, dispositions, everything, between the two girls. Because they were of an age they were forced to be much with one another. All this Elizabeth detailed to Mrs. Gardiner and in so doing she was satisfied of its truth. Mrs. Gardiner, having no cause to be otherwise, was easily persuaded, agreeing that Georgiana and Kitty had almost nothing in common.

The arrival of the carriage put an end to further conversation. They issued into the hall to find Georgiana and Kitty awaiting them—the one pensive, indifferent; the other becomingly flushed and eager to be off. Jane was there also to see them go, and wish them all an agreeable day. There were renewed expressions of regret that she would not be with them and that she should be missing the pleasure and interest of a new scene, but Elizabeth, who had risen that morning with a headache, would have been glad to change places with her sister and truly envied her in being able to stay at home. Yet, go to Clopwell she must; for without unduly over-rating her importance, she knew that whatever success could be hoped for from the party would depend upon herself—upon all the resources of her tact, her ability to lead a conversation so smoothly and lightly as successfully to round awkward corners and avert anything like stagnation, and thus to keep the spirit of the occasion in fullest flow. As for her indisposition, even to hint at it would be to spoil everyone's pleasure; so she resolved to say nothing about it in the hope that it would mend as the day went on.

The sun was high in a cloudless sky as they drove away from the house; everywhere the eye turned the landscape was bathed in its rays, and not a breath of wind stirred the air. Grateful indeed was the shade of the trees as they passed under their overarching branches. But even through the woods the heat was great, the motion of the carriage doing nothing to mitigate it, and the fatigue of holding a parasol aloft left little inclination for talk. Elizabeth and Mrs. Gardiner exchanged slight observations from time to time; Georgiana remained silent and lost in thought; while Kitty, hardly able to conceal her excitement at the prospect of viewing a mansion of which she cherished hopes of becoming the mistress, was too much engaged in watching for the mass of rock marking the boundary between the parishes of Pemberley and Clopwell to speak to anyone. When that had been seen, denoting that they had now passed into Clopwell itself, she could look round about her on all that the scene afforded of beauty and interest. Exclamations of delight burst from her and fell for the most part on unheeding ears. Elizabeth kept her eyes shaded with her parasol and Mrs. Gardiner, a native of Derbyshire, though pleased to be driving through a landscape familiar to her youth, privately thought that Clopwell could not compare with Pemberley's rich diversity of woods and crags and running water.

Thus they proceeded to within a short distance of the village, when the smart trotting of a horse along the road began to be heard, increased in noise, and prepared them for the gallant approach of none other than their host. Elizabeth and Mrs. Gardiner saw him first, but before they could do more than acknowledge his salutation he passed behind the carriage, and wheeling his horse round, drew beside them to ride the rest of the way like a true cavalier and knight of fair ladies. Bending down towards Elizabeth, he said that as soon as the gentlemen had arrived, and had been supplied with refreshment, he had set out to meet the carriage and bring it by the shortest road to his house. Elizabeth smiled and said what was gracious and proper, but by this time Mortimer was directing an eloquent gaze upon

Kitty who, divided between the desire not to show an inelegant delight and her anxiety to neglect no occasion for strong encouragement, succeeded in summoning to her aid the signs of bashfulness as well as the evidences of complaisance.

The rest of the journey was soon accomplished and the carriage entered the principal gates of the small park surrounding Clopwell Priory. Set upon level ground and much less imposing than Pemberley House, its ancient and diversified aspect yet struck the eye with the force of a picturesque beauty often denied more pretentious buildings. Through successive additions and destruction of part of the original edifice by fire, its earliest date at first sight was with difficulty determined, but a tower or keep at one end proclaimed its having been fortified in an age more barbarous than the present, when, so Mortimer informed the ladies, imparting what he had been told in child-hood, the monks had sometimes to be as warlike as other men to defend their own by force of arms. A small lake spread its waters at a little distance from the front of the house, near enough to reflect the wall and a part of the roof as in a mirror. It was full of great carp, Mortimer said, some of which were believed to be almost as old as the house.

From Mortimer's apologetic description of his ancestral home Elizabeth could never have imagined it as she now beheld it for the first time. She exclaimed at the sight of it, and Mrs. Gardiner joined with her in expressing wonder and admiration. The two girls, sitting back to the horses, were cheated of the first astonishing view, but now turned their heads to see what caused so much rapture. The carriage, meanwhile, skirted the lake and clattered over grass-grown flagstones to the front door. By the time it drew up, Mortimer had dismounted and was ready to hand the ladies out, and escort them indoors to a room where the gentlemen were comfortably disposed in chairs talking over what remained of a cooling beverage in their glasses.

A collation consisting of a variety of cold meats, pastries, jellies and fruit set out in the principal apartment was the first part of the entertainment. The meal was entirely informal, as Elizabeth had previously advised the youthful host on hearing of his difficulties. The guests sat where they chose, and the gentlemen waited on the ladies. Mortimer, having contrived that Elizabeth should sit on one side of him and Kitty on the other, looked all happiness. Turning to Elizabeth, he assured her solemnly that he could wish for no greater honour than her presence. "I am indeed fortunate," he said, "for wherever you are, Mrs. Darcy, there is always gaiety and good humour. There is never a dull moment."

If the spirit of the party in general was of ease and enjoyment, not everyone looked equally pleased. Major Wakeford, always grave, was graver than usual and more silent, and though he exerted himself to reply with a show of interest when spoken to, he would relapse into muteness on being left to himself. Acworth, on the contrary, who either moped when others were gay or gave way to an overdone hilarity, displayed an unforced cheerfulness which Bingley himself could not have bettered. He sat between Georgiana and Mr. Bennet, and as it was the latter's habit to address the company in general, Acworth spoke chiefly to Georgiana. What he said was clearly heard and never otherwise than could be said to anyone, but Elizabeth thought that his manner bordered on intimacy and reproached herself that she had not foreseen the conjunction of the two persons who of all others should be kept apart. She looked at her husband, but he was conversing with Mrs. Gardiner and betrayed nothing.

Though determined not to be caught watching and listening by Acworth, she could hardly help the straying of an eye or ear in his direction. Georgiana was heard replying to him with simplicity and candour natural to her when she had overcome her shyness. Her manner then was equally devoid of coquetry or reserve, and exhibited her in an endearing light to those who knew how to value her. Acworth, too, it had to be confessed, was at his best in her society— quiet, easy and sincere. But this was not to comfort or reassure; it but added to Elizabeth's anxiety. To rid herself of anything like the appearance of it she turned to Mortimer and expressed her admiration of his house.

"It may be all very well on a fine summer's day when the sun shines outside," he replied, "but in winter it is quite another matter. It is dark and dismal enough then with these low ceilings and panelled walls and all this great old-fashioned furniture."

"But it is the antique look, so in keeping with the great age of the house, that charms me," said Elizabeth. "I would not change it in any material particular. Nor should you, Mr. Mortimer. Some lighter hangings beside the windows and perhaps one or two tapestries and china ornaments would do all that is needed."

"What it lacks," said Mr. Bennet, "is the woman's touch that beautifies without adding one jot of comfort. A few female fripperies scattered untidily here and there would make a world of difference."

An expostulation from Kitty was followed by a dispute in

which everyone joined as to who were the most untidy—men or women—Mr. Bennet maintaining that women were incapable of order and method, and Mrs. Gardiner and Elizabeth warmly defending their sex. Bingley very traitorously went over to the side of the ladies and declared that for his part he never knew where he put anything and always had to ask Jane. Darcy gave it as his opinion that untidiness was chiefly due to laziness and was therefore about equally divided between the sexes.

"I detest perfectly tidy people," said Acworth in an accent of disdain and with an air of being very clever. "They are always dull and dictatorial from self-complacency."

"I do not agree with you," said Elizabeth dryly, conceiving this to be aimed at her husband. "It may just as well be said that witty people are never otherwise. Brevity, which is the soul of wit, as we are told, must arise from an orderliness of mind as opposed to the mental confusion which issues in rambling and repetition. How can the outward and inward parts of a man be at variance?"

"I can think of at least two instances to the contrary," said Mr. Bennet. "One is Dr. Johnson, a great wit and a great sloven, and the other is myself—an infallible logician, but too inveterately lazy even to sort my papers which are therefore always in a muddle."

"There cannot be too much caution in attempting generalities about human nature," said Darcy, speaking with his usual calm. "A man alone knows why he behaves as he does, but often enough he either does not seek to know the true reason or, not liking it, wraps it in a disguise of his own making."

This proved to be the last word on the subject, for as

everyone must agree as to its substantial truth, it discouraged further debate. Elizabeth saw Acworth turn his head sharply towards her husband and look away again with a peculiar twist of the mouth. The impression she received was all the stronger for not being understood. But she could not stay for conjecture. With Mortimer sitting beside her, it behoved her to live up to her character for gaiety and good humour, and although her head ached no less than it had done, but rather more, she exerted herself to talk and keep dullness at bay.

Shortly afterwards the party rose from the table. It was soon ascertained that the ladies, without exception, were desirous of looking over the house, and Mortimer, of course, felt himself under obligation to attend upon them; but Mr. Bennet, Bingley and Major Wakeford declared for the open air, very likely preferring their own unmixed society, and Darcy, who was familiar with Clopwell Priory from his boyhood, offered to guide them about the demesne. Acworth, after a show of indecision, followed Mortimer and the ladies. In a house of narrow passages and twisting staircases it was often impossible to proceed except two by two. Thus Mortimer found himself leading the way with Kitty on account of Georgiana having attached herself to Elizabeth, while Mrs. Gardiner and Acworth brought up the rear. Elizabeth at first took Georgiana's arm, then fearing her action might be inconve-niently construed, dropped it in favour of her hand, and thus linked together in sisterly fashion they continued for some time. As they went along, Mrs. Gardiner, always alert and interested, held Acworth in a flow of talk, chiefly of comment on what they saw. Civility did not always constrain the gentleman to appear at his best, and his replies remained few and short, yet neither Mrs. Gardiner's determined cheerfulness nor her resolution of not taking offence was ever impaired. It almost looked as if, ignoring the disparity between her thirty-nine years and his twenty-seven, she was bent on making a conquest of him. Elizabeth was mystified, but her headache inclined her to let all happen without trying to understand.

When they had wandered through the apartments on the ground floor which were all much alike in the style of a bachelor's habitation, Mortimer led his guests up the main staircase to a landing before a door which, on being opened, disclosed a room larger and lighter than any they had yet seen, with a beautifully moulded ceiling displaying in a central medallion the Mortimer coat of arms and a large oriel window, elegantly though sparsely furnished as for a lady's occupation. Kitty instantly burst into raptures and Elizabeth and Mrs. Gardiner, though quieter, were not much less admiring. The effect of light and space delighted them. In answer to their questions Mortimer said that the room had been his mother's drawing-room, and that after her death which had occurred many years ago it had been disused, and during his father's lifetime kept locked up.

"My father held the key and no one was ever allowed to enter it," he said. "When he died and my brother came into possession I found the key and satisfied a curiosity I had always had to see it. The floor, the furniture—everything was covered thick with dust. Our housekeeper, who came with me, said that it was all just as it had been when my mother was alive, except that her portrait had been brought from another place and hung where you see it now over the mantelpiece."

They all clustered round to see the portrait. It was by no means a first-rate painting in oils of a young woman remarkably like Mortimer himself. Mrs. Gardiner and Elizabeth looked at it with sympathetic attention. Kitty expressed her admiration of the late Mrs. Mortimer's beauty, but Georgiana, after a moment's regard, turned away. Acworth, having no interest in what he privately considered a very bad picture, wandered to the opposite wall where stood a large oaken coffer. Turning his head, he saw Georgiana pass near him and smiled.

"Will you hazard a guess as to what this chest contains?" he said to her. "For myself I would say that we should find all Mrs. Mortimer's wardrobe packed away in lavender and camphor."

"It is only too probable," said Georgiana. "What else would have been put away there in a locked room?"

"Then we are *probably* both wrong," he rejoined. "Let us ask Mrs. Darcy and Mrs. Gardiner their opinion. Better still let us satisfy our curiosity at once by asking Mortimer what's inside. Mortimer," he said, raising his voice and indicating the chest, "we are in a fever to know what you have got put away in here."

"I'm afraid I don't know," answered Mortimer, "for I have never thought to look."

Kitty cried out at such a lack of interest. "Do pray open it, Mr. Mortimer," she entreated, "or we shall all die of disappointment."

Mortimer turned the key of the chest, and lifted the lid, disclosing a piece of faded purple damask material several times folded, which on examination proved to be a curtain. Beneath that lay another exactly like it, and then two more, comprising a set of four.

"Alas," said Acworth in Georgiana's ear, "what a shock to our romantic anticipations."

"I had none at all," she replied, "either romantic or otherwise."

When the fourth curtain was taken up, however, it was seen that the lower part of the chest was full of unused materials, including lengths of silk brocade and taffeta in various colours, more figured damasks and handworked squares and ovals of tapestry with other products of the needle. Elizabeth collected from what she saw that Mortimer's mother had been not only a skilful needle-woman, but also a woman of some taste, and had perhaps designed the refurnishing of her house before death had intervened to prevent it.

"All this must have lain untouched these two and twenty years," said Mortimer, gazing at the array of stuffs in astonishment.

"How fortunate that they are neither discoloured nor injured by moth," said Mrs. Gardiner. "You are indeed in luck, Mr. Mortimer. Here is everything you can desire to adorn your house throughout."

"Oh, Mr. Mortimer, do let us advise you," cried Kitty. "I declare my head is full of ideas already. You are to have this room for a drawing-room again, you know, and the yellow brocade must be made into curtains for that noble window. If only we could banish you for a few weeks and then invite you to see what we had done."

Here, if ever, was an opportunity for a speech from heart to heart, but Mortimer was unable to find words and could only look his emotions of gratitude and pleasure. Kitty, in return, could only show a proper amount of maidenly confusion which, had there been no witnesses, might have led to interesting results. But they were most lamentably not alone, and after a moment's indecision, not knowing where to look or what to do, she turned to assist Mrs. Gardiner in putting back the contents of the chest. Elizabeth walked away to another part of the room to conceal her amusement at this comedy of easy courtship which could leave no one in any doubt as to how it would end. By a sudden movement she found herself face to face with Acworth. He also was smiling in much the same manner as herself, and prompted by much the same thought, as the meeting of their eyes testified. She immediately remarked that the room was very hot from the sunshine lying full upon it.

Acworth assented. "We have been in here long enough," he said. "Where do we go now, Mortimer?" he asked a moment later. "Have you no other chests of household treasures to show us?"

Mortimer was obliged to confess that he was very largely ignorant of what his house did contain other than what was in daily use. "All that I take to be women's business and not for myself to meddle with," he said.

"So much the better," said Acworth, "for it leaves our expectations undiminished and everything to be discovered. We warn you that not a nook or cranny shall remain unexplored. A complete survey of every room, passage, closet and attic must be made without delay. Left to yourself, you will never do it."

As the rest of the party followed Mortimer to the door, Elizabeth turned for one last look at the beautiful prospect of hills rising beyond the trees in the park which the window commanded. The sensation of being alone, if only for a moment, was very refreshing, and she was visited by a strong desire to escape from the others and go downstairs again in search of some place where she could rest in peace and solitude. She lingered, battling with the impulse, conscious of an increase of her indisposition, but knowing that she owed it to her host, to her role of principal guest, to continue with him. At last, resigning herself to do what was expected of her she turned to quit the room. She had before that instant believed herself to be the only person left in it, but now she saw that Acworth stood near the door apparently waiting for her.

"Now is the opportunity to escape," he said smiling, and coming forward. "All this ransacking of an old house is not much to your taste, I fancy."

"I have not any intention of escaping," she said lightly.

"Pardon my saying that you look pale—owing to the heat and closeness of the room, no doubt. Would not you like me to conduct you where you can sit quietly while the others finish their exploring?"

This reading of her thought astonished as well as discon-certed her, but likewise fixed her determination not to be conducted anywhere by Mr. Acworth except to the rest of the party. His smile had become satirical and continued too long.

"You are very kind, I am sure," she said, summoning to her aid all her presence of mind, "but I am perfectly ready to go on. Where are the others? We ought not to keep them waiting." She walked past him as she spoke and went through the door.

As he came close behind her she thought she heard him say in a very low voice, "Surely Mrs. Darcy does not credit me with designs upon her privacy." Whether she heard aright or not, such a speech could only be ignored and she walked on without another word, but equally without show of hurry or concern. Fortunately, before she had got farther than a few steps she was met by Mortimer, coming back to look for her. They were now to mount to the next floor, he said, and he had been afraid that, left to themselves, she and Acworth might lose their way.

Seldom had she met an acquaintance with more delight or given such a welcoming smile. Although owing allegiance to another lady, Mortimer coloured with pleasure. She made her excuses very properly for keeping him waiting; he replied, as he ought, with discreet gallantry. The rest of the party was then rejoined and on they went.

Chapter 13

NEVER IN HIS MOST sanguine moments had Mortimer imagined that his party would be the success it was proving. The day beforehand he had been plagued by doubts of his ability to keep the ladies from being bored; but so far from finding little to interest them, they were pleased with everything they saw. Urged on by Acworth, they explored every passage, mounted every staircase they came to, and opened every door whether of cupboard or room. Many rooms they entered were scarcely furnished and they found no more chests, but occasionally their persistence was rewarded by some curiosity, such as a rusty suit of armour left to lurk in a dark, little visited corner; and once their attention was directed to a sliding panel which cunningly concealed a flight of steps to a priest's hole.

At length they reached a room, not much larger than a closet, lined on one side with shelves, on which a quantity of odd pieces of crockery and china had been stowed away. Many of them were only common and coarse, but a few were of rare quality and design, and these passed from hand to hand to be admired and identified as of some particular make and date. Exclamations, conjectures, questions filled the air, and a constant jostling and movement made the room seem overcrowded. Elizabeth took up a plate and carried it aside to examine at leisure its charming pattern of birds and flowers, but became so lost in other thoughts while gazing at it that she ceased to perceive it or to know what was going on around her. A sudden decrease in the noise of voices made her sensible of her surroundings once more, and she looked up to find herself alone with Mortimer and Kitty.

They were standing before the single window which illuminated the room and, from being very high up in the house, gave an extensive view of open, rolling country towards the south. Mortimer was engaged in pointing out various objects in the landscape of local interest, and was earnestly communicative of everything he could think of to say about them. Perhaps never before had he found so attentive a listener as he did in Miss Kitty Bennet. Elizabeth felt herself to be entirely forgotten. The strange and novel sensation was not unwelcome as it encouraged the indulgence of a strong desire to steal away unobserved. Having put the plate back in its place on the shelf she walked quietly out of the room, a backward glance assuring her that the two young people remained wholly unaware of her retreat.

She went downstairs with a perfectly good conscience in search of the seclusion and rest she longed for. Mrs. Gardiner, she assumed, had accompanied Georgiana and Acworth to another room along the passage. As she passed through it to the head of the staircase she listened for their voices, but could hear no sound of them, and from that she concluded that they had gone to another part of the house. She did wonder whether they had returned to the ground floor as she was doing, but continuing her way thither she arrived in the hall to find it as silent and deserted as she could wish.

There were not even any servants to be seen, and on opening the door of the parlour where the meal had been served she saw that the table had not yet been cleared. A door in the opposite wall probably admitted to another sitting-room. She could not remember whether she had entered it on the tour of the house, but she thought not. She turned the handle, the door opened and she looked into a small, rather dark chamber pervaded by a faint odour presently recognisable as proceeding from the fumes of tobacco and beer commingled on numberless past occasions, and reminding her of arrival in inn yards at the end of a day's journey. The room had a look of shabby comfort and everyday use from the objects scattered about it. A pair of boots stood on the floor in front of a chair, a gun had been left lying on a table. Elizabeth concluded from what she saw that this was Mortimer's own private retreat, that no one would intrude upon her here, and sitting down upon the windowseat, she opened the easement and gazed out upon the refreshing scene formed by the lake and the trees scattered about the park.

The sky was now overcast by clouds, not a breath of air stirred the foliage, and the dark green water of the lake gave a melancholy tinge to the surroundings. The solitude and silence for which she had craved began to be felt too intensely for pleasure, and she began to wonder where her husband and the others with him had gone to. While she looked to this side and that, Major Wakeford came into view, walking slowly with his head bent towards the ground. Reaching a bench under a tree near the edge of the lake he sat down upon it and for several minutes remained motionless and, as it seemed to her, staring in front of him. He was too far away for her to see his countenance, but his perfect stillness spoke an intensity of thought; and then, the sudden movement with which he rested the elbow of his one arm upon his knee and covered his eyes with his hand, the extreme of dejection.

Fixed by a spectacle she could not understand, Elizabeth watched him with growing surprise and disquiet. If the signs of unhappiness did not deceive her, from what could such unhappiness proceed? Until the last week he had appeared really cheerful, on easy terms with everyone in the house, and ready to share in those pursuits and pastimes which a gathering of young people, all intimate together, serves to promote. But now, reflecting upon his behaviour during the last few days, she recalled fits of abstraction, silences maintained while others talked, a look of heaviness and dullness amid their laughter. In all this she had not seen anything to rouse apprehension of serious trouble, and cudgel her brains as she might, she was still unable to recollect any particular circumstance which could have been so very painful to his feelings.

The only idea which occurred to her as providing a not unlikely explanation of the matter was that, no longer beguiled by the novelty of his surroundings and the cheerful animation which pervaded the Pemberley scene, he suffered once more from the melancholy in which Darcy had found him. The explanation did not satisfy her and on further reflection she repudiated it, for she could now assign the alteration in him to a certain evening when others besides herself had remarked upon it, although at the time she dismissed it from her mind as having no real significance. Nor did it appear much in keeping with his known courage and fortitude that he should relapse into his former depression for no better reason than a change of temper.

Casting her mind back to that evening, she remembered Acworth saying to Georgiana, "He did not like our music, and for some people to dislike is to be displeased." At the time she had felt the observation to be both impertinent and inapt, but she now wondered whether it had not been nearer the mark than she had been willing to concede, whether in fact the intimacy thus disclosed between Georgiana and Acworth had not displeased him. It could scarcely be doubted that he had no high opinion of Acworth, in which case he must view Georgiana's consorting with him alone so frequently, as had transpired from certain remarks and admissions, with strong disapprobation. Yet that could hardly account for his continued loss of spirits.

An increase of headache brought on by so much exertion of thought suspended further cogitation, and she leaned her head against the window-pane and closed her eyes. Ideas continued to spring up in her mind but were repelled as baseless. Was Georgiana partial to Acworth? Had Wakeford been inclined to fall in love with Georgiana? Opening her eyes again, it was to see that Wakeford had disappeared; his place on the bench had however been taken by her husband and her aunt.

They were evidently deep in conversation and she wondered what was engaging their attention until she remembered that unlucky business transaction which was detaining her uncle in

London. Mrs. Gardiner had probably some message for Darcy relating to its progress or lack of it; for such was her interest in her husband's concerns, and such his confidence in her understanding and discretion, that there was little he did not impart to her. While Elizabeth watched them, feeling a sense of injury at not knowing what was being said, they rose from the bench and began walking towards the house. But when they reached the flagged space before it, instead of entering the front door they turned and paced up and down still talking, though so far away that most of what they uttered was inaudible.

Mrs. Gardiner's voice could never be heard except faintly, but Darcy's clear, slow accents were distinguishable in words whenever he came within a certain distance of the window where she sat. Such phrases as "I had not suspected this further obstacle" or "a situation demanding the utmost circumspection" were plainly applicable to nothing more interesting than some such matter as the sale or acquisition of land or house property on which Darcy was employing her uncle. But when she heard him say "he showed no surprise when taxed with it, but rather relief," this construction was by no means so plausible. Straining her ears for the next snatch to be caught, her curiosity grew mightily with the next sentence she heard fall from his lips. "Nothing must come into the open if my plans are to go forward." She could endure to be mystified no longer, and, putting her head out of the window, she called to them.

Darcy turned immediately and came towards her, followed by Mrs. Gardiner. He said nothing until he reached her when, looking through the window, he saw that she was alone. "Whatever are you doing here by yourself?" he asked in astonishment.

"I might as well enquire what you have been talking about," she retorted. "I came away from the others believing my aunt to be still engaged in chaperoning. I had no idea that she had a rendez-vous with her nephew."

She laughed as she spoke, but she thought that Mrs. Gardiner looked rather confused.

"Mrs. Gardiner has brought intelligence from your uncle of a nature that he did not care to entrust to the post," said Darcy calmly.

"Is that all?" she said in simulated surprise. "Do you know I have been watching you for this long while and imagined you to be hatching some plot. A more promising pair of conspirators I never saw."

She looked to see her husband change colour or betray some other sign of compunction, but he maintained the most perfect composure, and she added, "It was all about this business which is keeping my uncle in London so long, of course."

"Yes," said Darcy simply. "Unfortunately it is delaying him longer than he expected. You are pale," he continued, observing her with some concern. "Do you feel tired? Have you been over-exerting yourself?"

"Very probably, for such a tender plant as I am supposed to be," she answered dryly. But the headache which she had temporarily forgotten returned in full force and she found herself unable to press home the attack. "To be perfectly candid I should like to be going home," she confessed.

"It is time we all did," he said, looking up at the sky where the clouds hung low and threatening. "There is a storm coming up; we ought to be off as soon as possible. Where are the others who were with you? Where is Mortimer?"

Elizabeth told him, as she believed, that Mortimer, Acworth and the two girls were still ranging the house. Only then did she remember that Acworth and Georgiana had separated from Mortimer and Kitty, for from supposing them at first to be accompanied by Mrs. Gardiner she had given no further thought to their whereabouts. The idea that they had gone off alone together gave her a twinge of uneasiness, but she kept it to herself, since the event might prove them all joined together again.

Mrs. Gardiner offered to go in search of Georgiana and Kitty, while Darcy was to find Mr. Bennet, Bingley and Wakeford and bring them back to the house. Hardly had he set off than Mr. Bennet and Bingley appeared walking towards him, and behind them, though from another direction, came Major Wakeford. Elizabeth beheld him approaching with anxious enquiry. To her relief, as he came up, she saw him looking very much as usual and no graver than was habitual with him.

With everyone gathering for departure, she got up from the window-seat and made her way into the hall. There she met Kitty and Mortimer coming downstairs and looked up into their faces with a gaze more questioning than she intended, and certainly not importing what they thought it did. Mortimer instantly went very red, but Kitty merely smiled. On being asked whether they had not met Mrs. Gardiner, Mortimer was for going back to look for her, when the lady came into view on the stairs. She had gone east instead of west at the top of the stairs and thus had missed the young people until the sound of their voices below brought her after them.

It was now necessary to enquire for Georgiana and Acworth. "Have they not been with you recently?" Elizabeth asked, knowing perfectly well they had not.

"Not this hour or more," Kitty answered unconcernedly. "We supposed that you and they and my aunt had all gone away together."

"Then where can they be?" exclaimed Mrs. Gardiner. "Mr. Mortimer, are you sure they are not upstairs still?"

Mortimer ran upstairs again, and while the others waited below he could be heard opening and shutting doors and calling Acworth by name. In the meantime the gentlemen had all come into the hall from outside, and having heard from Mrs. Gardiner what Mortimer was doing, they stood and waited for him to reappear, bringing with him the missing members of the party. Elizabeth was in a state of perturbation she could hardly keep from becoming visible. A disappearance so complete was in itself sufficiently disturbing, but she felt also the indecorum of the proceeding, and persuaded that Acworth must have manoeuvred it for no worthy purpose, blamed herself for most culpable negligence. She should never have quitted Georgiana's side. Her eyes stole to her husband's face and beheld him looking amazed and displeased. It was no comfort that her father was with difficulty keeping his countenance. Bingley, after fidgeting from one foot to another, went off to hasten the saddling of the horses and the bringing round of the carriage.

After what seemed an intolerable length of time, though it really was not more than a few minutes, Mortimer returned alone and quite bewildered.

"They are nowhere in the house," he pronounced. "I have

looked in every possible place. They must have gone out onto the grounds."

Darcy thought it unlikely. "In that case one or other of us would certainly have seen them," he said, and looked at Bingley and Major Wakeford for confirmation.

"I have not seen either of them," said Wakeford steadily and quietly.

Going to her husband Elizabeth told him all she knew, explaining that the exploring party had kept together until the china closet had been reached, after which it had scattered. But here Mortimer, visited by a sudden and hopeful idea, broke into her account of how, owing to Mrs. Gardiner's departure, Georgiana and Acworth had been lost sight of.

"They may have gone up the tower," he said. "Acworth did question me about it, I recollect, and I told him that a fine view could be got from the top if one had the patience to climb so far. But I warned him that the steps were worn and slippery in places, so I did not believe he would attempt it."

In reply to a question from Darcy he added that the way into the tower from the house was now completely closed and that entrance could only be gained from an outer door.

"Let us by all means ascertain whether they are there or not," Darcy said, with a calm which masked some considerable anger. "If you do not mind leading the way, Mortimer, I will follow you."

The two of them went away directly, and a moment or two later Major Wakeford decided to go after them. Mr. Bennet, who saw nothing to be concerned about except the state of the sky, stood in the doorway contemplating the signs of the impending storm. Elizabeth and Mrs. Gardiner remained standing near the foot of the stairs. Mrs. Gardiner, fixing her eyes on Elizabeth, seemed about to speak from some uncommon anxiety, but Elizabeth, fearing some criticism of Georgiana, implied if not open, implored her with a look to say nothing in the presence of Kitty.

Thus an interval passed in uneasy silence. Retracing in her mind all that had occurred in their passage through the house, Elizabeth recalled a door on the topmost floor which, on being opened by Acworth, had disclosed a steep flight of steps. He had enquired of Mortimer whither it led and was told only to an attic. Acworth had appeared instantly to dismiss the idea of mounting it, but now her suspicion of the man inclined her to see him deliberately misleading those about him in the pursuit of some scheme of his own. In Mortimer's absence it was not possible to know whether in the course of his search he had gone up to the attic or not, but she believed the chances were he had not in the conviction natural to him that no lady of delicate and dainty habits would expose a spotless white muslin dress to its murk and dust. For an instant or two she was undecided whether to go there herself, or to wait for the men to come back from their ascent of the tower, until urged by a sudden increase of alarm she declared her intention to her aunt of trying one place she knew where Mr. Mortimer might not have thought to look.

"I had better go alone," she replied in answer to Mrs. Gardiner's offer to accompany her, "for if my husband returns before I do, you will be able to explain the matter to him."

She had not gone far upon her errand when a clap of thunder reverberated through the house. Shaken as she was, she kept on her way. A glance through a small window as she passed it showed the trees in the park lit up by a sulphurous glare and dashed by a violent wind. The heat and an oppression in the air made her quite breathless as she ascended the many stairs up the house; her knees began to tremble, her heart to palpitate, and had she consulted these various unpleasant sensations she would have turned back. Nevertheless she toiled on until the last flight of stairs was surmounted and she had reached the door of the attic. It was ajar, and only a slight push was needed to swing it further open and enable her to see into a place as dim as a cavern. Pausing on the threshold to recover her breath, she could hear Acworth's voice, but where she stood neither he nor Georgiana was visible to her.

"You astonish me," Acworth was saying. "How you can endure the frivolity, the emptiness of the life you lead here I am unable to comprehend. You have powers vouchsafed to comparatively few, and you waste them upon people who can neither understand nor appreciate them."

Georgiana made some reply which Elizabeth could not catch and Acworth proceeded:

"It is a duty you owe to society to cultivate so great a talent as you possess. Here at Pemberley you have not the opportunity—"

"I do not know that I wish to cultivate it further," Georgiana interrupted.

"Not wish to? Why not? But you need not tell me. It is contrary to your notions of how a lady such as Miss Darcy should comport herself. Your friends would disown you, you would be forever disgraced in their eyes if you were to devote yourself to any serious pursuit, instead of being content with a smattering of accomplishments. You may not believe me, you may even credit me with unworthy motives, but I tell you in very truth that it tortures me to see you waste yourself as you are doing. Pemberley—what is it? It is an idle beauty, a trivial, heartless elegance, a decaying order. I would save you from it. Before it is too late, leave it. What is to prevent you? Money you have in your own right, you would never starve as some have done."

"It is altogether absurd to speak of such a thing," said Georgiana impatiently. "My brother would never sanction it."

"Your brother—no! He would condemn you to some thick-headed squire of a husband—to misery, to degradation. If I were your brother, how different would be your lot. You would know the happiness of honest endeavour, you would live among people who disdain luxury as unworthy to be compared with the delights of poetry, of music, of all that ministers to the heart and soul of man. Think, Miss Darcy, I implore you—"

Elizabeth clutching at the doorpost for support as she listened, while her heart beat so rapidly as to suffocate her, had found herself unable to move from the spot. At length, horrified by what she heard, she forced herself to step forward into the room. There, in a corner, seated at an ancient spinet, was Georgiana, while Acworth, his arms folded upon the lid of the instrument, leaned eagerly towards her.

"Georgiana," she articulated faintly. At the sound of her voice Acworth raised himself and turned swiftly round, and Georgiana rose from her seat and came towards her. Elizabeth saw them looking at her aghast, as if she had been a visitant from another world. She felt very ill, but she held herself upright by a supreme effort and spoke again, though in a voice not much above a whisper.

"We have been looking for you everywhere. Your brother—
it is time to go home."

She felt herself swaying. Acworth stretched forth an arm,
Georgiana hurried to her side. The same moment footsteps were
heard on the stairs and Darcy and Mortimer entered one after
the other. The relief of seeing her husband was so great that it
overpowered her senses and she knew no more.

When she came to herself she was lying on a sofa in a room
downstairs, and Mrs. Gardiner and her husband were beside her.
Rain could be heard falling heavily on the flagstones outside and
the air was become perceptibly cooler. As she opened her eyes
and gazed about her, Mrs. Gardiner spoke a word of encouragement, and Darcy bent down and placed a glass of cordial to her
lips. A few sips of it did her instant good; she sat up and asked
whether the carriage had come. She was eager to be at home, but
Darcy said that it was still raining too hard for a start to be made,
and that in any case she ought to rest a little longer. She therefore resigned herself to wait with what patience she could. As she
lay back with her eyes closed, the conversation she had heard in
the attic returned to memory, but so confused was her mind that
she began to wonder if she had not imagined the half of it. But
for Mrs. Gardiner being there she would have begun speaking to
her husband about it; as it was she could only remain silent.

She was already looking better, and Darcy, knowing Mr.
Bennet to be in a state of anxiety about his daughter, went into
the hall to tell him of her improvement. Mortimer, Kitty and
Bingley stood in a knot talking together; Wakeford, his back
turned to the rest, was studying a framed map of Derbyshire
which hung upon the wall, while Georgiana, as far as possible

removed from everyone else, gazed upon the floor with grave and conscience-stricken mien. Mr. Bennet happened to be standing close to the door from which his son-in-law had issued and looked up at him with an expression of concern which changed to one of relief as soon as Darcy had spoken.

Almost before Darcy had finished his account of Elizabeth, Acworth came up and began a rapid apology for having kept everyone waiting.

"It was my fault entirely," said he. "Miss Darcy and I, having unaccountably lost the others, in search of them, looked into an attic and saw the spinet. To our amazement the instrument had not so much suffered that it could not be played upon, and I persuaded Miss Darcy to try it. In this way time passed without our knowing. I would not for the world have occasioned so much alarm to Mrs. Darcy—to yourself—as I appear to have done."

Darcy beheld his agitation, his feverish, imploring gaze with an unmoved countenance. "It was unfortunate," he said very quietly, and turned away.

Acworth made a movement after him to regain his attention, but thinking better of it resumed his former position against the wall.

At the end of half an hour the rain ceased and the journey back to Pemberley could be begun. It was accomplished by the ladies in silence. Neither Elizabeth nor Georgiana had any desire to talk; Mrs. Gardiner respected their evident wish to be let alone, and Kitty, though longing to indulge her excited feelings in chatter, had to bottle them up very much against the grain.

How grateful to Elizabeth's eyes was the first glimpse of her own house. But alas, the trials of this ill-starred day were by no means over. No sooner had she descended from the carriage than she was met by Jane, who hurried towards her with a look so harassed that it was immediately apparent to every eye that something dreadful had happened.

The news was soon told. Two hours previously Lady Catherine de Bourgh and her daughter had arrived all unexpectedly. Lady Catherine, as might be supposed, was extremely indignant at finding no one at home to receive her but a mere Mrs. Bingley, and although Jane made every endeavour to appease her, the lady continued very angry and would accept no excuses whatever. She asserted that she had always intended to come to Pemberley on this day—the eighth of June—and that any mistake on her part was inconceivable. Never had she been treated so scandalously. She knew, however, whom she had to thank for this mark of incivility.

"She would take no refreshment," said Jane, "and demanded that she and her daughter be conducted to the apartments they were to occupy. Reynolds attended them there and perhaps has been able to soothe her ladyship's wounded feelings. Such apparent neglect must have been so very vexatious to her notions of what is due to her, that I cannot wonder at her speaking as she did."

The brunt of Lady Catherine's wrath had fallen upon poor Jane's meek and unoffending head. But so far from resenting all the injustice of it, the angelic creature was able to rejoice that her beloved Lizzy had escaped the flagellation, which she herself had endured.

Chapter 14

UNEQUAL AS SHE FELT to meeting Darcy's formidable aunt, Elizabeth summoned all her courage to sustain the encounter. Her husband, seeing that she was still far from well, would have had her keep her room for the remainder of the day, but although nothing would have pleased her better had there been no Lady Catherine in question, she pretended to have so far recovered as to be able to perform the duties of a hostess without too much fatigue.

"It would never do if I failed to appear downstairs the first evening of their arrival," she said. "Do consider what a handle it would give Lady Catherine. I should never be able to hold my own with her again. She would think I was frightened of her."

Darcy would hardly admit her argument, but he saw that it was perhaps better to give way to her than to enforce his authority. She was in a state of nerves when no peace of mind was possible until the meeting with Lady Catherine was over. He yielded, therefore, with the understanding that she was not to

exert herself any more than was absolutely necessary, and particularly not to talk too much.

"Nothing that you can say or do will please Lady Catherine
half so much as the sound of her own voice," said he. "Let her talk
as much as she chooses and she will soon forgive and forget any
fancied slight."

"I shall not have the smallest objection," she replied, "so
long as I am not obliged to listen to every word. I do not talk for
my own pleasure, but for that of others."

Darcy smiled. "Very well," said he, "that is understood. Now,
if you are determined on going downstairs we had better go."

"A touch of rouge is sometimes of assistance," said Elizabeth,
looking at herself in the mirror. "What do you think?"

"Certainly not," said Darcy taking her hand and leading her
to the door. "You know I do not approve of it, and besides I
prefer on this occasion to have you looking pale and languid and
all eyes, so say no more, but come."

They descended to the saloon. Mrs. Gardiner, Bingley and
Jane were there before them, and soon they were joined by Mr.
Bennet and the two girls. Major Wakeford and Mr. Acworth
entered last, and it was noticeable that each avoided the group in
the centre of the room and went apart, though to different stations.

Dinner was ready to be served, but Lady Catherine and
Miss de Bourgh still delayed their appearance. The knowledge
and sense of Lady Catherine's displeasure affected everyone's
spirits, and showed alike in Bingley's forced laughter and talk-
ativeness and in the determined cheerfulness of Mrs. Gardiner.
Georgiana, pale and silent, sat beside Elizabeth with her eyes
fixed on the door. Mr. Bennet, who in general never showed

what he might feel, kept looking uneasily at Elizabeth. Only Kitty, thinking of Mortimer and all the tender meaning conveyed in his whispered adieu, was without any care at all.

The period of waiting was at length terminated by the entrance of Lady Catherine and her daughter. Darcy and Elizabeth immediately advanced towards her; the ladies exchanged curtsies, and the gentleman kissed first his aunt's and then his cousin's hand with grave ceremony. The presentation of followed. When Lady Catherine had suffered everyone present to be made known to her she turned her back on them and engaged Darcy in conversation. Elizabeth meanwhile spoke to Anne de Bourgh. The first endeavour of the Darcys was to clear up the misunderstanding that had so unfortunately arisen. Anne de Bourgh was civil enough to present at least an appearance of accepting Elizabeth's explanation, but her mother was not so easily mollified.

"You ought to know, Darcy," said she, "that I never make a mistake of the sort you are trying to impute to me. I am the very soul of method, and every engagement I make is clearly and accurately noted down for daily reference. With all the calls on my time where should I be if I did not? I am always telling your wife's friend, Mrs. Collins, that she is not nearly particular enough in such matters." The last sentence was said in so loud a tone as to reach all ears and cause Elizabeth to flush with annoyance.

Her nephew was spared the necessity of a reply by the appearance at that moment of Master Richard Darcy in his nurse's arms. This was a diversion Darcy himself had planned with reasonable hope of success. Taking the child from the nurse he brought him to Lady Catherine with justifiable pride in his son's size and beauty. Richard, a little shy at the sight of so many people gazing at him, made a lovely picture of cherubic gravity. That Lady Catherine was already melting was highly apparent. She began to smile widely, exhibiting a still excellent set of teeth. Darcy, watching the effect of Richard's charms upon the lady, was unfortunately not prepared for the effect of *her* display of good humour upon the little boy, nor did he become aware that anything was amiss until, looking aside at his wife, he saw upon her countenance an expression of alarm. Lady Catherine advanced her smiling visage and was about to kiss Richard upon the cheek when a shriek burst from him. Burying his face against his father's head he began to cry aloud, and when Darcy tried persuasion on him, and Lady Catherine, not yet offended, seconded his efforts by exhorting dear Richard to be a good little boy and look up, screams and wails issued from him which, though intelligible to nobody else, were audible to his parents and his grandfather, as "Go—away, naughty woof. Go—away."

Remonstrance as well as cajolery proving useless, Darcy delivered his son back to his nurse, who, as fully ashamed of her charge as his nearest relatives could be, bore him back to the nursery. The spectators of the scene began smiling in an embarrassed manner and finding excuses for Richard's deplorable behaviour. The storm had probably upset the poor little boy, it was his bed time, and he was doubtless tired and fractious. Mr. Bennet alone had thoroughly enjoyed the incident, for he was in the secret of Richard's affright at the sight of Lady Catherine. The lady, in fact, with her large and prominent teeth, bore no small resemblance to the picture in Richard's story book of the wolf pretending to be Red Ridinghood's grandmother, which Richard demanded to have explained to him every time his grandfather visited him in the nursery.

After this inauspicious prelude, dinner passed off better than could have been hoped. Lady Catherine sat beside Darcy and addressed herself to him in a loud and authoritative tone on subjects of a family or domestic nature which could have no interest whatever for anyone who was not privileged to be one of her intimates. The effect of her discourse upon those who had never before experienced her style was to keep them utterly silent. They had to listen whether they would or not. Anne de Bourgh was on Elizabeth's right hand, and answered only in monosyllables to the polite enquiries of her hostess, in that way speedily exhausting every subject that could be brought forward. Soon Lady Catherine had all ears to herself.

She made it known that she had just come from the residence in Warwickshire of some very old friends—Sir John and Lady Beaumont—and was full of praise of everything seen there. The house, of noble dimensions, equal to Rosings and perhaps even larger, had recently been re-furnished throughout in the most modern style and in well-nigh ducal splendour. The park was ornamented with the most magnificent trees, the pleasure gardens laid out with the utmost taste, and replete with the greatest variety of shrubs and plants ever assembled in one place. But the peculiar glory of Bardesley Park was a noble avenue of beech trees stretching from the front of the house for at least a mile, at the centre of which Sir John Beaumont had erected a pagoda. So high was this pagoda that it rose even above the trees and could be seen from all quarters for many miles around.

"You must build a pagoda here at Pemberley," said she. "I know the very spot for it. Rising from beside the stream it would make a most striking addition to the surroundings. Your mother, Lady Anne Darcy, would have been delighted with a pagoda in the grounds."

"My father's aim was always to preserve the natural beauty of the park," replied Darcy. "It was once suggested to him that he should build a Gothic ruin, but he scouted the idea."

"So would I," said Elizabeth. "I could not endure the sight of a *new* Gothic ruin among our trees."

"I will not say that I care for ruins myself unless they are prodigiously well done," Lady Catherine graciously conceded. "But a pagoda! Darcy, you must build one, I insist."

Darcy merely bowed, but Elizabeth, hot with indignation, would have made a rejoinder had not her father, who was sitting on the other side of her, said in her ear, "Never mind, Lizzy. Let them build an avenue of pagodas a mile long, each pair higher than the last."

She had to smile, but looked aside directly to see whether Miss de Bourgh had overheard. Either she had not or had not understood. Elizabeth had long since come to the conclusion that Anne de Bourgh was not so much proud and disagreeable as stupid. But she was wont to reflect that thirty years of such a mother would reduce any daughter either to idiocy or revolt.

When the ladies quitted the dining-room for the saloon, Elizabeth braced herself anew for one of her ladyship's characteristic onslaughts. But she had reckoned without her elder sister's unexampled thoughtfulness and unselfishness. In some manner altogether unlike Jane, whose delicacy was proverbial in the family, she managed to attract Lady Catherine's attention entirely to herself. Pleased with the deference she was receiving, and deciding at once that Mrs. Bingley was after all a genteel, pretty sort of woman, vastly superior to either of her sisters, Lady Catherine began subjecting her to one of her famous catechisms. Jane was required to state how long she had been married, the name and extent of her husband's estate, what portion she had brought him, and how many children had been born of the union. On hearing that Jane had brought two into the world in the space of three years, whereas Mrs. Darcy had produced but one in the same period, she heartily commended her, but subsequently tempered her approval on hearing that they were both of the inferior sex.

"You must go on, Mrs. Bingley," said she. "You must really continue. I do not like to think that your husband has no son to succeed to the estate. A dear friend of mine, Lady Maria Bassett, had six children, all daughters, before the seventh, which was a boy."

"And did she then stop, madam?" Elizabeth could not resist enquiring.

"By no means," answered Lady Catherine. "She had three more children, all sons."

"Poor woman," said Elizabeth, "what a reward of her fortitude and perseverance to have ten children to plague her!"

"You mistake the matter if you think so," her ladyship replied tartly. "Lady Maria was an excellent mother and her sons and daughters were the most obedient, well-behaved and well-spoken children I ever saw. Not only that, they grew up to be a credit to their parents and the comfort of their old age."

A silence fell, which Elizabeth broke by asking Georgiana to play for her aunt. She came forward at once to do what was required of her, but performed so listlessly that it must strike anyone well acquainted with her usual expressiveness. Lady Catherine was nevertheless loud in her praises, declaring that a very great improvement had taken place since the last time of hearing her niece. But even she could not but remark Georgiana's lack of animation.

"You do not look at all well, Georgiana. I would prescribe a change of air. When we return to Rosings you must come with us. I will speak to your brother."

Georgiana looked quite aghast at the proposal and while expressing her thanks very properly, spoke haltingly of the numerous engagements which must stand in the way of her quitting Pemberley for many weeks to come. But Lady Catherine beat down all her excuses.

"Nonsense, child," she said smiling. "What engagements can you have that may not be broken? Six weeks to two months at Rosings will set you up for the rest of the year. There is no finer air, anywhere, I believe."

Georgiana coloured and was silent. She looked pleadingly at Elizabeth who said immediately, "Georgiana does not like missing the ball, Lady Catherine. Can you imagine any girl of her age forgoing such an enjoyment as that? Otherwise I am sure she would be most happy to accompany you."

"A ball!" cried Lady Catherine. "Do I understand there is to be a ball at Pemberley? Why has it not been mentioned to me before?"

"We should naturally forbear to trouble your ladyship with a matter which could have no interest for you, or for Miss de

Bourgh in view of the delicate state of her health," Elizabeth said, already repenting her invention as she saw in array the ill-consequences that might flow from it. "Besides it will not take place within the period of your stay here."

Everyone stared in amazement at the extraordinary tidings that the Darcys were giving a ball in the near future. They usually gave one in the late autumn at Pemberley and again while they were in residence at their house in town, but a summer ball was a novelty indeed. Elizabeth, seeing all eyes fixed upon her, and fearing betrayal by some ill-considered observation, hastily proceeded, "Of course if your ladyship could have honoured us with your presence it would have given us the greatest pleasure."

Unfortunately Lady Catherine's usual spirit of contrariety did not on this occasion assert itself. It is possible that she descried in an assembly of such proportions opportunities not to be cast away. She herself had met Sir Lewis de Bourgh at a ball. It was to be supposed that all the neighbourhood would be invited to Pemberley for the event, and among the guests what gentlemen of rank and importance might not be included, eligible in all respects for the hand of her daughter? Rapidly she determined upon the best means of circulating precise information as to Anne's splendid fortune, and her features assumed their most gracious expression as she replied, "But I do not at all see why we should not stay for the ball. We can perfectly well postpone our return home. You would feel equal to it, would not you, Anne? There is no occasion for you to be dancing all the time."

Miss de Bourgh's lips were seen to move, but her reply was inaudible.

"Then that is settled," said Elizabeth as cheerfully as

possible, though her heart had sunk very low. She had committed herself in a moment of folly to an undertaking which had no charms for her. And what would her husband say?

When the gentlemen came in very shortly afterwards, the sight of their happy unconsciousness of what was in store for them made her more than ever sensible of the enormity of her conduct. Any moment might bring forth disclosure from Lady Catherine herself in a voice which must penetrate to the four corners of the saloon. That she would claim Darcy's attention as soon as he came within speaking distance was moreover a foregone conclusion, and it was almost a certainty that the subject of the ball would be uppermost on her lips. Luckily Darcy was hindmost in the procession advancing up the room, and Elizabeth was thus given time to enquire of her ladyship how she had left Mr. and Mrs. Collins. This was inevitably to destroy all Lady Catherine's complaisance and to provoke a tirade, but it can sometimes appear that the fire is preferable to the frying pan.

Lady Catherine replied that both Mr. and Mrs. Collins were in excellent health, but it was soon made plain that nothing else of good could be said of the hapless couple. On Darcy coming up however, her strictures were diverted from her particular griev-ance to a general consideration of the woes of patrons. "Oh, Darcy," she cried, "there you are at last. Now tell me, where in these days is there to be found a clergyman who is fit for such livings as Hunsford and Pemberley? I grant you that Mr. Collins is very bad, but on looking round so are they all. Have you been able to fill Pemberley yet?"

Looking his aunt steadily in the face as if to enforce

understanding of the purport of his reply, Darcy said he had hopes of being able to make a presentation to the living in the very near future. The special emphasis laid upon the last three words caused Elizabeth to open her eyes wide and then to look for Mr. Acworth. He was standing some distance away from their group, and in conversation with Jane and Bingley was unlikely to have heard anything. She wondered immediately whom her husband could have in mind, but concluded that he was chiefly concerned to forestall an attempt on the part of Lady Catherine to thrust Mr. Collins upon him. Yet it was most unlike *him* to deviate from the strict truth. "Meddlesome people like Lady Catherine make liars of us all," she reflected.

Tea made its welcome appearance almost directly afterwards. Distracted from the theme of Mr. Collins, Lady Catherine once more became a danger, but happily the composition of some little cakes roused her curiosity and led her on to speak of recipes known only to herself and the housekeeper of Rosings. In the general movement towards the table, Elizabeth had been able to exchange a look with Jane which assured her that she was perfectly understood in that quarter, and to drop a word in the ear of her aunt with similar satisfactory result. She knew that Georgiana, whose comfort at such a cost to herself she had procured, would say nothing even remotely touching on a ball at Pemberley; as for Kitty she was too much afraid of Lady Catherine to start any subject in her presence. Recipes of cakes and concoctions peculiar to this, that, and the other great household were therefore sedulously canvassed by all the ladies present, and with so much appetising detail that Mr. Bennet protested against such wanton titillation of his palate. Lady

Catherine, artfully praised by Elizabeth for the cooking at Rosings into the best of humours, pronounced the cooking at Pemberley to be nearly equal.

"Your mother, Lady Anne Darcy," she said to her nephew, "insisted on the same excellent table as she had been accustomed to in her own home, Carringford Castle. I rejoiced to see in some of the dishes which were served to us at dinner that her memory is still honoured."

After tea Darcy made up a table of whist for his aunt with Mrs. Gardiner, Major Wakeford and himself. Mr. Bennet wandered off to the library to read in the solitude he preferred; Elizabeth sat down beside Anne de Bourgh. The rest of the party started to play Speculation and soon the game was in full swing with some lively bidding between Bingley, Acworth and Kitty. Acworth who had been very silent during dinner as if not wishing to attract attention to himself, suddenly began an absurd imitation of a gambler whose all is at stake, portraying by turns with exaggerated gestures and grotesquely distorted features the fever and frenzy, the jubilation and despair attending the least happy chance or slightest reverse. Bingley, highly diverted, egged him on by pretending to remonstrate with him; Georgiana played as though she observed nothing or was impatient with their clowning, but Kitty laughed so immoderately that she could hardly hold her cards. Anne de Bourgh and Elizabeth were near enough to see everything, and Anne looked on at Acworth's performance in an amazement that verged upon alarm until Elizabeth explained, almost as she would to a child, that he was acting a part for the entertainment of his fellow-players. She appeared relieved, but not at all amused, and continued to gaze at Acworth in wonder. Suddenly he dropped the pretence, his features settled into repose, he became gentle and sedate. What Miss de Bourgh thought of him now was not to be ascertained, but she still watched him with grave interest.

When the game was finished, a second one was proposed and Jane, with characteristic thoughtfulness, took the opportunity of asking whether Miss de Bourgh would now care to join in. It was expected that she would refuse; on the contrary she rose from her chair and a place was made for her between Acworth and Jane. Very soon, spurred on by the gentleman and fortified by his advice and encouragement, she was bidding with the rest. His manner to her was marked by a happy blend of liveliness and deference and Anne seemed pleased by it. She smiled when he spoke to her, and accepted his instructions as to what she should do with unquestioning faith in their efficacy, and as success nearly always attended her she began to look quite triumphant.

Left sitting alone by her own expressed wish, Elizabeth could survey at her leisure all that went on between the players. Had fate on this day only cast her for the role of spectator, she had been amply provided with material for reflection for days to come. The sight of Acworth, his present innocent behaviour and his apparent unconsciousness of anything in the past that could be taken exception to, threw her into fresh doubts as to his true character. She had believed herself to have arrived at a tolerably correct understanding of it, concluding him to be passionate, impetuous, unstable, conceited, capable of subterfuge when in straits, but not of calculated deceit. But now she wondered whether he was not indeed artful to a degree hitherto unsuspected by her, whether his approaches to herself, which he must know she would repel, did not mask some deeper and more far-reaching design. Was he laying siege to Georgiana's affections in the guise of a disinterested concern for her true felicity that he might hereafter secure her fortune to himself? She felt that he was not above some such project and the conversation she had overheard in the attic suggested it. Fortunately Georgiana could be deemed safe from him in the openness and uprightness of her character, and her good sense had showed itself in the impatience of her replies to his representations. Elizabeth moreover took comfort from the reflection that no real danger to her need be apprehended since both herself and Darcy were alive to its possibility.

But such a conclusion was not to make her easy about Georgiana. Something was amiss; something was on her mind. At the distance she was from the table Elizabeth could observe the players without fixing her gaze on any one of them. Georgiana looked dispirited, even oppressed by her thoughts. She played absent-mindedly, her eyes astray, and was constantly having to be given the cue to play by Bingley or Kitty. What could it be that was troubling her?

Suddenly Elizabeth's meditations were cut short. Lady Catherine's spirits had risen as her cards prospered, and having won every rubber she had attained to complete charity with all the world. She smiled upon Mrs. Gardiner, although she was her niece-in-law's aunt who lived in an unfashionable quarter of London where ladies of rank cannot visit; she was equally gracious to Major Wakeford, and lauded the virtues of the military. Finally she commended Darcy for the project, communicated by his wife, of giving a ball at midsummer when the days are long and the nights are short and carriages may roll home by the light of dawn.

"It has never before been done at Pemberley, I believe," she said, "but I am not so narrow-minded as to oppose an innovation merely because it is one. Anne is quite charmed with the idea. Unfortunately she is soon fatigued by any exertion beyond the ordinary, but there is nothing she would enjoy more than dancing if her health permitted it."

It was this speech which came to Elizabeth's ears from the other end of the saloon and transfixed her with horror. She was too far away from the speaker to make any interposition whatever, but she turned in her chair to see how her husband had received the blow. In agonised suspense, she waited for his reply. Some moments, long to her anxiety, elapsed ere it was heard. Then, in his wonted, deliberate accents, he said:

"As you so justly apprehend, madam, the giving of a ball at midsummer has much to recommend it. The invitations have not yet been sent out so far as I am aware, but it has only *very recently* been decided upon."

For the second time that day Elizabeth thought she must swoon. But by tightly clasping her hands together and sitting very still she was able in a few moments to overcome the sensation, and on approaching Lady Catherine a little later to congratulate her on her successful play she could present a tolerably composed appearance. At her husband she dared not as yet look direct, but a quick sidelong glance showed him smiling, or at any rate not so very much displeased.

"I do not know how it is," said Lady Catherine, "but I am

always prodigiously lucky at cards. I have had the most amazing hands this evening. It is the same with Anne. Her luck never fails."

Elizabeth thought of a certain proverb, but forebore to quote it. No one could say that poor Anne de Bourgh had been lucky in life or lucky in love.

Chapter 15

THE NEXT DAY OPENED with rain falling in a steady down pour from a sky of unbroken cloud, threatening confinement indoors for many hours to come.

Elizabeth awoke so unrefreshed, so far from recovered from the indisposition of yesterday that Darcy insisted on her resting until she felt better. The inclination of her spirit was all against any suspicion of running away from her newly arrived guests, but she was secretly not sorry to he overruled. Firmness in a husband when it supports instead of opposes the pleasanter course is wholly admirable. She consented with a good grace to obey him. To remove any scruples she might still have he promised that in her absence he would hold himself entirely at Lady Catherine's disposal, to amuse her if she were dull, to placate her if she were angry, and to listen to her as long as she wished to talk.

The sense of respite which this assurance gave had a reviving effect upon her spirits. But although the state of Lady Catherine's temper was a matter of importance, very much more so to her conscience was the question of what should be said and what left unsaid relative to Georgiana's unfortunate escapade with Acworth. Loyalty to her husband demanded in principle that nothing known to herself should be withheld from him; on the other hand, he was on his own confession keeping her out of his full confidence, even though temporarily. There was also some consideration owing to Georgiana, and it seemed only fair that she should have the opportunity of giving her own account of what had taken place before it could be rightly judged. But she longed to hear Darcy's opinion on so much as they both knew, and had half expected that he would express it unasked. He had not done so, however, whether from intention or negligence, though she thought the latter unlikely. Her own fatigue and the agitation consequent upon Lady Catherine's arrival would account for his silence. On a sudden impulse, as he was quitting her for the breakfast-parlour, she asked him what he thought of Georgiana and Acworth's disappearing into the attic at Clopwell.

"It did not look well," she said, "but I am sure Georgiana meant no harm."

"In the ordinary way there would be nothing to cause disquiet. But," he added smiling, "why two persons should choose such a dirty place for their mutual entertainment I cannot conceive."

"The spinet was the attraction, I suppose," said Elizabeth.

"An obvious one," he answered, looking at the door almost as if he wished to escape.

"Then you do not think there was anything very much to take exception to?"

He appeared to hesitate. "In judging the actions of people," he said, "we are so much governed by our feelings that what we condemn in one person we shall excuse in another. Now, Elizabeth, you are not to talk any more. There is no need for you to vex your head about Georgiana, Acworth, Lady Catherine, or anyone else. Do not forget that there is a ball to prepare for."

"I hate the very mention of it."

"You distress yourself unduly. Although I have every excuse to stay away, I shall be there. More than that, I shall welcome our guests as though I were delighted to see them."

He went away, and Elizabeth was left to reflect that on the subject of Acworth he had been very evasive. But what could be said of herself? An infection of mystery was in the air, clouding judgment and perhaps even one's moral sense.

At breakfast the principal theme was the wretched weather and the lugubrious prospect of a whole day to be spent indoors. The leaden colour of the sky, the sodden colour of foliage and grass and the soft continuous rain encouraged gloomy feelings. Kitty was depressed because she foresaw that Mortimer would be prevented from riding over from Clopwell. Bingley sat silent for several minutes on being reminded by Jane of the excellent opportunity afforded for writing some long deferred business letters. Lady Catherine compared the climate of Derbyshire unfavourably with that of Kent. "There is more sunshine in Kent than in any other part of the kingdom," she said. "For that reason it is called the Garden of England." No one disputing the statement, she continued: "the scenery of Derbyshire is much praised for its grandeur, I believe. For my part I do not admire precipitous cliffs and jutting rocks."

"I entirely agree with you, madam," said Mr. Bennet. "Fortunately the features you mention are excluded from these grounds. No rocks jut here."

Darcy here interposed to give his opinion that the sky would clear before noon, and at this happy prognostication every countenance visibly lightened.

The meal over, Bingley challenged Acworth to a game of billiards. Mr. Bennet wandered away with the newspaper, and Major Wakeford took an umbrella and set off for a walk in contempt of the weather.

Lady Catherine defeated her nephew's good intentions by retiring to her dressing-room, accompanied by her daughter, to read and digest a report received from Mr. Collins on the state of affairs in Hunsford parish, and to indite a list of instructions in reply thereto. The other ladies, unmurmuring as ladies of lesser importance usually are, settled down in the little drawing-room to while away the term of their confinement indoors with needlework and conversation which Kitty contrived very soon to bring round to Clopwell and all that it contained. Admiration ran away with her tongue and sparkled in her eyes. At the end of a quarter of an hour of unbroken eulogy, Georgiana, who had hitherto spoken no word, folded up her work and, getting up from her chair, murmured almost inaudibly that she must go to her practice.

On arriving in her room she opened the pianoforte and placed a piece of music on the desk, but after playing a few bars her hands dropped from the keyboard and she looked aside at the window on which the rain was splashing and remained gazing outwards with troubled eyes. It was thus that her brother found her on coming quietly into the room a little later. She made a quick movement as if to commence playing again, but the pretence was instantly seen by him for what it was, and served only to confirm a suspicion silently harboured for several days, that she had something on her mind. He could not help connecting that preoccupation with Acworth, though he could not be certain. Believing that it might continue forever unknown unless she could be led to speak freely and openly, he resolved that the present opportunity for procuring her relief and the allaying of his own anxiety must not be neglected.

To win her confidence by making it appear that he had no particular design in interrupting her playing, he began by speaking of immediate small matters—Lady Catherine's unexpected advent, the plans which the bad weather must vary, Elizabeth's indisposition, the ball and all the labours attendant upon it. Then he looked at her music and asked her to give him an idea how it went. After that, it became natural to touch upon the duets with Acworth. She answered so frankly and with so little thought of there being anything wrong in the hours spent alone with a comparative stranger that his mind received complete relief. But mention of Acworth could give rise to reflections upon the want of decorum that marked so much of his behaviour.

"He is one of those volatile, uncontrolled persons of whom it can never be assumed that he will do what is right and proper in any given circumstances," he said. "For example, a man left alone with a young unmarried woman should observe the utmost care and delicacy in regard to her. But Acworth is so careless of appearances that it probably has not occurred to him that to make you conspicuous—as he did yesterday at Clopwell—is to do you a great disservice."

Georgiana coloured deeply and looked down. She had remained seated at the pianoforte while Darcy, after a turn or two about the room, was now standing with his back to the window.

"Are you speaking of our going up to the attic?" she asked gravely. "We found the spinet and he asked me to try it—" she broke off in some confusion.

"There was no harm in that," Darcy said observing her attentively. "But to remain up there so long, past the hour fixed for our return, and to keep the rest of the party waiting is an instance of what I mean."

"Has anything been said? Would it be thought—by anyone not knowing me very well—that I was accustomed to behave like that?"

"Certainly not," he answered. "There is no one here who does not know you too well for such an idea. The most that might be thought is that it showed an unguarded simplicity."

"But a stranger could have misjudged me," she persisted, crimson and distressed.

"One who did not know your character might. Censorious people do not spare their strictures. But what stranger is there here to misjudge you? I would advise you to put the whole incident out of your head, Georgiana. Any displeasure I may have shown at the time was due to the delay occasioned and to Elizabeth's running about the house in search of you when she was not fit for it. Nevertheless, before we close the subject, I must warn you to have as little as possible to do with Mr. Acworth in the future. He will not be here very much longer. Until then, treat him with civility, but do not let him inveigle you away again from the rest of the company." After a short pause he added, "He is not at all as he was represented to me. Need I say more than that?"

Georgiana bent her head in unhappy reflection. Without looking up she said presently with evident constraint, "I have no special desire for his society. His gifts I do admire, but that is all. I wish that to be generally and thoroughly understood."

"Nothing could be less equivocal," he said smiling. "I will not deny that I am relieved to hear you say so. And now I will interrupt you no longer. You must wish me away."

She shook her head with an attempt at an answering smile. "If it stops raining I shall go for a walk through the grounds for the sake of fresh air," she said.

"You hate confinement as Elizabeth does. Never were there two such confirmed ramblers."

He then went away, satisfied that she was in no danger from Acworth. Her distress and confusion had not gone unmarked, but he attributed that to the shrinking of her native modesty and shyness from the public notice she must feel she had unhappily brought on herself—a feeling which would pass.

It was now time to be enquiring after Lady Catherine's degree of comfort and state of entertainment should she have descended from her dressing-room. On looking into the little drawing-room he found her seated there with Mrs. Gardiner and Mrs. Bingley, instructing the latter on the only correct way of blending the different coloured silks of her embroidery. "Taste," said her ladyship, "is not to be imparted, but there are certain rules of congruity which, if observed, cannot fail to procure a reasonably good effect."

She broke off her discourse at her nephew's approach and the turn of her shoulder conveyed unmistakably that the attention of the two ladies was no longer required and their continued presence in the room rather deprecated than not. Seeing this, Mrs. Gardiner and Jane felt it their duty to withdraw as unobtrusively as they could. More mindful of the feelings of their host than Lady Catherine of theirs, they recollected, as if it had been temporarily forgotten, a promise to visit the nursery.

Lady Catherine was ever impatient of beating about the bush. Before Darcy could engage her upon the safe and easy topic he meditated broaching, she demanded peremptorily to be informed as to Georgiana's prospects of marriage. It shocked her to hear that no single suitor had as yet proposed for her niece's hand. That there was gross negligence on the part of *someone* she did not doubt. Was it not a chaperone's first duty to provide the proper occasions and facilities for bringing the young girl in her charge into the presence of the most eligible gentlemen of her acquaintance in such a manner as to recommend her to their favourable attention? A girl of twenty with such excellent connections and a fortune of thirty thousand pounds to be hanging on like a nobody was proof that no attempt to settle her had been made. It was simply disgraceful. The disgraceful circumstance of her own daughter's forlorn condition did not at first strike her, but it could not long fail to do so, and she said haughtily,

"Anne's case is different. Her choice is narrowed by reason of her immensely greater fortune. An heiress to a great estate has a very much more limited range than even Georgiana Darcy."

Darcy could only bow in a show of polite acquiescence. Happily Lady Catherine's outraged feelings or some element of mortification in them reined in her eloquence, and the pause which followed, indicating, as it did, a change of subject, enabled him to ask her whether she wished to renew her acquaintance with the Miss Robinsons. To this she replied that she would take an early opportunity of waiting upon them—that very day if the weather mended.

"The eldest Miss Robinson is so truly respectable," said she, "her ideas on all matters so nearly correspond with my own that it is a pleasure to converse with her. I could wish that there were more like her in these days of laxity and slighted authority. And so this Mr. Acworth is to be the new rector of Pemberley."

"From whom did you learn that, madam?" Darcy enquired.

"From Georgiana. I asked her what he was doing here and she replied in some roundabout way that I cannot remember that he had been recommended for the living. The name of Acworth was instantly familiar to me, and on hearing that he was a younger son of the late Lord Egbury I perceived at once that he had inherited the family countenance. He seems an agreeable young man. You are indeed fortunate in having Lord Egbury's son as the clergyman of Pemberley. It is but seldom in my life that I have made a mistake, but I was most certainly deceived in Mr. Collins. His pretensions to gentility were founded upon his prospective inheritance of the Longbourn estate which of course is too small to confer any consequence upon its possessor. To hear Mr. Collins talk one would have supposed it to be a great family place."

In reply Darcy offered the general observation that pretentiousness and conceit were to be found in every sphere of life, not excepting the highest.

"As regards Mr. Acworth," he continued, "he was invited to Pemberley for a period of some weeks without prejudice to any ultimate decision affecting the disposal of the benefice—either on his side or mine. There is reason to believe that he has no intention of remaining here."

"That is a pity, for he is eminently suitable. Have you tried persuasion? What are his objections? Georgiana did tell me that he is recently a widower and that he is often very melancholy in consequence. If that is so, he should marry again. Would not he do for Georgiana? But perhaps you dislike the idea of a widower for her?"

Darcy replied emphatically that such a thing was not to be thought of. "In any case," he said, "I should never urge her into any marriage—even the most advantageous—contrary to her inclinations."

"I think you are overscrupulous," said his aunt. "But I will say no more." Her features showed some displeasure, and without any change of countenance she enquired after Elizabeth's general state of health.

"This modern habit of breakfasting in bed for nothing at all is what I cannot approve of," said she. "I never did it myself when young, and now that there is rather more excuse I should be ashamed of the indulgence. But I thank heaven that I have always enjoyed the best of health. Your dear mother used to say to me, 'Catherine, you are indeed wonderful. You never give way under any circumstances.'"

"Such a constitution is undoubtedly a gift all too rarely bestowed," replied Darcy. "Fortunately my wife's health is in general as excellent as your own. Like yourself, too, she will never give way to indisposition if she can help it. Ill as she felt this morning she would have risen at her usual early hour had I not insisted upon her resting some hours longer."

"In that case I have no more to say," returned the lady. "I am glad to hear that you retain your authority, for from observation I should have supposed the opposite. Anne's character is so different. She does not seek to shine by comparison with others."

As Darcy could think of no reply that would be acceptable without offending his conscience, he got up from his chair and walked to the window to examine and report on the weather. From there he was able to communicate the welcome intelligence that the sky was clearing rapidly. Lady Catherine was therefore graciously pleased to agree to a carriage being ordered for her.

"Miss Robinson will be delighted to see us, I believe," she said. "It will be the most charming surprise for her."

About half an hour later Darcy handed his aunt and her daughter into the barouche that was to convey them to the Parsonage. As he stood to watch them go he descried the figures of two persons crossing the bridge over the river. In a moment the receding carriage obliterated them, then they were seen again and perceived to be Georgiana and Wakeford. Walking rapidly they approached the house. Neither spoke to the other and it was observable that they kept some distance apart. The nearer they came, and the more distinct the view of their countenances, the stronger grew Darcy's impression that there had been some disagreement between them, so much so that he turned and mounted the steps into the house that he might not increase their embarrassment by openly encountering it. Before he could utter a word, had he wished, Georgiana passed him quickly and crossed the hall towards the staircase, and when he looked round for Wakeford, it was to see him reach the door of the library and disappear through it.

In default of any explanation, an occurrence so strange and unlooked-for was bound to be disquieting. Delicacy forbidding enquiry, and recollection supplying no key to comprehension, Darcy resolved to think no more about it for the present. It was some hours since he had seen Elizabeth and a wish to know how she was now feeling directed his steps towards her room.

He found her dressed in readiness for dinner and saw with delight that she was looking once more her usual healthful self. She was reading, and without lifting her eyes from her book, she said, "Listen to this," and began reciting some lines of poetry descriptive of a mountain scene. He heard her with pleasure for the beauty of the verse and her clear, expressive, yet unaffected rendering of it. But in the same way as music will set the mind drifting along alien currents of thought, so under the spell of Elizabeth's voice in the surrounding stillness, the events of the past twenty-four hours came thronging into memory, took possession of his faculties and thrust away all else. At length he was brought to himself by hearing her say, "Fitz, you are not listening."

"My mind had slipped off for the moment, I confess," he answered.

"You always did sacrifice gallantry to truth," she said, smiling. "Where were your thoughts, may I ask? With Lady Catherine?"

"They might well be, for she has lost none of her energy, nor her interest in other people's affairs. But I was not in truth thinking of her." And after some slight hesitation he told her of Georgiana and Wakeford, of the manner of their return to the house and their appearance of estrangement.

"It would seem impossible," he said, "for what could they have to quarrel about? It is besides not in the character of either. They did not go out together—of that I am certain. Wakeford left the house immediately after breakfast, and Georgiana not much above an hour ago."

"Then we are to infer that they met, walked back together and on the way quarrelled. No, that will not do. Georgiana would not dare, neither can I believe it of Wakeford. He has appeared silent and preoccupied of late, it is true, but why should he quarrel with poor Georgiana?"

"Indeed I hope not," he answered. "It would add one more tangle to the other complications gathering under this roof."

"Other complications?" she returned, raising her eyebrows.

"Are they not always the effect of Lady Catherine's presence? Has she not already produced a ball? My excellent aunt must have her finger in every pie. She has now gone to visit the Miss Robinsons, and I shall be surprised if she does not return with some scheme for the disposal of the living."

Whatever else invisible or imponderable there might be in the carriage on its return from the Parsonage, Lady Catherine had visibly brought back Mr. Acworth. Darcy and Elizabeth were descending the staircase when the sound of arrival at the front door was heard. Following Lady Catherine and Anne into the hall came the gentleman, and then and there was enacted a scene of polished gratitude on the one side and gracious conde-scension on the other.

"If ever I can be of use where it will be truly appreciated I am only too happy," said she. "It is a rule with me that persons in our rank of life should be first in setting an example of obligingness. And it was really no trouble at all. My daughter and I were not in the least incommoded. So say no more about it, I beg of you."

Chapter 16

ELIZABETH'S REAPPEARANCE AMONG HER guests brought felicitations on her recovery, even from Lady Catherine, and a resumption of social pleasure. The evening began well. Mortimer, now a daily visitor, came to dinner and fixed all his looks and attentions upon Kitty in the approved manner preparatory to a declaration. The same four sat down to whist after tea as before, and Lady Catherine's good fortune in the cards she held, and the excellent support given by her partner varied not. All Mrs. Gardiner's customary good humour was needed to sustain reverse after reverse with tolerable equanimity, for not only were her hands and Major Wakeford's undeviatingly bad, but Major Wakeford, to her amazement and chagrin, lost one or two tricks that might have been theirs.

The rest of the party, including Elizabeth, played Speculation again in deference to Anne de Bourgh's expressed desire. As on the previous evening Acworth sat beside her and in the intervals of play conversed with her about Kent which he said he knew well from having been at school there as a child. He mentioned the name of the place, West Gitting, a village near Maidstone, and discovered to his surprise and that of his companion that it was within ten miles of Rosings. The circumstance proved quite animating and set up a sort of intimacy between them, for they could return ever and again with undiminished interest to an inexhaustible subject which had also the merit of excluding everybody else, not one of them having ever in their lives heard of West Gitting before.

"I went there when I was seven or eight," said Acworth in a soft, confidential tone. "My brother and I were entrusted to the care of the clergyman who eked out his stipend by taking one or two pupils into his house. It was a secluded spot, the church and vicarage lying some distance away from the village. We were very happy there on the whole."

He sighed gently and his countenance spoke the sad conviction of happiness being no longer possible. Once or twice Elizabeth thought she caught his glance, melancholy and almost accusing, resting upon herself. She took good care to show no consciousness of having seen it and, in fact, felt the greatest impatience with his behaviour.

Anne did not have much to say, but she listened with instant attention whenever Acworth addressed her, and now and then from her own knowledge supplied the name of a village or mansion on the road between West Gitting and Rosings. All this flow of reminiscence was both distracting and meaningless for the other players, and at the end of the game, Acworth being wholly taken up with determining the precise location of a house about which a little argument had developed, Bingley began showing

Mortimer a card trick and asked him whether he could guess how it was done. Mortimer with a shake of the head had finally to confess himself beaten, whereupon Jane, who knew, would have told him had not her husband restrained her.

"No, Jane. Not a word, not a syllable. Now Lizzy and Kitty—and Georgiana too—you are to set your wits to work to solve the mystery. Ladies always say they have sharper eyes than men."

Kitty protested that she abominated card tricks and saw nothing diverting in them at all, but Elizabeth, displeased with Acworth's ill-breeding in keeping the table waiting while he turned his shoulder to everyone but his neighbour, made a parade of accepting Bingley's challenge. He had picked up the cards and was shuffling them when Acworth suddenly turned round in a manner which showed him perfectly aware of all that had gone on without his participation, and asked for the cards to be handed to himself.

"I can perhaps show you something you have not seen before," he said. Then turning to Elizabeth with a slight inclination of the head he asked, "Have I Mrs. Darcy's permission?"

"By all means," she answered, perhaps more archly than she intended, "on condition that you let us in on the secret afterwards."

"Would you rob Samson of his locks?" he replied smiling.

Elizabeth averted her eyes, infuriated with herself for having provoked the sally. With a heightened colour she turned to Bingley and laughingly adjured him to be on the alert.

"I am the more likely to be made look very foolish," he answered in like manner. "Acworth means to confound us all, and if he doesn't I for one shall be disappointed."

For the next half-hour every eye was riveted upon Acworth as he executed prodigies of sleight of hand, each surpassing the last in the power of amazing and mystifying the beholders. All were spellbound, not excluding Elizabeth, who found his hands as expressive as his features in evoking sensations appropriate to the turn of the performance—whether of suspense, admiration or surprise. When at last in a moment of talk which arose between him and Bingley she looked round to speak to Jane, it was to discover Georgiana gone from the table and, on a further survey, from the room. She asked Jane whether she had seen her go and received an answer in the negative. Nothing further was said just then and perhaps ten minutes passed while Acworth repeated his last performance at Bingley's request. Suddenly Kitty observed unconcernedly, "What a long time Georgiana is away. It must be half-an-hour since she went."

Elizabeth now remembered that during dinner she had seen Georgiana sitting with downcast eyes looking strained and wretched. The necessity of attending to a lively conversation between Bingley and her father, lest the latter should express himself in a manner requiring tactful glossing over, had immediately obliterated a mere impression until the present instant. The conviction arose in her mind that something had occurred to make Georgiana more unhappy than ever. But before searching for its probable cause a plausible explanation of her sudden and silent disappearance must first be thought of and related. A headache, though a convenient sort of ailment, was so hackneyed that it might be seen through. An attack of faintness? No, for that could never have passed without visible symptoms of distress, a hue and cry for smelling salts and a bustle of ministrations. A neuralgia then, akin to a headache, but more excruciating, a more specific and therefore more convincing illness. The neuralgia was imparted to Jane in an undertone, not so low that it could not be generally heard.

Jane expressed sorrow and sympathy; Bingley was quick to echo her concern. Mortimer, glancing at Kitty, said he trusted Miss Darcy would soon recover from such a painful complaint. Kitty said she thought Georgiana looking very ill these several days and it was to be hoped she was not going into a decline. Acworth looked genuinely grieved. "She is a being who would suffer as exquisitely as she enjoys," he said half to himself. Anne de Bourgh alone appeared unmoved.

It was enough to make the author of the neuralgia believe in it herself. But from all that had passed before her eyes she knew that Georgiana's suffering was not of the body, but of the mind. Something must have wounded her feelings beyond endurance, something so closely locked in her heart that it could never be learnt from her own lips. In the meantime conjectures were better suspended.

By the time Lady Catherine noticed her niece's absence, Georgiana's neuralgia had been established in every other mind and had even been located at a certain spot in the right temple. Imagination and some verbal distortion had thus played their part. Major Wakeford alone said absolutely nothing but looked very grave and thoughtful. Lady Catherine expressed herself anew in the desirability of a change of air and the invitation to Rosings was again issued, and in a tone of command.

"I will take no denial," she said with an imperious look at Elizabeth. "As we are not returning until after the ball, no obstacle can now exist."

Although Elizabeth hated the very appearance of submission to dictation, she could not but be sensible of the probable benefit to Georgiana of a change of scene at this juncture, and she hastened to make all proper acknowledgments on her sister's behalf short of vouching for her acceptance of the invitation.

A little later the Darcys' guests separated for the night and Elizabeth could gain the privacy of her own room. At leisure to think over all that had passed during the evening she became so uneasy that she dismissed her maid until rung for, and made her way to Georgiana's door. She knocked gently though distinctly, but received no answer, and presuming Georgiana to be asleep made no further attempt to gain admission. Nevertheless her uneasiness remained, and feeling totally unable to rest she gave way to the desire of having instant conference with her husband and went downstairs in good expectation of finding him alone. When visitors were in the house to occupy much of his time during the day, he not infrequently stayed up an hour or more attending to his correspondence after everyone else was upstairs, and tonight he had told her that having a letter to write for early despatch on the morrow he might be rather late in retiring. She hurried to the library and found him there as she had anticipated. But he was not alone. Major Wakeford was with him.

They were standing close together in the middle of the room and facing one another in a conversation which they broke off as soon as she entered. The constraint and embarrassment in

Wakeford's face told her that some personal matter of a serious, and perhaps painful nature, had been under discussion. An apology for interrupting rose to her lips, but before it could be uttered Darcy took a step towards her and spoke first.

"I am glad you came, Elizabeth," he said gravely. "Wakeford has just told me that he must return to Devonshire without delay. He is to leave here early tomorrow morning."

Elizabeth's astonishment for a moment rendered her speech-less. She stared at Wakeford in bewilderment, then at her husband as if doubting her ears. "Surely this is a very sudden decision," at length fell from her.

"It is perhaps sudden in announcement," Wakeford said, avoiding her gaze and looking down. "But the necessity is of longer duration and must not be withstood. For some time I have felt that my duty lies at home. My father needs me; I hear in every letter of his declining strength. Thanks to your care and kindness I am no longer a useless clod; I can assist him in the management of his estate instead of being the burden I was formerly." After a slight pause he continued, "Do not think me ungrateful. I shall ever feel the impossibility of repaying the bene-fits I have received at your hands."

There were signs of some inward and incommunicable distress as he spoke; his voice was harsh, though subdued, his face flushed and his mouth compressed. He finished abruptly and bowed his head, apparently unable to say another word. Elizabeth sought her husband's eyes and they looked at each other in a silent colloquy which taught her that he comprehended the matter as little as herself.

"I owe you every apology," Wakeford presently resumed. "This abrupt announcement—this hasty departure. It must seem very strange—very inconsiderate."

"We are only sorry that you are obliged to go away," said Elizabeth quietly. "We shall all miss you extremely."

Wakeford turned away as if unable to encounter her gaze.

"I have urged him to stay, if only for some days longer," said Darcy. "He needs no assurance how greatly we value his society. But of course we must not seek to persuade him against his own sense of duty."

After another short silence Elizabeth began brief enquiries about the arrangements for the journey. Wakeford replied that his packing up had been done earlier in the evening and that he proposed, with Darcy's permission, to start after an early breakfast. The first stage of the journey was a long one if he was to arrive at his destination at the end of the second day.

It was on the tip of Elizabeth's tongue to ask if his family expected him so soon, but an intuition that the question would be an awkward one for him to answer stayed her. There was in fact nothing to be said except a repetition of what had gone before. After another awkward moment or two Wakeford withdrew, leaving Darcy and Elizabeth at liberty to say what they chose.

"What can it mean?" she cried as soon as they were alone. "There must be more in this than he would have us know. Have you the least idea?"

Darcy shook his head. "He told me no more than what you heard him say," he replied.

"How exceedingly awkward he looked, too. In fact he has been most unlike himself latterly, but more particularly since yesterday. At Clopwell—" she broke off as the recollection of his dejected behaviour beside the lake struck upon her with the force of a shock. She had not spoken of it, for the circumstance had been driven out of her mind by succeeding events, but now she related it with every assurance of faithfully representing what she had seen.

"It may be true that his presence is desired at home, but only the most urgent reason could decide him to go at such very short notice. Do not you think so yourself? One would imagine—"

"I have scarcely ever known imagination to hit the mark," said Darcy. "And where the case admits of so many different interpretations it is better not employed."

"You are altogether too cautious. How much evil and unhappiness have proceeded from a lack of imagination."

"Have your say then, or I shall be accused of monstrous cruelty."

"Well, one would imagine that he was suffering from some affair of the heart that had gone badly. Let us suppose that he had proposed to a woman who had rejected him. Would not that be a motive for instant departure?"

"It might be," replied Darcy, "although I should have given Wakeford credit for more self-control. But whom would he propose to?"

"True, there is only Georgiana, for Kitty is appropriated by Mortimer. But Georgiana! Fitz, can it possibly be that? She, too, has been behaving very unaccountably of late. You must have observed yourself how pale and melancholy she has been looking. This evening she vanished from the room without a word and I had to invent an excuse for her. How else could I explain her absence? And have you forgotten what you told me about her returning to the house with Wakeford this afternoon, and how they appeared as though they had had some violent disagreement? It has crossed my mind more than once that he was jealous of Acworth, that he resented her apparent preference for Acworth's society. Depend upon it, that is what has happened. He has proposed, and she has refused him."

"It is not very likely," said Darcy.

"How not likely?"

"Wakeford is a poor man and his sense of honour is such that he would not propose to a woman of fortune."

Elizabeth paused to consider his statement. "No," she said soberly, "I must believe that. Such scruples are absurd, I think; but that is neither here nor there. But there is the appearance of estrangement still to be accounted for. How is it to be explained? Can it be that he remonstrated with her about Acworth—about their being found together in the attic at Clopwell, and that she resented it?"

"It is possible, but scarcely probable," he answered. "Georgiana's disposition is too mild for resentment of reproof. She is, on the contrary, afraid of giving offence, almost of a too tender conscience." He went on to tell Elizabeth of his conversation with his sister earlier in the day, and her declaration of her absolute indifference to Acworth. "That she was not indifferent had been my fear," he confessed.

"It was also mine," she said. "Well, it is some comfort to know that she is safe from that quarter. But are not we as much in the dark as ever—or are we making a great deal out of trifles? Am I to speak to Georgiana, or leave her to herself? I believe I can answer for you in advance. You will say that it is better not to interfere."

"I do say it," he said with a smile. "But you have her confidence, and if there should be anything on her mind she will tell you of her own accord. Is not that your experience?"

"Generally speaking, it is. But as you are so fond of saying, there are exceptions to every rule. In a word, I will make no promises, but be guided solely by circumstances. And since I have warned you beforehand, you cannot quarrel with me."

"Heaven forbid," said Darcy. "I have neither the time nor the inclination for it. Quarrelling is a sort of entertainment for people who have nothing better to do."

This was the end of their conversation. Elizabeth would willingly have gone on talking, but Darcy still had his letter to write, and she left him in peace to get it done. In spite of continuing perplexity about Georgiana she went away lighter in heart for having confided it to his ear. Reposing in his calm and steady judgment, and sensible of his deep affection, his warm solicitude for her happiness, nothing could dismay her very much while he was at hand to counter every adverse circumstance which might threaten the comfort and well-being of their family life.

Chapter 17

MAJOR WAKEFORD QUITTED PEMBERLEY the next day at an early
hour. Only Darcy and Elizabeth were downstairs to see him off.
After he had eaten a hurried breakfast he enquired for the
chaise, evincing an anxiety to be away with all speed. The
chaise with his luggage, safely bestowed and secured, was in fact
already at the door, and he had but to enter it. But now there
occurred a short delay, for as he, with his hosts, was crossing the
hall, the post happened to be delivered and there proved to be
a letter for him.

The superscription denoting extreme urgency, he opened it
at once. As he read the brief contents, his countenance altered.
He was not the man to exclaim or show emotion in the presence
of others, but some conflict of feeling was apparent before he
could repress it. Folding the letter again he said with great
gravity, "It is fortunate that this reached me before I had started.
I am summoned to another destination, to Gloucestershire. My

aunt, Mrs. Chalmers, is very ill indeed—cannot live long, the writer says—and is asking for me."

The change of plans which the letter produced entailed little in the way of discussion, for the route now to be taken followed the same direction and differed only from the former in curtailment by about a third of the distance. Its cause, however, required something to be said of hope for a happier outcome of Mrs. Chalmer's illness than the letter indicated. The Darcys expressed everything that was proper, consolatory and kind, but as soon as the chaise moved off and its occupant was out of earshot, Elizabeth exclaimed, "it must be the aunt whose fortune Lady Tyrrell so obligingly bequeathed to him. If only that could be true. But there is another nephew with better claims, alas! Major Wakeford made that perfectly clear."

They returned to the breakfast-parlour to await the rest of the party who might be expected shortly to begin appearing. At each arrival the account of Major Wakeford's sudden departure had to be gone through, and Elizabeth found that in referring its motive to the news of his aunt's serious illness, and her desire to see him, it was at once placed in a light which gave it the aspect of an obligation fulfilled in the only possible way. What she or Darcy would have said lacking the explanation so timely provided there was now no need to consider, but it would have tasked all her ingenuity and his scrupulous regard for veracity.

In varying degrees of surprise, concern or philosophy was the intelligence received. Lady Catherine declared that it showed commendable respect on the part of a nephew for the wishes of an aunt; Jane, struck by the despatch of his going, saw in it the impulse of a truly affectionate heart desirous of shortening suspense by immediate action. Mr. Acworth, his features expressing derision, observed that a wealthy relation stretched upon a bed of sickness was likely to prove an irresistible magnet. He spoke low so as to be heard only by Georgiana who sat next to him at the table, but Elizabeth caught his words and the look of contempt with which Georgiana listened to them. She alone had had nothing to say on the subject although she attended to everything that was said by others. Pale and heavy-eyed as she appeared, Elizabeth fancied that her prevailing sensation was one of relief.

But Major Wakeford and his journey to his aunt was soon forgotten in the agitation excited by events of another kind. On gaining her sitting-room Elizabeth sent word to Mrs. Reynolds that she was at leisure to speak with her on household matters. On the housekeeper answering the summons it was immediately apparent that something of an extraordinary nature had occurred. With every endeavour to preserve a decent composure the poor woman could not subdue the evidences of her distress and concern. Before Mrs. Darcy had time to utter a word she burst into speech.

"Oh, ma'am," she cried, "there has been an accident to one of the maids and unfortunately it is Mason. She was going down the back staircase in the west wing, and just where it turns and is rather dark she fell over a broom which had been left lying there, and I do fear that she has broke her leg."

Elizabeth's first thought was to enquire whether Mr. Reed, the apothecary who attended the servants in any ailment, had been sent for. Mrs. Reynolds was able to satisfy her on that head—she had taken the liberty of despatching one of the grooms. Elizabeth was truly concerned for Mason; she was not very young and therefore the more likely to suffer from the effects of the great pain she must be in.

"But how could such a thing happen?" she asked. "There must have been very gross carelessness on the part of someone." She had been on the point of saying "or wickedness," but checked herself.

Mrs. Reynolds looked most unhappy. "I am sure I do not know, ma'am," she replied. "I have questioned everyone who was about at the time and can make nothing of it. Such a thing has never before happened in all the years I have been in the House and I do assure you that I feel the disgrace to myself more than I can express. And poor Mason is so put out, ma'am. The first words she said when we took her up were, 'But who is to dress madam if I cannot be there?'"

The circumstance of a broom left lying across the turn of a staircase roused suspicions which Elizabeth could not dismiss, however unpleasant, for she was like Lady Catherine in this, if in nothing else, that she would not, if she could help it, be ignorant of anything which occurred in her own house. A few questions elicited, if not much, enough to strengthen her secret belief that the accident to Mason was premeditated, and the name of the culprit therefore sprang to her mind. Whether Reynolds had suspicions of her own she refrained from asking.

"I have been thinking what is best to be done, ma'am," said Reynolds. "Miss Georgiana has lately been sharing Billing with Miss Bennet. Mason did say that Rachel Stone was proving herself a likely girl under direction for serving and such like, and perhaps Miss Bennet would not mind doing with her so that

Billing could wait on yourself and Miss Georgiana. But I hardly know whether that would do either. It is a puzzle to be sure."

"Billing must manage with Rachel's assistance," said Elizabeth. "After a day or two Mason will be able to give some help with her needle. How has Rachel been behaving of late?"

"I have had no more complaints of her, ma'am, and I do begin to think a little better of her, if only her looks were more modest. After you spoke to her, and so kind as you were, she seemed to improve."

"I am not yet perfectly satisfied that she is a reformed character," said Elizabeth gravely. "Her attendance upon me will give me an opportunity of observing her. I feel a special responsibility towards that girl which I cannot go into now, Reynolds. However, you may remember the circumstances of her coming into our service. At this moment I have no time to say more than that I rely on you to acquaint Billing of the temporary arrangement."

As soon as Reynolds had gone, Elizabeth went in search of Georgiana and Kitty with the idea of telling them what had happened. At this time of morning the girls were usually to be found with the rest of the party in the hall where plans for the day would be devised, talked over and arranged to accord one with the other. On this occasion Mrs. Gardiner and Jane, Mr. Bennet and Bingley were gathered at the farther end of the hall looking through a window, Kitty was nowhere to be seen, and Georgiana stood apart by herself deep in thought and lost to all that was going on around her.

In curiosity to know what was engaging the attention of the group at the window Elizabeth first moved in that direction.

Turning round at her approach, Mrs. Gardiner told her that Kitty was walking in the park with Mortimer.

"Jane and I caught sight of them," she said, "and really they do make a pretty promising couple."

"It seems a shame to watch them," said Jane, "but perhaps at such a distance as this they would not mind."

Elizabeth's private opinion was that Kitty would have not the least objection. Drawing near the window she saw the interesting pair for herself as they walked slowly up a grassy slope, keeping to the shade cast by a line of great trees. Mortimer was bending towards Kitty in the very attitude of making a declaration, while Kitty hung her head as bashfully as a young girl should in so delicate a situation.

"It will really be an excellent match for Kitty," said Mrs. Gardiner. "He is a very good young man, though perhaps not as clever as some. But then to live at Clopwell Priory! I have taken a wager with your father that they will come back engaged."

"And quite time too," said Mr. Bennet. "Of all things I do detest the worst is a long-drawn-out courtship while your shy and timorous swain works up his courage to the proposing point. What have they been waiting for all these days? Mortimer must know he is caught."

"For shame, Papa," exclaimed Elizabeth half-laughing, but apprehensive too of what he might say next.

"I do not agree with you at all, my dear," he replied coolly. "There is no shame in any natural process such as procuring a husband. It is every young woman's proper business and the sooner she accomplishes it the better. For that I have the highest authority—your mother."

"I am sure," cried Jane, "Kitty would never marry unless her heart prompted her."

"Fiddlestick, my love. *You* would not perhaps, and that is as much as you can say. Consider the example of Charlotte Collins, and her sister Maria Lucas, and a lot of others I could name. What has prompted them? Nothing but the desire of being married. For that any man will do."

"Very true, sir," said Bingley, "but Jane will never believe you. She lives in a world where folly and wickedness occur, but never in any of her friends."

"Well, Jane, be happy in your own way," said her father. "For my part any young man who takes a daughter off my hands is an object of gratitude. Now there will be only Mary to settle in life."

"Then it is a pity you did not bring her where there were still two unattached young men," said his son-in-law.

"I am certain Acworth would not have bestowed a single glance at her after the first. If ever there was a connoisseur of female beauty, it is that young gentleman."

"You might have had better hopes of Wakeford, then. I do not think he would consider it proper in a wife to be very pretty."

"Charles," cried Jane, really scandalised, "how can you?"

"Oh, my dear, there is no harm in a joke which everybody understands."

"Everybody may understand it, but it does not follow that it is in good taste."

"There is nevertheless some sense in what Bingley has said," observed Mr. Bennet seriously. "Wakeford is evidently one of those puritanical persons who sees danger in delight and perversity in beauty. He would regard a handsome woman as a temptation to be resisted. But then—for I suspect that like all puritans he has strong passions—though he resisted he might fall."

"I agree with Jane that in charity one should not discuss the absent," said Elizabeth quietly, for mention of Wakeford recalling Georgiana's presence in the hall, she felt for the embarrassment or worse that any further stroke of unconsidered speech might inflict on tender nerves. She turned after speaking to look for Georgiana, but she had gone—to her room probably to practise. Having still to inform her about Mason's accident and the new arrangement of sharing maids, she quitted the hall and went upstairs after her.

Georgiana was discovered walking up and down the room with her hands tightly locked together and staring before her with a look of such anguish that Elizabeth was struck dumb with amazement and dismay. For a moment or two they gazed at one another. On trying to pronounce her sister's name Elizabeth found her lips trembling. Georgiana seemed turned to stone, but suddenly she was so overcome that she burst into sobs which racked her frame. Elizabeth stood quietly beside her, knowing that until she had wept awhile she would not speak; but by a touch, a gently uttered word, she strove to soothe her.

"What is the matter?" she murmured. "Tell me if you wish to—if you can. I long to help you."

At last Georgiana said brokenly, "I do wish to tell you, Elizabeth. It is all so dreadful that I thought I never could—and yet I must. I can bear it no longer."

Stammering and confused, at times incoherent and barely comprehensible, she told her story, but Elizabeth, her faculties stretched to the utmost, began at last to piece it together into an intelligible sequence of events.

On Major Wakeford's coming to Pemberley Georgiana had at first shrunk from him less on account of his austerity of manner and speech than because of his crippled and maimed condition. Her solitary pursuits had preserved some childishness of thought which, with her extreme sensibility, made her regard such misfortune as she witnessed for the first time as dreadful and beyond possibility of mitigation. Major Wakeford was an object of pity, but more of awe, and for some time she could not overcome her shyness of him. Then as he gradually regained the use of his leg and began to enter into the life around him, her fear of him diminished and she found herself talking to him as naturally as to anyone else in the house and taking some pleasure in his society. His reserve, too, began to melt; he would seek her out of his own accord and converse of things in which she avowed an interest. They discovered tastes in common—a love of all natural objects, of birds and beasts, and all the varieties of vegetation, of the light and sparkle of running water and the silken surface of a lake. In exploring each other's minds they drew insensibly nearer, without any of the constraint that so often marks the intercourse of two persons of the opposite sex in the course of mutual attraction.

Elizabeth imagined that Wakeford did not suspect himself of harbouring any feeling towards Georgiana but that of brotherly affection, and perhaps—though a doubt did remain in her mind—it was no more. But in his esteem she had risen high; he admired her for her gentleness, her modesty and seriousness as well as for her accomplishments, and she probably inspired in him the idea of an almost flawless character. Such men seeking moral perfection and persuaded that it can be found do exist, and Wakeford was one of them.

Then suddenly all was changed. A difference in Wakeford's manner became discernible from the evening when Georgiana and Acworth had performed their duet. Thence-forward he ceased to address her except in observing the forms of civility, and no longer approached her voluntarily as he had been used to do. Georgiana was first surprised, then hurt; she searched her conscience for any cause of offence, and finding nothing to repent of, almost resolved to ask him what she had done to displease him. But no opportunity came her way and her courage was not equal to making one. Not only her courage, but her confidence in herself failed her; she felt powerless against his set purpose of shunning her society.

At last, however, they met one day by chance in the picture-gallery. Wakeford instantly made a movement of with-drawal, but Georgiana, rendered desperate, stood in his path and impulsively uttered the question she had so often rehearsed in secret. He replied awkwardly that she was mistaken—he was not in the least offended, having indeed no cause. "Then why do you avoid me?" she demanded next. He seemed to hesitate, she related, whether to answer or not, and while he delayed, Mr. Bennet appeared at the entrance to the gallery and came strolling through it, as he often did, to admire his daughter Elizabeth's portrait. The matter was thus decided; nothing further could be said between them, and covered with confu-sion at having betrayed herself unavailingly she got away as quickly as she could.

The nature of her self-betrayal was never explicitly stated, but Elizabeth understood well enough that she had discovered herself to be in love with Wakeford. No other inference was possible. Wakeford, modest though he was, must have guessed as much, and from a scrupulous sense of honour had acted in such a manner as to discourage any hopes of requital.

She had leisure for these reflections; for Georgiana broke down and wept again, and it was some minutes before she could go on. Nothing further had happened until the day of the expedition to Clopwell. At mention of Clopwell Elizabeth was moved to ask how Acworth had behaved in the attic. She was unable to collect much more than she had heard and observed for herself, for Georgiana had scarcely heeded him in the unceasing flow of her own wretched thoughts, and had imputed whatever was strange or even preposterous to the habitual extravagance of his speech when alone with her. Acworth in her opinion was on the whole a pitiful figure of a man.

"I am sorry for him," she said. "He has great gifts but no proper means of using them. I do not think he intends any harm at all to anyone; but he makes enemies. It is his constant theme that he is so often misunderstood."

"He invites misunderstanding," said Elizabeth dryly.

Georgiana went on to describe the scene when her brother and Major Wakeford burst into the attic and Elizabeth had fainted. Her brother had been wholly occupied in attending to his wife; Wakeford had avoided looking directly at Georgiana, but she felt him to be very angry, and the knowledge of having exposed herself to his disapprobation and contempt made her utterly miserable. The rest of the day—the return home in the rain, Lady Catherine's unexpected arrival, the necessity of appearing her usual self throughout the evening made all seem like a bad dream. She passed a sleepless night.

The next day she came downstairs to breakfast hardly knowing how to support the ordeal of being in the same room with Wakeford. On quitting the breakfast-parlour she was pursued by Kitty and, unable to shake her off, had to listen to a stream of chatter about Mortimer. In the course of comparing him to other young men—greatly, of course, to their disadvantage—Kitty embarked on a tirade against Wakeford for his silence, his gloom, his assumption of moral superiority to everyone else and a host of other unamiable qualities. Georgiana defended him, and this led to an exchange in which Kitty's incautious tongue ran away with her. She said as usual a great deal to no purpose, but among other opinions without rational foundation she asserted that Wakeford was in love with Georgiana, and having become jealous of her apparent preference for Acworth, was now sulking.

Kitty may or may not have been serious; she may have said what she did to raise a laugh, but the idea of such jealousy having never before been conceived by Georgiana, it made a powerful impression on her mind as affording an explanation of everything that had distressed and perplexed her. A light was thrown upon words, looks and actions which had been incomprehensible at the time, but now arose in her mind to confirm the flattering supposition. Among the more trivial details thus recalled, the circumstance of being found alone with Acworth in the attic at Clopwell gained an importance not to be dismissed. It must have given material support to the view that Acworth was to be favoured.

Hope dawned once more, for a cause having been assigned to the misunderstanding, it could now be set right. She had seen Wakeford quit the house after breakfast and walk off into the rain; from an upper window she had observed the direction he had taken. Without any positive assurance of meeting him abroad she resolved to go out into the grounds as soon as the rain ceased on the chance of doing so.

For some time she rambled about, keeping within sight of the house and all the paths leading to it that she might not miss him when he returned. But at last, becoming sensible of the impractibility of the scheme from the little privacy it would afford for any intimate conversation she gave it up, and with it all hope of an encounter, and walked away into the woods.

At a distance of about two miles off she came out of the trees on a road which ran beside the park boundary and there met Wakeford face to face. She was unable to say whether Wakeford had showed perturbation, the turmoil of her own sensations having left her without the power of judgment. In such a place they could hardly pass without speaking, and after standing awhile with averted eyes to utter a few commonplace observations on the weather and the state of the paths it was inevitable that they should turn together to go homewards.

Not much was said in the beginning of their walk. Georgiana's heart was beating wildly and she could not control her voice. Wakeford seemed unwilling to converse. Had he exerted himself to talk they might have reached home without incident, but Georgiana began to interpret his silences as a determination not to have anything to do with her, and this had the effect he would probably most have wished to avert. Her indignation reached a point when further reticence suddenly became intolerable and she asked him abruptly what he had against her.

For a moment, she related, he appeared overcome by astonishment and confusion—it was evident that he did not know what to say. Then he replied harshly that she must be mistaken, he had no feeling of that sort whatever. "Then why," she cried impetuously, "do you never speak to me now? Why do you avoid me? Your behaviour to me has so changed that everybody must notice it. What have I done? It is only just that I should know."

Wakeford seemed at a complete loss. He repeated in a low voice that she was in error, but his countenance was giving the lie to his statement. Georgiana was now almost frantic; she had reached a pitch of agitation when she cared not what she said.

"A week ago," she continued with the same vehemence, "we were able to talk freely, without reserve. Then suddenly all was different. If I had been guilty of some crime you could not have shown greater aversion. My conscience is clear; I have done nothing to merit such treatment. But I can guess what has offended you, though altogether unjustifiably. You think I am partial to Mr. Acworth because I allowed him to come to my sitting-room on several occasions to play his violin with me. It is no such thing; I have no feeling towards him; he has no power at all over me, only yourself—"

Having blurted out this admission Georgiana was unable to proceed. Wakeford said no word; she dared not so much as glance at him and the silence became dreadful. Then in a voice of the coldest constraint he began to assure her that she was mistaken; he had the highest opinion of her—the very highest. He added gravely that he did not think Acworth the best companion for a young lady, but he was relieved to know that he could not influence her. "I beg you to believe that I have your truest happiness very much at heart," he said steadily.

Tortured by shame Georgiana walked on without speaking, while Wakeford said not a syllable more. The longer the silence between them lasted the more difficult it was to break it until it became impossible. The final words had in fact been uttered, for they avoided each other during the rest of the day and next morning Wakeford had taken his departure.

Such was Georgiana's story. It was now for Elizabeth to administer what consolation she could.

"I know what you must be suffering, poor child," she said. "At present you believe your unhappiness will endure for ever and that life can hold out no prospect that will make it worth living. But time is indeed a great healer and not long hence you will begin to experience some relief. For when hope is dead, resignation takes its place, and in resignation there is balm. You may even find that your attachment was after all only transient. Seriously," she continued, "I do not think you would have been happy with him. I doubt whether you would have suited each other. He is much older than yourself—older indeed than his years. He lacks cheerfulness. He would have taken you away from all you hold most dear, from your beloved home and the friends that love and understand you to surroundings which by all accounts are of an old-fashioned rusticity, where your gifts would have remained buried and forgotten. For the violence of first love does not last, Georgiana. Either it becomes something higher and nobler founded upon a deep harmony of thought and feeling between two beings, or it departs, leaving behind it only certain ties of interest and custom."

Much more she said to the same effect while Georgiana

listened with bowed head and became calm and composed. Resignation was perhaps already doing its work.

There came a moment when it seemed best to leave her alone, for her wandering gaze seemed to be asking for solitude. She had not slept the last two nights, and after seeing her laid upon her bed and lightly covered over Elizabeth stole away.

Deeply affected by Georgiana's suffering, she herself was in no humour for any society but her own and would gladly have remained apart for the next few hours, but on her way to her dressing-room she was overtaken by Jane who came to announce an event which everybody had expected.

"Oh, Lizzy," she said with an air of serious happiness, "I was just looking for you. Kitty and Mortimer have now come in from their walk and say they are engaged. Father was in the library, and they went to him at once and obtained his consent. How pleased Mamma will be!"

"Kitty is indeed fortunate," said Elizabeth coolly. "An amiable, easy-going husband and Clopwell Priory into the bargain. And now, I suppose, I must hurry downstairs to welcome Mortimer into the family."

Chapter 18

KITTY'S ENGAGEMENT BROUGHT HER into a prominence which she would have found wholly delightful had it not drawn upon her Lady Catherine's particular attention. In her ladyship's apprehension a portionless miss (for what is a thousand pounds?) was quite beneath her notice in the ordinary way; but an engagement, whoever the parties, must always excite the strongest feelings, whether of jubilation or the reverse, and Lady Catherine was not slow to express her very great surprise at Mr. Mortimer with the utmost frankness, or to prophesy that the marriage would turn out badly, assisted by her conviction of never having been proved wrong in any single previous instance. This, however, did not discourage her from giving Kitty the benefit of that advice which her superior wisdom made so extremely valuable.

"It is customary for a young lady to be married from her own home," said she, "but in the present case I do not recommend it. Your sister, Mrs. Darcy, who has a tolerable taste in dress—

though not equal to Miss de Bourgh's—can give you all the assistance you may require on that head. All preparations can be made here. You need not return to Hertfordshire."

Lady Catherine had learnt from her former dealings with Mrs. Darcy to reserve the most candid of her utterances until the lady was not present to hear them. She now became sensible of being at a serious disadvantage among her niece-in-law's relations, in finding them a vexatious check upon that freedom of speech she so greatly cherished. Mr. Bennet was so misguided as to prefer his own opinions as to what was for his daughter's good; Mrs. Gardiner, though with all the deference due to exalted rank, likewise declined instruction, and even Mrs. Bingley could not be brought to agree entirely with her ladyship's views concerning the unsuitability of the match. There remained her own nephew and niece. Georgiana appeared either not to be giving her whole and undivided attention or to be rather deaf; and Darcy, though invariably polite, couched his replies to her observations in terms which left nothing further to be said. Alone with him one day, she profited by the occasion to speak out plainly.

"Mrs. Darcy will be well-advised to press on the wedding with all despatch. Mr. Mortimer is a simple, unaffected young man—I like him excessively—but he may begin to feel that he could have done very much better."

"I cannot imagine that Mortimer would hold himself superior to a connection by marriage with the Darcys of Pemberley House," said Darcy thoughtfully.

Sad would have been Lady Catherine's predicament but for the most civil attentions of Mr. Acworth. Polite, unassuming, sympathetic, he was all that she could desire to keep her in a cheerful humour. At her request he walked and talked with her and her daughter, sat beside either one or the other at table, and occasionally drove out with them in their carriage.

She began to speak of him with enthusiasm. "He is a most delightful young man," she said to Georgiana, "so truly the gentleman. There is a something about the members of our aristocratic families that cannot be mistaken."

As Georgiana did not reply, and indeed looked as if she desired to escape, her aunt continued in her kindest manner, endeavouring to overcome her supposed reluctance to disobey the wishes of her brother in marrying a widower.

"I understand that he was not married above a year," she said. "That can hardly be called a marriage at all, and I would not regard it as such. Were I consulted I should have no hesitation whatever in saying that you could be happy with him."

Confused and distressed, Georgiana begged her aunt to desist from persuasion. "There is not, and never could be anything between myself and Mr. Acworth," she said with some vehemence. "I like him very well in some ways, but not in that way. I do not intend ever to marry."

"Nonsense, child," replied Lady Catherine. But from that time, despite her disinclination to drop an idea once adopted by her, she said no more on the subject and appeared to forget it.

Since the expedition to Clopwell Priory, Mr. Acworth's demeanour, perhaps from motives of prudence, had undergone a striking change. No longer did he obtrude himself upon the notice of those about him by a parade of sentiments and opinions likely to shock them, but in the course of a single night he had become silent, retiring and conforming. An alteration so strong could not pass without general remark, but it remained for Jane to rejoice. The improvement must be lasting, and as such tend to convince all who had hitherto doubted it, of the inherent goodness of human nature. In glowing terms she spoke to Elizabeth of the transformation that they had been privileged to witness.

"And what, do you suppose, has brought it about?" asked her sister.

"It may, nay it must be that in a period of reflection he has seen the error of his past ways, and is now seeking to mend them."

"Well, there is another explanation, and you shall hear it. My own belief is that his altered behaviour is merely a ruse to draw attention to himself. He is insatiable for notice, and having exhausted one form of display, has now hit upon another."

"You will never be serious, Lizzy," said Jane smiling. "Fortunately I know that you do not mean half that you say."

Coming upon her husband shortly afterwards, Elizabeth called on him to share her own private amusement at this fresh instance of Jane's incorrigible optimism.

"Jane is happier today than she has been this long while," she said.

"Indeed!" replied Darcy. "And what, may I ask, has produced her present felicity?"

"She has become convinced that Mr. Acworth is a reformed character. Her faith in mankind is therefore justified and established. One may well envy her."

"Decidedly," he returned. But instead of smiling at her dancing eyes he looked grave and some feeling of constraint was visible, while he turned uneasily in his chair.

"I have recently had some conversation with him," he said. "He agrees with me that it is not in his interests to stay here much longer, but the date of his departure is not yet fixed. Some days must still elapse."

"So soon?" cried Elizabeth. "What a relief! My poor Fitz, how your patience and forbearance must have been taxed by that young man in some of his moods. I feel now towards him as if he were already departed; one can speak freely but without rancour of his improprieties of speech and behaviour—everything that has rendered him obnoxious. At least I could, but Lady Catherine and I are calling at the Parsonage this afternoon, and I must go and get ready."

As she was quitting the room Darcy said, as if upon a sudden recollection, "I must tell you that Mr. Gardiner has written that his coming, which he hoped would be within a day or two, must be further delayed. His business still detains him."

"It is very long," said Elizabeth, raising her eyebrows.

"Yes," he replied. "A hitch has occurred—unavoidable. A relapse—the illness of the other gentleman concerned."

Elizabeth was really in a hurry to be upstairs dressing for her drive and could not stay to question him as she might have done.

"It is disappointing," she said, "for I begin to fear that he will not come at all. Does my aunt know?"

"Yes, she knows."

"I wonder she has not spoken of it to me. But wherever Lady Catherine is, the concerns of other people can have no place. Adieu, my love, I must indeed go. I assume that you send your compliments to the Miss Robinsons."

Lady Catherine had a numerous acquaintance around Pemberley from having stayed there frequently when her sister, Lady Anne Darcy, was alive. Every dame and dowager within ten miles was a very old and dear friend of hers, grown dearer in retrospect, perhaps, than in the past. She delighted in visiting them all, and each day the carriage bore herself and her daughter away to some touching reunion. Elizabeth did not always accompany them, but sometimes she thought it expedient to do so, and that morning, Lady Catherine having announced her intention of descending upon the Parsonage later in the day, her conscience prompted her to seize the opportunity of paying off her own duty in that quarter. Her ladyship, she discovered too late, had made up her mind to a longer visit than usual that she might have a good long talk with that excellent Miss Robinson. Very often did the carriage stop at the Parsonage, but sometimes the Miss Robinsons were merely called to the door, or at other times Lady Catherine entered the house but to make a few friendly enquiries on her way to somebody else's mansion. Approving most heartily as she did of the Miss Robinsons, she was not disposed to neglect the prior claims of rank and consequence in the bestowal of her attentions. The ladies of the Parsonage must wait their turn.

That turn had however come, and Lady Catherine set off in a complacent and gracious humour. No one, thought Elizabeth, as she sat beside her, had ever extracted more unalloyed pleasure from her kind actions. The sense of conferring a boon was felt in the highest degree, and that proportionate gratitude must follow was never doubted.

The Miss Robinsons had been warned to expect Lady

Catherine and her daughter and were dressed in their best to receive her. After the first formalities had passed and chairs had been proffered and accepted, cake and wine were brought in, partaken of by all and pronounced by Lady Catherine to be excellent. Some talk of home-brewed wines ensued—none could compare with those made by the Rosings housekeeper— and after a polite acquiescence to save breath and dispute Elizabeth found herself with nothing more to say upon the subject. She had taken a seat near the window which looked out upon a very pretty view of the garden, now at the height of its flowering. Glancing outwards over her shoulder in the design of bringing forward a fresh topic between herself and Miss Sophia, she saw Acworth issue from an espaliered walk and approach the house as though about to enter it. So sudden was his appearance that she was unable to repress a start. Before she could turn away her head again he had reached the window, stopped and looked in. Instantly she lowered her eyes and resuming her former attitude observed upon his presence to Miss Sophia.

"I did not know that Mr. Acworth was here," Miss Sophia said without surprise, "but he is so much at home with us that he comes and goes as he chooses. Sister and I are quite accustomed to see him walk into the room unannounced."

From her manner of speaking Elizabeth collected that she, at any rate, was ignorant that very shortly the gentleman would no more be seen walking in and out of the Parsonage. Before she had leisure for further reflections the door opened and Acworth walked in. On seeing the company he looked astonished and began an apology for his intrusion, but Lady Catherine welcomed him with such unfeigned delight, and was so pressing in her invitation to him to join them that with a show of embarrassment he obeyed and seated himself modestly in a corner of the room. If obscurity and neglect were what he truly desired, Lady Catherine was not in the least disposed to gratify him. She ordered him forward with playful authority and kept him talking by asking his opinion on every subject that was mentioned. The Miss Robinsons eagerly seconded her exertions and soon he was made to appear the principal person in the room. Elizabeth thought that he did not much like these attentions; he looked distinctly uneasy and soon began glancing towards the door as if he wished to be away again.

Lady Catherine had never made a secret of her pleasure in the society of handsome young men. She loved them all, and was persuaded that they loved her in return. They probably experienced varying degrees of warmth in her affection, for she was noticeably more encouraging as a rule to those of higher rank or greater fortune. Although Mr. Acworth was indubitably the son of an earl, he was the youngest of several brothers, and were appearances to be trusted, had no more than the bare means wherewith to support his situation in life. Notwithstanding these drawbacks Lady Catherine was as attentive to him as if he were his eldest brother and as rich as Croesus. Had she been a younger woman an observer might have supposed her enamoured. Regarding herself as beyond criticism, and therefore scorning concealment, she made none of his power to charm her, and whenever she addressed or looked at him her countenance proclaimed her very strong partiality. She could not behold him without smiling broadly.

Such open admiration at length proved too much even for Acworth's vanity, and having consumed his cake and wine, after a suitable interval he asked Miss Robinson's leave to retire to the study that he might write a pressing letter. Elizabeth rather expected that Lady Catherine would show displeasure or pique—it was plain that she did not want to lose him, but as at the moment he could do no wrong, she commended his industry while relinquishing him with regret.

As soon as the door had closed behind him she burst into eulogy of his several perfections. He was the most delightful young man in the world, so truly the gentleman, so extremely clever and accomplished, an acquisition to the highest society. Miss Robinson, while heartily agreeing and supplying superlatives on her own account, lamented his delicate health. He would have been the very rector for Pemberley, but most unfortunately the climate of Derbyshire did not suit his constitution, he feared what he had heard of the winter. Miss Sophia, with ears only for the subject which interested her beyond all others, made one or two vain attempts to draw Mrs. Darcy into the chorus of praise. Any other conversation at the same time was in truth well-nigh impossible, the vigour, authority, and vociferation of Lady Catherine precluding it.

Curiosity and diversion as well as disdain kept Elizabeth silent. She wondered how far Lady Catherine and Miss Robinson would go in defiance of the sense and moderation proper to their age. But at length it occurred to her that Anne de Bourgh, likewise silent, might want for entertainment, and seeing her eyes stray towards the window, she invited her to a chair near her own. After a little hesitation Anne came, and looking out upon the garden observed that it was very pretty, much prettier than the one at Hunsford. Having said thus much she seemed disinclined to say any more, and cast down her eyes in what appeared a reverie. Elizabeth therefore had no choice but to continue listening to Lady Catherine and Miss Robinson.

"Sir Lewis de Bourgh could never endure the winter at Pemberley," said Lady Catherine. "We spent one Christmas here—I shall never forget. As soon as Sir Lewis was able to travel after the festivities were over we returned to Rosings. There he revived immediately and I recall his saying that it would be the last time he visited Derbyshire. He spoke truly— it was the last time. Mr. Acworth has the same delicate appearance as Sir Lewis—he is far from robust. The mild climate of Kent would, I am persuaded, suit him infinitely better than Pemberley. The short distance of Hunsford from London makes it extremely eligible as a place of residence. He would be able to visit his brother, Lord Egbury, and other friends in town whenever he chose."

Elizabeth looking just then at Anne saw that although her eyes were still fixed upon the ground she was listening intently to her mother.

"Poor young man," said Miss Robinson. "How well your ladyship understands the matter."

"At Rosings he would be rated at his true worth," continued Lady Catherine. "He would receive rather more consideration than—I flatter myself that I enter into his thoughts and feelings perfectly."

"I am sure he could not have a better or kinder friend, madam," interjected Miss Robinson. "I and my sister have done our best to make him at home in our own house, but unfortunately we are not everybody."

"You can do much, my dear Miss Robinson," replied Lady Catherine, "but you cannot improve the climate of Derbyshire. Even I cannot do that. If everyone were as reasonable as yourself! There is such a thing, you know, as an exchange of livings."

"An exchange of livings!" echoed both the Miss Robinsons.

"Certainly. Nothing is easier. It must be done every day. Mr. Collins, I am sure, would be perfectly agreeable to the transfer, and even if he were for a moment undecided, I have no doubt I could overcome any hesitation on his part."

"But, your ladyship," cried Miss Sophia in a state of alarm, supposing the business to be already accomplished, "what are *we* to do? For you know we had settled it that if Mr. Acworth stayed we could all live together in this house; but Mr. Collins is a family man according to what we hear, and if he came he would very likely require us to quit the Parsonage immediately."

"I do not see the least necessity," said Lady Catherine kindly. "The matter could be compromised to the satisfaction of all parties with a little good will—the slightest disposition to yield a point on the part of *some*. This house, so suitable for yourselves, would be much too large for the Collinses; they would be at a loss to furnish the half of it. Some smaller house could doubtless be found that would satisfy *their* modest requirements."

"Yes, indeed," said Miss Robinson. "Yew Tree Cottage is still empty, I believe."

"Capital," cried Lady Catherine. "Nothing could be better, I am sure. Now if only what we have planned with such ease as we sit here could readily be put into execution, how many people would be benefited! You and I, Miss Robinson, see what should be done. It remains only to convince others of its suitability."

At this point Elizabeth resolved that such insolent disregard of the proprieties as that Lady Catherine and Miss Robinson should dare to settle Darcy's business for him in his wife's presence could no longer be tolerated. Commanding herself to speak calmly, even lightly, she broke into their conversation.

"It is fortunate for Mr. Acworth's modesty, madam, that he is not present to be embarrassed by your kind schemes for his future happiness. May I congratulate you on your discrimination of his valuable qualities. But as regards Mr. Collins, I do not for one moment suppose that Mr. Darcy would consider a second application from him after refusing a first."

The effect of her words was what she expected. Lady Catherine drew herself up haughtily, but could not disguise her amazement, or her discomfiture at being told something of which she had been ignorant.

"Do I hear aright?" she enquired, deeply offended. "Am I to understand that Mr. Collins has dared to apply for the living of Pemberley without first consulting me?"

"Apparently so," Elizabeth replied with a smile. "I must apologise for my better information, my husband having shown me Mr. Collins' letter."

"I am surprised that Darcy did not inform me of it," said Lady Catherine in accents of resentment. "But as he refused the application he may have thought it unnecessary to distress me. If there is anything I abhor it is deceit of any kind. That and ingratitude are not to be borne. I had not thought, however, that Mr. Collins was sunk so low as to go behind my back."

Elizabeth made no reply, and Lady Catherine, anxious to turn from a subject which had occasioned her some loss of dignity, informed Miss Robinson that she wished to see the garden.

Nothing could ever be done at the Parsonage without fuss or trouble, and the Miss Robinsons must be properly bonnetted and shawled for the open air before they could usher their visitors through the garden door. A sort of procession was then formed. Miss Robinson and Lady Catherine led the way, and Miss Sophia, Elizabeth and Anne de Bourgh were to dawdle along behind them. But they had not gone more than a few yards from the house when Mr. Acworth suddenly stepped through the study window, and overtaking them, asked Miss Sophia whether he might join their party. Before half a sentence of delighted permission could be uttered he had offered his arm to Anne de Bourgh, and Elizabeth now walking in front with Miss Sophia heard him endeavouring to converse with his companion by asking her the names of the plants to be seen as they went along. As in most instances she was able to inform him confidently and correctly, the conversation between them became almost animated. From horticulture they soon passed away, and Acworth set himself to entertain the lady with a flow of lively anecdote and description which Elizabeth, obliged to give her attention to Miss Sophia, could only hear as sounding infinitely entertaining. Whenever he talked thus his countenance was enlivened with a sparkling of eyes and a play of the mouth which gave it a peculiar charm. Anne said little in return, but on the whole company stopping to admire an apricot tree which promised an abundant fruiting, Elizabeth saw that her usually pale face had quite a becoming colour and looked almost happy.

The visitors did not stay very much longer. Acworth handed

the ladies into the carriage but declined a seat in it. He must walk, he said, for the sake of his health. He had quite got into the habit of walking in the woods for the refreshment and peace it gave him. There was no persuading him otherwise, nor mistaking his positive intention not to be inveigled into accompanying them. Lady Catherine saw nothing to be offended at, but Elizabeth thought that Anne looked vexed and disappointed.

On the drive back to Pemberley House Lady Catherine could not leave the subject of her favourite. "I really cannot bear to think of parting with him," said she, "for I do not know when I have seen a young man who pleases me as much as he does. He must come to Rosings as soon as we return home on a long visit. Would not you like that, Anne?"

Anne murmured her usual listless assent, but her expression became thoughtful. Once she smiled to herself; it was a peculiar smile and instantly checked after a furtive glance at Elizabeth who, though seeing it, contrived not to meet her eyes.

As for Elizabeth, while replying to Lady Catherine whenever it became necessary, she sat revolving in her mind the suspicion, so strong as to amount to conviction, that Anne was in love with Acworth. The symptoms, subdued though they were in such an insipid creature, were not to be mistaken. It was not extraordinary, for Acworth had exhibited himself at his best to both mother and daughter, and his best was singularly pleasing. He could not, of course, have any serious intentions; his character forbade it, and he had besides made it perfectly plain that he had not.

But there are none so blind as those that will not see, and

once Lady Catherine had taken it into her head to desire a thing she was not easily to be baulked of its attainment. So completely charmed with Acworth was she that she might very soon think of making him her son-in-law if she had not already conceived the idea. Everything pointed to this consummation—his eligibility in point of birth and connections and the mother's determination to marry off her daughter as soon as possible. The only objection to the match was one that Lady Catherine could at present know nothing of—his shocking propensity to make love to every woman he met. But perhaps in this instance even that would not be accounted so very great an obstacle, since once he is married a man cannot help being a husband, whether good, bad or indifferent; and Lady Catherine, very much a woman of the world, might be willing to compound an occasional flirtation or straying out of bounds provided nothing of the sort was enacted before her eyes.

Chapter 18

ON REACHING HOME LADY Catherine and her daughter went
straight to their own apartments, but Elizabeth, feeling unwilling
to rest or settle to any indoor occupation, would have walked out
again to be active and in silent communion with her own
thoughts, had not the chance of an encounter with Acworth
presented itself as a risk to be avoided. Such companionship as
would have been welcome was equally denied her, for Darcy, Mr.
Bennet and Bingley were away for the day fishing in a neighbour's
waters and would not be home much before the dinner hour,
while Mrs. Gardiner, with Jane and Kitty had driven into
Lambton to shop and visit some friends, and Georgiana had
proposed visiting an old servant of the family who had attended
her in childhood. Only the children were to be found in their
own quarters, and anticipating her last visit in the day to them by
a short half-hour, she went to the nursery.

  She opened the door to find Georgiana with Richard in her
lap singing to him a song that had charmed her own infant ears,

while Jane's little daughter Harriet leaned against her knee. Richard sat perfectly still gazing up at his aunt with a solemn expression in his eyes, so enthralled that he did not see his mother until she was close upon him. But her arrival soon changed everything; he must be jumped about and rolled over and romped with according to a rule that he would by no means have broken, and the game must moreover continue until the appearance of the children's supper put an end to it, and even then his mother must sit beside him or watch him proudly feed himself with his own silver spoon. Then, and not till then, might she be allowed to go without an immoderate clamour.

Elizabeth's doubts about her son's character would arise from time to time in spite of Darcy's assurances that at Richard's age he had been exactly the same. But a child of such remarkable intelligence who was always thinking of something fresh to do could hardly help being a trouble to those about him, and enlarging upon the latest evidences of his forward understanding, she led Georgiana away from the nursery as far as the hall. There a common wish to be out of doors was expressed; they stepped out upon the gravel of the terrace and soon were in the garden walking between the rosebeds.

Since the day when Georgiana had confessed her unhappy love for Wakeford, Elizabeth had not had any further private conversation with her. To ordinary view Georgiana was not much different from her ordinary self; there were no signs of weeping or sleeplessness. But the state of the heart is not easily perceived, for habit and obligation can lend a mask of indifference to the countenance and can even summon an appetite at the sight of food. Hope and despair were equally absent from her aspect, and although she could hardly be expected to take pleasure in the diversions going forward around her, she did not shun them. What she must be feeling inwardly, Elizabeth could only guess at and commiserate.

The roses were blooming that season as never before and were now at the height of their profusion. Wherever they walked a rich diversity of colour met the eye on every side. Elizabeth gazed, lost in delight, and was almost startled when Georgiana suddenly addressed her.

"Elizabeth, I have something to tell you which you may be glad to hear. I have quite got over the feeling I had for Major Wakeford. It may seem strange to you, indeed it does so to me, but it is none the less certain."

Elizabeth caught her arm and pressed it affectionately. "Oh, Georgiana," she cried, "I cannot tell you how happy I am to hear you say so. I feared you must be suffering still. But how has it happened?"

"I believe I have *willed* myself out of it. It was chiefly what you said that weighed with me. You tried to convince me that the match would not have been a happy one and after a little I began to see that you were right. So by refusing to let my thoughts dwell upon him, by incessant occupation and staying in company, even though I would rather have been alone, the cure was effected. I am no longer sensible of any pain or regret."

Elizabeth marvelled, but in silence, that so severe a wound as it had seemed at the time had been so rapid in healing. Was the cure true and perfect, she wondered, or but the temporary insensibility that follows upon an excess of suffering? Fortunately it was not likely to be re-opened by Wakeford's return.

"It is strange that I used to think you had a partiality for Mr. Acworth," said she smiling.

"Mr. Acworth! Oh, no. I could never care for anyone who was not a great deal better and wiser than myself, and he is not that. I do indeed like him for many things; he can be a delightful companion, amusing, witty, and yet full of serious feeling, but he is too wayward and changeable. And I do not think he is to be trusted—especially since I saw him one day with Rachel."

"Rachel Stone!" ejaculated Elizabeth.

"Yes, I came upon them one day in a passage in the east wing. He had his arm around her and she was looking up at him in a very saucy manner. They did not see me—at least I believe not. I had just turned a corner when I saw them in the distance, and I felt so embarrassed that I withdrew at once."

"You said nothing at the time, Georgiana."

"No, because I did not like to speak of it. It would have sounded so much worse than perhaps it was, for I have heard that gentlemen do behave rather familiarly to serving-maids without meaning any harm. I did, however, say something to Rachel when she next came to my room. I said that I had seen her talking to one of the gentlemen visitors and that I hoped she had not done so except as a matter of service."

Elizabeth had to laugh at such a mild reproof to a girl so bold and brazen. "What did she say?" she enquired.

"She said she had no notion who the gentleman could be, but she was sure she would not have been speaking to him unless he had required something of her."

"That last part is probably the literal truth," said Elizabeth. "The circumstance reflects more discredit on Mr. Acworth than

Rachel, but I would not hold a brief for either of them. When did it happen?"

"Two or three days ago."

"Then since the improvement in his manners we have all applauded. Like children when deep in mischief he has become very quiet. But I will confess to you, Georgiana, that I am very sorry that I took Rachel into my service. I begin to see that it was a mistake. She is not a good girl and may prove a bad example to the other maids. As soon as Mason can resume her duties I shall place her elsewhere."

"I do think she is rather artful," said Georgiana.

"Well, I know I shall be thankful to have Mason back again. Reynolds says that she is in the greatest anxiety for fear of not being able to dress me for the ball."

"I cannot say I much look forward to the ball," said Georgiana.

"Nor I," agreed Elizabeth. "But I dare say we shall find it agreeable enough when it is upon us."

The evening passed away in the manner ordained by Lady Catherine for the promotion of her pleasure and likewise of her designs upon Mr. Acworth, which were now perfectly open and unmistakable. The lady's intentions to the gentleman were positively overwhelming and plainly embarrassed him, and looks were exchanged between one and another when she distinguished him in a way to cover him with confusion. Ridiculous as it was, and even laughable, it bred a discomfort in Elizabeth amounting to consternation, and it surprised her that her husband should show no sign of the concern he ought to feel, and could look on and listen with steady indifference while his aunt paid court to the most unsuitable object she could have selected.

What Anne was thinking was not easily determined. She behaved discreetly inasmuch as she maintained her usual rather insipid composure, as if hardly knowing what was afoot; but an occasional look of quiet complacency diffused over her features spoke of Lady Catherine's manoeuvres being not unpleasing to her. On the whole Elizabeth was sorry for Acworth. No man enjoys being wooed by a would-be mother-in-law even when his inclination is not averse to the daughter, but in the present instance the latter idea was too improbable to be considered for a moment. Once Elizabeth caught him glance at herself, look away and bite his lip and frown.

"What are your schemes for tomorrow, Mr. Acworth?" Lady Catherine called out to him towards the end of the evening. "If you are not otherwise engaged I must positively have you call with me on my very old friend, Lady Mary Harlowe. When she was here on Thursday she told me she had been at school with your mother, Lady Egbury, and was most urgent that I should bring you to see her."

Looking acutely uncomfortable, Acworth muttered something inaudible in reply.

Soon afterwards Lady Catherine rose to retire for the night. "Late hours do not suit Anne," said she. "When nerves are of such delicate refinement as hers long periods of repose are indispensable," adding as an afterthought, "but she is able to support fatigue a great deal better than she could a year or two ago. I am excessively astonished at the improvement in her health."

There had been a general uprising at the first sign of Lady Catherine's withdrawal, and the party was collected in a loose throng near her ladyship awaiting the cue for bow or curtsy.

Elizabeth had just stepped aside from bidding Lady Catherine good-night to give place to Darcy when she happened to catch sight of a look of peculiar significance in Anne de Bourgh's countenance. It seemed directed at someone and was both sly and pleased. So startled was she that she turned her head sharply to discover the recipient of the look. She saw Bingley laughing with Kitty and Mortimer, and Acworth moving away behind them. So Anne had arrived at intelligence with Acworth! "She is progressing," thought Elizabeth, "she is learning how to play her fish."

There was some lingering after the Darcys' most important guests had withdrawn, some reminiscent chatting about the day's sport between the gentlemen, some canvassing at large of plans for the morrow; but at last there was no more to be said, and no further desire but for sleep. This for Elizabeth was the hour when she might hope for unrestrained communication with her husband, when after hours of unremitting circumspec-tion she could say freely all that was in her mind—and even more—at no risk of being indiscreet or misunderstood, and hear what he had to say in reply, whether it was something to tell that added to their common knowledge, or an expression of his riper judgment. But no sooner had she reached her dressing-room when a message was delivered importing that something was amiss with Richard; he had suddenly been taken ill. Hastily removing her dress and throwing a wrapper about her she sped to the night nursery, all else forgotten in her anxiety for her son.

She found to her comfort that Mrs. Reynolds was there before her, and although Richard lay writhing as a young child does when in pain, the experienced old woman was perfectly composed, and showed nothing of alarm. Her countenance expressed all the compassion one must feel for helpless suffering, but also full assurance as to what should be done.

"I do think he must have eaten something he ought not to have had," she said in a low voice. "As I recollect, the children came to my room for their lollipops after their walk, and there was a basket of green gooseberries which had just been brought in for the servants' dinner. I did not see him go to the basket, but it was standing where he could reach it, and his little fingers are that quick he might have taken a few before I could have seen him."

"Mr. Roper!" exclaimed Elizabeth. "Is anyone about to fetch him? One of the servants must be roused."

"As you wish, ma'am. But I do not think it hardly necessary. A dose of medicine will give relief, I am sure it will. It is the same I used to give Mr. Darcy and Miss Georgiana when they were bilious or had eaten imprudently. If you will excuse me, ma'am, I will go and fetch it."

While Mrs. Reynolds was gone Elizabeth stood by Richard's cot watching him in a misery that more than equalled his own. He was not crying, but whimpering and tossing from side to side. She endeavoured to soothe him, but nothing could pacify him. It seemed to her a most alarming sign that he should want nothing of his mother. Her anguish made every moment seem an hour and she began impatiently and distractedly to call for Mrs. Reynolds when the housekeeper reappeared carrying a bottle and a spoon.

The dose was administered while Richard roared and woke up Jane's two children who until then had been fast asleep in their own little beds. They also began to cry and had to be tended and reassured. As the noise of Richard's paroxysms increased, to Elizabeth it appeared that he could not possibly survive; but seeing that Reynolds was still in confidence that he would recover, she exerted herself to remain calm. Thought was almost suspended while she watched and waited, and when she exclaimed suddenly, "Should not his father be sent for?" it occurred to her for the first time to wonder that he was not at her side.

But thought was again banished, for suspense came to an abrupt end. Nature, assisted by Mrs. Reynolds' medicine, rallied to Richard's relief and the cause of his disorder was forthwith removed. He lay at length quiet and exhausted, and as Elizabeth sat beside him and held one of his hands he fell peacefully asleep. Not until she was satisfied that she could relinquish his hand without waking him and stood up to steal from the room did she discover that Darcy was behind her.

"I was with Acworth and knew nothing of this, or I would have come sooner," he said as he led her away.

She was by now so spent that the name of Acworth awoke no echo in her mind. Lady Catherine, Anne, the Miss Robinsons—every idea connected with him was forgotten. She could think of nothing but her thankfulness that Richard was alive, out of pain and asleep. Seeing her fatigue, Darcy spoke only of the child and her need for repose.

"Reynolds says that Richard got at some green gooseberries. The rascal is at an age when everything edible he sees goes into his mouth. Do not distress yourself any longer, my own. Tomorrow he will be none the worse for it."

Elizabeth marvelled at his comparative unconcern. Did he not reflect that the gooseberries might very well have been poisonous berries? But she was too fatigued to take it up with him, and soon all was forgotten in the oblivion of exhaustion.

Chapter 20

On awaking the next morning, Elizabeth's first thought was for Richard, and though it was as yet earlier than her usual time for rising, she summoned her maid, and as soon as she was dressed went to the nursery.

Richard was still asleep, and although to a mother's anxious eye he did not look perfectly recovered, she was soon satisfied by his quiet and regular breathing that he was very much better and only needed ordinary care to be himself again. Having given instructions that he should not be roused until he awoke of his own accord, she went downstairs intending to take a turn in the garden before breakfast.

As she reached the foot of the staircase the door of the breakfast-parlour opened and Acworth came out followed by Darcy. She saw with surprise that he was dressed for travelling, and next that the front door was being held open by the servants and that a chaise waited without. Unable to comprehend what she saw, she remained standing and speechless, but Acworth looked round and instantly turned from his course and came towards her.

"I am quitting Pemberley forever," he said with an attempt at calm. "I feared—I had given up hope of seeing you before I left. It is scarcely probable that we shall meet again in this life. Farewell. May that happiness which has ever been denied me continue yours, now and always."

He spoke quietly, but with such melancholy in voice and aspect that she could find nothing to say in reply, until, sensible that Darcy had come to her side, she rallied her presence of mind and offering Acworth her hand, with calm propriety wished him a good journey. Its unexpectedness could hardly be spoken of from the suspicions it aroused, her own voice seemed insincere in her ears, and it was necessary to avert her eyes from his for they were fixed upon her with a despair which seemed to solicit an answering pity. For a moment he stood grasping her hand as if undetermined whether to go or stay, then raised it to his lips, turned precipitately and was gone. Darcy went slowly after him, and standing by the door of the chaise held a short colloquy with him as with an ordinary departing guest. Acworth entered the chaise; the horses started and bore him away.

"What has happened?" Elizabeth exclaimed when her husband rejoined her. "Why this sudden departure?"

"It had become necessary," he answered. "Lady Catherine—"

"Whatever will she say when she learns that he has gone?" she burst out.

"We shall soon hear. But to fix upon him as a son-in-law! It is no mere conjecture—I had it from her own mouth yesterday evening."

"It is impossible that a match between him and Anne could be considered. Unfortunately I am afraid that she has shown signs of liking him. But he has—could have—no intentions. There is nothing in her but her fortune to attract him."

"A man may have intentions without much personal inclination for the object arousing them," Darcy replied dryly. "A great fortune can be a great temptation, even though another woman claims his heart. But there could never be any question of such a match, as he himself is perfectly aware. If Lady Catherine knew all, she would be the first to acknowledge it."

"Whatever do you mean? Has something fresh come out that proves him worse than you supposed?"

"Much has come out. I cannot begin to tell you now, Elizabeth. Here comes Bingley. Another time—"

Before he could finish his sentence Bingley was with them, beaming with health and good spirits, eager for breakfast and for every enjoyment that a summer day can afford. They passed into the breakfast-parlour where gradually they were joined by the other members of the party until all were assembled excepting Mr. Bennet and Lady Catherine and her daughter. Mortimer, who had got into the habit of riding over to breakfast two days out of every three, came in with Kitty. Then Mr. Bennet made his appearance, and having uttered his usual comprehensive "Good morning to you all," turned to his daughter, Elizabeth, and said immediately, "So Acworth has gone away."

"How did you know?" cried Elizabeth.

"I happened to look out of my window as I was dressing and saw him getting into a chaise," replied her father. "That is how I know."

The exclamations and questions that instantly arose

required something to be said in explanation of this sudden and unexpected flight from Pemberley as it appeared to the enquirers. Why had he decamped? Whither had he gone? Was he coming back? Elizabeth, even more than those who knew less than herself, felt a curiosity to hear what Darcy would say in reply. That he was in a dilemma between the conflicting claims of veracity and discretion she could see from the fixity of his eyes which avoided everyone present.

"Acworth found himself compelled to leave very unexpectedly," he said. "He would have returned to London within the week in any case, but his private affairs were the cause of his going several days sooner."

Acworth gone became a being of the past. He began to be spoken of as one speaks of the dead.

"He was an odd fellow," said Bingley, "but I did not dislike him. If he was no sportsman he was certainly no prig either. He could tell a story in the drollest way imaginable, and his mimicry of persons was excellent."

"Nearly everybody improves on being better known," said Jane.

"Either improves or becomes insupportable," rejoined Mr. Bennet. "It is to Acworth's credit that he did neither. He remained very pleasingly dubious."

Elizabeth, at pains to look unconcerned while feeling an unsubduable agitation, began to be impatient for Lady Catherine to come down that the storm which she knew must burst forth on hearing tidings so destructive of hopes of a son-in-law should burst and be over. But it was her ladyship's prerogative to keep everybody waiting. At last, however, she did come, and her daughter with her, and the whole party could now gather round the table.

A few moments passed before Lady Catherine noticed Acworth's absence. She was in high good humour, in a mood of gracious condescension to everyone on whom her eye lighted, and Anne likewise seemed more cheerful than usual. Hope, if it was hope she entertained, had given her countenance something resembling animation and rendered it more interesting and attractive than it had ever before appeared. Able to guess the cause of her complacency, Elizabeth was heartily sorry for her. But she had no time to dwell on Anne's feelings when the sad business of a vanished suitor was unfolded; her real concern was all for her husband. Of stern necessity he must make a most unwelcome announcement, and as the unvarnished truth could not possibly be stated, he must so gloze it over as to do violence to those principles of candour and rectitude which lay at the foundation of his self-esteem. Deeply sympathising she watched him, she saw him turn towards Lady Catherine and open his mouth to speak, to say what must produce a most searching and awkward catechism in the answering of which he could hardly avoid uttering a direct falsehood. But before he could get out the first word Lady Catherine forestalled him.

"Acworth is surely very late in coming down this morning," she said indulgently. "Poor fellow, I trust he is not ill."

"It is indeed unfortunate, madam," Elizabeth quickly replied, "that Mr. Acworth has been obliged to quit us very unexpectedly, having been called away to London on the most urgent private business. As he could not stay to take leave of his friends in person, he asked me to express his very great regret for an omission he could not but deplore."

She dared not look directly at her husband, but felt him gazing at her, though whether more in sorrow or amazement she could not tell. Lady Catherine's whole person seemed to expand, while her eyes rolled in offended majesty.

"How is this?" she cried. "There was never a word of it last night. Why was I not told? I can hardly credit that he would go away without seeking to acquaint me of so important a decision. What does this mean, Darcy?"

"Your ladyship is doubtless aware that family matters may be of so delicate and intimate a nature that they cannot be canvassed in public," Darcy replied in his usual steady accents.

Lady Catherine seemed mollified. "True, very true," she said, her glance sweeping along the faces confronting her. "His modesty, his reserve would forbid it. With the exception of Anne I have never known anyone of a more refined sensibility. Poor young man! But I am confident we shall soon hear from him; he will not leave his best friends in ignorance of his concerns. Poor fellow, I thought he was not in his usual spirits last evening. He knew that he was to part from us and shrank from giving us pain. You must not be unhappy, Anne. It will not be long before we see him again. If he does not return here we shall all meet in London."

Everyone remained silent, though not from the same motives, for some were silent from prudence, others were awed, while others again were occupied in keeping a straight face. She continued in this strain for some time longer, until she had talked herself once more into perfect cheerfulness. It was not necessary to supply further fictitious details; she imagined them all. Elizabeth forbore to look at Anne, but when at last unable to avoid it, she turned her eyes that way, she saw that the daughter was no less contented than the mother. There was not the least sign that her composure had so much as been ruffled. It was cause for thankfulness indeed, and Elizabeth's relief that all had passed off so much better than might have been expected made her positively light-hearted.

Lady Catherine at length ceased, others began to speak, and suddenly Mortimer's strong slow voice was heard above all the rest.

"Do you know," said he, addressing the table in general, "I met Acworth's chaise as I was coming here. As soon as I saw it I wondered who could be quitting Pemberley at that hour, and as the horses were walking, for it was on the steepest part of the hill when I came up, I might have got down and spoken to him, but he was leaning back with his face in his hands, so I did not like to."

"Poor fellow," exclaimed Lady Catherine, unable to conceal her triumph, "what he must have been suffering!"

Elizabeth felt her cheeks grow hot in a discomfort impossible to overcome while Acworth continued to be spoken of. It seemed as though the subject were not to be let alone; when Lady Catherine left off, Mortimer, prompted by Kitty, must needs begin describing what he had seen all over again. Had it been any other matter to occasion awkwardness she could have signalled an entreaty to her husband to lead away from it, but the recollection of his having witnessed Acworth's emotion on parting from her deprived her of the courage to do so. Her father added to her confusion by murmuring in her ear from his seat beside her, "So you are not the only breaker of hearts, Lizzy!"

But the suspense of wondering and fearing what would be said next was shortly ended. With great self-denial Darcy introduced the name of his uncle, Lord Hartingford, into the

conversation, and it did not require much resolution to keep
Lady Catherine's tongue busy with a topic always fascinating to
her—the dignity, ancientness and importance of her family and
all those connected with it; and though it was well-nigh inexhaustible, for more than half the aristocracy of the kingdom
came within its purview through intermarriages, he was able to
contrive a juncture when the session was manifestly over, and a
concerted movement away from the table was seen to be desirable. Elizabeth was at liberty to leave her guests on the plea of
having to see Richard again. As she was passing out of the room
her husband came to her, and drawing her aside said quietly,
"When you have seen Richard come to my father's room. Come
in about half an hour." She nodded and went on.

It was difficult to contain her impatience until the whole half-
hour was over, for she was wild to be alone with him that they
might speak freely and she could hear what he had to tell her. It
passed, however, in the crowded scene of the nursery where,
besides the three children and their four nurses, there was Jane
visiting her two little girls and Reynolds come to see how Master
Richard was doing. Richard had to be looked at and felt and
coaxed to eat his breakfast and have a confabulation held over
him. Time wore away, and on looking at her watch Elizabeth found
that she was actually keeping Darcy waiting.

When she opened the door of his room he was walking up
and down as was his way if much perturbed. On seeing her he
stood still and looked at her searchingly.

"What is the matter?" she asked, going up to him and taking
his hand. "What has happened? I am quite frantic with suspense."

He looked down into her eyes. "I have to speak to you about

Acworth. I could not do so before, but now that he has gone you shall hear the truth. You understand that I sent him away?"

"Yes, I did—I guessed it. But it was impossible to tell them so. Something had to be said—something to be invented. I rushed into the breach. Ought I not to have done so? Perhaps I am more tender of your conscience than of my own."

Half in expectation of a remonstrance she found herself clasped to his heart. "That is a token of affection indeed," he said.

"Is any really needed?"

"No, not really. But a man likes to hear reassurance ringing in his ears."

"You are not asking much," she retorted. But she comprehended perfectly what moved him and continued, "And so does a woman. When you say that such and such a young lady is handsome or witty, I wait and wait—often in vain—for you to say that of course she cannot hold a candle to your wife."

"You know very well that for your husband you are a being apart, superlative and unique. There, does that content you?"

"Yes," she said smiling, "provided you go on repeating it at least once a month at every new moon."

"I must make a note of it. But I was to tell you about Acworth."

"What decided you that he could stay no longer in view of Lady Catherine's designs?"

"Let us sit down. It is a long story, but I will make it as short as I can. To begin with, let me say at once that he is not Stephen Acworth. You remember that I was never at ease in my mind about him. The discrepancies between what I had heard of his mind, manners and disposition and what he proved on acquaintance were so great and so many that they could not be dismissed as proceeding from my own error. Even on the journey hither from London I began asking myself, 'Can this indeed be Stephen Acworth?' The question was at first rhetorical, but gradually it became the expression of genuine doubt. I observed him narrowly and one circumstance after another increased it. As an example, on one occasion he said that he had been at a certain college of Oxford and then corrected himself, obviously recalling that Stephen Acworth's college was not that one, but another. That was stupid and he betrayed his consternation. After that he was more particularly on his guard. But good actor though he was, he was not good enough to sustain the character he had assumed with perfect consistency through days and weeks. His attention faltered or his patience wearied, and gross inconsistencies appeared. I had heard of Stephen Acworth as being deeply religious; this man, after a few attempts, gave up every pretence of it. When he first came he showed himself scarcely conversant with the manners and customs of our rank of society, but it became noticeable that he began to acquire these as he went along. What perplexed me was his unquestionable likeness to the late Lord Egbury—as Lady Catherine once observed, he had the family countenance. But at length a suspicion of the truth dawned upon me as I remembered something I had once heard. So convinced was I that the man was an impostor that I wrote to your uncle and enlisted his aid. It was arranged that he should call at Lord Egbury's house in Cavendish Square and ask for an interview with Mr. Stephen Acworth, and if he were not at home, enquire his present whereabouts. This he did. He was informed that Mr. Stephen Acworth *was* at home but not yet sufficiently recovered from his recent illness to be able to receive visitors."

Elizabeth had listened spellbound, with her eyes fixed upon her husband's face as he spoke. Impatient to know everything at once, she now exclaimed, "Then who is the man we have known as Stephen Acworth?"

"I am coming to that almost immediately. First let me explain how it came to be disclosed. In due course, after several letters had passed between the parties, Mr. Gardiner called by appointment at Cavendish Square and saw Stephen Acworth in person. Your uncle's tact and delicacy are known to you. He had, however, a very difficult mission to perform, especially in view of Stephen Acworth's state of health. But the first constraint and reserve got over, and the news broken to Mr. Acworth that he had been impersonated, the fullest and frankest exchange of information took place. Your uncle had one-half of the story, Stephen Acworth the other; between them they pieced together the whole of it.

"The man who came here representing himself to be Stephen Acworth is a natural son of the late Lord Egbury by a foreign opera-singer, known to his associates as Horace Carlini."

"That explains the something foreign in his manner and appearance," she interrupted excitedly. "It was what I could never understand. Did not you remark it also?"

"Yes, from the very beginning of my acquaintance with him. His mother, I believe, was French. She died, however, when he was scarcely seven years old, and Lord Egbury placed him at school with a clergyman in Kent to whom Stephen had been sent for his early education. There he went by the name of Horace Acworth and was supposed to be a nephew of Lord Egbury's. In this way the two boys grew up together, and became much attached to one another in spite of many divergences in character and taste. But these would be less marked in childhood. When he was seventeen Stephen left his tutor for Oxford, and Horace was given the opportunity of going there likewise to prepare for one of the learned professions. But this opportunity he refused. Stephen Acworth told your uncle that from his earliest years Horace had displayed an uncommon gift for music, and young as he was when taken away from the surroundings in which he had lived with his mother, he wished to return to them and exhibit himself in public as a performer on the violin. Lord Egbury, most foolishly and wrongly, as one must think, let him have his way, and gave him the allowance of a younger son to assure his independence. You can imagine what happened. He fell among people who introduced him to all the vices of the town, and encouraged him to squander his money in every sort of extravagance and excess."

"What else was to be expected?" said Elizabeth, with some indignation. "His father must certainly be held to blame for it. He was in the highest degree responsible for his downfall."

"You will think so all the more when you hear what followed. Lord Egbury died suddenly without having made any testamentary or other provision for him. No doubt he intended it, but put off the business until too late. Horace thus found himself penniless and without any regular employment. In this predicament he applied to Stephen for help—to the only member of the family who would acknowledge his existence, and admit his claim to compassion. As the innocent will, Stephen took upon his own shoulders the responsibility of the guilty party; he sought to make reparation for the evil his father had wrought, by assisting his brother to live, while urging him to reform his degraded mode of existence. You must not think he would have given your uncle any such account of himself; he spoke only of his deep concern for his unhappy and much injured brother and his desire to help him. It seems that Horace's life in town had brought him among members of the acting profession for which he had discovered some talent. He believed that his best chance of self-support lay in this direction, and Stephen, willing to believe it also, by one means or another obtained for him an introduction to Mrs. Siddons."

"So he became an actor! No wonder he deceived us as well as he did. He may even have got some enjoyment out of it."

"At first, perhaps, but not when he discovered what he had undertaken. However, to continue. For some time he got on well and appeared to be on the way to establish himself. Then suddenly and unaccountably he fell back into his old courses, was dismissed from the theatre, and took to living how he could with what assistance Stephen was able to afford him. After his—Stephen's—marriage this was perhaps no longer possible on the same scale, but however it may be, Horace resorted to habitual gaming, borrowed money here and there on the strength of a pretended allowance from the Acworths, and accumulated debts running into thousands of pounds. At length, as was bound to happen, his creditors no longer believed his tales and lost patience, and in the extremity he found himself he procured a large sum of money from a moneylender, having forged the name of a colleague of the theatre to a note of hand, thus incurring one of the severest penalties prescribed by the law.

"At this time—last May—Stephen had come to London

after the death of his wife. He was aware that Lord Egbury had written to me and was expecting me to call. He was already sickening for the fever which was to threaten his life, but his indisposition was attributed to grief and the state of his health was not understood. In the meantime Horace had taken refuge in the house for fear of arrest. His hope undoubtedly was that Stephen would be able to extricate him from his difficulties, or at least the worst of them. But Stephen's condition rapidly worsened and he became unable to understand anybody's business except in the most general sense. He assured Horace that he would do what he could when he was better, but Horace was desperate, and in imminent danger of discovery. Matters had reached a pitch of extreme urgency for him when I called at the house. As Stephen was now confined to bed he asked his brother to see me and explain his inability to wait on me. It was thus that the temptation to impersonate Stephen arose and proved irresistible. What the ultimate consequences would be he does not appear to have considered. It was enough that a temporary way of escape was provided."

Darcy paused and Elizabeth said reflectively, "It is a most extraordinary tale. I suspected something wrong, some sort of deception, but never for one moment what you have told me. I suppose you had all this from my uncle."

"Part of it I had in letters from him, but a great deal more was communicated to me by your aunt after her arrival here. Your uncle did not think it prudent to commit to paper so much that was extremely confidential."

"So that was what you were talking about at Clopwell, when you and my aunt were walking up and down in front of the house!"

"Yes, that was it."

"And I was not to know. But why, pray?"

"My only thought was to spare you embarrassment. Had you known what you know now, you could not have borne to continue meeting and speaking to him as you had to without finding it very disagreeable."

"No, that is true. I could not. It would have been dreadful. But how could you tolerate his presence among us after you had found him out? Why did you not send him away immediately? Or did you not confront him with it at first?"

"As soon as I knew for a certainty that he had impersonated his brother without the latter's connivance—for that had to be taken into account as a possibility—I did have everything out with him. He confessed to the deception with a wealth of excuses as you may imagine, and appeared to expect instant dismissal. But I had promised Stephen Acworth in answer to his own request that I would give his brother safe asylum until his affairs were so righted that he could return whence he came. Entangled as they are, and even bringing him within the arm of the law, much still remains to be done. Your uncle has undertaken the business for Stephen Acworth, who has given him power of attorney in all that relates to it, and is to send word as soon as Horace Carlini, as he prefers to call himself, can with impunity show himself abroad in London. But Lady Catherine upset all calculations and by the openness of her designs made it impossible for him to stay here a day longer. It was therefore arranged between us last night that he should depart early this morning and remove to a distance of twenty miles where he would be unknown but still accessible when the promised intelligence arrives. He confessed that he had scarcely any money, having got through what his brother supplied him with at their last meeting, so I advanced him sufficient to maintain himself in the meantime."

"You have treated him with really tender consideration. I hope he is grateful."

"He professes to be, though I must confess that charity was not my only, or even my first motive. For the sake of everyone involved, nothing of all this must leak out. But you know, Elizabeth, as soon as I knew him for what he was I began to like him better. I began to understand Stephen's concern for him."

"But should you not say that Stephen Acworth's concern reflects more credit on himself than on his brother?"

"Most certainly, he appears most nobly and worthily throughout the whole transaction. But as regards Horace, I have lived long enough in the world to see that there is only a hair's breadth between vice and virtue."

"You still have the power to astonish me," exclaimed Elizabeth. "Do you really condone what he has done?"

"No, I do not condone that, but I am able to support Stephen Acworth's view that he was sinned against—at any rate in the beginning."

"In other words, you have forgiven him for his outrageous behaviour to yourself."

"That is the only thing one can forgive," said Darcy, smiling.

"Then I am absolved from such magnanimity. Beside you I am hard and implacable. And the worst of it is that the world will never know you for what you are because it does not become your wife to publish it. It is too much like boasting."

"I am quite content that it should be so. My happiness,

thank goodness, does not depend on public applause. I am domestic, unambitious, and live but for the enjoyments of hearth and home—no very heroic character."

"It is a subject about which we cannot possibly argue; we can only flatly disagree. Tell me, is Lady Catherine to know the truth?"

"Not at present. I do not think it can be safely entrusted to her."

"On that head we do agree. But the living! Is Stephen Acworth disposed to accept it after all?"

"I am happy to say that he has accepted it. Though we have not met, we have learned to know each other, perhaps better than through years of ordinary acquaintance. It is not yet certain when he will come, but his arrival cannot be long delayed now."

Elizabeth drew a deep breath. "What a load is off my mind," she said seriously. "I have not felt so happy these several weeks. It is true that there must still be daily encounters with Lady Catherine, but even they are numbered. As for the Miss Robinsons—I must not openly rejoice, but how I do. And yet I begin to be sorry for them. What a contrary thing the human heart is."

"When it is the heart of Elizabeth Darcy," said her husband.

Chapter 21

MORTIMER WAS NOW SO thoroughly at home at Pemberley that he came and went as he pleased, and in whatever society he found himself spoke out whatever came into his head without restraint. As his ideas were seldom of striking novelty, his observations commonly attracted but little attention, but now and then he had the good fortune to make everyone who was near enough to hear him listen to what he said. This always afforded him great satisfaction, for it encouraged him to feel that he was making progress in the art of conversation.

In the evening of the same day of Acworth's quitting Pemberley the party gathered in the saloon round the teatable had fallen into one of those silences that become more binding the longer they last. Even Lady Catherine remained fixed in thought unutterable, while Elizabeth, who was seldom at a loss to set conversation flowing, gave in momentarily to the languor which usually follows upon an over-excitement of the nerves. A full minute had passed when a slight movement on the part of

Darcy betokening an endeavour to say something, however trivial, was arrested by Mortimer's suddenly observing that two departures from the same house in much the same manner within a fortnight was very singular indeed.

"The country folk hereabouts say, 'If twice, then thrice,'" he added.

"Oh, pray don't repeat what such people say," said Kitty, excessively shocked that they should be mentioned at all in the elegant surroundings of the saloon.

"But they are often proved right," Mortimer persisted. "I could tell you a thing or two from my own knowledge." And undeterred by the shade of disapprobation on the fair face of the lady beside him he proceeded to relate some hair-raising stories of the horrid happenings connected with such ill-omens as of birds flying into houses, the breaking of a mirror, and seeing the new moon through a window.

"Misfortune can always be depended on to occur when required," said Mr. Bennet, "while prognostications of good commonly fail to produce it, at least in my own experience. How often have the certain signs of money coming to me preceded the receipt of a heavier bill than usual. Superstition is for strong minds; weak ones had better flout it."

But in spite of ridicule or of what anyone could advance in disproof Mortimer stuck to his point, and his steadfastness was rewarded by complete and striking confirmation, for the very next day Lady Catherine received a letter from Mr. Collins of such disastrous import that no sooner had she read it than she ordered her carriage and directed the packing of her trunks.

The letter, the greater part of which was read aloud at the

breakfast table, informed her that a thief or thieves, assisted, it was feared, by a newly engaged footman, had broken into the house during the night and stolen a large quantity of valuables. The wretches having got away with their booty without disturbing a single member of the household, discovery was not made till the following morning. A thorough search of the whole house, conducted, it appeared, by Mr. Collins himself, accompanied by the housekeeper and butler, had disclosed many precious articles vanished, including some of the oldest and choicest wine in the cellar.

Wounded in all her feelings as a lady of rank, the mistress of a great estate and paramount authority in her own parish, Lady Catherine exhibited a spectacle to constrain pity and awe. But her presence of mind deserted her not, and her majesty of deportment was rather increased than sunk by this stroke of outrageous fortune.

Darcy at once offered to accompany her to Rosings and placed himself unreservedly at her disposal in all that required to be done. At first she would not hear of it and categorically declined assistance. She was fully accustomed, she said, to deal with any and every matter that might arise in the house or on the estate—she believed she was the equal of any gentleman in the country. In the end he prevailed over her reluctance and she was brought to concede that his advice and support could be of importance to her. It was therefore settled that he should go.

Elizabeth very naturally assumed that Anne de Bourgh would travel with her mother, but when Lady Catherine rose from the table to go upstairs to prepare for the journey, Anne merely left her chair for another near the window.

"Are not you coming, Anne?" said her ladyship in some surprise. "I can assure you there is not a moment to lose. We quit the house within an hour."

"There can be no necessity for me to come, Mamma," replied her daughter. "You know I cannot support the fatigue of travelling post as you will do. I prefer to stay at Pemberley."

The sharpness of her tone in speaking and the look of mingled fear and obstinacy upon her features was such as to strike everybody unpleasantly. Elizabeth suspected that this was the first time in her life that she had so much as proposed a course in opposition to her mother who, completely taken aback by the novelty of her daughter expressing so very decidedly a will of her own, could only stare in astonishment. To ease the uncomfortable feeling produced, Mrs. Darcy interposed with the civil hope that Miss de Bourgh would continue at Pemberley as long as it suited her.

"And besides, Mamma," said Anne coldly, "you would not wish me to miss the ball."

Lady Catherine had in fact forgotten that it was to take place and in little more than a week hence, but mention of it had a certain effect upon her. Of late, owing to other plans occupying her mind, she had ceased to look upon the ball as an occasion for matrimonial schemes, but she could notwithstanding reflect that there is no harm in having more than one string to one's bow. Further reflection might also persuade her that in all the business to engage her attention on arrival at Rosings Anne, helpless, nervous and irritable, would be better out of the way for the present. She therefore acquiesced in her staying at Pemberley with more grace than might have been expected.

In the bustle of preparation for the journey Elizabeth had no time for speech with her husband until he was about to enter the carriage beside his aunt.

"Dare I remind you of the ball?" she asked. "Dare I hope that you will be back in time for it?"

"You can count on me for that," he replied, "even if I have to return to Rosings afterwards. You do see, my love—don't you?—that my aunt has a claim upon me—that I could not do otherwise."

"Oh, yes, I see it perfectly. I am the most reasonable being in the world, I believe. Adieu, my dearest. Be sure you write very soon and tell me everything."

The absence of Darcy from their midst unfavourably affected the spirits of those left behind, or would have done, had not the removal of Lady Catherine gone far to console them. But Mr. Bennet positively regretted her loss as a bereavement, and said he did not know how he was going to support life without her.

"She is a most admirable lady," he asserted. "What spirit, what pertinacity, what invincible self-complacency are united in one person! Not only to be always right, but to know it so well—that I do applaud in her. Her discrimination of character—so just—and her scorn of surrounding opinion make her a most valuable adjunct to any society so blest as to contain her. I could almost wish I were in Mr. Collins' shoes."

On the subject of Acworth, to which he recurred now and again, he was no less emphatic.

"That is a very astute fellow indeed. He will make his way in life—there's no question. A man who can get round women without apparent effort, as he does, will be always in clover."

Elizabeth wondered what her father's true opinion would be if he knew all. But it had been settled between her husband and herself that upon several considerations the imposture ought not to be made public, but disclosure strictly confined to those persons actually concerned to know the truth, as the need for it was proved and on condition of their preserving the utmost secrecy. In particular it was seen to be necessary that Lady Catherine should be informed very fully as soon as possible in view of the project she had formed of an alliance between her daughter and the supposed Stephen Acworth, a duty which Darcy intended discharging at the first opportunity. The prevention of an open scandal was principally desirable in the interests of the real Stephen Acworth on his appearance in the place where he had been impersonated, but almost equally so for the sake of the fair fame of Pemberley House. Howbeit Darcy was most anxious to minimise the effects of the imposture upon the person chiefly liable to suffer from them, and apart from Lady Catherine whom it behoved to know everything, he believed that only so much as would account for the substitution of one Mr. Acworth for another should be divulged, even to members of the family circle.

What precisely should be said, whether that a near relation of the Acworth family had substituted himself for Stephen Acworth, on the latter falling seriously ill, in order to evade his creditors, and had subsequently confessed to the deception, Darcy had scarcely had time to decide, but Elizabeth comprehended that his absence must impose on her a silence respecting recent events not to be broken. It was some comfort, however, that she could speak freely to Mrs. Gardiner as being privy to the whole grand secret, and whose retentive memory treasured up details that Darcy might have forgotten to relate, especially concerning the real Stephen Acworth.

"In the course of their meetings your uncle found him every-thing that could be wished in point of character and general understanding, though his grasp of business is perhaps deficient owing to lack of experience. He lives too much above mundane considerations to seek his own advantage. His delicacy of feeling might by some be called womanish, but I do not know that to be such great dispraise."

"He would appear to be all that my husband hoped for," said Elizabeth. "This affair will have a happy conclusion after all, I foresee. Now there is only one thing left to wish for—no, there are several things. First, that the ball should be over; second, that my husband should settle down at home, and not run hither and thither about the country on other people's business; third, that Georgiana should be happy, for in spite of her seeming tran-quillity I do not think she is so; fourth, that Anne de Bourgh would go home. She is behaving in a most peculiar manner. It is agreed that we are all to be sorry for her, but it does not make me like her any the more."

Miss de Bourgh's chief peculiarity lay in a studied avoidance of her hostess. Deprived of her mother who ordered every moment of her day, it might naturally be supposed that she would be at a loss for occupation, and Elizabeth had started by offering her all the attentions one bestows upon a specially honoured guest, endeavouring to ascertain her wishes and proposing various schemes for her entertainment. But Anne made it plain beyond mistaking that she wanted none of her. Every day after breakfast she asked for a carriage to drive her either to the Parsonage or some other neighbouring house, and showed the utmost determination to go alone, for on Elizabeth's first offering to accompany her, contrary to her own inclination and purely as a matter of courtesy, she evinced something that could only be called displeasure. Frequently it happened that she stayed out until close upon dinner time. Where she had been all those hours she omitted to say, for she did not open her lips more than was absolutely necessary for the prosecution of her own affairs. Her manner was not only forbidding, but furtive, as if she were harbouring a guilty secret. It was a nice point to decide whether she were witless or slightly deranged, and Elizabeth was tempted to the conclusion that the latter state of mind was answerable for her otherwise unaccountable behaviour. Jane read the matter differently.

"Consider the novelty of being able to go where one pleases and do as one chooses. Anne de Bourgh has been kept in all things like a child. No doubt the delicacy of her health has induced in Lady Catherine an excessive vigilance over her, and maternal solicitude may have led her to overdo her care of her daughter. It is only natural that free, perhaps, for the first time in her life, Miss de Bourgh should resent even the appearance of restraint upon her liberty."

"You may be right," said Elizabeth. "It is certainly the most charitable construction upon her manner of going on. But I should have thought that ordinary good breeding would have prompted a little more politeness to myself and her fellow guests. Upon any view her conduct is exasperating. When it pleases her she can ask a favour of me. Lady Catherine took away her maid with her, and Anne who had shared the maid was left without any. She therefore came to me and asked for Rachel Stone. At first I thought that a request for a girl so young and inexperienced was a piece of modesty, but far from it! I offered her Mason or Billing; neither of them would do, only Rachel Stone. Of course I gave way."

"Do not you think," said Jane, speaking with a slight hesitation, "that she may be pining after Mr. Acworth?"

"I see no signs of it, and as I half expected that she would betray disappointment, I am not likely to have missed any indications of the sort."

A curiosity not altogether unjustifiable decided Elizabeth to call some time at the Parsonage and discover, if possible, what attraction drew Anne there. One day when Mrs. Gardiner and Jane Bingley had driven off to Lambton on a shopping expedition, and she was otherwise at leisure to do as she chose, she gave herself the indulgence of going down to the village on foot, meditating as she went along upon the vicissitudes of this most eventful of summers. Having paid one or two visits to old family pensioners and thus provided herself with an excuse for an unexpected and informal appearance, she arrived at the door of the Parsonage and rang the bell. Several minutes, long to the patience of a lady not accustomed to be kept waiting, elapsed before Thomas opened the door and ushered her into the dining-room. There Miss Sophia was discovered sitting alone, and on seeing who came in, visibly started and displayed extreme confusion.

"Oh dear," said she, stammering and agitated, all her features working and suffused with a pink blush, "we had not the least idea—that is, I am so very pleased to see you, Mrs. Darcy. You are indeed quite a stranger. I am sure Sister—would you be so very good as to excuse her—she is rather particularly engaged. But had she known—I am sure—However—" Here either her ideas or her voice failed her and she ceased abruptly.

Concealing her amazement Elizabeth sat down and began all the usual polite enquiries after the health and concerns of the Miss Robinsons. In due course she reached the subject of Miss Sophia's flower-garden, surely a safe one. But all Miss Sophia's stammering and agitation returned as she replied that the garden was very well, but not what it had been a fortnight ago, that just at the moment it was not at all worth looking at. As it was perfectly clear that she had some reason for keeping Mrs. Darcy out of the garden on this occasion, Mrs. Darcy was so obliging as to introduce another topic. She began to speak of Lady Catherine de Bourgh's sudden recall to Rosings, gave the latest intelligence of the spoliation of that august dwelling and ventured a few reflections on the wickedness of the times. By such degrees did she arrive at mentioning Miss de Bourgh. It must be the greatest comfort to Miss de Bourgh that she had the Miss Robinsons at hand whenever she had exhausted the resources of Pemberley House. It was indeed something to have friends who made one feel so very much at home, who could be depended on to extend an unfailing welcome whenever one dropped in.

Miss Sophia replied haltingly that Sister and she were always pleased to see Miss de Bourgh. As Mrs. Darcy had said, she had quite got into the habit of dropping in for a little chat. Sister and she missed Lady Catherine excessively. It was all a most dreadful business, and she hoped that those wicked thieves would soon be hanged.

While she was speaking Miss Sophia glanced about her nervously, peered out of the window over Elizabeth's head, stopped as if she knew not what she was saying, and in other ways betrayed a strong desire that her visitor would go away. Such manifestations could hardly be ignored. Refusing a belated offer of refreshment, Elizabeth rose to her feet, and leaving her compliments for the elder Miss Robinson, withdrew in a manner designed to allay the least suspicion that she had noticed anything strange in the mode of her reception.

But as she crossed the road from the Parsonage gates and entered the park and struck into the path through the wood the feeling uppermost in her heart was of indignation. The obvious explanation of Miss Sophia's maladroit behaviour was that her calling at the particular time had been regarded as unwelcome— as an intrusion. In all likelihood Miss de Bourgh was being entertained in the drawing-room and on hearing the doorbell clang had expressed the wish that no other caller should be admitted—she was fully capable of that. As a compromise Miss Sophia had been deputed to receive the unwanted visitor in the dining-room and get rid of her as soon as she could without being downright uncivil. The discovery that it was Mrs. Darcy who was to be treated thus discourteously had thoroughly flustered her. Without the wit, the presence of mind, or perhaps the courage to vary the instructions of her sister, she had in fact bungled the business ludicrously.

Having completed to her satisfaction this portrayal by her imagination of the circumstances of her visit as both credible and probable, Elizabeth began to view the matter in a humorous light and, as she went along, to make of it a story such as she might relate to her husband, enlivened by those touches of fancy which transform a mere dull recital into a theme for laughter. Thus employed, her eyes fixed upon the ground and only half sensible of her actual surroundings, she remained unaware that someone was rapidly approaching her along a path converging upon her own until an abrupt intimation, that she was no longer alone, but was being followed, made her turn round. There, at the junction of the paths stood a man. It was Acworth. Thus she still thought of him.

The shock of his appearing in this place when she had believed him to be many miles away caused her cheeks to blanch and her limbs to stiffen. "Mr. Acworth!" she exclaimed faintly. "What does this mean? What are you doing here?"

He made an eager movement towards her. "I did not mean to alarm you," he cried. "I would not for the world. I followed you because I must speak to you—this once, if never again. What others may think of me I do not greatly care, but to you I do seek to justify myself, or if justification is not truly possible, to lessen your contempt of me. I entreat you to listen."

She looked at him doubtfully, and as if answering an unspoken question he continued hurriedly, "I returned to Pemberley this morning and was at the Parsonage when you called. As I did not wish anyone to know of my presence in the place I asked leave of the Miss Robinsons to retire when the doorbell announced a possible visitor, but they would not hear of it, and so Thomas was directed to show anyone desiring to enter the house into another room. As soon as I learned who had come I quitted the Parsonage under pretext of fearing discovery, but in reality that I might intercept you as you returned through the park."

She was not so overcome by the surprise of the encounter that his explanation perfectly convinced her of its truth. It raised too many questions for that. But while refusing to exhibit the complaisance of a willing dupe, she must equally avoid displaying mere curiosity as such.

"Do the Miss Robinsons understand the part you played here?" she asked gravely.

"No," he replied. "Mr. Darcy did not think it necessary that they should be told as they were not directly affected."

"Perhaps he did not foresee that you would revisit the scene of your—your—forgive me. What else can it be called but your imposture?"

He shrugged his shoulders. "Call it what you will. I do not deny that it was. But when you know all—"

"You took a great risk," she went on inexorably. "The chance of my calling at the Parsonage might appear remote from your knowledge of my habits, but Lady Catherine and her daughter have been constant visitors there as you are well aware. For aught you knew they might have been there today."

After a perceptible hesitation he replied, "The intelligence of Lady Catherine's departure had reached me in my retreat. Would it not be natural to suppose that Miss de Bourgh had also quitted Pemberley?"

"Yes," answered Elizabeth, deciding on a bold stroke, "it would be perfectly natural. And it must have taxed your ingenuity indeed when, if I collected her intentions rightly this morning, you found her already with the Miss Robinsons."

"Not very much ingenuity is needed where Miss de Bourgh is concerned," he said, looking down. "I believe that my real purpose in revisiting Pemberley was to see you once again, if I might. As you say, I know your habits, your love of wandering through the woods unattended. Oh, do believe that I speak the truth," he cried, raising eyes that flashed with an intensity of feeling. "Nay, hear me," he demanded vehemently, as she sought to stop him. "You, secure in your own happiness, can hardly deny the consolation of speech to one so wretched, so accursed as myself. You have heard what I have done, what my life has been—every vice has doubtless been laid to my charge. But you have not heard what I have suffered, what drove me in my despair to those courses which the happy and prosperous condemn so self-righteously. What was it but my love of yourself, that torturing passion doomed to frustration from the outset. Do you remember how one day near this very spot as we were walking together I told you the story of a man, representing him as a friend of mine, who fell in love with a woman on beholding her as she stood with a party of friends in the vestibule of a theatre? I hoped you would understand. That man was myself, the woman no other than yourself. Would you have me tell the story afresh?—how I lived but to see you again, only to learn that you had given yourself to another. From that day all happiness, all hope was over for me."

He paused, panting for breath, but before Elizabeth could utter a word of expostulation he rushed on again impetuously.

"You have been told that I came here feigning to be Stephen Acworth in order to escape the consequences of folly and crime. That is true; I did. But the inducement beyond all others was the opportunity afforded of seeing you, living in the same house with you, holding speech with you. What might come of it I hardly asked myself. A madness took possession of me and I acted without thought or care for the future. Alas, hope soared to be dashed to the ground. From the very first you showed your mistrust of me, inspired, if I mistake not, by Mr. Darcy. You took your tone from him. Because I did not ape the ways of your country gentlemen, because I dared to confess to unfashionable accomplishments you disdained me as if I were scarcely fit to come into your presence. You were a great lady—you had a husband, you held me off."

"Mr. Acworth," interrupted Elizabeth, "you have no right to speak to me in this manner. I am truly sorry for your misfortunes, I do make allowances for your conduct, but you must be perfectly aware that you laid yourself open to mistrust on an occasion that we can neither of us forget, and these reproaches are totally unmerited. We are now meeting, as you have said, for the last time. Do believe that I wish you a happier future."

She held out her hand in farewell, but he seemed not to see it.

"I have so much to say to you," he said, looking at her despairingly, "and this opportunity must not pass away before I have said at least some part of it. Whatever you may hear of me in the future, do not believe that I shall for one single instant be inconstant to your memory. Your image will be ever before me as of the one woman—incomparable—who has taught me the holiest feelings of the heart. For that I do thank you, without that lesson I might have gone through life ignorant of what it can hold of beauty. Say that you forgive me, not only for what I have done, but for what I may do again."

She said something in reply, she hardly knew what. He fell upon one knee, seized her hand and pressed it to his lips. There he remained bowed before her, neither speaking nor moving. Suddenly he sprang to his feet and without a glance or a word rushed away through the trees and was lost to view.

Elizabeth turned and continued her way towards home, but so painful was the tumult of thought and feeling agitating her that she had not gone far before she found herself unable to proceed another step, and she sank down upon a slab of moss-covered rock that projected from the ground against the path and endeavoured to compose herself.

Tears came but afforded no relief, reason could give no firm declaration but was as unsettled as her sensations; she was unable even to summon up a clear idea of what had happened. She longed to confess everything to someone who would understand and absolve her from all blame and rid her conscience of its irrational sense of guilt. But no one was at hand, and when she cast about in her mind no one would do but her husband who was absent. Convicting herself of having been aware from her first meeting with Acworth of his sentiments towards her, she began to censure herself unsparingly for withholding from Darcy the least circumstance of which he could justly have complained. Oh, why had she not been candid with him? To leave him in ignorance of Acworth's return, of the encounter in the wood, of the substance of their conversation was unthinkable, but that imposed on her the obligation to say also everything that hitherto had been left unsaid. She had no fear that he would show anger; she could not bear to think that he might hence-forth regard her as undeserving of his trust.

While these thoughts raced through her head she could not altogether forget Acworth's distress. No woman, however happy in her married life, can remain indifferent to a man who professes to love her without hope of return and swears to cherish her memory until death. His suffering must excite pity, her recollection of him be tinctured with some part of tender-ness. Elizabeth would rather have hated and despised Acworth; it was an affliction that she could do so no longer—he had to that degree impressed himself on her heart. The impression made by his speech, his gestures, his passion and despair were not perhaps indelible, but thus they would seem at every pricking of memory.

Her first sight of him in the vestibule of one of the London theatres she now remembered, although beyond a passing vexa-tion it had no significance for her at the time. With Sir William Lucas and his daughter Maria she had that day come to London from her home in Hertfordshire, and after spending the night at her uncle's house in Gracechurch Street, the party was to travel the next day into Kent to stay with Mr. and Mrs. Collins at Hunsford Parsonage. In the evening her uncle and aunt took them to see Mrs. Siddons in a performance of *Henry VIII*. After the play, while they stood in the vestibule waiting for their carriage, she turned involuntarily to see a man gazing fixedly at her. She removed her eyes immediately, but her brief glance showed the stranger wearing the sort of hat and cloak affected by members of the acting profession, and although the large brim of his hat half concealed his features she recognised him as having taken a small part in the play she had just seen. Her aunt at that moment made an observation drawing off her attention and the incident had passed out of her mind into complete oblivion until Acworth recalled it to her. Her sensation of having seen him before on his arrival at Pemberley was now explained, and equally her inability to recollect where she had seen him, for who would have discovered the strange looking young man of the hat and cloak in his latter guise of a soberly clad young clergyman.

How long she sat occupied with these and other thoughts she hardly knew, but at length, fearing it must be getting late, she rose up and hurried through the wood. As she came out under the open sky the view of the great house standing amidst its lawns and gardens calmed the agitation of her spirits; as she approached its walls her courage revived, and when she had passed through the doorway into the quiet and safety of home she felt as though awakening from a frightful dream.

Chapter 22

A WEEK WENT BY and the day of the ball arrived. From an early hour Elizabeth began to look for Darcy's return, but morning and noon passed away without bringing him. She had no fear of his not keeping his word to be with her in time to receive their guests, as her faith in his ability to overcome every obstacle that might hinder his progress could not falter. In tranquil expectation, therefore, of seeing him at any moment appear before her, she sat during the afternoon in the little drawing-room with her aunt and Jane and Georgiana engaged in needlework. The ladies were embroidering a set of infant's caps, each employing her own invention, and they were comparing designs and deciding that Georgiana's was the best when the butler entered and approached his mistress.

"Is your master come?" she instantly enquired.

"No, ma'am," he replied. "It is Major Wakeford. He is in the library."

Astonished beyond measure at this unheralded return, and wondering whatever it could portend, Elizabeth quitted the room and hastened to the library. One glance at Georgiana had told her very little, having revealed only a head bent rather lower than before over her work, thus concealing any change of countenance. Fortunately the perfect delicacy and discretion of Mrs. Gardiner and Jane could be depended upon to spare her the embarrassment of a train of conjectures to account for Wakeford's unexpected arrival, though neither was aware of her having any particular interest in the matter.

It was strange to see Major Wakeford standing in one of his remembered attitudes and looking very much as if he had never gone away. That first impression soon passed; there was a change in him. His aunt must have died; he was in mourning. He seemed nervous—almost as if uncertain of his welcome. Elizabeth greeted him warmly; she explained that Darcy was absent but was immediately expected home, and then said with a smile, "I trust this means that you have returned to stay with us for a further period."

"You are all kindness," he replied, "but I do not know whether I ought to accept your invitation. I reached Bakewell rather more than an hour ago, and engaged a room at the inn for this coming night. Before leaving Bath I wrote to Darcy. Am I right in supposing that he has not yet read my letter?"

By a standing arrangement Elizabeth was empowered by Darcy to deal with all letters which came for him whenever he was away, but one or two, delivered since yesterday she had left on the writing table with seals unbroken since he would so soon be at home to dispose of them himself. These she took up to show Wakeford, and one of them he was able to claim as having been written by himself.

"I wrote to him announcing a material change in my pecuniary circumstances," he said. "My aunt died about an hour after I reached her house. I had no expectation of benefiting under her will beyond, perhaps, a small legacy, but in point of fact she has left me the greater part of her fortune. Why she chose to alter the disposition of her property no one knows—certainly not myself. It is true, however, that her other nephew already possesses a considerable property of his own. But that is neither here nor there. Today I am in a very different situation from what I was when I last had the pleasure of seeing you, and although I cannot boast of much else that would recommend me as a suitor for the hand of his sister, I have less diffidence now in seeking Darcy's permission to pay my addresses to her."

He delivered this speech with his customary soldierly directness, but Elizabeth thought she could detect the signs of deep feeling, both in his voice and in his countenance. Her first sensation was of joy, her next of doubt whether he was not too late, whether, as Georgiana had said, she had not indeed starved to extinction her former attachment.

"I cannot, of course, speak with any authority for my husband," she said with considered gravity, "but I can go so far as to say that he is chiefly desirous that Georgiana should be truly happy in any choice she may make."

"Yes," he answered, looking down. "That is what I have asked myself continually on the journey hither. Could I make her happy? Equality of fortune is not everything. I am deeply conscious of that."

"Am I right in supposing," Elizabeth asked after a rather awkward pause, "that it was your lack of fortune only which deterred you from coming forward before?"

"Yes," he replied with a look of anxiety that touched her. "Only that, I assure you. I felt that poor as I was, maimed and unable to follow any profession, it would be very wrong in me to seek to engage the affections of any young lady, still more so one who might be expected by her relations to make a great match."

"You are very modest," Elizabeth said gently. "Indeed I wish you well." But she wondered whether the old-fashioned formality of his style would prove sufficiently persuasive in wooing a girl who was not thoroughly predisposed to accept him. She could not imagine that he had the least idea how to set about the business in such a manner as to bring it to a successful conclusion and longed to give him a word of advice or warning. She did not however feel justified in speaking at all decidedly on a subject that held so much perplexity to herself, and to pass from it she began to tell him of the ball that was to be held that night. She had not got out more than a sentence and a half when the door opened and Darcy came into the room.

He had been informed by Baxter of his friend's presence in the house and showed no inordinate surprise but sincere pleasure. After the first salutations had been exchanged, some hesitation or reserve in Wakeford's manner began to raise a question as to the real motive of his return which could not be directly asked, but became the more palpable in Darcy's studied avoidance of any enquiry likely to be construed as angling for information. At length, interpreting a glance from Wakeford at herself as giving her permission to speak for him, Elizabeth told her husband briefly of the change in his circumstances and his object in returning to Pemberley.

Darcy masked any astonishment he might feel and gave his consent readily but without much encouragement. "My sister must speak for herself," he said, "for this is a matter in which I should by no means attempt to influence her." But on learning that Wakeford purposed returning to the inn at Bakewell he pressed him to take up his quarters at Pemberley and allow a servant to be sent for his luggage. Wakeford made some slight demur on the score of his inability to take part in the ball, but soon yielded to no more than a little persuasion.

After some further, rather laboured conversation Wakeford, doubtless perceiving that his host and hostess might wish for some private talk on a subject of such high importance as a proposal for Georgiana's hand, asked leave to retire to the room that was to be assigned to his use. No sooner were Darcy and Elizabeth alone than she began immediately.

"What actually is your opinion, Fitz?"

"To be perfectly candid, much as I like and respect Wakeford, he is not what I had in mind for Georgiana."

"I thought as much. But is there anyone else whom you do think good enough?"

"I cannot say that there is. However, as I think I made clear, I would by no means stand in their way. But what of Georgiana?"

"That is uncertain. As you know, she thought herself at one time to be in love with him. We know now that he went away because he became aware of it but felt he could not in honour propose marriage to her, and believing as she did that he was indifferent she determined to cure herself. She told me that she had done so—that she no longer cared for him, but she may be only deceiving herself."

"As I see it," said Darcy, "Wakeford can but ask her. It must be left to her to make up her mind whether to accept or reject him."

"What you really mean is that there is to be no pleading of causes. You suspect me of being sympathetic towards Wakeford."

"If he cannot plead his own cause, no one else can do it for him."

"No one is wise when they are in love. Need I remind you of your own stupidities?"

"Be just. You did not always behave so very intelligently yourself. When you hated me you drew me on, and when at last you changed your mind you showed it by a persistent avoidance of my eye and the most chilling silence."

"That proves my point."

"I do not think so. Our feeling for one another was strong enough to triumph over our own stupidity, if you like to call it such, and make all clear between us."

"And the upshot of all this is that it is best not to meddle between two persons, even when they don't know their own business."

"They probably know it better than you or I do."

"At any rate," said Elizabeth seriously, "I must tell Georgiana why he has come. That is not to meddle, I hope. I defer to your superior judgment, my love, for that relieves me of all responsibility. A strong, decided character like yours thoroughly enjoys responsibility, whereas the weaker vessel, like myself, gladly gets rid of it. And so I look to you to take care of your cousin this evening and see that she is provided with partners and everything for her comfort. I do not think she is very well today. She is pale—that is, paler than usual—and seems nervous. What an odd creature she is. How did you leave Lady Catherine?"

"Not very well, either. The state of affairs at Rosings has been a severe blow to her. Her spirit and determination are still admirable, but I could see her struggling against fatigue."

"Did you tell her the truth about—Acworth?"

"The name he commonly goes by is Horace Carlini. Yes, I did. It was neither an easy nor a pleasant talk. At first I had hard work to convince her that her erstwhile favourite lacked even respectability of character. When at last I succeeded her indignation at being deceived, as she termed it, knew no bounds and she upbraided me for having misled her. It is strange that a true explanation of why I acted as I did—out of consideration for Stephen Acworth's feelings and to enable him to give Carlini one more chance to redeem his character—should sound lame, but so it was. She said that to have kept her in ignorance of the facts was an affront to her understanding."

"You should have told her for her own consolation that you kept your wife in the same dark ignorance."

"I should have done no such thing," retorted Darcy. "Like yourself I give no handles to Lady Catherine."

Elizabeth laughed, but grew pensive again almost immediately. There was Georgiana to be prepared for what awaited her, and so it behoved her to separate again and reluctantly from the dearest of companions. She went away to find Georgiana, and discovered her in her own room in retreat from the mere possibility of meeting Wakeford before she was ready for it.

Her first question, "Oh, why has he come?" spoken almost angrily, gave the measure of the dread she felt. There was no indifference here, but whether her former regard had not turned to a settled repugnance was not so certain.

As once before to Darcy, Elizabeth related the great change which had occurred in Wakeford's fortunes, his application for her hand in marriage, the reasons which had formerly kept him from declaring his sentiments and his earnest desire to make them known to her now that the chief obstacle to their union, as he conceived it, was removed.

"I hold no brief for him," she said. "Only ourselves know truly why we act as we do. But in justice to him I would say that he sincerely believed that he did what was right in holding off before."

"Oh yes. I know that for him duty and honour are first and foremost. But isn't it honour that moves him now? If he had felt any real regard for me would he have humiliated me as he did? Wasn't it in the highest degree cruel? He must have known how ashamed of myself he made me feel. For that I can never forgive him, nor could I feel any confidence in him ever again."

"Everyone is prone to error, and in love especially people commit follies and blunders. I don't wish to advise you, however, Georgiana, but to prepare you for what cannot very well be avoided. You do not wish to run away from him as if you had really done something to be ashamed of. I myself should call it a noble impulse which the event has justified. You must summon your pride to sustain you—the pride of a Darcy. The ball will befriend you, for you must dance all the time, which he cannot. I doubt whether he is able to, and in any case his aunt having so recently died would make it improper for him to do so. You will meet at dinner, but we shall all be there and I will keep him talking to myself. From his point of view he could hardly have chosen a worse time for his venture. The advantage will be all with you, and without much exertion and little or no awkwardness you can make it apparent that you wish to have nothing to do with him. I should not wonder if tomorrow he goes away quietly without importuning you at all, having read his dismissal in your manner. But you know, I shall feel sorry for him, for I cannot help liking him."

The effect of Elizabeth's representation of the case was to make Georgiana much less agitated than before. She listened to every word, appearing to reflect deeply. She still looked somewhat troubled, but Elizabeth could see that she had recovered sufficient command over herself to behave in Wakeford's presence with due propriety and tolerable composure.

"Very well," she said at length. "I will see him and even speak to him if I must. But there is really no alternative."

"I am afraid not," said Elizabeth. "It is a thing that must be done and got over."

She stayed no longer, for time was advancing, and she must commence dressing for the ball, in itself a ceremony of care and art. While Mason was arranging her hair she was moved by the reflection that no one else would ever do it so beautifully to wonder whether Rachel Stone was equal to all that Miss de Bourgh required for a special occasion and to speak her doubt of it aloud.

"She thinks she is equal to anything, ma'am," Mason said in a tone which spoke of affront having been taken. "Just before we were to go upstairs she told Billing and me that she wanted no interference or instruction from either of us. She said—excuse the expression, ma'am—that Miss de Bourgh would not have us poking our noses into her affairs."

"Indeed," replied Elizabeth in a manner to convey the very strongest reprobation of such impertinence. But what Mason had told her decided her against going to Anne's room in case it might be regarded as an intrusion, and as soon as she was ready she went instead to fetch Georgiana that they might enter the saloon together.

They were the last of the party to appear, everyone, including Major Wakeford, being there before them. The terrible moment when Georgiana must acknowledge his salutation arrived and passed. They met, they spoke. Georgiana's face blanched as he came before her, and his had not much more colour in it. They moved apart again immediately, and fortunately Mr. Bennet, who had been wandering round the room in one of his incommunicable meditations suddenly drew everybody's attention to himself by coming to a halt before the ladies where they stood in a group together and ejaculating, "Ha, a veritable rainbow."

The description was not inapt. Mrs. Darcy was in pale yellow, with diamonds sparkling in her dark hair and round her throat, Mrs. Bingley in green, Mrs. Gardiner in violet, Georgiana and Kitty in white, as became young girls, and Anne de Bourgh in crimson. As Elizabeth had told Darcy, Anne was not looking at all well, and her heavy-eyed indifference was in strong contrast to the glowing cheeks and vivacious glances of the others. Even Georgiana was now as flushed as before she had been pale.

At dinner Wakeford sat beside Elizabeth and a flow of conversation was tolerably well maintained between them. After one of the slight pauses that now and then occurred Wakeford said quietly but with such distinctness as to be heard at the other end of the table,

"So Acworth is now at Bakewell."

"At Bakewell?" Elizabeth exclaimed, hardly able to credit her ears. Simulating indifference she enquired, "Did you then meet him there?"

"Yes, I met him at the entrance to the inn. He told me he had quitted Pemberley and was staying there for a day or two, but would soon be off to London."

Acworth within six miles of Pemberley! It was a disturbing thought. The question instantly arose as to what he could be doing there since Bakewell was certainly not on the road to London, but caution prevailed over curiosity and she forbore to question Wakeford further. She glanced at her husband and fancied she saw her own feelings reflected in his countenance. He said nothing, however, and turned almost immediately to speak to his cousin. His observation was received in silence; she appeared not to have heard a syllable, but toying with the food on her plate in her usual languid manner looked as if she knew not how to hold herself up.

Elizabeth had sometimes thought that much of Anne de Bourgh's ill-health was assumed in order to escape exertions that were unpleasing to her. Established as a semi-invalid she could be as lazy as she chose without being criticised. Latterly, and particularly since Lady Catherine's departure she had seemed in better health, but this evening she looked positively ill.

Elizabeth felt so concerned for her that on the ladies returning to the saloon she asked her whether she would not like to retire.

"I am afraid you have one of your very bad headaches," she said as gently as possible. "Perhaps you would like to disappear from view. You should not stay if you do not feel equal to it. Pray do as you choose."

Anne hesitated so long that she appeared to be deliberating. In a voice of constraint and without raising her eyes she replied that she did not feel so very ill.

"If I do not feel able to support the fatigue of staying up so late as the end of the ball I shall take advantage of your kind permission. Should I retire very early I trust no one will think it necessary to follow me."

In some surprise that such a proviso should be mentioned Elizabeth assured her that her wish would be respected. As the lady closed her mouth with the manifest intention of not speaking again for that time and clearly desired to be let alone, she went away to speak to Georgiana.

"Everything has passed off well so far," she said, after drawing Georgiana aside. "But do not too openly avoid him."

"I will do my best," Georgiana answered, her face clouding. "But oh, how I wish that this evening were over."

Elizabeth could but echo the sentiment from the depths of her heart. Desiring as she did to see both Georgiana and Wakeford happy, or at least relieved from misery, she was most cruelly divided in her sympathies between them, since the relief of one must procure the misery of the other. Her main concern was naturally for Georgiana, but how she was to endure witnessing Wakeford's final disappointment she preferred not to think.

Chapter 23

THE TIME HAD NOW come when every private thought must be put aside. Shortly after the gentlemen joined the ladies in the saloon the guests began arriving, and soon the first small cluster round the Darcys had swelled to a throng, and the separate, intelligible strains of friends and acquaintance greeting one another and falling into light talk were blended in an indistinguishable buzz of voices. Dancing young men set about securing pretty partners and carried them off across the hall to the ballroom; the older people got round the card tables or found seats to watch the dancing. After the usual delays the first dance was formed and the violins struck up a lively tune.

It fell to Elizabeth to lead off with a certain Sir Charles who danced with punctilio while directing upon her a smiling gaze in certain expectation of those pearls of wit for which the most charming woman in Derbyshire was justly famed. She returned his smiles, but although she talked with persevering sprightliness she was unable to throw off anything so remarkable as to please her own ears. Luckily her reputation came to her aid, and Sir Charles continued to display all the admiration it merited.

After they had gone down the dance and she had a moment of leisure to look about her, she saw that Anne de Bourgh was standing up with Bingley, always the most considerate of partners, and that Georgiana's portion was the eldest young Vernon. Major Wakeford, she supposed, had been secured for one of the tables of whist. But no, while her eyes were directed towards the door she saw him stroll into the ballroom, as if he had but the moment before strolled out of it, and take up his stand among a group of older men who preferred talking among themselves to dancing or playing cards.

Lofty and spacious as it was, the ballroom became very hot in the course of an hour or two, and one of the long windows, that farthest from the card players, was thrown open to the night at Elizabeth's behest. As soon as a dance was over the young people, disregarding what their elders might say about the dangers of night air, flocked towards it, and some of the most venturesome stepped outside upon the gravel walk to look for the moon or their favourite constellations. Such stargazing was all very well for the hardiest, but careless young men and easily led young girls can soon stray beyond the limits of the prudent or the allowable, and by degrees the chaperones with looks and observations began to make their disapprobation felt. Darcy, ever watchful, thereupon directed that the window should be closed, or very nearly, but before the servants were to execute his order, he stepped outside himself to make sure that no loitering couple should be left shut out.

A figure, the figure of a man to judge by its height, standing in the shadow cast by an angle of the house was visible, but not very clearly, upon the path a few yards away. Advancing, Darcy found that it was Wakeford, and able to guess pretty well what his friend was feeling and thinking, he spoke his name quietly and without any note of surprise.

"You find this sort of thing no more to your taste than I do," he said, after accosting him. "From time to time we give these entertainments for the benefit of the neighbourhood and oblige our acquaintance to go to the same trouble in return. I have no doubt it will go on until three or four."

"Some of your guests have already departed," replied Wakeford, "although it is not long after twelve. I heard the clock strike not three minutes since, and as it did so a carriage drove away from behind the house."

"From behind the house!" Darcy ejaculated. "That's extraordinary; it is usual to leave from the front door. Someone, probably, wishing to slip away easily without fuss," he added, dismissing the matter as explained.

Wakeford made no rejoinder and Darcy, recollecting the business of the window, returned to the ballroom to direct its being closed. Having done so, he came out of the house again and found Wakeford still standing where he had left him.

"I have been thinking, Darcy," he began almost immediately, "that I did unwisely to come before you had answered my letter. I should have waited for some assurance of a favourable reception before venturing here."

"I doubt whether that would have been the wiser course. Boldness, precipitancy is said to pay in these cases."

Wakeford's silence spoke his lack of conviction, and after a pause Darcy continued,

"It is probably very unwise to lay down a general rule respecting a matter which affects everyone differently. To be candid, how Georgiana regards you I do not know. Even Elizabeth, who has her confidence in most things, says she does not."

"I feel very much as I did on the eve of my first battle," said Wakeford. "Beforehand I had been all eagerness and confidence, but as the moment of going into action arrived my blood began to run cold. A change has come over Georgiana and I feel that I no longer know her. It may be better for me to go away tomorrow."

In ignorance of what had actually passed between Wakeford and his sister, for Elizabeth had told him only so much as he needed to know, out of consideration for Georgiana's feelings, Darcy attributed his bewilderment to the novelty of a situation he could never have experienced before. To be in love for the first time at thirty-two is to be overpowered by emotions which properly belong to callow youth, and he was doubtless ashamed of being driven by a force he did not comprehend.

"I would by no means seek to influence you," he replied, "and I do not feel justified in offering any advice. While this ball is in progress you can only watch my sister dancing with other men as she must do whether she likes it or not, just as they feel it an obligation to offer themselves as partners. You have my best wishes, Wakeford. I cannot say more."

Wakeford uttered a quiet "thank you," and a silence then ensued which indicated that everything had been said on either side for the present. After a moment or two Darcy, excusing himself, returned to his other guests.

On looking round the ballroom for his cousin he could nowhere see her, but as Elizabeth had prepared him for her early withdrawal from the scene he felt no surprise at her absence. He had observed how wretchedly ill she appeared, and with what an effort she had gone through the first two dances with Bingley. Afterwards, although he had offered to introduce other partners to her she had resolutely declined to stand up again, and had sat beside the Miss Robinsons staring before her with a strained fixity of gaze and deadly pale. That was the last he had seen of her, and in pity for her evident suffering he was relieved to find that she had stolen away. He almost wished he could do likewise. In his view the last hours of a ball must beget in all but the most indefatigable dancers a feeling of weariness and satiety, a fervent longing that the violins would cease scraping out their well-worn tunes and that the incessant noise of laughter and chatter be silenced. He would have marvelled that Elizabeth should still seem fresh and lively when by rights she should be drooping, had he not learned long since a woman's power of endurance in the great cause of social duty.

But the guests began to melt away with the dawn, and at length the door closed behind the last departure. Suddenly feeling utterly exhausted Elizabeth mounted the stairs in the agreeable anticipation of much desired sleep. Behind her in the hall below Wakeford stood talking to her husband. She could not hear what was said, but from Wakeford's despondent look she could guess tolerably well what it was. Georgiana, if she had not absolutely rejected him in so many words, must have made it plain that she would not do otherwise.

At that point in fatigue when her head refused thought she came to the door of her room. There in trembling agitation stood Reynolds awaiting her, there as well, less trembling but in a state of horror as deep and awestruck was Mason.

"Oh, ma'am," cried the housekeeper, hardly able to articulate for the heaving of her bosom, "I hardly know how to tell you what has happened. I would not disturb you at this hour but for its being so shocking. Oh, ma'am—"

"What has happened?" exclaimed Elizabeth. "An accident— Master Richard? Tell me at once."

"It is not Master Richard, ma'am. It concerns Miss de Bourgh and Rachel Stone."

"Good heavens! What has occurred?"

The story which Reynolds now began to relate fell upon ears so little prepared to receive it that its purport was at first rejected as incredible and impossible. Elizabeth heard that between eleven and twelve o'clock Rachel had been summoned to Miss de Bourgh's room by the ringing of her bell. It was to be expected that she would remain there, an hour or more, but when nearly three hours passed and she did not return, the housekeeper judged that some enquiry was necessary. It was ascertained that Rachel had neither come downstairs, nor had she gone to the bedroom she shared with the other young maids. Reynolds therefore took upon herself to go upstairs and discover if possible what was keeping her so long with Miss de Bourgh.

Approaching the door of Miss de Bourgh's room she saw that it stood ajar, and this circumstance so strange in itself emboldened her to open the door still farther and look into the room. A single candle upon the dressing-table was so nearly burnt out as to be flickering in its socket, but it gave enough light to see not only that the room was untenanted, but that it had been left in disorder. Wardrobe doors and drawers hung open exposing their ransacked interiors, discarded articles of wear lay where they had been cast upon the bed or on the floor amid the odds and ends of rubbish that a packing-up to go away throws out to be tidied up afterwards. Everything spoke of the frantic haste of flight.

As Reynolds gazed horrified, hardly able to credit what she saw, the candle on the dressing-table flared up and then went out, leaving her in darkness. She came away in all the distraction of knowing not what to think, still less what to do. The ball would not be over for at least another hour, and until then it was not possible to gain speech with either her master or her mistress. Yet something must be attempted, if only for her own satisfaction, and fetching Mason from a doze in her chair in the servants' hall, the two women went upstairs, fortified by each other's company, to see if they could by any means arrive at comprehending what had happened.

While hunting round the room in the hope of finding something to enlighten them, they came upon a letter which had been left lying beside the candlestick on the dressing-table. It was addressed to Mrs. Stone, and as Rachel could neither read nor write, must have been written for her by another person, presumably Miss de Bourgh. After some debate with Mason whether she should open and read it Mrs. Reynolds decided that it was not for her to do so, but that it should be preserved and handed to Mrs. Darcy.

The finding of the letter marked the conclusion of the housekeeper's narrative. It was now produced and Elizabeth entered her room to read it while the women waited outside. Rachel, in the language and handwriting of Miss de Bourgh, informed her mother that she was quitting Pemberley in the service of a new mistress and was going to live with her either in

London or Kent. As she might be some time on the journey thither a further letter should not be expected just yet. Rachel sent her love to her mother and sisters and begged her mother not to be uneasy about her as she had got a very good place where she would be well treated and live happy. Then there followed these words which were perhaps intended as a message for others besides Mrs. Stone.

"We are travelling at first into Scotland as Miss de Bourgh has business there before she can return to her own home. When this is concluded she will communicate with her relations."

Elizabeth read this sentence twice over although its significance and intention were so clear as to strike her immediately. Miss de Bourgh had eloped—with whom? Only one name occurred to her for there could be no other, and her chief wonder was that with so many circumstances to suggest something of the sort being in the wind, she had been so little suspicious, so little penetrating, that such an outcome as now burst upon her should find her all unprepared. Anne de Bourgh had eloped with Horace Carlini. It was quite natural, almost to be expected. She was in love with him and he was not proof against her fortune. He must have persuaded her to it, knowing that Lady Catherine's partiality could not possibly survive knowledge of the truth about himself. Whether Anne knew it as yet was in doubt, but Elizabeth could give Carlini credit for making every disagreeable fact appear in the guise of totally unmerited misfortune, thus exciting her pity and increasing the ardour of her affection for him.

Such musing did not detain Elizabeth longer than a few seconds. While still reading the letter she comprehended the need for instant action. Her first duty was to find her husband and tell him everything, or at any rate as much as she knew;

indeed her thought flew to him with mad impatience for his presence, his attention, his counsel. She ran out of the room to seek him, leaving the women standing outside the door and met him coming through the gallery. Her distraught looks would have astonished her could she have seen herself; she saw their effects in his face as he caught her arms and asked her what was the matter.

Commanding herself to speak intelligently, she repeated Reynolds' story, and then, for she was still clutching Rachel's letter in her hand, gave it to him to read.

Darcy heard her calmly and in silence for the most part, merely asking a slight question or two on some detail she had not made perfectly clear, and having read the letter, he led her back to her room. Reynolds and Mason were still waiting in the same place, and before following his wife through the door he stopped to speak to the housekeeper. Without emotion, for she was past any fresh sensation, Elizabeth heard him order breakfast for himself at eight o'clock and a chaise for a quarter of an hour later.

"I have every confidence in your discretion," he concluded. "You will, I know, ensure that the events of the night go no further than need be. Your mistress will acquaint the Widow Stone of her daughter's departure."

"You intend to follow them?" Elizabeth said on his rejoining her.

"Yes, I must go after them—there's no question. They will have had several hours start, but they will not travel so fast as I can do, and before the end of the journey, before they cross the border into Scotland, I shall come up with them. By that time Anne may have repented of her rash action and will consent to be escorted to her own home."

"I feel certain she will persist in her folly."

"That may be, but neither she nor Lady Catherine must ever be able to say that she was not given the chance to change her mind."

"You are perfectly sure that she has gone with Ac—Carlini?"

"There is no doubt of it, I fear. All that we know points to it. Lady Catherine encouraged her to like him—very likely to view him as a possible husband. Yesterday he was seen in Bakewell by Wakeford—not six miles away."

Elizabeth, all thought of sleep banished and hardly conscious of the passage of time, now began to detail everything she could remember to have witnessed in Anne's behaviour since Carlini had quitted Pemberley which, regarded as merely eccentric at the time, now bore a very different complexion. Her daily disappearances to the Parsonage or upon solitary excursions in the carriage, her studied avoidance of her hostess and fellow guests, her insistence upon Rachel's inexperienced and inadequate services for sole attendance upon herself, now made up a coherent story, the interpretation of which was not far to seek. She and Carlini had doubtless been meeting secretly with the help of the Miss Robinsons, though it was improbable that these ladies were aware of their scheme to elope, and the flight had been planned for the night of the ball, as affording an excellent opportunity to get away undetected. Rachel Stone had been drawn into the business as a confidante, Carlini having discovered in her an infinite willingness to be persuaded into anything, and had become a useful aider and abettor. Anne's feebleness and helplessness, indeed, could not have carried all through without Rachel's continued assistance.

"I can't think how I could have been so blind to what was going on," she said. "My eyes are as sharp as most, I suppose, and yet he completely took me in. He actually pretended to be in

love with me, knowing full well that I would avoid him in consequence, that he might prosecute his schemes undisturbed."

Darcy shook his head. "No, that was no pretence, Elizabeth.
An ephemeral passion it may be, for men of Carlini's sort seldom
know constancy to one woman, but real enough while it lasts.
And perhaps because fated to remain unsatisfied it will linger on
longer than most of his flames. It may even have played a part in
driving him on to do what he has done—in the desperation of
feelings he has never attempted to control."

"You are more than just to him," she said. "Apart from the
injury he would have inflicted upon you if he had been able, the
family embroglio is only one of the evils which must result from
his conduct. Nothing now can remain hidden; everything must
come out into the light of day to be spread abroad with every
hurtful addition which malice or ignorance can invent."

"I am afraid so," he replied. "It is well-nigh impossible by
taking thought to provide against every contingency or to
contradict beforehand whatever may be falsely reported. Our
reputation must rest upon our so bearing ourselves that it may
be seen that we at least have dealt honourably and done what
we conceived was our duty. And now, Elizabeth, you must take
some rest. You will have enough to do and to endure when I am
gone, and you will need strength for it. Come, my love, let me
see you asleep."

The strange vigil ended at last in dreamless repose. Elizabeth
slept on far into the morning, neither moving nor waking when
her husband left her to start upon his journey to the north.

Chapter 24

THE MORNING WAS FAR advanced when Elizabeth went downstairs after a light breakfast taken in her own room. It was a clear, brilliant day, with a gentle breeze stirring the foliage of the trees and bringing the scent of grass into the house—such weather as would have made her rejoice but for the heaviness of her thoughts. From the moment of waking, when the recollection of all that had happened during the past night flooded her mind, the consequences to be apprehended from Anne de Bourgh's flight had borne them down, not the less so because so much uncertainty must continue for days to come. The hardest blows were yet to fall, as to which her imagination could supply her with a wealth of detail, while fear remained that the worst had not been foreseen.

There was no one about the house, or so it seemed, no one to be found in the breakfast-parlour or the library or elsewhere, and after wandering through various rooms in half hearted search of someone to speak to, and feeling totally unable to give her attention to any settled occupation, she betook herself to the nursery to see the children, although it was past her usual hour for it, and they might be having their morning sleep.

They had just been laid down to rest and Jane and Mrs. Gardiner were coming away after visiting them. Elizabeth turned and accompanied them as far as the hall. There they encountered Mr. Bennet returning from his morning stroll. He, as might be supposed, was on his way to the library, but on seeing his daughter, Elizabeth, for the first time that day, he stopped for some talk.

"So Darcy has gone back to Lady Catherine," he said. "What a fellow for duty he is, to be sure. And as the reward of virtue Miss de Bourgh has given him her company on the journey, we hear—set off at eight o'clock this morning. A truly sudden decision on the face of it, but I am not surprised. She made it so clear that she hated us all. You look amazed, Lizzy. Do you mean to tell us this is the first you have heard of it?"

Elizabeth was more than amazed, she was struck dumb by knowing not what to say in reply. As she could not remain silent she asked her father how he had heard the news.

"I had it from Jane," he replied. "She was up at her usual hour, it seems, and saw them go."

"No, Papa," interposed Jane. "I did not see them for I was not downstairs till much later. It was Reynolds who told me they had gone."

A light broke upon Elizabeth, and if it had not been to raise awkward questions she would have laughed aloud. As it was she found it difficult enough to prevent the liveliness of her feelings from becoming visible in her countenance.

Turning away with affected nonchalance she walked to the window to admire the weather.

"What a beautiful day," she exclaimed. "There is such a look of freshness everywhere. What has become of the others? Charles, Georgiana, Major Wakeford—where are they?"

"I saw Georgiana walking with Major Wakeford along the terrace shortly after breakfast," said Mrs. Gardiner. "They were not long together, I fancy, because only a little later Jane and I met her with Kitty in the flower garden."

"Major Wakeford spoke of having to return to Bath today," Jane added. "He was surprised to hear that Mr. Darcy had left home again so soon, and particularly at his not having mentioned it last night. On his enquiring for you, I told him you might be taking a long rest after the fatigues of the ball, and he said he would defer his departure until he had seen you."

"Where is he now, then?" asked Elizabeth.

"Charles persuaded him to take a rod and go with him to a part of the stream beyond the waterfall."

Wakeford gone fishing with Bingley! It did not sound as if he were in a very desperate frame of mind, whatever the briefness of his interview with Georgiana and his intention of going away might imply. There was something here requiring explanation, but her most pressing desire at the moment was for authentic information concerning the story, or rather the general belief of Anne de Bourgh's having quitted the house with her husband to return to Rosings. Excusing herself therefore on the ground of having to speak with Reynolds on household matters she went to her dressing-room and sent word to the housekeeper to come to her. The summons was obeyed with a celerity which spoke of having been momentarily awaited. Within an instant or two Reynolds was standing before her mistress, looking pretty much as she always did, and as if there had been no horrid discovery in the night to shake her composure.

"Your master quitted the house soon after eight o'clock this morning, I believe," Elizabeth said, without looking at her directly. "No one but yourself and Baxter attended him, presumably. It is being said that he was accompanied by Miss de Bourgh. How can that be?"

"Oh, ma'am, that is certainly a mistake, but as I could not bring myself to say anything but that Miss de Bourgh was gone too, the ladies and gentlemen concluded that was how it was— that Miss de Bourgh was with Mr. Darcy and had gone back with him to her own home. And so, ma'am, I did not like to contradict them, for it seemed a good thing that it should be seen in that light."

Elizabeth was not herself unversed in the uses of prevarication to meet an embarrassing occasion, and this appeared to her to be an instance which needed no justifying. Repressing a gratified smile, she next enquired,

"But the other servants—what do they know, or rather, what do they not know?"

"Mason and me talked it over privately, ma'am, and we thought it would be as well if Miss de Bourgh's room were to be made tidy and the bed to look as if it had been slept in for the housemaid to see when she went in this morning. And then I asked Baxter to arrange that none of the footmen should be about when Mr. Darcy came through the hall and entered the carriage. We did not at first quite know how to account for Rachel, but

Mason said that Miss de Bourgh being rather a peculiar lady—
excuse me, ma'am—it would be believed if we said she had had
Rachel to sleep with her and go away without a word to anybody."

Reynolds eyed her mistress with some anxiety as she
concluded this confession of unheard-of duplicity, but Elizabeth
could feel nothing but gratitude for this latest and most signal
proof of devotion to the family she had served for so many years.
For Darcy's sake, and perhaps in a lesser degree for her own,
Reynolds and Mason, and Baxter no less, had taken upon their
conscience the uttering and acting of a falsehood, and then she
reflected that Mason's devotion to herself was exemplary, and
the saving of her mistress' conscience was equally comprehended
in the sacrifice.

"Indeed I think you did quite right," she said seriously. "You
have given me time to consider the matter at greater leisure than
would have been possible otherwise. I feel sure also that Mr.
Darcy would commend your action." To allay the misgiving this
use of her husband's name produced, she continued, "As we are
still very largely in the dark as to what Miss de Bourgh meant by
going away as she did, it is only right that the very strictest
secrecy should be observed about last night."

Mrs. Reynolds assured her mistress that she perfectly understood what was required.

The next step, Elizabeth decided, was to visit Rachel's
mother, but until she reached the cottage she remained uncertain whether to let the letter addressed to Mrs. Stone go out of
her hands or not. The errand was not at all to her liking. It
seemed, however, as though the stars for this day had ruled that
all her expectations were to be upset. Mrs. Stone was neither

overcome with grief at the loss of her child nor even surprised at the manner of her going. She had known for some days as a great secret, it appeared, that Miss de Bourgh had offered to take Rachel into a distant part of the country, although she had not thought that it would be so soon. Elizabeth formed the opinion that she was a careless, weak woman, with a family too large for her to manage at all well, and so Rachel would not be greatly missed. Further, she discovered that Mrs. Stone, like Rachel, could not read or write, and this being the case it seemed very unwise to entrust her with a letter which if shown to neighbours of more understanding and learning, might give rise to the wildest rumours. She quitted the cottage, therefore, with the letter still in her pocket.

As she did not wish it to be thought that her solitary concern that morning was with Mrs. Stone she called at one or two other cottages before returning home. She had not forgotten that Major Wakeford might be waiting to see her before taking leave. He had been seen walking with Georgiana, but shortly afterwards they had separated. Then he had gone fishing with Bingley. From these few facts it was unsafe to come to any positive idea of the outcome of their conversation, but it did occur to her that Georgiana, moved by his assurances, discovering in fact that her feeling for him was not dead, might have asked for time to consider her answer. This would account both for his decision to quit Pemberley that day, and for his evident inclination to linger awhile. She was prepared for some such explanation when, on entering the house from the carriage, she met Wakeford himself.

He approached her with his usual grave, direct gaze, and having wished her good-morning and enquired after her health, he came at once to the point.

"Mrs. Darcy, I have to tell you that I find myself obliged to leave you again. I should in any case have found it necessary to return to Bath to conclude the business there, but a doubt existed whether after a brief absence I should not find myself at Pemberley again. It is now settled beyond a question that this cannot be."

"You have spoken to Georgiana?" Elizabeth exclaimed involuntarily.

"Yes, I asked her for an interview this morning. She heard me very patiently, but her refusal was unequivocal and I had no option but to accept it and withdraw."

He spoke quietly and equally without chagrin. Elizabeth expressed in the most feeling words she could find her regret for his disappointment, but before she had finished her speech the conviction dawned that he was not inconsolable, and she began to wonder whether, after all, as Georgiana had maintained, he had not come forward from a sense of duty. Perhaps he had never truly loved her, or more probably he had fallen in love with his idea of her character, as, men of his simple sort may do, afterwards discovering the reality to be so much different that it was as if one woman had been substituted for another. The truth of the matter she was never to know for certain, as she could not see into his heart, but that was to remain her belief.

Not long afterwards he departed amid the good wishes of all for his future health and happiness. He had not been at Pemberley again long enough to be missed, and the only person whose thought followed him was Elizabeth. Knowing as much as she did, and yet so little of all there was to know, she could not help wondering what sentiments his reserved nature had harboured towards herself—towards everyone else. He had spoken of sincere gratitude for kindness received, but that was a mere obligatory form of words. The truth of it was felt in the strong clasp of his hand at parting.

It was natural that he should be spoken of by those who had just bidden him farewell, and the briefness of his visit brought forth the sort of remarks that might be expected. Georgiana had arrived in the hall a minute or two before he left, and was the first to slip away. Elizabeth had watched her as she performed her own part in the public leave-taking, but although she was pale and seemed nervous there was no trace of any weakening of the decision she had made. While everyone else flocked out on the steps to see the chaise start she had remained in the hall, and when the others sauntered back, talking, she walked rather quickly to the staircase and disappeared.

Elizabeth found her in her room looking out of one of the windows. She put her arm round her waist and said lightly, "So you have given him his congé, Georgiana."

"Yes, it was not so dreadful as I had feared. He was very considerate."

"And you have no lurking regrets?"

"None whatever. Seeing him again cleared up all my doubts. I am sure that I could never have been even tolerably happy with him. What we shared in common—an interest in natural objects—was so little compared with the differences that must have developed between us. I cannot perfectly explain how it all arose—I mean about what I felt at one time, but I think it was an attraction of opposites made stronger by previous repulsion. When he had gone I came to myself and what I then chiefly suffered was horror at having—but you know. And besides I could never bear to live anywhere but here. How could I leave Pemberley? You could not, you know you could not, Elizabeth."

"But if it had been a question of choosing between Pemberley and your brother, I know which it would have been."

"I hope he may soon come home."

On a sudden impulse Elizabeth told her the whole extraordinary story of Horace Carlini—of his birth and upbringing, his outcast existence in London, the follies and vices which had led him into the desperate straits from which he had sought to extricate himself by impersonating his half-brother Stephen Acworth, and lastly of his presumed elopement with Anne de Bourgh. It was necessary to expound the motives for that complete secrecy which so far had enshrouded the affair, and this led to a consideration of the real Stephen Acworth's character. Georgiana expressed her warm admiration of his disinterested affection for his wretched brother. His endeavours to reclaim him in spite of every discouragement did him the greatest honour.

"He must have found himself in a quandary," said Elizabeth. "He earnestly desired to save his brother from the consequences of his misconduct, but he could not do so without the help of the man to whom his brother had behaved so disgracefully. There has been some quixotry on both sides, I believe, and see how it has been repaid. The object of their concern has himself cut the

Gordian knot by carrying off the person and fortune of a lady who happens to be the cousin of one of his benefactors."

"You are quite certain he has eloped with Anne?" asked Georgiana.

"What else can we think? No other conclusion can be drawn from what we know."

"Yes, and he is capable of it, moreover. I recollect that he made a laughing pretence of a sort of offer one day—at least I construed it as such—and when I showed that I thought his language out of place, he pretended he had been joking."

"Was this at Clopwell?"

"No, one day when we had been practising together. In that flowery manner he sometimes used he spoke of our joining in a duet for life. And then afterwards, to prove that he had not meant what might be inferred he said—but why repeat it?"

"Only because you have provoked my curiosity, which can never bear to be tantalised."

"He said, 'I like you far too well, Miss Darcy, ever to fall in love with you. I respect and admire you from the bottom of my heart.'"

"Indeed! How extremely reassuring! And then, if I recollect, on a later occasion he proposed that you and he should run away and live like brother and sister. And not on nothing, I suppose. Your money was to provide food and lodging, not to mention the little expenses of a gentleman. Money—a great deal of it—was Anne's sole attraction in his eyes, for in spite of all his wonderful sentiments he is thoroughly mercenary. But why did you say nothing of this before, Georgiana?"

"He begged me not to repeat anything that might be misconstrued by those who did not understand him, and would regard a figure of speech as a literal statement."

"There is one short word for a figure of speech as it comes out of his mouth," Elizabeth observed. "Fortunately it is impossible that we shall ever see him again."

Some days were to pass before she heard from her husband, days of tranquillity, if somewhat weighted by suspense. At length a letter, dated from Carlisle, arrived for her.

Darcy wrote that he had surprised Anne and Carlini at an inn the evening before, having come upon their tracks some days previously. They had travelled faster than he had expected, and he found Anne in a state of great fatigue, but inflexibly determined to proceed to the consummation of their design. Carlini had at first shown fear, but afterwards attempted to brazen the matter out with the effrontery of which a frightened man may be capable.

Darcy continued,

"He said that Anne had come away with him in the full knowledge of the circumstances of his birth and his present difficulties, and in fact hinted that the proposal to elope was initiated by her as he would not have dared to suggest it. This is very possibly true in the sense that by laying siege to her affections, and afterwards playing upon the infatuation he had inspired, he led her on to utter the decisive words. However it may be, from what was said, and what I observed for myself, I formed the conclusion that there was really no option but for them to be allowed to finish what they had begun, and so tomorrow I shall accompany them over the border that I may be able to testify to the marriage having taken place in my presence. This I do for Anne's sake. But there could not truly be any fear that Carlini would risk the loss of so valuable a prize as he has obtained.

"As soon as the ceremony has been performed I shall go straight to Rosings. The task of breaking the news to Lady Catherine cannot be otherwise than extremely disagreeable, but it must be done. How long this part of the business will detain me is at present in doubt. Lady Catherine may expel me from her presence forthwith; on the other hand, she may consider that she has a right to use me in any way that occurs to her, for which there is some foundation.

"Adieu, my beloved. Be very sure that I shall not stay away from you and Richard a moment longer than is absolutely necessary."

Several more days went by. One morning Elizabeth received two letters by the post. One from her husband she opened first and learnt that he was now at Rosings, and had just come from a most painful interview with Lady Catherine who, as was perhaps only natural, blamed everybody but herself for what had happened. Her rage against Carlini was boundless, and she had declared her resolution of never allowing her daughter to enter her presence again. Her chief lament was that the de Bourgh estate could not be alienated from Anne, since she deserved to be left without a penny.

"There appears nothing I can actually do for her," Darcy concluded. "But she will not hear of my going, and until she has to some extent recovered from this truly outrageous stroke of fortune I do not see that I can."

The other letter was in a handwriting Elizabeth did not recognise. She opened it with only casual wonder as to its contents and read as follows:

I address you across a gulf which no action of mine could have rendered more unbridgeable than it was already—a gulf willed and widened by yourself. Yet while life shall last nothing can ever erase your image from my heart, and my dying breath shall whisper your name. I once told you that cheated of one love, I could console myself with another. It is not true. You have taught me the last lesson of constancy. At your shrine I end my pilgrimage.

When you have read these words destroy them. I know that they will remain imprinted upon your memory for evermore.

—Horace Carlini

Her cheeks flaming, her heart racing, she tore the letter up into the smallest possible pieces, and then burning them in the grate, saw to it that they were utterly consumed. Afterwards she wondered whether she should have kept the letter to show to her husband, but the thing was done. Never, she thought, could she bring herself to repeat what had been written—to Darcy, to Jane, or anyone else. "Is this a last attempt to sow discord, misunderstanding between my husband and me?" she thought. "Madman that he is. But he is safe, he knows that no retaliation is possible. The spoils are his."

As often when her feelings were agitated beyond control, she burst into tears, and as usual when she had cried a little, she felt better.

Sunday came and Monday passed, but brought no further tidings from Rosings. The house was peaceful though dull, lacking the presence of its master and the animation of expected events. Elizabeth had taken upon herself, after consultation with her aunt, to give the other members of the family circle an account of Carlini's proceedings up to the time he had been sent away from Pemberley. Further than that she did not think it expedient to go until the consequences of the elopement had taken shape out of the uncertainty which still invested them. Mr. Bennet refused to be amazed, saying that he had expected some queer business from the first moment of setting eyes upon the young man, and Bingley, after he had got over the first effects of the revelation discovered that he had thought the same. Jane could find nothing but pity in her heart for a being so misguided, while Kitty could find nothing hard enough to say about him. Mortimer spoke last.

"He always struck me as not being quite the gentleman," said he. "That was what puzzled me more than anything else, because, you see, he was supposed to belong to a titled family— in a proper manner, that is. But now everything that I did not like is explained."

On Tuesday morning Georgiana and Mrs. Gardiner were walking upon the lawn in front of the house when, casting their eyes towards the eminence from which the road wound down to the bridge, they saw a carriage approaching. It was still some way distant, but only a few moments' scrutiny was needed to assure Georgiana that it belonged to Pemberley, that, in short, it was bringing Darcy home.

"It is my brother," she cried. "Oh, where is Elizabeth?"

Leaving her companion to follow more sedately, she ran back to the house and after a breathless hunt through several rooms found Elizabeth at length, and drew her to the front door just as the horses could be heard pulling up with a clatter of hooves and a jingling of harness. They were in time to be standing on the steps, Mrs. Gardiner with them, when Darcy alighted.

He had not come alone. Behind him stepped forth Mr. Gardiner, an unexpected sight most joyful to his wife, and only less so to his niece. But before the first ecstatic words of delighted surprise had fallen from their lips, a third gentleman got out of the carriage and required to be greeted.

On first beholding him Elizabeth almost visibly started. For one moment she thought that Carlini had incomprehensibly returned to Pemberley. She saw a slight, dark-complexioned young man with black hair and lineaments such as Lady Catherine would have described as tracing the Acworth family countenance. Then she observed that the eyes regarding her were blue instead of black, and that the features, less marked than Carlini's, were expressive of a character both firm and gentle. Even before her husband spoke his name on making him known to her, she was conscious that she was looking at last upon Stephen Acworth. In another moment the likeness to Carlini had dissolved never to reappear.

Another beside herself had nevertheless shared the first impression. Turning to look at Georgiana who now came forward, she saw her gazing at the newcomer dumbfounded, almost incredulous. Recovering herself, she merely curtsied and drew back in rosy confusion.

They all next went into the house. Refreshments for the travellers were brought, and while they partook of claret and cold meat, the ladies sat down with them to encourage their appetites and ply them with questions. There was much genial conversation and a general sense of a happy reunion.

The first moment that Elizabeth could speak to Darcy privately, she exclaimed, "My dear Fitz, he is perfectly charming."

"I thought that you would say that," he replied. "Fortunately he is not only charming, he is—but why should I deprive you of the pleasure of finding it all out for yourself. It would be too cruel."

Within a reasonable period, allowing for the usual formalities to be observed in such cases, Stephen Acworth entered upon his incumbency of the living of Pemberley, and took up his abode at the Parsonage. There for a time he lived alone, attended by a few devoted servants whom he had brought with him from Mentmore. In general he appeared cheerful, though with spirits subdued by all he had suffered of loss, illness and anxiety, and before long the Darcys were able to witness a steady improvement in his health, and could rejoice that he was become thoroughly at home in his surroundings and happy in their society.

The advent of a second Mr. Acworth upon the scene so soon after the disappearance of the first gave the busybodies of the parish much to say, but as nothing could ever be learnt which might throw light upon the obscurity enveloping the subject, such gossip as spread about died away for want of matter. The Miss Robinsons, enlightened by Darcy as to the first Mr. Acworth's true character and cautioned by him to keep it to themselves, were able to refrain from mentioning him, though one day Miss Sophia, finding herself alone with Elizabeth, confided to her that Sister and she had been dreadfully deceived in a certain young man. "How little we thought," said she, "when he used to come visiting us, and was so agreeable, that all the time we were nourishing a viper."

After assiduously but fruitlessly searching for a house to satisfy their demands for every imaginable convenience, the sisters found one in the most select part of Lambton which, though far from answering all their requirements, was the least unsatisfactory of any they had seen. The rooms, to be sure, were rather small for their large furniture, but by perseverance and contrivance they succeeded in squeezing it all in to the last piece. At Lambton they found a circle of acquaintance who deferred to their importance, and thereafter were not often seen at Pemberley.

For some time little was heard of Anne and the man she had married. But by degrees, through one channel or another, enough leaked out to give the Darcys a very fair idea of how they were going on. It was learnt that they were residing in a fashionable quarter of London, and Carlini, unable to give up the company of his former associates, now behaved as their patron and made his house a place of resort for musicians, actors and poets, among whom some were already famous. The extravagance of his hospitality earned him all the notoriety he could desire, and at the opera, the theatre or the concert-room he was become a familiar and striking figure. Of Anne not much could be ascertained. It was said that the delicacy of her health forced her to live very quietly, and she was therefore seldom to be seen in public places.

Lady Catherine continued to reside alone at Rosings in a state of implacability towards her daughter and her daughter's husband. But after a year and a half of estrangement Anne became very ill, and believing her life to be in danger, begged to see her mother. A child—a son—had been born. She recovered, but the idea of a grandson worked a revolution in Lady Catherine's feelings, and not only did she consent to be reconciled with her daughter but extended her forgiveness to Carlini on condition of his taking the name of de Bourgh. To this he offered no objection, and although he would never agree to settling down as a country gentleman, he was prevailed upon to spend a few weeks at Rosings every year during that part of the summer when no concerts were being given and the theatre and opera houses were closed.

As in the past, the Darcys kept up their custom of going to town for several weeks of the season, but whether young Mr. de Bourgh took care to avoid an encounter or that he moved in a different circle, they never saw him at any of the entertainments they attended. One day Darcy, walking in Pall Mall, met him coming towards him in the company of a friend. Mr. de Bourgh, talking loudly and with a display of animation, passed him without the flicker of a glance in his direction.

Kitty Bennet was married to Robert Mortimer in the autumn following the formation of their engagement. In spite of Lady Catherine's injunctions she did return to her native Hertfordshire for the wedding, which went off with all the éclat bestowed by the presence of the Darcys and the Bingleys, to say nothing of innumerable other relations and friends. Felicitations on the excellence of the match poured in on the Bennets from every side, and their superlative luck in marrying off three out of their five daughters so very advantageously was a principal theme of conversation in Meryton drawing-rooms and parlours for several weeks.

Major Wakeford sold the property at Bath bequeathed to him by his aunt and returned to his father's house in Devonshire. On his father dying shortly afterwards, and his succeeding to the estate, he continued to live there with his mother and three unmarried sisters. He himself never married, but the continuance of the estate in the family was secured by the marriage of his younger brother whose wife presented him with several sons and daughters. Darcy and he exchanged letters from time to time, but Wakeford never stayed again at Pemberley.

Georgiana was destined to remain at Pemberley for many years. At the end of two years she married Stephen Acworth and moved from her brother's house to the Parsonage. From the first moment of meeting they had felt drawn to one another, and the mutual sympathy discovered at the beginning of their acquaintance ripened imperceptibly into a true and tender affection. They were alike in many respects, but principally in being of a greater refinement of sensibility and delicacy of mind than the ordinary run of men and women, and if they shared a fault it was in their disinclination for any society but their own or that of the family at the Great House.

About six months after the famous midsummer ball a second son was born to the Darcys. They had hoped for a daughter but it was not to be. Elizabeth had never been one to sigh for long over what could not be helped and she soon consoled herself with the reflection that Grenville would make a better companion for Richard as they grew up than a sister. She had yet to learn the inexhaustible resource of little boys in contriving and carrying out all manner of mischief. Fortunately Darcy, though an affectionate parent, was not a weak one, and when the young rascals went too far they were summoned to his presence, and there were taught at his hands the salutary uses of chastisement.

After one such correction Richard said stoutly, "Mamma, Papa did not really hurt me—at least not very much."

Like his father he could not bring himself to say what was not exactly true.

Finis

About the Author

D.A. Bonavia-Hunt was born in London, the daughter of a gifted clergyman, and educated by a governess and in private schools. She lived with her brother, the Vicar of Stagsden, Bedfordshire, in the English countryside during the time that she wrote *Pemberley Shades*.